DISAPPEARING ACT

BAEN BOOKS by MARGARET BALL

Disappearing Act
Brain Ships
(Omnibus with Anne McCaffrey and with Mercedes Lackey)
Mathemagics
The Shadow Gate

DISAPPEARING ACT

MARGARET BALL

DISAPPEARING ACT

A Baen Books Original

Baen Publishing Enterprises
P.O. Box 1403
Riverdale, NY 10471
www.baen.com

ISBN: 0-7434-8853-9

Cover art by Bob Eggleton

First printing, October 2004

Library of Congress Cataloging-in-Publication Data

Ball, Margaret, 1947-
  Disappearing act / Margaret Ball.
      p. cm.
  "A Baen Books Original"—T.p. verso.
  ISBN 0-7434-8853-9 (hc)
  1. Life on other planets—Fiction. 2. Political corruption—Fiction. 3. Space stations—Fiction. 4. Women—Fiction. I. Title.

PS3552.A45535D57 2004
813'.54—dc22

                                                          2004013801

Distributed by Simon & Schuster
1230 Avenue of the Americas
New York, NY 10020

Production by Windhaven Press, Auburn, NH
Printed in the United States of America

10 9 8 7 6 5 4 3 2 1

DISAPPEARING
ACT

Chapter One

Tasman

Maris idled along the broad walkway of Fourteen, admiring the window displays, admiring her own reflection in the windows, and keeping one eye on the target, several shops ahead of her. She really *should* have had all her attention on the target—but top-level ladies never moved that fast, and it wasn't as if Maris had all that many chances to sashay along the shopping aisles of Fourteen as if she were a toppie herself, somebody who belonged there. Johnivans had fitted her out good for this expedition, too, and she just couldn't pass up the chance to see herself looking like a real toppie. Her bodysuit was used, of course, but at least it fit proper and she'd insisted on passing it through the sonic cleaners until only a few indelible stains bore witness to its previous owner's life. The turquoise and fuchsia spiral stripes still had plenty of glitter to them. And over that she had draped a sarong of real pseudosilk, purple with a border of gold sequins, whose artfully careless knot had cost her half an hour's sweating concentration. If it weren't for the unruly dark curls held back with a twist of bright orange silk, Maris thought, she wouldn't know herself—and even those weren't

1

half bad for the current job, one of the toppies' current fads was for "natural"-looking hair that they zapped with electrocurlers to get the effect of a careless mop. In fact, the target's hair looked very similar . . . though she probably shook the artificial curls out into sleek, shining folds at the end of the day instead of struggling through them with a comb. Maris glanced ahead to see if she could tell the difference between electrostimmed curls and her own messy hair, and saw only a gap where the target had been standing a moment ago.

Her insides sank; she felt as dizzy as if the gravity had failed and sent them all into free fall. Losing a target while she mooned over hairstyles and the clothes in the shop windows . . . Johnivans would never forgive her! Worse, she'd never forgive herself for having failed him like this. After all he'd done for her, to screw up on her very first real important top-level assignment . . . Maris moved forward as quickly as she dared, trying to look like a toppiegal in a hurry instead of a panicked scumsucker who was way, way above her proper depth, glancing into each shop in search of a short, slender woman with black curls over a shiny silver bodysuit. Not in the candied fruit stall, not trying on sandals, not . . . she could have disappeared into the fitting rooms behind this display of resort sarongs, but the instinct that made Maris such a good lookout told her no, not there, this target wasn't here to shop for fancy clothes any more than Maris herself. She had been idling along, looking in the shop windows but not really interested . . . meeting someone? But where—ah, a narrow walkway opened to the left between two shops, probably a service passage, and a thread of silver had snagged on the decorative stucco of one wall. She must have ducked through there, must have had an assignation behind the shops; something funny there, exactly what Johnivans would be interested in. Maybe Maris could redeem her moment's lapse of attention and do even better, get close enough to overhear what they were saying; Johnivans had taught her that once people got into a conversation they stopped really *looking*. She sidled flat along the shop wall, stepping as delicately as a moth in case some sound betrayed her presence. She couldn't see anybody in the gap at the far end of the service walkway. Good, they weren't looking back for her—but something felt subtly wrong—and before she could figure out exactly what, she was flying through the air to land in the shadowy space beyond the walkway.

"I might consider letting you go," said a quiet, amused voice somewhere above the weight that pressed her face down into the gridded surface of the walkway, "if you tell me a sufficiently interesting story."

The fall had knocked the air out of her and the knee holding her down wouldn't let her get a decent breath, but Johnivans' patient training was there like internal steel to support her when all else failed. *Stay in character, never stop watching for a break, don't waste energy kicking yourself over past mistakes.* What would a real toppie think was happening?

"Don't be a fool," Maris gasped. It was hard to sound haughty and sarcastic when you could barely breathe, but she gave it her best shot. "You can't mug people this close to the shops. Let me up now and I'll give you a break, I won't call the guards until you've had a few seconds to get away."

The grinding pressure in the middle of her back eased. Could it be working? Small, strong hands gripped her shoulders and flipped her over. Maris stared up into a face eerily like hers—olive skin, black eyes, tangled mop of black curls—and worked on getting her first good breath of air in what seemed like forever. "You look as Sarossian as I am!" the woman exclaimed. "What— How . . . ?" She bit her lip, considering. "Well, even Saros breeds its traitors, I suppose. Right, then. If you really want to call Security," she said, "this is your best chance. You do that, and we'll both show ID, and I'll apologize for the unfortunate misunderstanding, and . . . well? You're not calling for help. Funny, I *thought* not—"

Maris had used the unexpected breathing space to do something far more practical than calling for guards who would slap her into a holding cell just for being this far top-level without proper ID. Working one foot flat on the floor for balance, one hand under her for propulsion, she shot upward and sideways, banged her head into the other woman's nose, got extra leverage by planting an elbow in one of the soft curving breasts outlined by that slick silver bodysuit, and corkscrewed out of the target's hands. She was on her feet and headed for the maze of service

tunnels behind the shops while the target was still cra-
dling her aching breast, lost herself deeper in the tunnels
than any toppie would venture, took long-unused maintenance ladders and dusty passages where the codes on
the security doors hadn't been checked in years, and didn't
stop to catch her breath until she was well down on Thirty,
in a place nobody but Johnivans' people even knew about
anymore.

For all the sixteen-or-so years of Maris's memory this
quarter of Thirty had been ignored by the toppies. Once,
years ago, she'd been told that a chance meteorite strike
smashed the loading dock beyond repair. These days, newbies
credited Johnivans with personally bombing the dock to
create a "useless" space inside Tasman for the Hideaway,
but Maris had doubts she would never express. Not that
it mattered, one way or the other. Whether or not Johnivans
had caused the original destruction, who else would have
been clever enough to take advantage of it the way he did?
His hackercrackers had twiddled Tasman's database so that
half the level was no longer on anybody's clean-and-check
rota, changed a few security codes on the outer doors to
discourage anybody wandering by, and—within the space
that was left, Johnivans had made a home for his people.

Most of Thirty had been left the way Maintenance abandoned it: comfortless bare stockrooms and loading stations,
chill with the knowledge of the deep, black, infinite cold-
ness that was just the other side of the airlocks and walls.
Anybody doing a routine check would trip a dozen alarms
in this outer area before they got to the chambers where
Johnivans stashed the good stuff; they'd die in the traps
he'd had set long before they could penetrate to the heart
of the Hideaway, the long room where Johnivans housed
and fed his people.

Even dreading the confession of her failure, Maris felt her
heart lift as she entered the Hideaway. Topside was new and
exciting, but everything here spelled *home*: the cavernous
spaces walled and floored in a patchwork of mats and carpeting and spoiled silks from rich men's baggage, the sharp
motes of dreamdust floating like a blue cloud in the air,
the rich scent of food being heated on the warmers that
Johnivans had placed everywhere to ward off the chill of
Outside.

The usual crowd was there: Herc and Little Makusu sharing a glowing tube of dreamdust, Nyx posing in yet another fantastic garment pieced from fragments of damaged brocade and velvet, Ice Eyes and Keito the Fingers playing with one of Keito's fantastic constructions of mirrors and holograms. The usual huddle of skeletal bodies, gang buddies who'd dreamdusted themselves to the point they no longer bothered to eat and would shortly die with those dreamy smiles on their thin faces, moved languidly on a pile of cushions in the far end of the space. Johnivans never stopped anybody killing himself with dreamdust or poptoys; he said those who chose to do that stuff weren't worth saving.

But Johnivans himself wasn't there.

"Look at this, Maris!" Keito hailed her. "I fixed the glitch, now the Thief and the Lady orbit each other, like *so*." He pushed a movable panel and glass changed to mirror; hidden wires clanged together, and two figures sculpted of light appeared in the center of the ragged sphere and began a stately dance around each other.

"It's wonderful, Fingers," Maris said with sincere appreciation. "You could be a toppie artist—your pieces are better than anything I saw in those snobby stores on Fourteen."

Ice Eyes raised his eyebrows. "*I'm* the artist here," he announced, "an artist of the Light Touch. This stuff of Keito's is just play. Here's your scarf back."

Maris put a hand to her head, then joined in the laughter as Ice Eyes bowed and handed the wisp of bright silk back to her with a flourish. "But, Ice, it's cheating to distract me with Keito's holotoys! You don't have those when you go collecting."

"Don't need 'em," Ice Eyes protested, "toppies are slow and stupid."

"Not all of them," Maris said, remembering what she'd come to report. "Where's Johnivans?"

"The question," said a slow, cold voice behind her, "is, where's the target you were supposed to be following? Did you lose her, or just decide to take a little vacation from your assignment?"

Maris turned and dropped to one knee. If groveling and contrition would save her from the worst of Johnivans' wrath, she didn't mind. She deserved it. "Worse," she admitted with her eyes fixed on the pointed red toes of his boots.

"There's something worse than disobeying *me*? You never cease to surprise me, girl."

Maris lowered her head until her forehead touched the top layers of carpet scraps. Dust tickled her nose, made her want to sneeze, and the acrid hint of Little Makusu's dreamdust tempted her with the promise of oblivion. "She tumbled to me following her."

"Get careless?"

"I must have—but I don't know how! I'm the best at follow-me-target, Johni, you know that, we've played it all my life, even *you* can't tell when I'm tracing you . . ."

"Hmm. So that makes you the best?"

"Nobody else here could track you through from Twenty-four to Twenty-one when you tried us, could they?"

"So if you're so good, who persuaded you to be *not* so good at it this time? Hmm?" A foot on Maris's head underlined the question.

"Nobody! I swear it. She's just—better than anybody we tracked before—or maybe she's got better tech. You said she was asking Little Makusu about smuggling pro-tech onto Kalapriya—well, wouldn't it make sense that a tech smuggler would have the best equipment for herself?"

She could tell Johnivans was considering this point seriously when the weight of his foot quit grinding her face into the carpet. Maris dared a glance upward and saw him frowning, but no longer angry. Not at her, anyway. She'd become expert at reading the signs.

"Nobody could pay me enough to dub on you, Johni," she insisted. "You know that. I owe you everything—do you think I've forgotten so easily? If I'm not one of Johnivans' people, I'm working the corridors, I'm nobody, I'm dead. You saved me from that and I'd never dub on you. Not to save my own life, certainly not for anything a damned toppie could wave at me!"

Johnivans' frown of concentration smoothed out into the broad smile that lit up her universe. " 'Course you wouldn't, Maris. I know that—I was just testing you, see? Now stop rolling on the carpet, you'll get your nice outfit dirty!" Strong hands lifted her up. Maris felt safe and protected again inside the strength of those arms, the warmth of Johnivans' smile. If he forgave her, if she was still one of his mates, then nothing else mattered. Sure, she'd blown the assignment, and she'd do whatever dirty, boring job he gave her as penance—but it didn't really matter. The tech smuggler might have outsmarted her, but Johnivans would outsmart the smuggler in turn. He always did.

"Do you think the target turned Maris?"

"No chance! Maris is *yours*. I think this woman outsmarted her, just like she admitted." But a slight frown lingered on Little Makusu's face.

"Maris," Johnivans remarked, apparently to the empty space in the middle of his private chambers, "is good. *Bunu* good; I trained her myself. So . . . either the toppie turned her, or . . . Maybe she's smarter than she looks."

"Maris?"

"No, moron, this wannabe tech smuggler. At first I thought she was *bunu* dumb, trying to start her own racket without paying her specs to me first, but now I'm wondering. Maybe she's got serious backing, just wants to ID who's running the game here so she can have us taken out. We need to know more."

"Want me to bring her here?"

"No. Take her to the Maus-hole. If you can."

"If I *can!*"

The warm smile lit up Johnivans' face. "Just kidding, Little M. But seriously now . . . take some help. Keito the Fingers, maybe Daeman if he's not too crazy today. Remember, she got round Maris. I don't want any of my people approaching her alone. And after you've stashed her," he added, "find out where she's bunking, and send Fingers to check out her quarters. I want as much background as we can get before I start questioning her. And one other thing . . ."

"Don't mention the op to Maris," Little Makusu said. "Just in case."

"*Bunu* right!"

Calandra Vissi could hardly wait until she got back to her suite on Five to compose and code her message back. Strictly speaking she shouldn't be sending anything at all, since what she had at this point was hardly vital information—but it was *something*, after all these days of dropping hints and broadcasting suggestions until she began to doubt there actually was a smuggling organization on Tasman for her to check out. But logic said there had to be. Tasman was an artifact of FTL travel, a miniature artificial world created at a point where converging singularities in the geometry of space made it extremely inconvenient *not* to have a nearby world for docking and refueling and transshipping passengers and cargo. Hence, Tasman—expensive, with its thirty levels of living and working quarters, its inability to produce anything for itself beyond the most basic hydroponics required to keep the air healthy. Expensive beyond words, when you considered the cost of shipping every single component, foodstuff, and other necessity from some distant world.

The only thing more expensive would have been *not* having Tasman, being unable to use this marvelous area of converging singularities except by laboriously docking two ships together for cargo exchanges.

That debate had been argued out in Calandra's great-grandparents' time, and Tasman had paid for itself—with docking and toll charges that everybody complained about, but everybody paid—within a generation.

Almost everybody, anyway.

In the early, bare-bones days Tasman could not possibly have housed a smuggling operation (unless it was run by the officials in charge of customs and excise, Calandra noted, having been trained to consider all possibilities). Now, four generations after the world had first been placed here, it had been added onto and improved beyond recognition. The core levels, One through Three, comprised a luxury world with every comfort that could be imagined to keep staff happy and slow down turnover, because it was much more expensive to train new maintenance and customs staff and ship them out than it was to provide the existing workers with synthetic lobster dinners, the latest holos, virtual tours by the current holostars, and anything else that could amuse people stuck on a world with no open spaces. The levels immediately around the core were equally luxurious, resembling nothing so much as a huge shopping mall that radiated out from Four's top-level stores with plush carpeting and discreet fountains all the way down to the crowded walkways and mass-market chain stores of Fourteen. Nothing *cheap*, of course; it didn't pay to import cheap goods to Tasman. Still, Fourteen didn't hold much to appeal to someone like Calandra. But it was nearly the lowest level open to the public—Fifteen and Sixteen were drab service areas frequented mostly by staff members bent on saving every penny of their salaries for the future, and from Seventeen down to the outer skin, the only comfortable areas were the lift tubes that led directly to the passenger bays, surrounded by dull and chilly storage and maintenance areas. So Fourteen was the best place, Calandra figured, for her to troll for contacts with the smugglers that *had* to be operating on Tasman by now.

Logic insisted they had to be there. In general: No place with so much wealth, tangible and intangible, pouring through it could be immune from crime; and history taught that excessive tolls and customs *always* generated smuggling. In particular: Kalapriya bacteriomats that didn't pass through the Federation's rationing and control system were coming from *somewhere*—and Tasman was at the only singularity point reachable from Kalapriya. However the black-market bacteriomats were being distributed, they had to pass through Tasman, and somebody there had to know how it was done.

Somebody who was already unethical, or he wouldn't be distributing black-market bacteriomats; somebody with the power to divert and conceal shipments of things that had to be moved in special climate-controlled, airtight containers; somebody who already had contacts on Kalapriya; somebody, in short, who could be expected to leap on the offer of a partnership smuggling prohibited technological luxuries onto Kalapriya.

The only trouble was, you couldn't look up "Smuggling—Tasman/Kalapriya" on the netbase and expect to find an informative entry; nor could you insert an offer of partnership into the ceaseless stream of public service announcements and commercial advertisements that clogged Tasman's main info channel. You had to be subtle, come at it sideways, think like a criminal. Drop hints, let it be known in the right quarters that she just might have certain devices that would be guaranteed to sell for a high price on Kalapriya if only she had a way of bypassing the Barents Trading Society's checks on all incoming cargos. And who knew what *were* the "right quarters"? Calandra had reasoned that there must be an underworld to Tasman and that the bacteriomats must be coming through that way, because all her boss's extremely discreet audits of Tasman's records showed no hint of any fiddling with the data. But in the last few days of bar-hopping and casual chatting and dropping hints Calandra had begun to wonder if Fru Silvan's delicate computer inquiries had missed something, if they should be checking out the highest levels of Tasman rather than the lowest.

And she really didn't want to go on to Kalapriya without the slightest hint of where to look.

So it had been a great relief when the girl started following her, some time that morning, and an even greater one when she passed up several perfectly good chances to steal Calandra's shopping bag. Even a credit chip left carelessly on the countertop while she turned her back and haggled with the jeweler hadn't attracted her shadowy follower. The girl *had* to be from the unknown gang she was trying to make contact with; there was simply no other logical explanation.

And she'd gotten away.

But that didn't matter, Calandra reassured herself. At last she had some progress to report! If her carefully casual inquiries had attracted somebody to investigate her, then logic was right and there was at least one strand of the web she was seeking here on Tasman. Pull on that strand, and she might find out enough to guide her investigation on Kalapriya itself . . .

Mulling over her next move, she forgot to check her proximity sensors—they were mostly a nuisance in a crowded public area anyway, she'd had to pay the closest attention to pick out the one faint blip that showed a repeated pattern behind her and gave that girl's presence away. And she hardly noticed when a sharp angle of joined corridors took her out of the main stream of foot traffic for a moment.

A sharp push between her shoulders made her stumble forward, putting her arms up to protect her head from hitting the tiled wall—but the wall fell open before her, and just before the world went black Calandra registered, too late, the red flashing lights of her sensors screaming *Attention, watch out, somebody's getting much too close.*

The first thing she knew was that it was *cold;* the second, that her head was exploding. No. It just *wanted* to explode, to get away from the pain, little shreds of Calandra flying out away from the aching center into the cold . . .

"She's awake," said someone. "I told you I din' hit her no harder'n I had to."

"Shouldn'a hit her at all," said a different voice in the same slurred accent Calandra had learned to associate with Tasman lifers, the ones who came and stayed and generally held the worst crew positions. Staffers had their leaves on their home worlds, their three- and five- and ten-year rotations, kept ties with home. Lifers . . . her brain was wandering.

"Doesn't matter, she'll be plenty awake for Johnivans to talk to." There was a nasty laughter behind that voice, a mocking accent on *talk* that made Calandra shiver despite her pretense of unconsciousness.

"You sure?"

"Yeah, watch this—" and a burst of pain flared up Calandra's right arm, coming from the hand, the middle finger bent impossibly far back until there was a snap and her stomach lurched. She moaned then, couldn't help it, and gave up the pretense of unconsciousness. Had to look, anyway, to see if her finger was still *there*—it was, but the angle made her feel sick again. Better not to look, then.

"Bright girl," said the man with the cold, mocking voice. Calandra studied him through half-closed lids, pretending to be dazed from the blow. *Maybe not* pretending, *I'm not functioning all that well.* Dark golden skin, black eyes with a hint of an oriental fold, broad shoulders. Not too big to tackle, if he were alone. He wasn't; the owners of the other two voices were looking over his shoulder. "See, it's not a good idea to lie to us."

"Didn't—" Calandra managed in a voice whose wobble dismayed her. She sat up slowly, hissing with pain when she accidentally moved her right hand.

"Oh, yes. Pretending to be out when you're not, that's a lie, that's no *bunu* good. Don't need another lesson, do you? Thought not. Learn fast, do you?"

"Daeman, Johnivans said not to question her till he was ready," protested one of the others, a slender youth with bright green hair in a fashionable topknot.

"D'I ask her anything, Little M? I'm not *bunu* questioning

her. Just getting her ready. Want her in the right mood, don't
we?" The broad-shouldered man—Daeman?—smiled down
at Calandra with a mad sweetness in his eyes that terrified her. *Sane criminals I can maybe talk my way around.
This one's not sane.* "In case you're wond'ring, lady, the
right mood is cooperative. Totally *bunu* cooperative. I gotta
tell Johnivans you're a quick learner, don't I, that you don't
need no more lessons in how to talk to the boss? Or do
I?" he mused. "See, I *like* teaching, and seems like you'd
be a good student. What do you think?"

"I think you started right, but you're making a mistake
with the threats," Calandra said, looking at Daeman but
pitching her voice toward the two behind him, who might
possibly be sane. "Your boss and I have mutual interests.
We need to talk."

Daeman giggled. "Oh, yes. You'll talk! You'll *sing* if we
ask you real *bunu* nice, won't you, toppie lady? You know
how nicely I c'n ask? You wanna demonstration?"

"*Daeman.*" The boy with the green topknot touched the
big man's arm. "Let her wait here, think it over. You scared
her enough, Daeman. You're scared, aren't you, lady?" His
eyes fixed on hers, sending some message. What? *Never cower
to bullies, it only encourages them.* But did that hold for
madmen? Probably not.

Calandra lowered her eyes and blinked rapidly, as if trying
to blink away tears. "Y-yes," she said, and it wasn't hard
to sound weak and scared. "Please don't hurt me again."

"Not before Johnivans gets here," Daeman said with that
high-pitched, frightening giggle. "He likes to be *sure*, know
what I mean? You think about that now, toppie slut. We'll
have us a party when Johnivans is ready."

And on that, unbelievably, they left. The door hissed
shut behind them and Calandra drew a long breath that
shook with grateful relief. With those three watching her,
the only advantage she could get over them was pretending
to be weak and hurt and too scared to resist, waiting for
them to relax so she could make a move. Alone, she had
a lot more advantages. Start by getting out of this place?
She briefly considered staying for the promised meeting
with their boss, what had they called him? Johnivans? Not
worth the risk. She did want to talk to him—but not on
his territory, with him thinking she was his prisoner, and

certainly not with that mad Daeman anywhere around. All right then. No telling how long she had, and there could be cameras hidden even in this barren, steel-walled cell. What was it, anyway—part of a corridor? Leaning against a cold wall, head lolling as if she were half unconscious, Calandra closed her eyes, thanked the land spirits of Saros for the Diplomatic Sector's tradition of thoroughness, and called up the implanted database that held maps of Tasman. Using a recent implant like this always gave her a headache; spikes of pain flared between her eyes, vanished and recurred while she scanned sectional maps of the outer layers. Yes, a corridor leading to one of the disused loading docks. *Of course*, an area neglected like that was a natural breeding ground for a criminal underclass. And the partition doors originally built in as barriers against accidental breaches of the skin still worked; she'd just seen Daeman and Little M and their friend leave through the one to her left. Probably a better idea to take the one to her right, then, assuming it didn't open on deep space. No, that was all right; the maps showed that none of the corridor partitions led directly to a loading dock. Two sets of double doors with an air space between, that was what she had to look out for—avoid those and she'd be all right. With the maps in her head, she didn't need to worry about being spaced—only about avoiding Johnivans and his friends. Especially his friends.

The other problem with new implants was their slowness to respond; it took time to grow the neuronal connections that let the hint of a thought of moving a small muscle trigger the right commands in the silicon part of her brain. Calandra had to blink twice, hard, to get the cross-sectional maps floating through her vision to change to a 3-D walkthrough beginning just where she thought she might be. And then it was a crummy threedie, jerky, lacking any of the detail that would allow her to select this particular corridor partition from any of the others in the dead area of Level Thirty. There was only one way to test her guess, and it would give her away if anyone was scanning. She would just have to hope that underworld criminals weren't as efficient as Diplomatic Authority.

Standing wasn't quite as easy as it should have been; that knock on the head? No matter, a little sway and stumble was quite artistic really, should convince anybody watching the hypothetical hidden camera that she was merely moving aimlessly about. Three hesitant steps took her nearly to the right-hand partition door, the one Daeman and his friends *hadn't* used. Calandra leaned against the door as though the effort of moving had exhausted her. Hell—her body hid one hand from view, but it was the right hand, which she didn't particularly want to use just now. No help for it; turning in a circle to put her left hand between her body and the security keypad would definitely look purposeful and alert a watcher. *What am I complaining about? I've still got four perfectly good fingers on that hand.* Okay, so using even one finger awakened pain demons that flew up the nerves of her arm keening and wailing disaster. Tough. The pain wouldn't kill her, wouldn't maim her, couldn't even keep her from accessing her new implants. She couldn't be sure that would be true of whatever Johnivans and Daeman might be planning to do to her.

A roll of her eyes upward and a twitch of her right eyebrow got the damned threedie walkthrough unstuck, let her scan through codes until she spotted the list she wanted, the corridor codes for Level Thirty. *Earthlady of Saros, if ever I poured wine from my cup for you, let it be the first one I try!*

Third code out of ten; not enough to make her feel securely under the Earthlady's protection, but not bad. And knowing which code worked also told her exactly where on Thirty she had to be. Just two more corridor cells and an inconspicuous ladder door could get her to Twenty-nine, then to Twenty-eight and higher, where there would be legitimate crew. Could the smugglers actually have been careless enough to leave that way out unguarded? *Probably—after all, they don't know I carry all Tasman's security codes in the top left corner of my forehead.* Not that the new chip was literally there, but that was where the headache had centered.

Diplomatic School emphasized, over and over, that *probably* wasn't good enough if you had any way to improve your odds. Calandra wiggled her right foot and felt the comforting thickness of the very slightly raised heel. Slip the dazer out now, to have in her hand when she went through the door? Or take her chances on this door, and hope she had time on the other side to get her weapon out?

She might be able to get at it now without alerting anybody. Calandra let herself slide down the wall, careful not to put any weight on the now unlocked door, and tucked her feet under her as she sat. The heel had been designed to let an agile woman casually finger the recessed printpad and slip the dazer out with a single gesture that looked as if she was just easing a tight shoe.

An agile woman with a fully functioning right hand.

Oh well—in three seconds, when she went through that door, anybody watching her would already know something was off. Calandra wriggled to cross her legs in front of her, pressed her right thumb into the print-pad, and awkwardly slipped the catch and pulled out the dazer left-handed; stood up in a smooth flowing motion that she owed not to Diplo School but to Madame Petropolous's Dance Class for Preteens; and pushed the door open with her right elbow, holding the tiny dazer in the palm of her left hand with the nozzle just peeking between two fingers and her thumb on the firing pad.

Another barren corridor section, this one with shipping crates piled along the inside wall. No shouts, no alarms— dared she take time to investigate even one of those tempting crates? By the time she got free and could come back with station authorities, any bacteriomats concealed in those crates could have been spaced—there to her right were the double doors leading to the defunct Loading Bay B7, plastered with faded stickers bearing the usual warnings: No Exit, Danger, Unsecured Area, Authorized Personnel Only, Vacuum-Rated Protective Gear Absolutely Required. All of which might or might not mean that the second, exterior set of doors to the loading bay had been damaged in the collision that wrecked B7; if Tasman Civil Authority was like any other set of bureaucrats Calandra had encountered, they would rather slap warning tapes all over the doors than actually test or fix anything. The one thing she felt sure of was that the smugglers would be well equipped to dump anything incriminating on a moment's warning.

If there was a sealed bacteriomat transport canister in one of those crates, and if she could get it to—not to Tasman Central Authority, they might be involved, unlikely as it seemed—back to her boss on Rezerval, then she would have more than redeemed the carelessness that allowed the smugglers to trap her. Calandra squeezed the dazer, resetting it to separate metal from metal rather than neuronal connections, and cut a careful seam round the four sides of the topmost crate. She caught the toppling metal side with her right forearm, just managed to get it to the floor without a betraying clang, set her dazer on top of the crate and rummaged through the packing pearls one-handed. Little pink and green and blue packing pearls flew out with every motion and swirled around her head, too light to succumb to Tasman's artificial grav fields. Somebody was going to have fun cleaning those damned pearls up; she hoped, viciously, that Daeman would be given the chore of recapturing them. With his bare hands. One at a time.

Metal and plastic, square-edged shapes, recessed print-pads . . . a rounded shape under her palms that felt right, a short tube about three inches in diameter. Aha! She pulled it out, congratulating herself as she recognized the cool white outer insulation of a biosample freezetube . . . and stared in frustration at the black-and-white dot code in the address space.

No name, no address, just a dot code. Calandra stared at the code until the dots swelled and shrank and spiraled before her eyes. *No*, she wasn't going to be able to memorize it, and *yes*, she was sorry now that she hadn't let "Doc" Ovsami at Diplo Central give her the latest in retinal camera implants, but so what? All she had to do was take the actual canister to any sorting and delivery substation to get the dot code translated into an address. And she needed to take the canister with her anyway, to a microbiology lab that could open it under approved protocols and identify the fragile cells in stasis within.

And with this information, it should be ten times easier to track down the source of the black-market bacteriomats. Calandra tucked the freezetube under her arm and headed confidently toward the next corridor partition door, the one that should lead to her way uplevel.

The listed code didn't work.

Could the list have been scrambled for some reason, so that the code for this partition didn't come immediately after the code for the previous? Not bloody likely. Try the one before, then, maybe she'd been reading the list in reverse order.

That one didn't work either.

And even as she was tapping in the other seven possibilities she knew they wouldn't work; either the damned smugglers had hacked into the system and recoded the doors or the list was out of date.

There *was* one other way out of this partition, though. They just might not have recoded the double airlock doors.

It wasn't a pretty exit, but anybody would think it beat hanging around to let Daeman torture her at his leisure.

Timing would be all-important.

Calandra took a deep breath of stale, recycled station air, appreciated it with every living cell of her body, and moved over to test the airlock doors leading to the absolute cold of space.

"She's *what*? Don't give me that? *Bunu* Diplos travel in style—she'd have been staying right up on Two or Three, not in some Level Five transit cubicle!"

"Maybe she's a Diplo, maybe she isn't," Keito the Fingers said. "We found the cards tucked into the lining of her travel bag. Maybe she stole them. Maybe they're forged. Maybe . . ."

"Scanner!"

Nyx had the equipment ready before the word was out. Johnivans fanned out the cards and ran them through the scanner slot one at a time, barely pausing to read the information that flashed on the screen. He stopped when the screen showed a face. "Little Makusu! This look like her?"

"That's her," Little Makusu confirmed with a glum stare. Curly black hair, black eyes, olive skin—like Maris, almost, only a Maris who was cleaned up and older and more confident.

Johnivans sighed and let forth a string of expletives in Hongko, more chilling for being uttered without apparent expression. With the same dead-calm voice he summarized, "So you've kidnapped a Diplo and let Daeman torture her. Diplos don't just go missing; when this one doesn't report in there'll be an almighty stink. Got any bright ideas how to fix it?"

"If she's found dead," Little Makusu said slowly, watching Johnivans' face. The Man didn't seem to be getting any *angrier*, at least. " . . . dead of natural causes . . ."

"How much damage did Daeman do?"

"Only a broken finger," Little Makusu said proudly. "I kept him under control."

"Brilliant. Any suggestions on how we make a broken finger into a wholly unsuspicious natural death?"

"The woman was nosing around where she shouldn't have been. An accident. An accident in Engineering— something that mangles her hand—or Maintenance, any kind of conveyor system ought to do it—something around a loading dock; she was too damn interested in how stuff gets on and off Tasman," Little Makusu improvised, feeling happier as Johnivans seemed to relax. "We'll work out something."

"Okay, get on with it, make a plan, let me know when you're ready. And fast! I want her found before she's reported missing, get me?"

"Uh—where'll you be, boss?"

Johnivans rolled his eyes upward. "Having a little chat with the lady. Now we *really* need to know what she's here for."

"Want Daeman?"

Another roll of the eyes. "And to think you're one of my *brighter* people. This whole enterprise must be under the special care of the God of Minor Fuckups. *No*, I don't want Daeman, he has no self-control. We can't leave any more marks on her until you've figured out how to arrange her accidental death. I'll have to find other ways of persuading her to talk."

God of Trouble sends by threes, Johnivans' grandmother used to say. So okay, they had a nosy stranger asking about smuggling pro-tech onto Kalapriya, that was one; after they'd shown their hand by kidnapping her, the woman turned out not to be a freelance smuggler who could disappear but a *bunu* Diplo traveling incog, that was two. Johnivans refused to be superstitious; but when he found the cell where Daeman and Makusu had stashed the woman empty, and the parcels stored there cut open, somehow he was not surprised. "I was wrong," he muttered. "We've been upgraded. We are getting the special attention of the God of *Major* Fuckups."

How had she gotten out? Not the way she came; she'd have had to get past his people, and they weren't *that* incompetent. He didn't think. Then again, anybody stupid enough to leave their catch in a corridor section with the far partition door unlocked . . .

"It *wasn't* unlocked," Little Makusu protested.

Johnivans gave him a bone-chilling glance. "You checked, of course."

"It's never unlocked. Nobody goes that way. Look, it's closed now, isn't it?"

On inspection, the door was not only locked; it flashed red warnings every time Johnivans touched the key pad. The door sensors reported vacuum on the other side; the airlock doors leading to the damaged loading bay must have been opened.

"It was left unlocked," Johnivans said flatly. "She went through into the next partition, but *that* door *was* locked. So . . . what exactly did you idiots do to her, that she preferred spacing herself to a little talk with me?"

It probably wouldn't be a good idea to point out that most people who knew Johnivans would make the same choice. Nor would it help to remind Johnivans that he'd *wanted* them to scare the woman before leaving her alone, for fear and imagination to weaken her defenses.

"Vacuum'll get Maintenance down here," Keito the Fingers said gloomily, and Makusu mentally blessed him for changing the subject.

"So? One thing's for sure, they won't find anything." Johnivans frowned and drummed his fingers on the door panel. "That gives me an idea . . . no, it wouldn't work . . . Get some of the boys to shift the rest of those crates, just in case Maintenance checks past the breach to look in here . . . Not that it'll help. We need to get them off-station; when a Diplo's reported missing, they'll look *everywhere.*"

"Not the Hideaway," Keito said. "Nyx took it off the data maps; the maint-bots don't even know it exists now."

Johnivans sighed. Deeply. Why were all his boys such fuckups? "For a missing Diplo," he said evenly, "it won't be maint-bots, it'll be human beings. And not all humans being as dumb as you lot, it's just remotely possible that one of them will notice some discrepancies between the space used in the database and the recorded volume of Tasman." He could see the work of years going down the drain; his organization scattered, no place to gather, no safe place to relax, nowhere to stash the goods he moved to and from Kalapriya. Ask the Consortium for help? Better not—they weren't the kind of people who responded well to a show of weakness.

"If the Diplo weren't missing they wouldn't search the whole station," Keito mused.

"If wishing were oxygen, I'd be able to breathe between the stars!"

"Maris looks a lot like that Diplo," Makusu commented, beginning to see a ray of hope.

"Yeah, but she'd never be able to pull it off. Diplos are *schooled*. They know everything there is to know—and all Maris knows is the underside of Tasman. They've got all those brain implants and mysterious powers, too," Keito pointed out.

"Oh yeah? That little lady didn't work no mysterious powers on yours truly," Makusu swaggered. "She was as scared of Daeman as anybody else would have been. You ask me, it's just a load of holocrap about the Diplos. They're just another kind of toppies, that's all, and Maris already passed for a toppie."

"Yeah? When?"

"When she was following this Diplo."

"Who caught her, may I point out!"

"Shurrup, both of you!" Johnivans growled. "A man can't *think* with your bickering going on—not that either of you would know anything about that. We might just pull it off. We've got the Diplo's cards; Nyx can change the prints and retina scans to match Maris, even put in Maris's picture. She's faked enough IDs for us, even a Diplo's can't be all that different."

"Yeah, but Maris can't possibly fool anybody that she's . . ." Keito's voice trailed off under Johnivans' withering stare.

"She is perfectly *bunu* qualified," Johnivans said slowly, "to pass for a *dead* Diplo. And that's all we really need— a corpse that matches the specs, to stop them searching."

"But Maris . . ."

"Failed us all, when she let that Diplo catch her. I don't have room in my organization for fuckups."

Makusu thought about the unchecked partition door and stopped protesting before Johnivans could think of some use for *his* corpse.

"But don't tell Nyx why we want the IDs faked. She likes Maris."

"So did I," said Keito, sadly, but accepting the inevitable. Better to lose one girl than to see the entire Organization go out the airlock.

"I wish you'd stop hanging over my shoulder while I work," Nyx told Maris. "You're getting on my nerves."

"You *asked* me into your luxurious closet," Maris pointed out. The workroom was actually a little bigger than a closet, but the specialized—and highly illegal—equipment lining the walls left about enough free room for one woman and a can of cold fizz. "And you didn't even tell me why you wanted samples. Trying something new for Johnivans, are you?"

Nyx hunched over her console, tapping the screen here and there with a long platinum fingernail to adjust parameters that were invisible from Maris's angle of vision. "I'm not supposed to talk about it."

"C'mon. He can't expect that you'll take finger and palm prints, retina scans, hair and blood and skin samples, and I won't even *notice*. Do you have to go through with this for everybody in the Organization? Are we all getting proper IDs or what?" Maris didn't really want to give Nyx a hard time—but she was nervous, waiting to hear what Johnivans had done to her assigned target . . . and what he was going to do to *her* for screwing up. That there would be a punishment she accepted without question; she just wished she knew what it was.

And she hoped, without too much hope, that he wasn't hurting the other woman too much. Of course if she was a smuggler from some rival off-station gang, trying to muscle into the Organization's business, she deserved whatever she got . . . but . . . she hadn't seemed like that bad a sort.

And thinking about any of this was unprofitable. Johnivans

would do what he had to do and she'd have to be crazy to question him. He'd befriended her when she was just a kid barely old enough to be recruited by a pimp and sent out to work the corridors. If she weren't part of the Organization that's where she'd be now, doing one crewman after another and handing over her credits to a boss who slapped her around if they weren't enough or if he was in a bad mood. Johnivans asked her to do some hard things sometimes, but nothing demeaning, and he was fair, and he looked after his people. She felt like a total jerk for even thinking of questioning whatever he had to do with that woman.

It was much, much less upsetting to hang over Nyx's workstation and try to figure out her special top-secret project.

"If you have to get samples from everybody in the Organization, there'll be no way of keeping the project quiet," she pointed out. "You really think somebody like Little Makusu is going to give you scans and cell samples without asking questions? Or *Daeman*?"

"Fortunately," Nyx said while she tapped the screen in a rapid tattoo that brought up flashing arcs of colored lines in constantly changing patterns, "I don't have to sample Daeman or anybody else. Just you."

"Just *me*?" Maris could practically hear the sound of her teeth hitting the floor as her jaw dropped open. She knew her place—about the lowest form of life in the Organization, even before she'd failed Johnivans in this assignment. "Girl, there's too much monoxide in your air mix! No way am I important enough to justify this much of your work. Even *before* I screwed up."

Nyx's elaborately painted face showed a small, secretive smile under the masklike decorations of green and platinum spirals. "Well, maybe you're not as much in disgrace as you thought. Listen, if anybody else finds out, I'll be the one in big trouble . . . but Johnivans can't have meant I can't tell *you*, seeing it's all for your benefit. Just don't let anybody else know, okay?"

Maris swore on the integrity of Tasman's outer hull, then spat on her hands and swore by the God of Minor Fuckups that she wouldn't reveal what Nyx told her to a living soul.

"Okay . . . I'm about done, anyway; just have to wait for all that data to process and print." Nyx pushed her stool away from the console and half turned to look up at Maris. The smile was dancing in her eyes now. "Looks like Johnivans has a real special assignment in mind just for you, lady. Know what I've just been doing? Know who that woman is you were following, the one Daeman and Makusu had to snatch after she rumbled you?"

"Don't remind me," Maris pleaded. "Way I fucked that one up, there's no way Johnivans would trust me with any solo project again."

Nyx's lips curved. "She's a Diplo. Name of Calandra Vissi, originally from Saros, in transit to assignment on Kalapriya. And you may have noticed that she looks a lot like you . . . You're going to take her place, Maris."

"Me! She doesn't look that much like me . . . I can't fake being a Diplo . . . the scans will show . . . arrghh. *That's* what you wanted all my data for." Maris gulped and shut up, her thoughts racing.

Nyx nodded. "First I had to set up the ID cards, then I hacked into the station records to make everything consistent. In a few minutes you'll have all of Calandra Vissi's ID—but with *your* picture, prints, and cellular specs. *And* they'll match what Tasman Central Authority think they recorded when she came on-station."

"There'll be other records, won't there? From her home world, from Diplo Central. You can't hack into all those . . . can you?"

"I *might*, given time," Nyx said with a brief scowl. "Never say can't! But Johni didn't tell me to go that far. It's a rush job, and the data only has to be consistent on-station, that's all I know . . . so whatever he's got in mind for you to do, it must be here on Tasman. Maybe he wants you to impersonate her with Tasman Central Authority and find out what she's been sent here for."

"Maybe . . ." Maris agreed. She should feel excited. Instead of punishment, this looked like a promotion! Only . . . too many things didn't make sense. She sidled to the door. "Thanks a million, Nyx. And I *promise* I won't tell anybody. Only, I need to be alone for a bit now. Think. You know? It's a lot to absorb."

"Okay, but don't go far. Your new cards should be popping

out any minute now . . . in fact, here they come. You want
to take them up to Johnivans yourself?"

The path from Nyx's workstation to the Hideout led
through a series of narrow, unused maintenance corridors
with partition doors rekeyed to codes only Johnivans' gang
knew. Maris tapped out the codes automatically, her mind
racing. Impersonating a Diplo? How could she ever pull it
off?

"Johnivans?"

"What's the matter, Maris? You look upset."

"Nyx told me," she blurted out. "About—"

Johnivans' face became momentarily a cold and chilling
mask, and Maris took a step backward, frightened of him
as she'd never been before.

"What, exactly, did Nyx tell you?"

"That you want me to impersonate this Diplo, maybe even
go to Kalapriya in her place. Don't be mad at Nyx," Maris
pleaded. "I—I kind of wormed it out of her, like."

Johnivans smiled and Maris thought she could actually
feel her heart resume beating. If she'd known Nyx telling
her would make him *that* kind of angry—but he wasn't angry
now, he looked like an indulgent uncle who's had his surprise present given away. "I would have broken it to you
more gently. Scared?"

"I can't do it," Maris said flatly.

"If I tell you to, you will."

"I didn't mean— Of course I'll do anything you want,
Johnivans, but—a *Diplo*? How can I possibly pull it off?
How could anybody?" Maris tried to collect her thoughts,
to explain. Diplos were—they knew everything, and what
they didn't know, they had magic chips implanted in their
brains to tell them. They could kill people by looking
at them and transport themselves without ships and,
and . . .

"Easy, kid," Johnivans said with his slow, warm smile
when Maris babbled out what was on her mind. "Most
of that talk about Diplos is mushroom feed. Hey, if they
were some kind of superpeople, think we'd have been able
to snatch this one so easy? They're just another kind of
snob toppie, that's all. Trust me, you won't encounter any
problems trying to pass for Calandra Vissi. Why don't you

go up to her quarters now and try on some of her out-fits? If they don't fit right we'll have to get them altered."

"Am I really going on to Kalapriya? That's her next assignment station."

Johnivans studied his fingernails. "Yeah. You're going exactly where she was going, Maris. And since the ID's done, I wish you'd get started. Know where her quarters are?"

Maris glanced at the handful of flimsies Nyx had handed her along with the cards. Level Five, corridor sixty-seven, room K. "Yes. But what if she shows up there?"

"I can personally guarantee you that will not happen."

"And can't you at least get me some Kalapriyan language plugs and an info-vid about the place? She'd be expected to know all that."

"You think you can fake a Diplo's language-learning implants with a few days cramming language plugs?"

"Can't hurt, might help," Maris said with more confidence than she felt. "And I can't be seen buying them, or order them off her account. It would look funny—she's supposed to already know that stuff. *Please*, Johnivans?"

"Sure, sure, I'll have Fingers get right on it."

That probably meant the plugs and vids would be gen-tly lifted from store stock or from some legitimate traveler's baggage, which seemed to Maris a silly risk to take when it would be easy enough to buy them—but she'd pushed Johnivans far enough already, and after all it was his decision. "And I'll go try on some of the Diplo's clothes," she said cheerily. "Just have Keito bring the plugs to her quarters, okay?"

Maris put on her "toppie" disguise just to make the jour-ney up to Calandra's quarters. She'd never been this close to Center before—and from the looks the real toppies gave her in the public lift tube, the shiny bodysuit and pseudosilk sarong that had enabled her to pass on Fourteen were barely acceptable on Five. Maris couldn't exactly define the dif-ference between her appearance and that of the toppies around her, but they looked somehow *polished*. As if some-body had put in long careful hours on arranging each strand of hair, buffing each gleaming nail, placing each beauty jewel in just the right place to bring out the best features of each smooth, confident face. She tried not to catch anybody's eyes as she hurried along the softly carpeted corridors of Five, glancing at tube and cross-corridor numbers out of the corner of her eye. Fifty, fifty-five, sixty, sixty-five, sixty-six, sixty-*eight*, that couldn't be right, what happened to sixty-seven, mustn't look lost or somebody would for sure stop her and ask what she was doing here, oh, *bunu* remodelers, sixty-seven had been bent around a lift tube to come out on the wrong side of seventy. Letters now, A–J this way, L–M that way, oh lovely, where was K, didn't toppies use the same alphabet as normal folks or—oh. Sixty-seven K was right in *front* of her, that was why there weren't any arrows pointing the way to it. With shaking fingers Maris inserted the key card Nyx had given her into the slot, placed her palm on the pad beside it. *Now* the alarms would go off, shrieking unauthorized access—

The door slid open so quietly Maris hardly heard the quiet *swoosh* of buffers across the deep-piled carpet. She took one wondering step inside, then another. And she'd thought *Fourteen* was luxurious—it was nothing to compare with this! How did you close the doors? She didn't want to risk a voice command. Oh, wave your hand over this sensor pad, the one with a picture of an oval door slit down the middle, and the iris closed. Wave again, and it opened. Maris waved a third time and told herself to stop playing with the room controls. Calandra Vissi wouldn't be fascinated by these controls, she'd be used to things like this or better—though what could be *better* was beyond Maris to imagine. In her head she started thinking how she'd describe the place to Nyx, how she'd convey the sense of luxury and safety executed in such an understated manner. Nothing like the bright patchwork of colors and textures in the Hideout; instead, soft blue-grey furnishings that seemed to grow naturally out of the soft grey-blue carpet. She dropped down on a sofa, half afraid her cheap sarong with its gaudy border of silver threads would stain or scratch the perfectly skin-soft upholstery. Chairs you could go to sleep in, she'd tell Nyx, the way they molded themselves to fit and support your body. Light that seemed to be everywhere and nowhere, somehow following the direction of your eyes so that whatever you looked at was gently illuminated and nothing glared. A full wall fitted with a flat-screen viewer set to create the impression of a deep forest glade stretching out into the distance. And *another* room opening off this one—no, two of them! A flimsy notice on one door invited the traveler to take advantage of the amenities in the Personal Care Suite. Maris glanced through the door and saw a gleaming array of faucets and mirrors and cosmetic toys. No wonder toppies had that polished look! Now she knew where they kept the polishers. Those would be fun to play with. Perhaps she'd get Nyx up here and the two of them could experiment with everything until they made themselves up into proper toppies from head to toe.

But first, clothes, in case they needed alterations. Johnivans thought of everything! Maris investigated the third room, fitted with a bed and hanging rods, with a small travel bag carelessly tossed under the clothes draped on the rods. Swathes of polysilk and other fabrics she couldn't even begin to name. From the way they felt between her fingers, the subtle odors arising from them, she thought some of them were actual organics. All the colors were good ones for her, strong ambers and warm browns set off with splashes of turquoise and emerald. Well, of course, she and Calandra Vissi had the same coloring—what was it the woman had said? Maris looked Sarossian, like her? Maris gave a mental shrug. That kind of talk was for toppies, people with families and dirtside homes. *Her* family was Johnivans and the Organization, and her place was Tasman—and her job, right now, was to try on one of these bodysuits and make sure it fitted.

It's going to take more than fine feathers to make a fine bird out of you, jeered a voice in her head as Maris slipped into an amber-colored suit and pulled the bodysuit closures together. A little tight up top, but nothing to worry about . . . as long as she didn't take a real deep breath. Maris inhaled experimentally and felt the bodysuit fabric relaxing around her chest, then molding itself more accurately to her shape. Hah, so even Johnivans didn't know everything—toppie clothes were self-altering, at least some of them! There was a wrap with a design of turquoise and aqua diamonds on a dark amber background that looked perfect with this suit; nubbly texture, but incredibly soft against her skin. And not—she tested with an experimental tug—self-altering. Made sense; you didn't want your wraps to give under pressure, they'd fall off. And she'd bet this was some kind of real organic anyway, not a teachable polymer.

With a little experimentation she was able to reset the wall screen from "forest glade" to "mirror" and check out how she looked. "From the neck down, very toppie," Maris concluded. Now she could see just how sleazy the "toppie" outfit Johnivans had provided had been, the crumpled bodysuit and the thin sarong with its stiff silver border, but at least the practice she'd had tying the sarong came in handy now as she adjusted the turquoise-and-amber over-wrap. From collarbone to ankles she was perfect. She stepped into a pair of the light sandals on the bedroom floor and was relieved to find that these, too, were self-fitting. As the uppers molded themselves to her foot shape the soles stretched out a little, accommodating a slightly longer foot than they were used to. The spongy texture was comfortable to walk on but the sandals themselves weren't really at all like the flimsy things she'd seen some toppie women balancing on; they were more like running shoes disguised as gold-strapped sandals, with the self-teaching polymer straps gripping her foot and ankle firmly, the flat cushiony soles giving a good grip on the carpet. Shoes you could run and fight in, made to look like high-fashion accessories . . . Like Diplos themselves: finely tuned diplomatic and military weapons disguised in a human skin. Maris might get the outside look right, but how was she ever going to fake the interior?

Well, for starters she could wipe that frightened look off her face, get her natural tumble of black curls restyled into a polished, artful tumble of curls like the toppie girls she'd seen on the way here, and . . . well, maybe she wasn't *quite* ready for that, to take the disguise out into the public areas of Five. Okay, there were things she could do right here in the suite first, like learning at least a few basic Kalapriyan greeting phrases, like "Hello" and "How are you?" and "What's *bunu* happening today?"

The comdesk wasn't so different from the ones Johnivans had appropriated for use by the gang; of course their call-codes weren't in any list this comdesk had stored, but Maris knew Keito's code. She buzzed his personal clip, got voice contact but no picture. "Keito, haven't you got those plugs for me yet?"

"Plugs?" Keito sounded—what? Blank? Surprised?

"Kalapriyan language earplugs," Maris said patiently, "and some info-vids on the planet. Didn't Johnivans tell you that I'm—" Well, maybe he *hadn't* told Keito all about her mission. Maris rearranged her sentence. "Didn't he tell you to get me those materials? Pronto? I'm sorry—" No. Little Maris, lowest-ranking member of Johnivans' gang, might apologize for asking Keito to do things for her instead of the other way around. Calandra Vissi probably *never* apologized. Besides, she needed those plugs. "I'm sorry you didn't get the order before I left the Hideaway. Now you'll have to send somebody up here with them. Five–sixty-seven–K," she repeated the address in case Keito didn't have that either.

"Johnivans didn't tell me anything about getting you— Oh. Right. Of course. Um, Maris, I'll, um, I'll be up with the plugs myself. Right away." Keito cut the contact abruptly, leaving Maris staring into the mirror wall with a puzzled frown.

She'd been some time finding the suite and then learning her way around it, trying on Calandra's clothes and all that. It wouldn't have taken Johnivans two seconds to com Keito and tell him what she needed in the way of support materials. And Keito didn't forget things. So what was going on, with him first sounding like he didn't know a thing about any language plugs for Maris and then promising to bring them up personally instead of sending a runner? Had Johnivans and everybody else gone crazy? Why was she the only person who seemed at all worried about how she was going to learn enough to impersonate a Diplo?

Trust me, you won't encounter any problems trying to pass for Calandra Vissi.

You're going exactly where she was going.

But what if she shows up there?

I can personally guarantee you that will not happen.

And he hadn't even bothered to pass on her request for plugs to Keito.

The girl reflected in the mirror grew so pale that she seemed to fade out in contrast with the rich, deep colors of her borrowed toppie wraps. She could only think of one way Johnivans could be so sure that she wouldn't give herself away. There was only one reason he wouldn't even bother to keep his promise to have Keito get her the plugs and vids she would need to carry off the deception.

Maris was too unskilled and uneducated to pass for a Diplo. But her DNA and retinal scans and fingerprints were all on Calandra's ID and in Tasman's databases. On Johnivans' suggestion, she was wearing Calandra's clothes. Her *dead body* would pass for Calandra's without any problem.

Johnivans wouldn't do that. He'd held her life in his hands for the years since he plucked her out of the corridors and let her into the shelter of the Hideaway.

Maybe he thought her life was his to throw away.

Maybe . . . With relief, Maris seized on the point that made nonsense of her wild imaginings. Makusu and Daeman *had* the real Calandra. If Johnivans wanted a corpse in the cabin, why wouldn't he just kill Calandra? Unless she'd escaped . . . Maris didn't think she'd escaped.

But what if she shows up there?

I can personally guarantee you that will not happen.

Daeman was a wild card, but Little Makusu was kind of sweet, if not terribly bright. Maris entered his com code and waited, twisting her fingers together, for him to answer.

"Yeah?"

"Hey, Little M, it's me, Maris. Listen, I need some info from that woman you snatched. You okay to go down to the holding partition and let me talk to her over your com?"

"Can't do that, Maris."

"Johnivans' orders? Because he *wants* me to talk to her, Little M."

"Naah. He didn't say that."

"How you know?"

" 'Cause you can't talk to the *bunu* cow now that she's spaced herself, can you, Maris? I mean—wait a minute—I don' think I was s'posed to tell you that, Maris."

"I won't tell anybody," Maris promised. *If I don't move fast, I won't even have the chance.*

And the last piece of the puzzle fell into place. Johnivans needed a body to pass for Calandra's. He didn't need anybody to pass for a living Diplo; that was why he could be so casual about Maris's ability to pull it off. Faith in her? Ha. Faith in her stupidly following orders without thinking about them until it was too late, more like it.

It might be too late *now*.

Maris stood in the center of the largest, most luxurious private space she'd encountered outside the Hideaway, shivering with deep chills that shook her from head to toe. The view of her own white face in the mirror didn't help; with a wave of her hand she reset the wall screen to a forest setting. All that luxury, and she couldn't even play with it. All she wanted was to walk into the illusory forest and disappear.

She'd known there would be a punishment for her failure in tracking Calandra.

She just hadn't expected it to be a death-penalty crime. *Johnivans*.

He'd given her a home. A place to belong. Well, he could take all that away again, and her life too; in a sense it already belonged to him. She probably wouldn't *be* alive now if if weren't for Johnivans. Corridor happy-girls didn't last long.

And she'd trusted him. She couldn't remember parents, knew Tasman Central Authority only as a distant threat, but Johnivans had been family and authority and home . . . and she'd felt happy and secure, knowing she had someplace she really *belonged*, people who accepted her . . .

People who were casually planning to kill her because her dead body fitted their schemes in a way her living self never could.

The chills became waves of pain that crashed through her body. She almost cried out with the pain . . . *It's not real. It's only feelings. Emotions. Don't feel. Think!*

Maris imagined herself shutting down like a console going into sleep mode, all the displays dimming, only one blinking light that was the one little part of her brain that processed information; all the memories and love and pain temporarily shut down.

And that light was blinking "Alarm Red." Like the stupid, obedient little girl she was, she'd brought herself exactly where Johnivans wanted her! What better place for Calandra Vissi to be found dead of natural causes than right here, in her own suite? Any minute now they'd be coming to get her, to turn her into Calandra, she could be a *good* imitation of the Diplo if she were dead, alive she could never pull it off. She had to get out of here *right now* and go . . . where? Was there any place on Tasman that Johnivans couldn't find her?

The com-chime jingled and Maris started convulsively. Too late—they'd found her—no. The forest glade was replaced with the image of a young man in Tasman Central Authority uniform. "Diplomat Vissi? With respect, Diplomat, we cannot hold your flight more than another ten minutes. If you do not respond to this last notification—"

Maris laid her palm on the com panel. It didn't flash alarms yelling "Impostor! Impostor!"

"Diplomat Vissi!" The uniformed boy wiped his forehead. "Why didn't you respond before?"

Because I'm dead. The real Calandra was dead and the fake Calandra would be, any minute—unless—

"Shall I notify the shuttle crew that you're on your way?"

"Yes," Maris said in a voice tight with strain. "No—wait!" Her head was whirling. "I—I've forgotten which exit bay to go to."

"Thirty–two eighty-three–B, ma'am. Shall I send someone to escort you?"

"Please." Maris thought she had managed an appropriate tone of hauteur; she moved her hand to close the display. Johnivans would find it hard to arrange her "natural" death if she were being escorted to the shuttle by someone from Central.

Or would he just consider the escort as one more witness to dispose of? *Don't be silly, even Johnivans can't get away with leaving a trail of corpses all over Tasman.*

She hoped.

And the escort was already at the door; that boy who commed her must have had someone waiting in the hall. Probably it wouldn't do his career any good to be the one on watch when a Diplo missed her connection. Well, she'd do him a favor as well as herself.

"One moment!" Maris swept Calandra's personal belongings off the long shelf and into the black travel bag, jammed a few of the hanging clothes in on top, picked it up and prepared to act the part Johnivans had prepared for her. Surely she could pull it off long enough to reach exit bay 283, board the shuttle—and then? Well, at least she'd be off Tasman. And once they reached Kalapriya, she'd shed Calandra's identity and lose herself on that world. A whole world had to be easier to hide in than a space station, and Johnivans would have no reason to kill her anyway. Once she'd boarded the shuttle as "Calandra," his worries about a missing Diplo would be over.

He could have thought of that. He could have given me that chance. No! No thinking; no feeling; just get to the exit bay. Maris nodded to the escort, handed him the black travel case to carry for her—surely a Diplo didn't carry her own luggage?—and followed him through the corridors of Tasman to the exit bay.

Chapter Two

Rezerval

Annemari Silvan sighed and tapped her deskvid again, harder, one perfectly shaped fingernail clicking impatiently in the lower left corner. You'd think Federation officials at Base on Rezerval would have the latest and best equipment; actually they had the latest, not fully debugged, annoyingly untested equipment. She'd wasted countless hours in meetings with Procurator Taddeo trying to get it across to him that just because they could *afford* to buy the latest "upgrade" of every program and system didn't mean they *should*; eventually she gave up and decided to accept that high Federation officials were also, thanks to Taddeo's lust for the latest and greatest technology, unpaid beta testers for comdesks, datafetchers, and anything else Taddeo could convince himself was a timesaving appliance.

Tap. Tap. Taptaptap . . . Reading the manual was a last resort and one that Annemari, with a twenty-year history in database design and implementation before she got pushed upstairs into administration, always felt vaguely ashamed of using. But sometimes there was no other choice . . . Oh. The new improved interface required you to tap the top right-hand corner to activate com mode before it would let you tap the bottom left to call up your address list. And exactly why that was supposed to be an improvement, who could guess?

And she was only fretting about the fiddle time wasted on new systems because that was easier and safer to fret about than the very real problems she faced as a servant of the Federation and the mother of an adolescent boy with his own set of problems. With one more decisive tap Annemari initiated a call to the desk of Evert Cornelis. Whose call code she knew by heart, so who was kidding whom about her need to figure out how the new deskvid brought up an address list?

"Haar Cornelis? I need a favor?" The upward, seemingly insecure inflection worked well with adult men; Annemari suspected, without wanting to think it over too much, that it had some connection with her slight, almost childish figure and a smooth face unlined by twenty-five years in Federation service.

"Anything I can do for you, Fru Silvan, you know that!" Evert's broad, ruddy face beamed at her from the deskvid, seeming to warm her entire cool, grey, steel-and-plastech office. "If it's about the new communications bill—"

"Nothing official," Annemari confessed. Time enough to explain the details when they were outside. "It's just . . . Niklaas is in the Med Center again for another round of tests. I promised I'd be there while they were doing the tests, and I was wondering? If you could possibly make time to walk over with me?" No need to fake the slight quaver in her voice. That was real enough. That she knew what effect it would have on Evert, and deliberately didn't control it, was despicable—but no worse than what she'd already done, and trivial beside what she was contemplating doing.

"I should be honored, Fru—Annemari." Perfectly Evert; on Federation business they were Fru Silvan and Haar Cornelis, on something as personal and unofficial as giving an old friend some moral support at the Med Center they were Annemari and Evert.

The Med Center was just a short walk across the park from the Federation offices; a pretty walk, lined with flowering trees and decorated with vistas of ponds and statues and follies. Annemari made casual conversation about the plantings, and how lucky they were as Federation officials to enjoy this luxurious setting, and wasn't it fortunate that whoever was in charge of the park didn't share Haar Taddeo's enthusiasm for newness or the trees around them would have been torn out and replaced by some genetic experiment melding apricots with bristlephlox, until they were nearly at the central pond. Evert very courteously went along with her, making no attempt to lead the conversation to what he must suppose were her real concerns.

And they—he—Niklaas *was* her main concern, always and only. But if the next round of medical tests had really been the problem, she wouldn't have gone to this much trouble to get Evert out of the building.

"Could we sit for a moment?" Annemari headed for one of the white-painted benches that surrounded the pond without waiting for Evert's response. He was far too much a gentleman ever to deny such a request.

"Have we time?"

"Yes, Niklaas's tests don't begin for nearly an hour. I wanted to talk to you, Evert, and *not* on the deskvid." Annemari ran a finger over the bench to test it for dust and gave the skirt of her beige silk suit an imperceptible twitch to keep it from stretching out of shape when she sat down. Satisfied, she seated herself beneath the grey statue of Hans Joriink, Hero of the Federation, rather improbably rendered in full battledress with very modern-looking weapons, and patted the place beside her.

"Cold things, deskvids, I've always thought." Evert sat down and put an arm round Annemari's shoulders and gave her a brisk hug. "Worried about the tests?"

"Always. But I didn't get you out here just to cry on your shoulder."

"At your service, any time," Evert affirmed. "Cry on, lean on, whatever else you want to do with a shoulder . . . maybe not dislocate it. Pretty near anything up to that, though."

Annemari forced a smile. "Evert, have you ever heard . . . well, rumors, hints, anything . . . about some people getting bacteriomats that weren't . . . that didn't come through the usual channels?"

"Galactic myths," Evert said cheerfully. "Sure there are rumors like that, but they're in the same class as all those stories about spacefaring dragons that eat ships, Indigenous Territories rulers who make live sacrifices of prisoners, and beneficent aliens who want to solve all our problems with their advanced technology. The fact is, the Barents Trading Society has the bacteriomat business locked in. And it's not as if they were holding on to a surplus that somebody else might steal and sell, you know. If they could produce more 'mats faster, they'd be only too happy to sell more. The market's a long way from flooded."

"I am," Annemari said quietly, "only too well aware of that."

Evert glanced down at her, concern showing on his kindly face. "Niklaas still not eligible?"

She shook her head. "You know the rules. He's classified as a self-inflicted injury. Absolutely last on the list for a 'mat . . . and there will *always* be new Hassenblatt's and Fournier Syndrome victims diagnosed who come ahead of the SIIs." She heard the bitterness in her voice, stopped before she could get into a full-blown tirade about the rules and the bureaucrats who enforced them.

"I've never thought that reasonable," Evert said. "He's a kid. Kids do dumb things. Having a roloprop accident shouldn't be . . ."

"There are any number of Fournier Syndrome victims who'd argue with you. After all, they did absolutely *nothing* to bring on their disease—except for having a genetic defect we didn't know to screen for when they were born." Annemari sighed. "The trouble is, I can see their point."

"We might be able to find some way around the rules," Evert suggested. "Damn it, if top Federation officials on Rezerval can't bend the rules a little . . ."

Annemari shook her head. "Dear Evert. You know that it works just the other way. We're exactly the people who *mustn't* bend the rules, precisely because we might be able to if we tried.

"I might try," she admitted, "but Niklaas won't hear of it. He knows where he stands on the list, he knows what it would do to my career if I tried to slip him into an approved category and got caught, and he says he will kill himself, and do it properly this time, if I try any such thing— he says he'd prefer that to the guilt of knowing he'd dragged me down with him. And I believe him," she said. "So you see—I didn't lure you out among the flowering paths to ask your help in anything quite *that* unofficial."

"What, then?"

"What if I were to tell you that the rumors about black-market bacteriomats were more than galactic myths, Evert? What if I were to tell you that I'd been approached by someone who claims to have them ready to install—at a price?"

"I'd want to know a lot more about the seller," Evert said.

Annemari sighed. "So would I. But I've been unable to trace him—her—or it. A self-destructing message on my home deskvid, no contact number, only a promise that they'll be back in touch after I've had time to raise the credits."

"How much?"

Annemari told him and Evert whistled. "That much? But—"

"I could raise it," Annemari said, "given time, and if privacy were no concern. But it's not exactly—if I go to the credit center for a loan, they'll want to know what it's for. And even if I lied, the coincidence of my needing a lot of money suddenly, and Niklaas's mysterious cure . . ."

"It could turn into a scandal almost as bad as getting caught trying to slip him up the list," Evert agreed. "So you need help with the credits?"

"No . . . Not yet. I haven't decided!" Annemari clasped her hands together so tightly the knuckles turned white. "It's unethical. It might be Niklaas's only chance. I haven't talked to him about it. I don't know how to persuade him even if I decided to do it. It could be a scam. Probably is. As you said—I need to know more about the seller."

"How?"

"I thought, when I couldn't trace the message, I might be able to investigate from the other end . . . look for their source. It seemed likely that somebody's found a way to steal some of the Barents Trading Society's stock. The 'mats must be coming from Kalapriya; somebody has to be smuggling them off, and they have to pass through Tasman."

Evert nodded. Tasman was a vital transfer station for any number of FTL routes, but it was the only station that offered FTL access to Kalapriya. Get the black-market 'mats to Tasman, and they could be sent off in a dozen directions. "That's where I'd start looking, too," he agreed. "What have you found out?"

Annemari pounded one clenched fist on her knee. "Nothing—worse than nothing! I'd had complaints about irregularities in the Barents Trading Society relations with the Indigenous Territories on Kalapriya."

"Orlando Montoyasana," Evert said instantly.

"Who else? Yes, I know, he sees sinister plots in every colonial system. Anthros are like that; they care so much about keeping the cultures they're studying pure and uncontaminated that they see tech contaminants under every rock. We've been ignoring his memos for years. But you see, we do investigate one every so often, just so he can't complain of being totally ignored. So I sent a Diplo to Kalapriya . . . Calandra Vissi, she's on my extended staff, you know her?"

"A very competent young woman," Evert murmured, "even apart from the augmentations."

"I tried to let Montoyasana know she was on her way, so he could be looking out for her and show her whatever "evidence" he has. But the man hasn't downloaded his messages for weeks."

"Probably off somewhere collecting more native rituals, and well out of ansible range. I don't suppose he's so popular with the Barents Trading Society that they're going to decode his mail and transmit it by heliograph. No modern communications outside the Society enclaves on the coast, you know."

"Maybe," Annemari agreed. "That's what I thought at first, too. But now, Calandra . . . Officially she's been sent to follow up on Montoyasana's complaints, to tour the Indigenous Territories and make sure no culture protection regulations are being broken or sidestepped. Unofficially . . . I asked her to go by way of Tasman, and to see what she could find out about smuggling links with Kalapriya."

"And?"

Annemari turned both palms up in exasperation. "And *nothing* since her first report from Tasman, telling me she'd arranged to be "stuck" a few days in transit to give her time to drop some hints about smuggling and see what she could find out."

"So maybe she hasn't found anything out yet."

"She would have told me that before she left for Kalapriya. Calandra's very conscientious; she reports in regularly—at least she used to."

"You're thinking she ran into something she couldn't handle on Tasman?"

"Not on Tasman, no." Annemari shook her head. "That much I *do* know. She caught the Kalapriya shuttle right on schedule; I've called up the passenger manifests, even made an excuse to talk with the young man who served as her courtesy escort to the shuttle gate. But she should have reported in as soon as she reached Kalapriya, and I've heard nothing for several days now. One person dropping out of contact could be coincidence, especially a researcher. But two disappearing from the same world—and when the second is a trained Diplo—I'm afraid, Evert. I'm very afraid Calandra may be in serious trouble."

"Couldn't get to an ansible?" Evert suggested, weakly.

"Oh, come on. The shuttles all land just outside Valentin, the BTS headquarters city. She could certainly have checked in by one of the ansibles allowed under the enclaves' exemption 'for technology vital to trade and government, and capable of being strictly segregated from indigenous cultures,' " Annemari quoted from Federation regulations.

"They have ansibles in the offices," Evert allowed, "but they do require their people to live in technology-consistent quarters. My aunt Sanne's always complaining about it— even though with all the Kalapriyan servants in the household, she has a lot less to do than she would in a smart-apartment on Barents. She married a fourth-generation Trader, you know, one of the van der Wessels, what's his name, Paalje, no, Pledger, that's it . . . the old Trader families go in for funny names. Why, you can tell a Trader even before he opens his mouth, that's what Sanne used to say, never mind their accents, they'll always have one of those made-up names like Johntoon or Raydeena. Of course that was before she married into the van der Wessels; she doesn't think anything, now, of having children called Cloud and Shower. I live in fear of the third christening, they're liable to call the kid Thunderbird. Sanne's younger than me, you understand, we Barentsians run to extended families, she's the daughter of my oldest brother and he's more than thirty years older than I am—"

"Exactly why I wanted to talk to you, Evert!" Annemari broke in at the first pause for breath. "I *knew* you would have the solution for all my little problems; you always do." Her secret vice of watching romance holos when she couldn't sleep at night was paying off; without all those goopy holos, she'd never have known how to flatter a man into doing what she wanted. "Your aunt Sanne sounds perfect."

"Not in my experience," Evert said. "Bit of a pill, actually, always going on about trivial little problems and making them into mountains. She can spend more time—"

"Perfect for what I need right now," Annemari interrupted ruthlessly before Evert could get into a long catalog of Sanne's peculiarities. "On Kalapriya, in a coastal enclave, married into a top Trader family. She'll know everything that goes on, and she'll have access to an ansible, and nobody will think it at all peculiar if she sends her nephew long chatty messages about life in Valentin."

"M'family would," Evert corrected. "Think it damned peculiar. Sanne's a lousy correspondent; I probably wouldn't even have heard about Cloud and Shower if she hadn't been counting on me for substantial birth-gifts."

"And if I know you, Evert, you were madly generous. So she'll want to be especially nice to you now, won't she?"

"She will?"

"So that you'll be equally generous with little Thunderbird when he—or she—comes along. Just ask her—by private ansible, Evert, *not* the Federation system—how things are going on Kalapriya and whether she's desperately busy with parties and receptions for the visiting Diplo. Then if she writes back complaining of all the extra work of entertaining Diplos and how hard it is to get carpets of rose petals in the right colors, we'll at least know Calandra is all right—"

"And if she says, 'What Diplo?' we'll know that something happened to Calandra either on the shuttle or right after she got to Kalapriya," Evert finished. "Very clever, Annemari!"

"I could never have thought of it without your help," Annemari said without even blushing. "Dear Evert, you're so clever—and so kind!" she added, more truthfully. "So you'll check with Sanne?"

"Tonight," Evert promised. "Could do it sooner, but if you want it kept on the quiet, better not run home now to use my personal ansible, eh? Although if a Diplo's gone missing, Annemari, it *will* be an official Federation matter, you know?"

"Of course I know that," Annemari said impatiently, "but there's no need to make it official just yet. I'd rather keep everything very discreet, just in case . . . well, if there *is* a black market in bacteriomats, we don't know who might be involved, do we? Somebody knew how to contact me on Rezerval—what if somebody at Federation headquarters is involved in this? Or what if . . ." She paused and clasped her hands tightly together.

Evert sighed. "Or what if you decide to acquire a 'mat from these people for Niklaas before you blow the whistle on them," he finished for her.

Annemari stared out across the pond. A flight of swifts swirled and turned above the water, making a graceful ballet of their daily hunt for water insects. Speed, grace, freedom . . . all that Niklaas was denied. "It would be unethical," she admitted, "but I have to consider it, Evert. You do see that, don't you?"

"Unethical to do it, maybe," Evert said, "possibly immoral *not* to do it. Of course you have to think about it."

"If they're stealing 'mats from Society stock," Annemari mused, "it would be exactly the same as using my connections to sneak Niklaas up the list; in effect, I'd be stealing from somebody with Fournier Syndrome or worse. But if—*if*—somebody has found another, better way to reproduce 'mats, something the Society doesn't even know about . . ."

Evert tried not to let his face show what he thought about the likelihood of this possibility. "Just let me see what I can find out about your missing Diplo, and what *she* can tell us about these black marketeers, and you worry about the other half of the problem."

"What's that?"

Evert rose to his feet. "How you're going to persuade Niklaas that accepting a black-market 'mat isn't just as unethical as jumping the list. And speaking of Niklaas, hadn't we better be getting on to the Med Center?"

CHAPTER THREE

Valentin on Kalapriya

Dwendle Stoffelsen took one last glance over the notes for his speech of welcome. It would never do to stutter or mix his words in front of a Diplomat—damned people probably had an entire dictionary stored in one of those little chips they had stuck in their heads. A *thesaurus*. In six *languages*. Along with canned speeches for every possible occasion. And here he was, eyes too old to focus on the words that flashed on the tiny prompters built into the podium, reduced to relying on a handful of old-fashioned flimsies and his own memory for what was likely the most important event of his career.

"Floris, can't you set the prompt screen to a larger font?" he demanded of the young tech who was setting everything up in the meeting hall.

"Sure, Haar Stoffelsen, if you want to be prompted one word at a time," the kid said cheerfully. "Heck, I can even bring up a font so big you'll get one *letter* at a time, if that's what you'd like. What I can't do is make the screen itself any bigger—that would require a new screen, and we'd have to get that shipped via Tasman."

Not to mention, he thought, that a bigger prompt screen

45

would have to be fitted into a bigger podium, and old Stoffelsen would look like even more of a doddering old fool than he was, standing behind a pedestal that dwarfed him. Why hadn't the old guy gone off-planet for a lens replacement as soon as his eyes began playing up, like any normal person?

Dwendle Stoffelsen was wondering the same thing, but unlike young Floris, he knew the answer. Some of the Society business he managed was just too delicate to be left in the hands of subordinates while he took the time to visit off-world medical facilities. And too dangerous! You couldn't trust these kids nowadays; they'd be poking into all his private files as soon as his back was turned. And there was no telling when some crisis might arise that needed his personal management. Why, he might even have been off-world at the time this Diplomat arrived! And what a disaster *that* would have been. One certainly couldn't trust Torston to handle a Diplomat properly, and as for Kaspar, he simply didn't understand the protocol and traditions of the Society. These kids new from Barents were too impetuous by half, always trying to solve problems with the first wild idea that flew into their heads. He shuffled the flimsies irritably. Even these notes were too hard to read. But there wasn't time to have them printed in a larger font; he could already hear the welcoming music outside.

The vaguely melodious sound of flughorns in the distance, supported by the rhythmic drumming of the boras, became a deafening cacophony of blare and thump as the doors to the meeting hall were thrown open. After the blue-uniformed guards entered there came a slender, dark woman almost dwarfed by the tall forms of the honor escort on either side. Good Barentsian lads, Dwendle saw approvingly; the best of the new generation, reared in and dedicated to the traditions of the Society. Standing between them, swaying with fatigue and most inappropriately dressed in some modernistic off-world outfit that was half skin-tight stretch fabric and half billowing draperies, the Diplomat didn't look like such a threat after all. Just a young woman who didn't know anything about Kalapriya or the Barents Trading Society, and who—with any luck—would leave knowing little more. Dwendle took a deep breath and waited for the blare of the flughorns to die down before he began his opening remarks.

"Diplomat Vissi, the assembled Fruen and Haaren of the Barents Trading Society welcome you to Valentin on Kalapriya. We are deeply honored by your visit . . ."

It was, after all, nothing he hadn't said hundreds of times before, if not to quite such a dangerous visitor. And as the formal phrases rolled on, Dwendle felt his confidence returning. This slight young woman could hardly pose any real threat; if it weren't for all those increasingly urgent ansible messages from Rezerval, he'd begin to think this whole visit was just a formality, the Federation's polite way of showing respect to the Barents Trading Society and the invaluable service they offered. *And not only the Society, now.*

Thinking of that, and of the wealth and power that would totally overshadow even the wealthiest of the conventional Society members, Dwendle went on almost automatically with the flowery phrases he had assembled from a hundred such speeches to make sure that no compliment, no phrase of welcome, would be lacking from the Barents Trading Society's formal greeting to this most unwelcome visitor. He gazed with mild irritation at the glazed eyes and expressionless faces of his colleagues. You'd think they could pretend a little more interest; maybe they *had* heard it all before, but he flattered himself that his vibrant voice and measured, dignified yet forceful delivery lent new life to the old words.

"And in conclusion . . ." he began, and was irritated yet again to see a flicker of joy on the faces in the front row. Just for that, he extended his "conclusion" by a good five minutes, repeating already-expressed hopes for a joyful visit and a fruitful collaboration between the Barents Trading Society and the Federation of which their home planet had the honor to be a member, reiterating the honor they felt upon being visited by a Diplomat from Rezerval and the deep desire of every member of the Barents Trading Society to serve the visitor in any way possible.

Maris didn't mind how long the old geezer talked; as long as he was speechifying, she didn't have to figure out what to do next. Not that she'd had a lot of options yet. She'd meant to be out of the shuttle seconds after it docked. Hadn't ever ridden a shuttle before; didn't realize how long it took to complete docking, how everybody

lined up and shuffled forward a step at a time, how she'd
be stuck in the line of travelers. You'd think a Diplo would
get special treatment, first one off—not that it would have
done her much good; the reception committee was waiting right there in the docking bay. Uniforms, lots of blue
uniforms, and so much gold braid it made her eyes hurt.
A sea of tall young men with hair as yellow as their gold
braid and tall old men going grey, or losing their hair
altogether, like nobody here ever heard of implants. Tall
blond people closing in around her, no way to slip away
on the short walk to the single exit door—which was
guarded, anyway, by more of the tall guys in the blue and
gold uniforms. On both sides. And outside, a blaze of heat
and light and white dust that half stunned her, even before
that godawful blare they called the Barents National Anthem
started up and they lifted her into some kind of box on
wheels with large animals tied to it.

Of course she *knew* what a sun looked like, she wasn't
ignorant. Johnivans treated his crew to the best entertainment holos even before they were released for public dis-
tribution. She just hadn't realized how big and bright the
thing was, and how it released waves of heat that settled
down on your head like a smothering blanket—and how
come, if the Barents Trading Society was so rich, they
couldn't afford a nice climate-controlled city? Nobody in the
holos had to experience this kind of raw dirtside life, not
unless they were brave pioneers colonizing a new world or
something.

At least the hall was climate-controlled. From the outside
it looked like all the other primitive buildings they'd passed,
built from some kind of creamy white stuff that dripped and
crumbled, topped with hard round red tiles; but inside it
was a reasonably normal kind of place, with smooth walls
and gentle lighting and, thank goodness, cool air.

And it, too, was guarded inside and outside by uniformed
men. Maris felt as though she'd been swimming through
a sea of tall blondes ever since she came off the shuttle.
The women were as bad as the men, big and buxom, with
yellow braids wrapped around their heads to make them
look even taller. And their clothes weren't anything like
Calandra Vissi's up-to-the-minute stretch bodysuit and woven
wrap. Instead they wore loose floating panels of some flimsy

organic-looking cloth, topped with falls of fine white lace that set off their pink-and-white complexions. No way Maris would be able to slip away and blend in with this crowd, even if they hadn't had six people watching her every minute since she stepped off the shuttle.

The old geezer had finally shut up; a discreet pattering of palms filled the hall, and suddenly they were all looking at Maris: hundreds, *thousands* it seemed, of bright blue eyes watching her.

Expecting her to stand up and act like a Diplo.

Make a speech, probably.

She *couldn't* make a speech. She hadn't had any practice. She didn't know the words. She talked like a Tasman scumsucker.

This was where they discovered her imposture and—what? Shipped her back to Tasman on the departing shuttle, most likely.

Not a good idea. Somehow she'd have to drag it out a bit longer, at least until the shuttle was gone; she didn't mind if they threw her out on a ship going somewhere else, just not back to Tasman.

Stand up. You can do that much, can't you?

The folds of her fashionably draped overwrap were damp with sweat from the brief ride outside, and the bodysuit was sticking to her in places she had never expected anything to cling. But yes, she could stand up. She could even find a few words of thanks to *what was his name, oh yes* Haar Stoffelsen *don't forget the others* and all the members of the Honorable Society who had found time to welcome her today. She apologized for being too tired from the trip to respond properly. "Maybe later," she said, and sat down more quickly than she'd planned, dizzy with fear and certain that her last words had come out in the Tasman twang as "Mybe lyt'r."

It seemed that whatever she said marked the end of the welcoming ceremony; the Society members all stood and came crowding round her, a sea of bright blue eyes and broad smiles that seemed somehow pasted onto their faces. The band crashed into action again. Maris winced and leaned back against her padded chair, then stood again as people started coming up to shake her hand. She dropped her eyes and murmured syllables that might have been polite greeting formulas. Weren't they ever going to finish saying hello—so that she could say good-bye and get out of here?

Her sway was not feigned at all, but it brought one of the matrons sitting on the stage behind her to her elbow. "Dwendle, you fool, the young lady's not used to our climate, nor dressed for it. Go on, all of you!" She shooed the elders of the Society, now all on their feet, away with quick impatient gestures. "Do you let me take her home now for a nice rest, heavens know the poor girl will need it before the banquet and ball tonight. Saara—drat that child, she's never here when I want her!"

"You told her to stay home, Mama," murmured a young woman even taller than Fru Stoffelsen, bending her head meekly even as she spoke.

"So I did, Faundaree! Well, heavens know somebody has to see to those dratted servants or they'd take a half-day holiday with all of us cooped up in here listening to Dwendle. Come along with me, m'dear."

"Ivonna, my love," Haar Stoffelsen protested weakly, "we'd planned a tour of orientation for Diplomat Vissi after the welcoming ceremony."

Maris belatedly remembered that *she* was Diplomat Vissi, and tried to look interested in the horrible prospect of being toured and oriented, but there seemed to be no need; Ivonna Stoffelsen ignored Dwendle's objections as if she hadn't even heard them. Quite possibly she hadn't; the lady had not stopped talking since she took charge of Maris, ordering the tall girl—Fawn, was that her name?—to see that the carriage was ready, telling a young man on the fringes of the crowd not to lounge like a Kalapriyan servant, but to get on to the Stoffelsen house and see that Saara had the young lady's rooms properly prepared and a light repast ready to send up.

"Yes, yes, Fru Stoffelsen," another of the interchangeably tall, fair young men interrupted, "but we *must* have Diplomat Vissi for the tour of the culture caves first. The tide, you understand."

Ivonna Stoffelsen puffed disapproval. "Well, *I* call it cruel, Benteen Teunis, dragging the poor young lady off to be seasick and lecturing her about bugs before she's even had time to find her land feet!"

"We don't want to waste the Diplomat's time, do we now?" Teunis took Maris's elbow and deftly steered her out of the crowd. "I'll return her to Jetty Six," he promised Fru Stoffelsen. "Tell your driver to wait there with a carriage and a pair of turagai."

Turagai, turagai, turagai, the big animals that pulled the boxes were called turagai, that was the kind of thing a Diplo with a language download would be expected to know. Maris repeated the word like a charm to keep her safe while Ivonna Stoffelsen indignantly proclaimed her intention of meeting the young lady personally at Jetty Six—"and you'd best not take too long with your bugs and slime, Benteen Teunis!"

"Microbes," Teunis said in a tired voice that somehow told Maris he'd heard this from Ivonna before. "Microbes, Fru Stoffelsen, and biofilms. And the reason we are all here."

"Diplomat Vissi," Dwendle Stoffelsen managed to interject before Teunis carried Maris away, "we will look forward to seeing you at the welcoming banquet tonight. My fellow Society officials and I will be prepared for an in-depth discussion of your mission so that we may learn how best to serve you."

Serve her up on a platter, he thought privately, *with an apple stuffed in her mouth*. Wasn't it bad enough that she'd *come* here, with all the implications of meddling and interference and undesirable questions that the visit of a Diplomat meant, but she also had to show how superior she felt to them all? Not even bothering to respond to his speech! Dwendle straightened his shoulders, feeling taller and stronger now that his horrible wife was out of the building. It was unthinkable that all he had worked to achieve should be called into question by this—this insolent child. Tonight they'd get the details of her orders out of her, and then he could consult privately with Torston and Kaspar as to how to arrange matters. Surely they could whirl her through Kalapriya, bury her under uninteresting details, send her away with the impression they'd told her everything about the 'mat trade while leaving her with very little real information. Have her tour the breeding caves, then send her on state visits to the native nobility of the Plains States until the heat and humidity exhausted her. They'd done it to other

important visitors. Diplomats couldn't really be possessed
of the superhuman powers rumor credited them with. Could
they?

Maris decided she had no real choice but to follow wherever this Benteen Teunis wanted to take her. She didn't
know enough about what a Diplomat really did to plan
her own schedule; presumably these guys did, so if she
just went along with whatever they had planned they'd
likely accept her for what she pretended to be. And sooner
or later there'd be a chance to slip away. They couldn't
very well keep her in meetings and on tours for every
watch of the cycle.

Could they?

Anyway, all she had to do now was follow Benteen
Teunis from the cool meeting hall, along a dusty white
path inadequately paved with big flat rocks. Sweat dripped
off Maris's forehead and dampened her curls into slick,
wet locks. But after they had walked a good two corridor sections' distance, she felt the warm air moving gently
against her face. Something smelled different, too. Aha!
They might talk about living under the planet's low-tech
restrictions, but *she* could tell now. Somebody, somewhere,
had turned the temp down and set a ventilator fan in
motion. The air fresh out of the ventilators always smelled
different . . .

"Ah, the sea breeze," Teunis said. He gave a deep sigh
of satisfaction. "I am grateful my work keeps me on the
water or in the caves most of the time; tell you the truth,
Diplomat Vissi, I don't know how my colleagues in the
Society can stand living in the heat of Kalapriya.

Sea? Maris mentally riffled through her memories of old
vids and found a number of quite unlikely images: scant-
ily dressed people standing on stages that rocked up and
down, waving shiny sharp things and yelling at each other.
Oh, yes—that had been in *Sea Pirates of the Iraveen*.

The sea pirates had been quite unpleasant people until
Captain Quirk of the Federation landed and reformed them.

With tanglenets and dazers.

"Ah—there aren't any pirates where we're going, are
there?"

Teunis laughed a bit harder than Maris thought the

question warranted. "No, the Kalapriyans are a peaceful people. At least within the Trading Society's sphere of influence. Piracy would interfere with our business, you see, so we—ah—discourage it."

Probably with tanglenets and dazers.

"Only simple fishermen use the coastal waters," Benteen Teunis reassured her. "And—ah—the Society, of course."

The cool, sharp-smelling air was all around them now, and Maris could see a line of blue-green between the white-walled buildings that lined the road. As they drew closer, the line got larger. Wider. Not really a line at all. Fields? Some sort of crop, waving in the ventilator breeze?

Water.

A *lot* of water.

And things bobbing up and down on top of the water like those stages in *Sea Pirates of the Iraveen,* only Maris didn't think there were any machines making the things sway up and down like that. She thought—

A particularly long, rolling, heaving sway felt like it was trying to carry her stomach with it, and she concentrated so hard on *not* noticing the movement of the wooden things that she barely noticed anything else: not the short, dark men around them coiling ropes and folding nets and talking in a strange birdlike chatter, not Benteen Teunis's hand on her elbow again urging her to step down into one of the little wooden things, not—

She *would* have told him, not on your life, I ain't going *on* one of them things, but she was afraid that if she unclenched her jaws long enough to say anything she would lose the entire contents of her stomach, just like some new dirtsider in zero-g for the first time, and pride kept her silent.

Two young men, as fair-haired as Benteen Teunis but with redder skin and younger faces, did things with ropes and pieces of cloth around them and Maris, teeth clenched firmly against the heaving swell of the water and its echoes in her stomach, barely noticed that the little box she was sitting in was moving away from the land, out into the unimaginable expanse of blue-green water. The Kalapriyan fishermen watched them, unmoving on the dock.

"Why do they not awaken the demon in the box?" Sunan asked.

His friend Ladhu shook his head. "They never awaken it until they are out of sight of the harbor. Perhaps the sea-demons cannot be called up near land, lest they leap ashore and escape from the outlanders' control."

"Or perhaps they think if they are careful enough, we will not notice that they use demons to push their boats?"

Ladhu laughed. "Even outlanders cannot be *that* stupid."

Benteen Teunis sighed with relief as they rounded a rocky crag that blocked the small harbor of Valentin from view. "All right, boys, you can start the motor now."

There was a rumbling noise like a small—a *very* small—shuttlecraft taking off, and the box suddenly tilted, pointy end up, leveled off just above the water level and began to move forward smoothly and much more quickly than before. Maris gave an involuntary sigh of relief. This felt so much more natural than all that sloshing and swaying and pulling pieces of cloth around against the wind.

Benteen Teunis gave her a friendly smile. "My apologies if the motion of the boat under sail bothered you, Diplomat Vissi, but we are under strict orders not to use the hover engines within sight of the natives. Can't risk cultural contamination, you know."

Maris nodded. She couldn't think of a properly toppie-class reply; he'd just have to think her a snob.

"It'll only take a few minutes now to reach the sea caves," Benteen went on without even waiting for a reply. "I'd better give you some background on how we harvest the 'mats—or no, I suppose you've already been briefed on all that?" His face fell as he realized that there was probably very little he could tell a fully trained and briefed Diplo.

Fortunately, there was *plenty* he could tell Maris.

"Nobody understands the local situation like a—um—local," Maris said brightly. "Tell you what, why don't you just pretend I dunno nothin' about yer mats an' give me the usual spiel?"

Idiot! She was slipping back into the sloppy Tasman way of speaking Galactic. But Benteen didn't seem to have noticed; he was too happy to tell her all about his beloved bugs. He talked microbes and biofilms and bacterial communities even when they reached the protruding tongue of slick, black stones leading into the first cave, even during all the business of docking and handing her over the side and mentioning that she just might want to watch out for the algae that made the cave entrance so slippery and oops, I forgot to mention that little bump just inside. Maris would have thought a rock hanging low enough to bang her head would have been considered a serious health hazard by the tall, solid Barents colonist.

"I'm s'prised you haven't removed that," she said, rubbing her forehead and glaring at the rather ugly mud-colored lump of rock that had been hiding in the overhead shadows just behind the cave entrance, now illuminated in Benteen's handlight.

"Oh, we couldn't do that," Benteen said, sounding shocked. "We haven't yet tested it for microbial life."

"I thought you *knew* what grows in here."

"The 'mat colonies, yes. But who knows what else might be here, might also prove of incalculable benefit to mankind?" Benteen gestured largely at the craggy rock formations surrounding them, turning the handlight as he did so to point out each type of microbial colony in turn. The pools of salty water on the cave floor held fuzzy blobs that looked to Maris like bits of somebody's lunch bar that had been left in a warm place for much too long; one of the walls was dotted with circles of pinkish-beige stuff; misty white nets trailed down from the top here and there. Personally, Maris would have described the place as seriously icky, not as a source of incalculable benefit to mankind. But then, what did she know? Apparently bacteriomats also came from this dank hole in the ground. And those had certainly been of major benefit to her, and Keito, and Ice Eyes, and . . . *Johnivans*.

Who had been father and brother and friend to her.

Who had been casually willing to throw her life away.

Waves of pain swept over Maris and she missed a good part of Benteen Teunis's explanation of the incredible biodiversity concealed in the fuzzy blobs and other odd things growing on the cave rocks. When she could pay attention again, he was earnestly explaining the difficulties of culturing the bacteriomats outside the cave environment.

The famous bacteriomats seemed to consist of two, no, three spots of greenish-grey film, hardly visible against the grey rocks on which they grew. The sparkling glass dishes placed all around them were far more noticeable.

"Looks like a shrine," Maris said when Benteen paused, evidently waiting for her comment.

"What? Oh!" He laughed. "No, those are our attempts to find some culture medium that the 'mats will like. You see, we can harvest from these three 'mats, but only when they grow large enough that we can take a ten-centimeter square and still leave something a little bigger. Take a sample smaller than that, and it dies in transit. Leave less than that, and the whole colony dies. We lost two of the five original 'mats learning that." The light shone briefly on a grey rock that had been scraped bare in two spots. "So far they—the 'mats—are still VNC."

"Meaning?"

"Oh. Viable but nonculturable." Benteen paused and chuckled self-consciously. "In layman's terms, you might say it means we still haven't figured out how to grow them outside the cave environment. We can keep them alive—in stasis—but they don't reproduce until they're implanted in a human brain." He went on to tell Maris more than she really wanted to know about synthetic media versus complex media, the school of thought which swore by Beccoham's G-22 Fetal Calf Serum and the opposing school supporting RQNJ 554, and the isolated nuts who insisted on using pure red agar with selected growth agents manually added.

None of which concoctions had as yet appealed to the bacteriomats.

"It's basically just a matter of trial and error," Benteen admitted. "Even on worlds we've known for centuries, successfully collecting microbes is as much folklore as science. Some researchers even leave vital medium ingredients out of their publications!"

"No, really?" Maris said, trying to sound appropriately shocked. If it was as hard as Benteen claimed to grow these bugs, and as valuable as they were—well, if *she* figured out how to do it, she for sure wouldn't be publishing her results for anybody and his brother to copy.

"Why, when I was in graduate school, I needed to collect some samples of the luminescent strains of Barentsian cyanobacteria for my dissertation research. And I tell you!

I tried to grow them on agar, and on Lochinver's LML, and even on Falcon's Medium with glucose, and *nothing* worked. Finally I got in touch with Professor Benedetti, who had collected the original cultures, and you know what he told me to put into the medium? Paper clips! Old-fashioned, unplasticized, wire paper clips. And it worked!"

Maris made admiring noises.

"But the *point* is," Benteen emphasized, "that so far *nothing* has worked with the 'mats. They like these particular rocks, right here in this cave, and this particular damp air probably supplies some catalyst we haven't identified yet; and they like human brains. Nothing else! That's why there's such a demand for them, because the supply is limited to what we can harvest from this site and the three other caves we've found with 'mat films. We've got researchers going up and down the coast looking for other cave sites, but for all we know, these four caves may be the *only places on the planet* where these particular biofilms are found. So you see, it would be impossible for somebody to be harvesting them without our knowledge. We have each growth site mapped before and after every harvest. You think somebody could come in here and cut a ten-centimeter square off one of these babies and I wouldn't even *notice*? It would be like taking ten square centimeters off my own skin." Benteen thought this statement over briefly. "Worse, really. It's *easy* to get skin replaced."

"Then how is it being done?"

"What d'you mean?"

Maris thought she'd been clear enough. "How is somebody getting extra 'mats to smuggle off-planet?"

"They *aren't*," Benteen said emphatically.

"Oh, but—" Maris stopped short. *Right, scumsucker. Explain to him exactly how you know somebody's smuggling 'mats? Calandra wouldn't know.*

"Oh, you know," she finally said. "One hears rumors . . ."

"Rumors, schmumors. I can tell you of my own personal knowledge that the supply is carefully controlled and every *single* bacteriomat sample is accounted for from the moment it leaves its cave until the moment it is shipped to Rezerval."

Fru Stoffelsen was waiting at the dock when they returned. She started talking before Benteen handed Maris up the steps, and she continued talking all through the hot, weary journey to the Stoffelsen chambers. Maris recalled little of the jolting ride but heat, sweat, the ubiquitous white dust, and Ivonna Stoffelsen's voice going on and on, expressing her low opinion of men in general, Barents Trading Society officials in particular and her own husband most of all; fools who thought being a Diplo, sorry, Diplo*mat* meant a young lady was a machine and not a young lady tired out from too many space transfers and in no condition to be subjected to speeches and tours of orientation and all that nonsense.

And yet this Dwendle Stoffelsen seemed to be a very important member of the Society. He certainly acted as if he ranked all the others, just as Johnivans ranked everyone else in Tasman's underworld. Maris tried to imagine what would have happened if she or Nyx or even crazy Daeman had brushed Johnivans out of the way and countermanded his plans, and looked at Ivonna Stoffelsen's buxom form with dawning respect. Either these people had a *very* strong tradition of courtesy to women, or they had some very egalitarian customs. Either way, Maris thought she could learn to like it here, and even felt a slight pang of regret when she remembered that she needed to sneak off as soon as she was left alone for a minute. But there was really no alternative. "In-depth discussion," ha! Even if she got a chance to look at Calandra Vissi's official orders, she had a feeling Dwendle Stoffelsen was going to want more information about her plans than that. A lot more.

Fru Stoffelsen's nonstop chatter was at least giving her some idea of what kind of world she'd stumbled onto. From the complaints interspersed between pointing out landmarks, Maris began to understand why life on Kalapriya reminded her of a holo about brave pioneers settling a new world. There had already been a civilization on Kalapriya when Barents "discovered" the planet: First Wave colonists, so long separated from interstellar civilization that they had developed their own culture and primitive technology. Due to previous disastrous encounters between long-separated First Wave cultures and the modern world, the Federation had protocols for minimizing the culture shock and easing these cultures into modernity. The state or world or confederation of planets that claimed rediscovery of a First Wave world was allowed to govern that world as a colony and to exploit its natural resources, but only subject to severe Federation restrictions. Technology beyond the level attained by the indigenous culture had to be necessary, approved by the Federation as necessary, and restricted to small enclaves that could be strictly segregated from the indigenes.

In some sense, Maris had known all this, known that much of Johnivans' income derived from smuggling prohibited technology onto Kalapriya. Since Tasman was the one point through which all Kalapriya traffic had to pass, and since Johnivans had a lock on Tasman's underworld, the pro-tech smuggling business was a very profitable one indeed.

And, of course, things that were smuggled onto a planet were not displayed openly. Maris would have said she knew that too, if anybody had questioned her. Only, just as the burning globe overhead was so excessively large and real compared to the suns she had seen in holos, the reality of Kalapriya itself far outstripped what she might have imagined a low-tech planet to be like. No visible technology higher than the best indigenous level meant no climate control outside of a few strictly guarded Trading Society official buildings, no powered walkways, no transport at all other than these boxes-on-wheels, no servomechs in homes . . . Ivonna Stoffelsen enlarged on these and other restrictions which, she felt, made the lives of Society officials and their families little more than one long sacrifice to the economy of Barents, and in so doing, gave Maris a better idea of what to expect on Kalapriya than any number of training vids could have done.

By the time the jolting box turned in at an avenue shaded on both sides by trees as high as any three levels of Tasman, Maris thought she was beyond surprise—but the gracious white structure visible at the end of the avenue took her breath away. "Your—the Stoffelsen family chambers—are in *that*?" She'd seen holos of a palace, once. Three-level columns holding up shaded porches, walls pierced with viewing vents a level high and a grown man's armspan across, billowing swathes of flowered fabric . . . this seemed to have no relation to the squalid living conditions Fru Stoffelsen had been complaining about all the way from the meeting hall.

"This," Ivonna Stoffelsen said with pride, "is House

Stoffelsen at Valentin. Nothing to compare with the home House on Barents, of course, but . . . the Stoffelsens are Old Trader Family, you understand? "Those lindenbaumen"—she waved at the trees shading the avenue—"were put in by old Joris Stoffelsen himself. Not really lindenbaumen, of course. Not allowed to plant anything from Barents. Natives call 'em something else, one of their unpronounceable outlandish words. But they have flowers that smell just like linden, so *we* call them lindenbaumen. Makes us feel we've got a little bit of Barents with us in our exile."

Faundaree made an odd strangled noise at this and Maris glanced anxiously at her, wondering if the girl was choking. "Ma's never been off Kalapriya in her life," Faundaree whispered under cover of Fru Stoffelsen's monologue. "None of us have. We're fourth-generation Society. She just likes to put on airs about being an exile!"

Despite Fru Stoffelsen's words, Maris had been escorted halfway through the sprawling house before their meaning dawned on her. This wasn't the building where the Stoffelsens had chambers—this *whole building* was theirs! Interior space such as she'd never dreamed of in her life: high-ceilinged, white-walled rooms, their shadowy darkness a relief to the eyes after the glare of the Kalapriya sun. One room opened off another in a seemingly endless procession, all with wide windows and some sort of mechanical flappers overhead creating an artificial breeze, all furnished with tables and chairs and shelves made from real organics. Maris knew the material was organic because Fru Stoffelsen complained endlessly about the ban on high-tech imports that made it impossible for her to offer her guest a suite with proper self-molding chairs and an autobed.

"I think this is *beautiful*, Fru Stoffelsen, honestly," Maris told her, standing in the center of one of the three spacious rooms that constituted her guest suite. "The space, and the quiet, and this wonderful furniture . . ." She ran her hand gently over the satin-smooth top of a chair back, appreciating the deep glow that emanated from the reddish-purple wood. "I've never seen anything like it."

Ivonna Stoffelsen bridled with pleasure. "Now that's real courteous, coming from a young lady that's likely already seen more worlds than you've had hot dinners, Faundaree! You could learn some manners from the Diplomat, Faun, instead of standing there gawking like a great country girl with nothing to say for herself, as if you hadn't been educated on Barents and everything! Now over here we have the washing facilities, such as they are, Fru Vissi, and poor makeshifts you'll likely think them—"

"Please, call me Mar—uh, Calandra," Maris caught the slip just in time, and let Fru Stoffelsen go on to explain away her awkwardness with the porcelain washstand and the bathing tub as the natural confusion of somebody used to the latest in high-tech refinements. "Really, after the tube-showers on Tasman, this is luxury," Maris said with perfect honesty. "All of House Stoffelsen is perfectly lovely, you have nothing to apologize for, Fru Stoffelsen, it's me should be apologizing for imposing myself on you this way. I could have stayed at a public—"

"Not one of them shelters the Society puts up for officials in transit, wouldn't be proper for a young lady on her own," Ivonna cut her off. "And what are you giggling for *now*, Faun?"

Faundaree hastily straightened her face and begged pardon. "It's just that the lady sounded almost like one of us for a minute, and then she slipped back into that awful Tasman twang, Ma."

"Uh—automatic mimicry," Maris improvised hastily, hearing the echo of her own unfortunate words. *Impowsing meself this wye.* She strove for an effect similar to the Stoffelsen ladies' broad, slow vowels. "I'm afraid it's one of the hazards of the profession; I seem to pick up the speech patterns of anybody I'm with." She gestured vaguely toward her head, as if to implicate one of the embedded microchips that were said to give Diplos such amazing powers.

Fortunately, the Stoffelsens didn't seem to know much more about what Diplos actually could and could not do than Maris did; in any case Ivonna was more interested in castigating her daughter for rudeness than in accounting for her visitor's slipping accent. Finally she allowed as how "Calandra" might want to rest before that evening's banquet and ball, chastized Faundaree again for standing there chattering when any fool could see the young lady was tired from her trip, and moved toward the door. Maris privately thanked the God of Looking After Unimportant Persons. If she could just be left alone for a little while, long enough to figure out how and where to disappear to—it was going to be more of a problem than she'd realized, with her olive skin and black curls she'd never be able to blend inconspicuously into a population of red-and-white-complexioned blond giants.

"Bless me, what was I thinking of?" Ivonna exclaimed, halting her progress toward the suite door. "You'll be needing proper clothes for the ball—die of the heat, you would, in something like you've got on now, Fru Vissi—I mean, Calandra. Didn't your bosses warn you about us having no citywide climate control?"

"Don't be silly, Ma," Faundaree interrupted, "Diplos know everything about everywhere, all planted in machines in their heads."

Maris smiled weakly. "There are an awful lot of exaggerated rumors about what we know," she said. No need to mention that in her case the rumors would be more than just exaggerated. "And your mother's right. A sudden posting—I didn't even have time to pack appropriate things for this climate." That at least she knew was true. None of the high-tech, high-fashion outfits she'd raided from Calandra's closet would be suitable here. Given the restrictions on inappropriate technology, they were probably illegal. "You know how these bureaucratic offices are, Fru Stoffelsen . . ."

"Don't I just! No consideration for anybody anywhere, and that's the truth! How much notice did you get, anyway?"

"This time yesterday," Maris said with perfect truth, "I had no idea I was coming to Kalapriya."

Ivonna Stoffelsen clucked some more about the well-known inconsiderateness of all bureaucrats everywhere and finally, half towed by her daughter, left with promises to send her second daughter, Saara, up with some suitable Kalapriyan-style clothes.

"Not too soon, I hope," Maris muttered as soon as Ivonna and Faundaree were out of sight.

"The Fru desires—?" piped up a fluting voice behind her.

Maris gasped and whirled to see a squatting form where she'd thought there were only shadows. The form elongated, fluttered, moved forward and became a slender-boned person even shorter than Maris, bowing deeply.

"Who the—*who are you?*"

The small person looked up at Maris. Its dark face was

placid. "This one called Kamnan, set here to serve Fru because speak ver' good Galactic. But could not understand what Fru said just now."

"Oh. Um. It doesn't matter. I don't want anything, could you just go away for a while?"

"Not speak good enough?" Dark, liquid eyes became even more liquid with welling tears.

"Speak *great*, Kamnan, you probably speak better *bunu* Galactic than me, but I—don't—want anything right now, understand?"

"Understand. Will wait." Kamnan sank back down into her—his?—corner, and Maris stifled a sigh. She hadn't figured on having to know how *servants* worked on top of everything else. Even in the holos, nobody had servants, not even toppies, except . . . well, except those old story-vids about pioneers. Okay, it made sense. If you couldn't have so much as a dust-sorber, let alone a molecular clothes box, then somebody had to push things to clean the floor and do whatever you did to get clothes clean without a moly-box, and it was probably not the most interesting work in the world, so if you were a toppie—and the Barentsians seemed to think they were *all* toppies—you got some lower-level type to do it for you. Which, in this case, probably meant a native Kalapriyan.

Maris felt quite proud of herself for working all this out unassisted. There hadn't been much call for thinking things out in Johnivans' gang; Johnivans himself did all the thinking; what he wanted the others for was to carry out his plans.

I *was a servant,* she thought suddenly, *his servant, and so were all the rest of us. I thought he was my friend, but he wasn't; he was my boss. He didn't save me from working the corridors because he cared about me, but because he thought I could be useful. All he ever did was use me— use all of us.*

That thought made something deep in her chest hurt; she felt more alone than she had since her days as an orphan without a gang, roaming the lowest levels of Tasman and stealing or begging just enough to keep alive. *Don't think about it now, think about practical things; think about where you are now.* There was certainly enough of *that* to keep her newly discovered intellect busy! This

Kamnan, who couldn't be sent away, who acted so sub-
servient and looked so different from the other people she'd
met, must be a Kalapriyan—all right, she'd already worked
that out, but what she hadn't seen at first was how useful
Kamnan could be. She could tell Maris all about Kalapriya;
maybe she could even teach her enough of the language
to cover up Maris's total lack of Diplomatic language
implants.

"Kamnan—" Maris began, and then was interrupted by
a flurry at the door.

"Masaidtobringyousomeclothestotryonyou'reaboutmyheight-
theyshouldfit. You'reFruViissiright? I'm Saara."

"Huh?"

"I *said*," repeated the pile of light-colored organic fabrics
filling the door, "I'm Saara."

The long bare legs under the fabrics moved forward; a
cloudburst of lightweight white fabric covered with tiny
flower prints billowed over the bed, and a girl just a little
taller than Maris looked her over gravely.

Maris returned the assessing look. Not a giant like the
rest of the Barentsians she'd met, this Saara, and instead
of a wreath of yellow braids her hair was cut short and
brushed up in a sort of defiant crest. And it wasn't yellow, either, but a mix of pink and turquoise stripes. The
girl was so slender that she gave an impression of being
extremely tall, but it was really just long graceful bones
and a way of carrying herself, that boss-of-all-the-world
look all Barentsians seemed to have.

"Yougottabehotinthatoutfitwantatrysomeoftheseon? *Well?*"
the girl added impatiently when Maris didn't respond
immediately. "You want to try some of these on?"

"If they're like your mother's and sister's dresses, I don't
really see the need," said Maris. Those loose billowing tents
of lightweight organics would fit anybody, wouldn't they?
And she was less than thrilled about wearing a white organic
tent printed with tiny little pastel flowers. With her coloring, she'd look like a short stick of broiled soypaste kebab
wrapped in way too much recycled flimsy.

Saara grinned. "You'd be surprised. Ten millimeters too
long in the hem, and you step on it every time you try to
walk anywhere."

A *very* short kebab, Maris thought ruefully. Even if she

liked these pallid prints, these dresses were designed for tall fair Barentsians.

"And if I hike it up and get it ten millimeters too short, I suppose that wouldn't be so good either?"

"My dear! Dreadfully *fast*, showing your ankles like that! And a Diplomat, too! Old hens," Saara added in her own voice, making a couple of clucking noises with her tongue.

Maris looked at Saara's own long, tanned legs and minuscule cut-off bodysuit without saying anything.

"Yeah, but *I'm* only a child," Saara said. "Sixteen next spring. I get until I turn eighteen before I have to wear this stuff. 'Course I got some proper lady dresses now, for like Ma's parties and like that, but I don't have to like wear it all the time, sowhenMasayscanIsparesomeIgolikesure, no problem, you know? Howoldareyouanyway?"

When Maris deciphered the question a flash of panic stopped her voice. *I don't* bunu *know how old I am, nobody ever said, nobody ever asked me that, nobody ever cared . . . oh, stop worrying, you ninny, she wants to know how old* Calandra *is.* But the answer to that was somewhere on the identity papers Nyx had handed her, and she hadn't studied them, she hadn't planned on "being" Calandra Vissi longer than it took to disembark from the shuttle . . .

"Sorry," Saara said with an embarrassed laugh as Maris failed to answer, "Ma keeps *telling* me to talk slower, but I get like wound up and I forget. I said how old are you anyway?"

By that time an acceptable evasion had occurred to Maris. "Old enough to have to dress like a proper lady," she said ruefully. "Can you show me how these go on?" What had looked simple at first glance turned out, when she picked up one of the garments, to consist of a bewildering profusion of under-panels and over-panels, hard knobbly round things, long narrow fluttery things, gathered bits and straight bits . . .

"Sure, and you can tell me all about other worlds. I'm going to be a Diplo, you know, when I'm old enough."

Maris blinked. "But don't you have to be—"

"Selected? Yes, but the School *would* select me, if they knew about me," Saara said confidently. "As soon as I'm old enough to take passage off-planet without my parents' permission, I'm going into the Real World, and—"

"What do you mean, the Real World?"

"Oh, you know. Anywhere but here. I mean, Valentin is like some kind of game we're all playing, pretending to be pioneers back in the Age of Expansion, playing at living without technology. *Nothing* happens here!" Saara said explosively. "Anyway, I'm not going to wait around for a Selector to happen to notice me; I'll just go to the School and explain that they *ought* to want me. I'm plenty smart enough and I know lots of useful things already, and I'm good at languages—only I suppose that doesn't matter if you get those chip implants, does it? Like, you probably speak better Kalapriyan than I do!"

"I think it extremely unlikely," Maris said firmly, resolving to get some language practice with Kamnan as soon as this unnerving girl went away. "The implants aren't nearly as powerful as most people think they are." Since Saara accepted this without question, she went on to say, "All they really give me is ability to learn the language faster than most people would." That felt safe enough. Maris's entire life had depended on being faster and sneakier than anybody expected, and why should learning languages be any different from the things she'd learned with Johnivans?

"Oh. You don't already—"

"Hey," Maris said with a forced laugh, "it's not like they open up your head and pour a dictionary in, you know!"

After a moment's disappointed silence, Saara laughed too. "Silly me," she said good-naturedly. "Up until this moment I had the idea it really worked like that. I guess a lot of things in the Real World don't work like I think. I guess if I just like stop talking and let you tell me how it is out there, I can learn a lot from you."

"Not nearly as much," Maris said, "as I hope to learn from you."

Chapter Four

Udara on Kalapriya

The Office of Lands and Properties Contracts had a lofty-sounding title, and a reasonably high place in the hierarchy of Udara's court bureaucracy—Chulayen's supervisor's supervisor had the title of Minister and reported directly to the Bashir—but the offices themselves were no better housed than any in Puvaathi, and worse than some. The three-story mud-and-timber building with its thick walls and deep, narrow windows had been converted from a family dwelling erected back when Puvaathi was just another one of the quarrelsome, feuding villages that made up the original Bashirate of Udara. Back when the Bashir himself had been a baby born into one of these sprawling compounds where four and five generations of a family lived together in a state of perpetual quarreling that mimicked the relations between villages and states—so Chulayen's father, the Minister for Trade, had described old Udaran life.

Having grown up with no family but his parents, a staid couple high in the Bashir's service who treated Chulayen with all the adoration usually lavished on a late-born son to a couple who'd given up hope, Chulayen himself had no clear idea of what life had been like in those old-style family

compounds. Crowded and noisy certainly, like his own rooms
down the hill now that the twins were almost seven and
the baby was beginning to crawl. Multiply that by twenty
or thirty, add old dowagers screeching about long-buried
feuds, put it all in the smoky darkness of this compound
and what did you have?

Probably something very like the Office of Lands and Properties, but without so much paper and ink, Chulayen thought
with an inner amusement that did not show on the smooth
brown mask of his court-trained face. His supervisor, old
Lunthanadi, was as cranky an old woman as anybody could
want, even if her trouble was too much to do rather than too
little. With a very small exercise of imagination he could cast
his colleagues as siblings and cousins jostling for recognition:
the young clerk-trainees were the toddlers, good for nothing
but to spill the inkwells they were supposed to be refilling
and misdeliver the memoranda they were sent to carry from
one department to another; and the shadowy, unseen figures
of the Bashir and his High Council could be the ancient great-
grandfathers who still held the land titles and the keys to the
money chest clenched in their bony fingers.

And fantasies like this did nothing to diminish the stack
of memoranda still on the writing desk before him, waiting for a word scrawled in the margin here, a tactfully
worded answer there, before they could be forwarded to some
other unfortunate soul or even, with great good fortune, go
to rest in the overloaded filing drawers along the west wall.

Chulayen squinted at the crabbed handwriting on the topmost document, held it close to the lamp to see it better,
and for the thousandth time contemplated announcing that
he was moving his office out to the verandah, where he
could work in decent light, breathe clean air, and see the
panorama of the city's countless flat-roofed dwellings spilling
down the mountainside before him. Quite impossible, of
course. There were highly confidential documents and very
important papers somewhere in this stack; one couldn't risk
having such things snatched up by a passing wind and blown
down the muddy lanes of Puvaathi.

Even though this particular letter, when he finally deciphered it, proved to be neither confidential nor important.

"I shall go blind before I'm thirty," he complained to
Sudhan, at the next desk. "All this just to read one more

complaint from some dung-shoveling villager who thinks the Bashir's decision to confiscate one of his fields for court costs was unjust! But I suppose that's what it is to live in the modern world. My father used to say that in the *old* Bashir's day anybody who dared to write a letter of complaint after a hearing in court would have had his nose and ears cut off."

"He wouldn't have written it anyway," Sudhan said, gloomily surveying his own stack of paperwork. "Back when everything had to be inscribed on scraped sheepskins, people wouldn't have stood for all this writing everything down and making copies in triplicate. In which case," he said, recovering his normal air of bouncy good humor, "we'd have been out of a job, so gods bless the man who invented paper! And now I look at it," he added, studying the sheet before him, "this particular piece of paper is more in your department than mine." He reached out a long arm and added the page to Chulayen's pile, making his own stack infinitesimally shorter.

"I'll do the same for you, first chance I get," Chulayen threatened. At least the document Sudhan had palmed off on him was in fair court script, an official judgment of some sort. Easy enough to read, but nothing to do with him; he was supposed to be evaluating appeals against previous judgments, not codifying new ones. A sinecure, since there had never been a successful appeal, but it showed the Bashir's dedication to doing the right thing. Someday the court *could* make a mistake, and when they did, Chulayen would be there to set it right.

He skimmed the page to get some idea whose desk he could dump it on, and frowned as he reached the bottom.

"Here, this can't be right."

"It's a pronouncement of the Bashir's court," Sudhan said. "Right and wrong have nothing to do with it—"

He broke off suddenly, hearing the rustle of Lunthanadi's full trousers, and almost choked while rewording the sentence to express more acceptable sentiments. "I mean, that is, pronouncements of the court are by definition right. We're not supposed to evaluate them, just file them."

"I'm not even supposed to be doing that," Chulayen said. "It should have been routed to a filing clerk, but all the same . . . Mother Lunthanadi," he appealed politely to the supervisor, "there's a mistake in this court pronouncement, what should I do about it?"

"Mistake? Hah. Those court scribes can't spell, I always said so! Send it back to be recopied, boy."

"Worse than a spelling error," Chulayen persisted. "This is a bad judgment. It's—the court has made a mistake, they can't have been informed of all the facts."

"Talking treason," old Lunthanadi said. "The Court of the Bashir doesn't *make* mistakes, Chulayen. And even saying they did make a mistake, once it's been pronounced and copied, it ain't a mistake, it's the law, and it ain't for us to question it, just to record and uphold it."

"Yes, but this really is a mistake. They wouldn't have done this if they'd understood—Mother Lunthanadi," Chulayen said, desperately willing her to understand. "Someday there will be an appeal against this judgment, and it will be a good appeal, and we will be forced to uphold it. Do you want your department to be the first one ever to support a successful appeal against a pronouncement of the Bashir's court?"

Lunthanadi held the paper out at arm's length and studied it. "And what makes you think you know more than the Bashir's own advisers about these Jurgan Caves?"

"I've *been* there," Chulayen said. "I've seen them. And you know it's not easy to travel there, at least it didn't used to be, before last spring." That was when the state of Thamboon had been peacefully absorbed into Greater Udara. Before that, Thamboon had been definitely hostile to Udara, a trouble spot on the borders from which seditious drawings and ballads entered the Bashir's territory. Of course, two years before *that*, Thamboon and Udara hadn't shared a border; the narrow strip of Narumalar had been a buffer between them . . . until the Bashir announced that the Narumalarans, alarmed at the aggressive actions of Thamboon, had requested the honor of becoming part of Udara. At the time when Chulayen and Anusha went there on a pilgrimage discreetly disguised as a general tourist trip, Udaran visitors weren't popular in either Narumalar or Thamboon; but he supposed the nasty aggressiveness of the Thamboon people had made Narumalar consider Udara the lesser of two evils. Certainly the Bashir, having taken in Narumalar, protected its people and borders as zealously as his own; why else would he have felt it necessary to absorb Thamboon?

Lunthanadi's lips twitched. "Ah, yes. I had forgotten Anusha's . . . enthusiasms. She's still involved in that cult, is she?"

"It's not exactly a cult," Chulayen said. "More of a . . . way of approaching life, you might say." Inside, he writhed with embarrassment. Following the Inner Light Way wasn't treasonous or even illegal; it was just not the sort of thing his class of people *did*. Mention the Inner Light Way and people got images of crumbling warehouses and a bunch of common Rohini and half-Rohini people, day laborers and maids and people like that, going into transports of ecstasy over the flames from a crude oil lamp. Anusha's continued involvement with the sect was a constant embarrassment to Chulayen, the sort of thing that might make his superiors feel that despite his impeccable Rudhrani lineage, he wasn't the kind of young man who could be trusted at the lofty level of the Bashir's personal council and their assistants. Normally he wouldn't have said anything at work to remind people of Anusha's religious enthusiasms. But in this case there was no way around it.

"We visited the Jurgan Caves," he said. "Eight years ago." *To pray for a son*, Anusha had said. *A holy pilgrimage to ask the blessings of the earth.* And the Earth had responded in Her usual way, with double blessing but no son: his beautiful twin girls, Neena and Neeta. Young devils, those two, with their glossy black pigtails dipped into any mischief-broth that might be stirring . . . but still a blessing. And now that they had a son, baby Amavashya, to carry on the lineage and say the ancestor-prayers when he and Anusha passed on, Chulayen could just enjoy his girls for the light and laughter they brought to his home.

"Very nice," Lunthanadi said, already looking bored. "You are a good husband to cater to Anusha's little hobbies. Some might say, too good."

Despite this broad hint, Chulayen felt he had to continue. "Mother Lunthanadi! This pronouncement says that the Jurgan Caves have become property of the State of Udara, to be mined for saltpeter."

Lunthanadi raised her bushy eyebrows. "And your little wife will have religious objections, I suppose?"

"Probably. I don't know. That's not the point! The caves are a natural wonder, Mother Lunthanadi. You don't have to be a believer of the Inner Light Way to see that. They are . . . there are whole chambers as large as this building, all lined with crystals, and lighted at noonday through openings in the roof, so that they sparkle like jewels on the breast of the earth." Embarrassed anew by his poetical flight, Chulayen reined himself in and tried to speak only of the practical issues. "The caves are hard to get to, high in the mountains. There's only a footpath leading to them, and it is a difficult path, the Thamboons won't—wouldn't—let anybody old, or handicapped, or pregnant women, even attempt it. Even if we desperately needed the saltpeter deposits, extracting and removing them would be a nightmare."

"Where there's need, roads can be built," Lunthanadi said slowly.

"Not *there*," Chulayen said with deep feeling. "The Thamboon mountains make Udara look like one of the Plains States. Half the rock is limestone, and crumbling, so you can't count on any path you used last year to still be there after the snow melt has washed down the mountainside. And if it *is* still there, it takes a Thamboon-born guide to recognize it."

"Ghaya tracks," Lunthanadi nodded. "Is that all, boy? We've all traveled in the mountains, you know. You're not an engineer, what do you know of road building? 'He who does not know how to dance says that the floor of the courtyard slopes.' "

"No self-respecting Udaran ghay," Chulayen said desperately, "would recognize a Thamboon mountain path as a usable track. And then there are the bridges, did I tell you about the *bridges*? Three strips of twisted grass rope if you're lucky—one to stand on and two to hold. If you're not lucky, maybe only *two* strips of grass rope. Or *one*." He swallowed hard, remembering. If Anusha hadn't been so shrill about his failure to support her beliefs, if he hadn't been so desperate to stop the nagging that the risk of death seemed an acceptable price to pay, he'd never have made it across the first bridge. "The Thamboons get loads across balanced on their heads. Do you really think we're going to export significant quantities of saltpeter that way?"

"Modernization," Lunthanadi said. "Development. Build better bridges."

"And we don't even *need* the saltpeter!"

Lunthanadi gave him a sharp bright glance. "We don't, eh? What are you, one of those loonies who thinks we don't need a national defense? I heard Inner Light types get that way—"

"I'm *not* an Inner Light follower," Chulayen said. "And yes, I know we need a strong defense force, and I know saltpeter is used in making gunpowder, but I also happen to know that our gunpowder stores have increased, not decreased, over the last five years. Despite all the enemies we've had to fight in that time."

"Precisely," Lunthanadi said. "Udara is surrounded by enemies. Not your place, nor mine, to argue with the Ministry for Defense. 'When they come to shoe the turagai of the Bashir, does the dung beetle stick out her foot?' We need the Bashir's army as never before, to pacify all those hostile states, and—what do you mean, the gunpowder stores have increased? Not your department, is it? Not even mine."

Chulayen swallowed again. He'd picked up that bit of information from Anusha's chatter after an Inner Light meeting where some low-level clerk from the Ministry for Defense had been saying things he shouldn't. But mentioning the Inner Light Way again would destroy any credibility he had left, and if he mentioned the clerk . . . talking about Defense Ministry stores at a public meeting was probably treason. Traitors deserved their swift punishment and removal from society, of course, but the poor guy hadn't meant any harm, he was just another nut case deluded by the pacifistic babble of the Inner Light Way.

"Just check," he challenged Lunthanadi. "You can do it. Minister Odaniya can request the statistics on saltpeter supplies and uses from the Minister for Defense. We all spend two-thirds of our time answering questionnaires and compiling statistics on this and that anyway; nobody will notice one more."

"Hmph! You worry too much about things that are none of your business, Chulayen. Remember, 'The wise adapt themselves to circumstances, as water molds itself to the pitcher.'" Lunthanadi turned away and waddled toward a junior clerk who had stopped his copying work to enjoy the argument. "Here now, young Bhiranu, d'you think the Bashir pays you to sit with your mouth open and see how many flies'll fall in? Your mother may have . . ."

With the ease of long habit, Chulayen tuned out the tirade and returned to his own desk, thinking so hard that he almost didn't notice Sudhan's winks. "*Told* you," Sudhan whispered, but then Lunthanadi whipped around and he became very virtuously busy reading and scribbling comments on his own paperwork.

As well to keep busy, Chulayen supposed. He reached for the next paper on the stack. But the court pronouncement that had worried him did not get routed to a clerk for filing; instead it found its way into the inner folds of the sash that held up his light, loose trousers. While he went through memos and letters mechanically, stamping each one with the appropriate phrase, scribbling his initials somewhere on the margin and consigning the paper to the appropriate box for the clerk-trainee to carry off for filing, the original memorandum seemed to grow and stiffen until it was all sharp edges and corners, poking him with every deep breath he took, refusing to be forgotten and filed away properly.

Lunthanadi had as good as accused him of being a—a *pacifist*. Chulayen's lip curled in an involuntary sneer. It was an ugly word, and one he had in no way earned. He was as loyal a servant of the Bashir as anyone in Udara, and of good Rudhrani stock on both sides of his family tree. He had never questioned and did not now question Udara's need for a strong army to defend its ever-increasing borders. His parents, already elderly when he was born, had well remembered the times of chaos in Udara when brother fought brother for the right to the throne, when venal councillors debased the coinage until you needed a barrow full of tulai to buy a turnip—and then likely couldn't get the turnip, because the farms had been despoiled by fighting among the war lords. They'd told him enough tales of those days to make him understand, perhaps better than most young men of his generation, just how fortunate Udara was to have a strong Bashir who maintained peace and good order in the community. Why, they could scarcely be better off had they lived in the legendary times of the Emperor! And now that he had a family of his own to care for, he was thankful every day that they were growing up in a strong, safe state. Neena and Neeta would never know the fear his mother had recounted at seeing blood running in the streets; little Vashi would never cry with an empty belly.

That was why he wanted somebody to understand the mistake in this judicial pronouncement, couldn't Lunthanadi see that? Not out of disloyalty to the regime, but out of the highest kind of loyalty, the kind that didn't want to see the Bashir's Council tainted by the record of a single unjust or unwise decision.

Also, it would be a great pity if the Jurgan Caves' wonderland of crystal chambers were destroyed by saltpeter miners before anybody figured out that it was virtually impossible to transport the product from Thamboon's mountains to the gunshops of Udara.

At the midday break Sudhan asked Chulayen if he was feeling ill.

"You've hardly moved a paper since that quarrel with Lunthanadi, you keep staring at the walls, and your lamp needs trimming." Sudhan nipped off the charred end of the wick deftly and looked again at Chulayen in the flare of improved light. "You're a funny color, too."

"Hardly moved—oh!" Chulayen really looked at his cluttered desk for the first time in some hours. Sudhan was right. That first burst of mechanical activity had ended as he sank deeper in thought; this afternoon he'd have to work double-fast to catch up with the new papers that had been deposited on his desk while he stared into space and thought.

Except that he wouldn't be here this afternoon, because out of all that blank nonthought had come an idea. He knew now what he had to do to protect the honor of the Bashir's court. "You're right. I don't feel so good. Tell Lunthanadi I went home sick, will you?"

"You're forgetting your dinner!" Sudhan pointed at the package of cold dhanadi balls, each wrapped around some tasty filling and the whole thing wrapped up in layers of green leaves that kept the food cool and fresh.

"You have it. I'm not hungry."

Sudhan shook his head at Chulayen's departing back. Pass up Anusha's cooking? The man was *definitely* sick.

In the hours that followed, most of them spent on the benches outside some office or other, Chulayen occasionally thought with regret of the packed dinner he had abandoned. Anusha might have her little faults, but even apart from the loyalty he owed to the good high-class Rudhrani girl his parents had chosen for him, she really was an excellent cook. Always in the kitchen, scolding their Rohini servant girl and getting her fingers burned and her hair smoky by insisting on preparing the meals herself so that they met her exacting standards. But he couldn't very well eat his dinner and then claim to be going home sick; he couldn't take the package home with him, or Anusha would want to know why he wasn't at work and where he thought he was going; and a High Rudhrani gentleman didn't eat in the street or sitting in the hall outside an office, like some Rohini day laborer. It simply wasn't done.

He couldn't go to the most logical person, either, the Minister for Land and Property; old Odaniya was a stickler for procedure and protocol and would likely refuse to talk to Chulayen altogether once he found out that Lunthanadi knew nothing of the visit. And the Minister for Defense wasn't likely to see a midlevel bureaucrat from another office, without an appointment and without recommendation.

But Chulayen's parents had boasted a wide circle of friends among the Bashir's most trusted ministers and councillors, men and women who would welcome Chulayen for the memory of his parents and would—he hoped—hear him out once he explained what was troubling him.

The welcome he received unreservedly; the understanding turned out to be a little harder to come by.

"Certainly, certainly, dear boy," his father's old friend Viripraj said. "Very—ah—conscientious—of you to concern yourself with these matters. But hardly my department, is it? Yours either, for that matter. You just route that on to the proper authorities, and I'm sure they'll see it's all taken care of."

"But who *are* the proper authorities?" Chulayen asked. "And if the Bashir's Council didn't know how inaccessible the Jurgan Caves are, how can I be sure that these authorities will understand?"

Viripraj's chuckle was rich as a well-aged red wine. Perhaps a wine a little past its prime . . . "Now, now, young Chulayen. You mustn't go setting yourself up as the only living expert on the world and how it should be run, not when you're talking to *me*. Not with somebody who saw you crawling around the floor in nothing but a cut-off shirt! Just give me the memorandum, and I'll see it reaches the proper person, and you can get back to work. Mustn't neglect your work, now, not with those pretty little girls of yours wanting marriage portions in a few years. What were their names again? Nila and Nela?" He reached out one hand, expectant.

"Neenalaladhi and Neetavaruna." The twins' lively brown faces and sparkling black eyes smiled in Chulayen's mind. Anusha often talked of taking the children back to see the Jurgan Caves and give thanks to the Earth for their fine healthy family—not now, of course, but in a few years, when baby Vashi was old enough to travel and when the situation in the former state of Thamboon had become somewhat more settled.

Perhaps, when they went, he could tell the girls how their father had preserved the Jurgan Caves so that they too could see the crystal chambers.

"Thank you," Chulayen said, standing, "but I mustn't impose on you to that extent. It was a great kindness in you to see me at all."

After Chulayen left, Councillor-Emeritus Viripraj sat thinking for a moment, then shook his head sadly. These young people, how rash they were, how incapable of seeing the whole picture! It was a harsh duty, but didn't he owe it to the memory of his old friend, Chulayen's father, to see the boy was brought to his senses? He rang a bronze bell and one of his confidential clerks came in.

"Follow that young man who just left," Viripraj instructed him. "If he returns to the Office of Land and Property Contracts, come back here and report to me. If he goes anywhere else . . . well . . . I suppose you'd better come back and report in any case." It wasn't time, yet, to send a note to the Minister for Loyalty. That could wait. The boy *might* show the good sense to take himself back to his own department and work through the proper channels.

"You do not seem to understand the unique position of the Ministry for Defense," Lal Neena Somiti said coldly. "It is my privilege, indeed it is every Udaran subject's privilege to defer to the Defense Ministry's requirements above all else—saving, of course, the Ministry for Loyalty." Her right hand moved in a barely visible avert-the-evil sign, hardly more than a reflexive twitch.

"When the requirements make *sense*," Chulayen said, "but this is a stupid pronouncement."

"It is not for such as you to call the Bashir's Council *stupid*. 'When they come to shoe the turagai of the Bashir—' "

" '—does the dung beetle stick out her foot?' " Chulayen finished for her. Lal Neena was as fond of old aphorisms as his boss Lunthanadi. "Lal Neena Somiti, if the turagai of the Bashir are already shod, might not even the dung beetle warn the Bashir that he is wasting money on a farrier? If they understood the position—"

"I am sure they consulted the requisite experts before making their decision."

"And had the 'requisite experts' ever been within half a kilo-lath of the Thamboon border?"

"There is no Thamboon border," Lal Neena pointed out. "The former aggressive state of Thamboon has now been peacefully absorbed into Greater Udara, by the mercy of the Bashir, may his name be remembered forever. Your talk comes perilously close to disloyalty."

"I only want to make sure this pronouncement isn't overruled on appeal!"

"It won't be," said Lal Neena. "You'd do well to think more of your own life and career, Chulayen, and less of meddling in affairs that are beyond your province." Her tone softened. "I'm only telling you what your own mother would, if she were alive to see what you're getting up to. Adapt yourself to circumstances, Chulayen, as—"

"As the water does to the pitcher," Chulayen finished tiredly. "And if the pitcher is broken, what becomes of the water?"

Lal Neena shook her head. "Go home, Chulayen. Go home *now*, and return to your office tomorrow. It may not be too late."

"First Somiti in the Ministry for Trade, and now you think he's going up the mountain to the north quarter?" Viripraj sighed. The boy was working his way through his parents' influential friends like a madman with a lighted torch in the dry brush. Pundarik Zahin lived in one of the mansions on the north quarter of the mountain, and he was always to be found there since the paralysis of his legs had forced him to retire from the Ministry for Defense. Doubtless that would be Chulayen's next stop. The best thing Viripraj could do for him now would be to see that he was brought to his senses as soon as possible. Harsh but necessary. "Very well. Send this note to Zahin—and see that you get there before young Chulayen does!"

"Sir, *you* could verify that the Ministry has more than adequate stocks of saltpeter!" Chulayen begged.

Pundarik Zahin stroked his long grey moustaches thoughtfully. "Adequate? Tricky word, that, boy. Adequate for what? Never know when we may need to repel aggression on our borders. Or put down uprisings within them."

Chulayen looked blank. "There's never been any unrest against the Bashir." The Ministry for Loyalty was well known for stopping troublemakers before they could get fairly started, and Chulayen had always felt they did an excellent job. He *liked* living in a peaceful and prosperous state; what idiot wouldn't?

"That's not to say there never will be any," Zahin pointed out. "Ministry for Loyalty can't be everywhere. And you know, those Thamboons, they're a wild lot, most of them are ethnic Rohini—naturally they're going to take a subordinate place to us Rudhrani, now that the countries are merged."

Chulayen nodded. That was the logical outcome, of course. Everybody knew that Rudhrani were smarter, faster, more logical, generally better fitted for management and government. Since most of the Thamboon people were Rohini, their country must have been struggling along with people unfitted by nature for the positions of leadership they were forced to assume. Of course Udaran-educated Rudhrani would be filling those positions now, and possibly some of the Thamboons were too short-sighted to see that the changeover was for their own good. Still—

"It's not going to make us any more popular in the former State of Thamboon," he said, "if we start by destroying a natural beauty spot which many Rohini consider also as a sacred place."

Zahin's bushy grey eyebrows shot up. "Sacred place? Perhaps that's *why* the Bashir's Council condemned the caves, my boy, ever think of that? Gathering spot for disaffected Rohini, these wild-eyed cultists. Better all round to set them to peacefully mining saltpeter—that's the kind of menial job Rohini are good at, after all—then they won't have time for all this Inner Light Way nonsense."

"But there's no way to transport the saltpeter, even if we did need it! It's just not profitable to bring anything big and heavy down out of those mountains. It would only be worth industrializing the caves if the product were something very small and valuable—" Chulayen stopped in midsentence. He had never seen Zahin like that, as if his face were carved from something harder than stone. This wasn't dear old "Uncle" Pundarik with the bad legs that he was arguing with; it was General Pundarik Zahin, conqueror of the half dozen states that had been combined to create Udara before Chulayen's birth. It was Defense Minister Emeritus Pundarik Zahin, still very much an active voice with the ruler whom he had brought to power and kept there through ten years of civil war.

"I really think, Chulayen," said this stranger, in a voice so carefully level that it was worse than the wildest tongue-lashing, "that you should go home now."

"Not back to work?" It was only midafternoon.

Zahin shook his head. If his face hadn't been so still, so carefully expressionless, Chulayen would have thought he looked sad. It must be a trick of the light. "No. Not today. It's too late."

"You mean—they've already started mining the caves?"

Zahin looked startled for a moment. "Well—that too."

As he made his way down the mountain, Chulayen pondered those last words of Zahin's. They were a strange echo of Lal Neena Somiti's. She had said *It may not be too late;* Zahin, *It's too late.* Too late for what?

The top of the mountain, the fine tall whitewashed houses surrounding the Bashir's palace, the peacock gardens and the fountains that cascaded down steep flights of terraced basins, were still bathed in golden afternoon sun. But as

Chulayen reached the lower levels, where Puvaathi village had originally been built and where it had exploded into a disorganized nest of office buildings, converted houses, street markets and kava houses, the slope of the mountain behind him caught and held the sun and turned afternoon into blue dusk. He walked from sunlight into shadow and felt the cool air of early of autumn on his face. Here the shadows turned muddy brown and dirty whitewashed buildings into blue palaces, made a veiled princess of a Rohini street vendor and a hidden treasure of a market stall's sacks of open spices. Chulayen took a deep breath of the clear mountain air with its underlying flavors of wood smoke, roasting meat, spices, and ghaya hair. Well, okay, not so clear maybe as it was up on the clean, cool, sunwashed mountaintop. But the mingled smells were comforting, were familiar, were *home*. His steps quickened as he turned away from the central crossings where shops and vendors clustered, toward a tangle of wood-and-mud houses that teetered precariously down the lower slopes of the mountain, one story tall on the west side and three on the east side. Behind a latticed window, someone sang mournfully from the song of Rusala.

> *Sada na rajian hakimi; sada rajian des:*
> *Sada na nove ghar apna, nafra, bhath pia pardes.*

> "Kings are not always rulers;
>   kings have not always lands:
> They have not always homes;
>   they fall into great troubles in strange lands."

"Buy a *yai pao*, honored sir?" whined the stooped old Rohini pancake vendor who usually worked just a few hundred steps from Chulayen's house, in the angle where three sets of buildings met and scattered down the slope in different directions. "My last one, honored sir, and with it for a free sauce, all the news of the day."

"Thank you, but the woman of my house would be annoyed were I to enter the house munching on dir—on fare not cooked by her own hands," Chulayen stopped himself from saying *dirty street food* just in time. It was right for a High Rudhrani gentleman to be courteous to all, even the lowest beggar; and at least this old woman was not begging, but trying to earn an honest living by selling the greasy pancakes sprinkled with slices of sharp fresh onion. The things *did* smell good, setting his stomach rumbling and reminding him that he had forgotten to eat earlier.

"So stand here and eat it while I tell you the news, grandson! You should not go home hungry and unprepared." Chulayen felt he really ought not to allow such familiarity, but such kindly concern emanated from her wrinkled face that he couldn't bring himself to snub her.

"No, no—I really must get home." As always when he got this close to home, Chulayen felt the familiar rush of anxiety, the old fear that he would return to an empty house, doors and window shutters shattered by rifle butts, empty rooms greeting him with the memory of screams. There was no reason for such fears—but the nightmare had wakened him time after time in childhood, and it had not gone away when he married and set up his own home; it had only inspired Anusha, after six months of marriage, to take up sleeping in the outer room where, she said, at least she could get some rest. During the day Chulayen was never troubled by such irrational fears, but each evening when he returned home his steps grew quicker, his breath shallower, until he saw Neena and Neeta running to greet him and knew that all was well with his family. And here he stood exchanging banter with a Rohini street vendor! He felt in the pouch at his sash and tossed her a tul. "Here, grandmother, give your last cake to someone who needs it."

"But the news—the news!" The old woman caught at the end of his sash, and Chulayen began to feel seriously annoyed by her impertinence. "The Arm of the Bashir has been busy today." That was the common people's term for the police employed by the Ministry for Loyalty.

"Then that is good news for all loyal subjects," Chulayen said automatically. No one spoke against the Loyalty's men, even if some of their actions did seem a bit excessive at times.

"*Is* it, Chulen? Is it?"

The small hairs at the back of Chulayen's neck prickled at this insinuating use of his nickname. "How do you know my name, grandmother?"

"Never mind that," the old woman said, "but if you are in such a hurry, then go—go to your house, Chulen, and then when you know how much you need my news, come back." Her black eyes sparkled bright in the tired, lined old face. Poor woman, probably she was used to augmenting her income from the pancakes by selling fortunes to ignorant common people who would be impressed by such tricks. There were a dozen ways she could have learned his name, she was on this street every day—

There was a black space down the street, a hole in the monotonous, irregular wall created by a dozen different colors of mud houses jammed too close together for anyone larger than a child to slip between the houses. A door-shaped hole with jagged edges . . . Chulayen's steps quickened. It was almost down by his house, something must have happened next door, Anusha would have been frightened, it couldn't be *his* house, no reason for the Ministry for Loyalty to come there . . .

Go home. It may not be too late.

It's too late.

The Arm of the Bashir has been busy today.

Chulayen stopped in front of the splintered ruin of what had been his fine arched door, gay with blue and red painted birds, and tried to make sense of what he saw. It didn't make sense, he was dreaming, this must be old Lammon's house next door that the Arm had broken into, a rich Rohini out of place in this decent Rudhrani neighborhood . . . Lammon's door had been unpainted.

It was still unpainted, still whole.

Empty house, empty rooms. A spatter of blood on the doorsill. The screams of his recurring nightmare rose in Chulayen's ears, deafening him to the small sounds on the street; his children's faces swam before his eyes, blinding him to shattered shutters and a bloody splash. The nightmare again; in a moment Anusha would wake him, he felt her tugging on his sleeve now . . .

It was only Tulaya, old Lammon's woman. "Come along inside now, dear, won't do no good to stand out in the street all mazed-like. Come you in and I'll fix you a good hot cup of kava and some of my barley soup. There's nothing to be done now, they'm long gone. Took 'un just afore shadowfall, they did."

"Neena? Neeta? Where are they? They always run to me before I get this far."

"All gone," Tulaya said. "Took 'em all, even the baby. Said they didn't want you, not yet. Said you'd know what to do if you want to see them again."

Empty rooms.

The memory of screams.

And no waking from the nightmare now.

Chapter Five

Valentin on Kalapriya

Saara stayed and chattered about life on Kalapriya until her mother called her away to dress for dinner. "And you should be dressing too, Calandra. Your escort will be calling any minute now. Ever such a nice young man, Gabrel, you'll like having him take you to the dinner and ball." Ivonna smiled. "I know, I know, you're here to work, but there's no law against having a little fun, is there?"

"I won't be going with your family, Fru Stoffelsen?" Maris asked in dismay. She had been counting on the Stoffelsen ladies' chatter to camouflage her during the evening's festivities. Then, surely, tonight she could figure out some way to get off Kalapriya and stop playing the Diplomat.

"That would hardly be proper," Ivonna Stoffelsen said.

Saara lingered. "Shemeansitlookslikewe'remonopolizing-you," she whispered.

"What?"

"*Monopolizing* you," Saara repeated in a slightly louder whisper. "YesmaI'mcoming!" she shouted, and left with a friendly wave.

Maris barely had time to scan Calandra Vissi's papers before Kamnan was fastening her into one of those complex

85

many-paneled drapes of light organic fabric, and this escort for the formal dinner was waiting downstairs.

Leutnant Gabrel Eskelinen. She gathered that "Leutnant" was a title connected with the blue-and-gold uniform he wore. So what did she call him? Gabrel? Haar Eskelinen? No, Fru Stoffelsen called the man "Leutnant Eskelinen" when she spoke to him. Maris covertly sized him up while Ivonna introduced them. Another tall Barentsian, hair so blond it was nearly white, cold blue eyes very light in a tanned face. The tan was the only thing that made him seem a little different from the rest. Young, but stiff as any of the old geezers who made the speeches.

What did toppies say when they were being introduced? Maris summoned up memories of old holos and held out one hand, languidly draped downward—sometimes the guys kissed hands, on those old shows. "A pleasure—"

"The pleasure must be entirely mine, Diplomat Vissi," the young man interrupted her. "We should depart now." A stiff bow, coming nowhere near her outstretched hand, and he wheeled and made for the door without waiting for her.

One of the ubiquitous Kalapriyan servants helped her up into the traveling box, and Maris studied her escort's profile as he guided the—the turagai, that's what they were called—down the long shady drive leading from House Stoffelsen to the public streets of Valentin.

Okay, she didn't know much about toppie manners, but she could tell *rude* when it was shoved in her face like that. Obviously this Gabrel Eskelinen disliked her.

Intensely.

She felt absurdly hurt, considering that they had only just met, so it couldn't be her *personally* he disliked, it must be Calandra Vissi. Or rather, Calandra's mission here. She supposed that was part of the job description for Diplos, getting up people's noses and asking inconvenient questions. Not to mention listening to interminable speeches, being sent to primitive dirtside locations without decent climate control, and having little machines stuck in your brain.

This Gabrel acted like he had something stuck up his backside as well as a bad whiff of Diplo up his nose. Maris supposed really she should be grateful to have a few minutes with someone who had no questions for her—but, irrationally, she wanted this one to *talk* to her. She didn't like being treated like a packing canister that had to be ferried from one port to another.

"So," she ventured as they turned into the mud-brown street outside House Stoffelsen grounds, "you got a lot of these, these boxes-on-wheels here?"

Gabrel Eskelinen looked down his long nose at the animals pulling the box. "There's no need to be sarcastic, Diplomat Vissi. You must know as well as I do that the term is 'carriages.' I'm sure a Diplomat would never be sent out without thorough briefing on the manners and politics of her assigned posting."

"Wish that were true," Maris said. "But as it ain't, maybe you could, like, fill me in on what's what on Kalapriya?"

"I am, of course, entirely at the Diplomat's service," Gabrel said in a tone suggesting exactly the opposite. "What in particular would the distinguished Diplomat wish to know?"

"You could start with what's got you so stuffed up," Maris suggested, "an' then go on to the gen'ral situation."

"I am afraid I fail to take your meaning, Diplomat Vissi."

"Why ye're narked. Canty-nosed. Zero-geed."

As Gabrel continued to look blank, Maris groped in her Tasman vocabulary for more synonyms, then realized that was exactly the wrong thing to do. Whatever specialized training Diplomats received, they probably didn't have a dictionary chip for Tasman scumsucker slang. She'd have to keep it simple.

"Why don't you like me?"

"I scarcely know you, Diplomat Vissi. It would surely be premature to make personal assessments based on a few minutes' conversation."

"Yeah, well, there wouldn't even a' *been* no *bunu* conversation if it was lef' to you, would there? Looks to me like I'm the only one making an effort here."

Gabrel's hands twitched on the long thick strings he held and the turagai came to a stop. He let the strings fall slack and turned to face Maris. "I have been assigned a duty," he said. "My duty is to escort the distinguished Diplomat wherever she may require during her visit to Kalapriya. I prefer not to allow personal considerations to interfere with that duty, and would appreciate your doing the same."

"Well, if actin' like a stuffed-up, narky, canty-nosed old geezer three times yer age ain't lettin' personal considerations interfere, what d'ye call it? Ye're bein' *bunu* rude and excuse *me*, but I'd kinda like to know why."

"Because *some* of us, unlike the distinguished Diplomat, have better things to do than interrupting other people's work for a pleasure jaunt disguised as a survey trip!" Gabrel spat out. At last there was some color in his face: two red spots over his cheekbones, and something like cold fire in the pale blue eyes. "For your information, Diplomat Vissi, I was engaged in extremely delicate negotiations with the head of one of the Indigenous Tribal Territories when I was recalled to dance attendance on you! As a result, our relations with the hill states may not be stabilized for years! You can hardly expect me to be pleased about this, can you?"

"If ye're pinheaded enough to take it out on me because ye don't agree with what yer bossman tells ye to do, then I'd say it's the Trading Society's good luck ye're not still doin' yer 'delicate negotiations!' " Maris snapped back. "Anybody with a temper like yers got no business tryin' to do diplomacy!"

"Look who's talking! *Diplomat* Vissi? I'd expect better manners from a Tasman scumsucker!"

Maris sucked in her breath, realizing just how fatally she'd given herself away. What now? Deportation back to Tasman?

"Um," Gabrel said awkwardly at last. "I'm—sorry. I went too far."

He thought she was silent because he'd insulted her.

Even now, he didn't guess the truth.

The pent-up breath escaped at last in a snorting attempt to suppress her laughter. Gabrel looked affronted for a moment, then began laughing too.

"We have both behaved poorly," Maris said, aiming now for a nice, polite, toppie voice and accent. "Can we start over, do you think, Leutnant Eskelinen?"

" 'Twould be my pleasure, Diplomat Vissi. Now, what particulars of Kalapriya can I give to add to your no doubt extensive briefing on our world?"

Maris had had time to think since the first time he asked this question. "There are ways in which no outsider can truly understand a world," she said, loftily, as though quoting a dictum from some old professor geezer at Diplomatic School. At least she hoped that was what it sounded like. "It would most beneficially supplement me—my—briefing if you would do me the kindness to explain Kalapriya to me as you would to any totally ignorant visitor. In that way, you see, I shall have the benefit of the native viewpoint."

"You mean the Society viewpoint," Gabrel corrected her. "We Barentsians have dealt with Kalapriya for only a few generations. Those of us who were born here may boast of being native-born, but the true natives are the Kalapriyans, the Rohini and Rudhrani—and very few in the Society trouble to understand *their* viewpoint, or even realize they have one!" He made some odd clucking noises and flapped his hands up and down; Maris was startled for a moment and then realized the last noises were addressed not to her, but to the animals before them, now in motion again.

She took a moment to reply, reminding herself to try and talk like a toppie in one of them old holos. "Now that," she said slowly and carefully, "is exactly what I mean. Nothing in my briefing comes from the native Kalapriyan point of view."

Gabrel gave her a surprised glance. "I thought you were here to follow up on Orlando Montoyasana's complaints."

Where was the God of Looking After Insignificant Persons when you needed him? Maris had forgotten all about the orders she had so briefly skimmed back at House Stoffelsen. "He ain't—isn't—a native, though, is he? Even though he claims to represent their interests?" *Nice recovery. Now try and remember who you're supposed to be.*

"Neither am I, if it comes to that."

"No, but—" she remembered his cause for disliking escort duty "—you've spent time inland, away from the area the Barents Trading Society controls. And I do want to know all about Kalapriya, not just the coast and Valentin." *Maybe there's some place away from all these blond giants where I can hide out for a while.*

"Yes. You'll need that if you're seriously investigating Montoyosana's allegations."

"You think I'm not?"

Gabrel shrugged. "It's never happened before."

"Oh. You get people makin' complaints to Rezerval and Diplomats sent in to investigate all the time, do you? And this ain't the way the standard investigation works?"

He gave her an irritated glance. "I didn't mean *that*. But most galactic visitors find life in the coastal enclaves quite primitive enough. They have no interest in exploring the interior, where travel is difficult and sometimes dangerous. Montoyasana himself hasn't been heard from in some weeks—not that I think anything's *happened* to him; he probably just stumbled on some fascinating native ceremony and wandered off without letting anyone know—but the point is, we've no real way to pull him out if he is in danger, not even to locate him."

Danger? What do you know about danger, pretty boy? Anybody tried to kill you *lately?* "I expect to go wherever the needs of the investigation take me," Maris said loftily. *Like on the first ship going anywhere but Tasman.* She wondered if Calandra Vissi's personal credit chips would be sufficient to buy her passage off-planet. Surely a Diplomat wouldn't be sent out without adequate funds for any emergency. She hoped.

"In that case you'll need to know a bit more about Kalapriya than the average tourist guidebook. Well, I suppose you do, being a Diplomat . . ."

"But I want to know *your* idear—idea—of the place. Leutnant Eskelinen. Wasn't that why they pulled you back from yer job to show me around? Because of you bein', like, an expert on the inland areas?"

"Well . . ."

Some things worked on Kalapriya just like they did on Tasman, Maris thought. Flattery was one.

Gabrel cleared his throat and began what promised to be a lengthy and informative lecture. "You'll know already, of course, that the Barents Trading Society directly governs only the coastal enclaves where our people breed and sort the bacteriomats for the interstellar trade. Just inland, along the coastal plain, the Indigenous Territories begin, all under native Kalapriyan rule . . . though in fact Barents has pretty good control of most of the plains states. The two major states bordering the coast, Vaisee and Ekanayana, were constantly at war with one another when we first settled Valentin, to the extent that neither one recognized our treaties with the other. There were also some problems with bandits. In the end we had to form our own army and go into those states to establish order. But they've settled down well enough now, and the smaller states along the coastal plains generally follow their lead. They all used to be provinces of the Empire—did your briefing cover that? No? I suppose they thought it was past history, hundreds of years ago, and not relevant. But it's very relevant to the Kalapriyans; half their songs and stories date back to those times. Not surprising. That was the only time of peace and prosperity they'd known until we showed up—the few generations after Dhatacharya united the tribes and named himself Emperor, until the degenerate Salbahan took the throne and oppressed the people so badly they assassinated him and vowed never to let another ruler control the whole continent. A mistake, in my opinion, but they really didn't much like Salbahan— and any time somebody looks like bringing the separate states together again peacefully, some malcontent makes speeches about Salbahan's return and the talks fall apart."

Gabrel thought over what he'd just said, while Maris tried to keep track of the names and ideas he'd just poured over her.

"Actually," he said in a while, "I suppose Dhatacharya's initial empire wasn't established all that peacefully, either. It would have been a matter of conquering the nation-states one by one, after all. But the point is, you're going to hear references to the Empire everywhere you go in Kalapriya, and rather more if you do go upcountry. Vaisee and Ekanayana are too comfortable under Society control to bother much with politics anymore. But the smaller states in the Hills—and the smallest don't amount to much more than a couple of villages and the grazing land in between— raid each other as a national pastime and justify it with songs about the heroic battles of the Empire. And in this generation we've got a chap with serious fantasies about restoring the Empire. A whole handful of small native states—the Seven Villages, Phalap, and most recently, Thamboon—have been absorbed into what the Bashir is beginning to call Greater Udara."

"Another Dhatacharya." Maris nodded, just to prove she'd been paying attention.

"In personality," Gabrel said drily, "he's rather more like Salbahan. But the leaders in the Trading Society here favor him, because he's accepted a Barents Resident to look after our interests—not that we *have* any interests in the hill territory, but still, I suppose we don't want these petty wars coming down to the plains and disrupting the coastal states.

When I was recalled, I was in Dharampal—that's another native state in the hills—trying to persuade the Vakil to accept a Resident. I was trying to convince him that the support of the Barents Trading Society might be useful to him now that "Greater Udara" has grown right up to his borders. The trouble is that the Bashir strongly opposes any other hill state taking a Barents Resident, for obvious reasons. And the Vakil of Dharampal can *see* the threat that Udara poses; he can't see, can't begin to imagine, the muscle the Barents Trading Society could bring to bear against Udara if there were any of our people up there to speak for the states that are being conquered. So he's being very, very cautious."

The beasts pulling their box—no, *carriage*—were allowed to amble while Gabrel went on about the political structures of Kalapriya. By the time they reached the meeting hall Maris felt she had learned quite enough about that subject to be able to play the Diplomat for the evening. As for the bacteriomat trade, it might be the ruling passion of the Barentsians, but it was nowhere mentioned in Calandra Vissi's orders. So at least she didn't have to pretend to know any more—or any less—than Benteen Teunis had told her that afternoon.

This time Maris was prepared for the climate-controlled luxury concealed inside the humble-looking white stucco meeting hall. She was not, however, prepared for the gala décor and the brilliant lights blazing inside. Since that afternoon the hall had been transformed, the rows of chairs moved to make room for white-draped tables covered with glittering glassware and serving dishes.

And the space between the tables was completely filled with tall, impatient-looking people. Maris shrank back as she took in their expressions.

"Oh gods, we're late an' they're narked, ain't they?" she whispered to Gabrel, momentarily too agitated to maintain her toppie accent.

"A Diplomat," Gabrel said in a discreet undertone, "by definition, is never late. The proper starting time for any function is when the Diplomat arrives. And don't show them you're scared; the old men will bully you if they think they can get away with it."

Maris felt grateful for his hand under her elbow, steadying

her as they moved into the room, and absurdly bereft when he was whisked away to a table for those of lesser standing while she was stuck at the head table between Dwendle Stoffelsen and a bunch of other old guys. Introductions were quick and businesslike; she caught the names Torston Huyberts and Pledger van der Wessels, but did not recognize or remember the titles of the official positions they occupied. *So what? I'm not supposed to be a* bunu *expert on the organization of the Society . . . am I?* Yeah, probably she was. Calandra Vissi probably had a datachip implant that had been freshly loaded with the Barents Trading Society's organization chart, names, titles, job descriptions, and complete *bunu* resumes! Oh well, it wasn't like they were going to interrogate her about the structure of their own business, was it?

No. It was a great deal worse.

"In order to facilitate your survey of the Society, Diplomat Vissi," Torston Huyberts began in a voice as oily as the soup that was placed before them by a slender, dark Kalapriyan servant, "it would be best if you could tell us now the precise scope of your inquiries and how you intend to carry them out."

Maris took a spoonful of soup. Too bad it wasn't something solid; she could play for time by chewing or pretending to choke on it or—gods, her mouth was screaming for the fire marshals! She grabbed for the glass before her and poured half the contents down her throat.

"Bread helps more than liquids," murmured Pledger van der Wessels. "If the distinguished Diplomat would care to try our native-baked *paan*?" He offered her a basket filled with flat things that Maris hadn't recognized as bread. She bit into one and discovered a soft, fruity filling that helped to assuage the minor explosions in her throat.

Torston Huyberts chuckled. "One forgets that our colonial habits are sometimes a little too *hot* for offworlders."

Was there a subtle threat in that, or was he simply enjoying seeing her discomfited?

"I 'spect I'll get used to it, Haar Huyberts," Maris said in her best toppie voice, a little husky still from the searing mouthful of soup. "However, perhaps it would be best to begin slowly."

"And is that how you plan to begin your inquiries? Slowly?

Few visitors look on Kalapriya as a pleasure jaunt to be prolonged."

He was definitely baiting her. Why? So she'd blurt out classified information? Maris smiled to herself. At least there was no danger of *that*.

"We can do this slow or fast, any way you and yer— your colleagues like, Haar Huyberts. I been—I *have* been assigned to make certain inquiries; I ain't about to leave until I get satisfactory results." *Like, maybe, tomorrow morning. If you define a satisfactory result as a ticket off this place* . . . Time to take the lead. If she asked enough questions, he wouldn't have a chance to tease her, would he? "Perhaps you could begin by explaining to me exactly how the bacteriomat trade works."

"Surely your briefing . . ."

"I like to hear the local point of view," Maris said. It had worked on Gabrel.

"Surely your tour of the caves with Benteen Teunis—"

"Haar Teunis was mostly interested in explaining the scientific aspects of the trade, not the business ones."

Both Torston Huyberts and Dwendle Stoffelsen seemed to relax slightly at this statement. Why? Did they know how somebody was evading the controls Benteen Teunis put such faith in, and shipping illegal 'mats to Johnivans? Surely not, because they began immediately to serenade her with more than any human being could possibly want to know about the business.

While the soup was removed and some kind of minced meat smothered in white sauce brought in, Huyberts explained the accidental discovery of the bacteriomats' potential when an explorer from one of the early contact ships slipped on their slimy surface in a sea cave and fell fifteen feet onto the lowest layer of rocks, breaking his head open and severing his spinal cord. When found, he was suffering from shock and dehydration and his face was half covered with a slimy mat of nanobacteria. The rescue crew reported the semiparalysis from the spinal injury and the fact that their attempts to cleanse the man's head resulted in shrieks of pain and hysterical arching of the upper half of his body, the part that could still move.

By morning, when a landing party from the ship was able to bring a boat around to the cave mouth, the bacterial mat had shrunk to a thin film covering the badly broken skull . . . and the explorer walked to the boat."

"Temporary paralysis of a bruised spinal column," said the ship's doctor.

"That nerve was *severed*," insisted the medtech who'd examined the man with portable scanners.

"Not now, it's not," said the doctor.

"Exactly. You ought to take a closer look at whatever's growing inside the cave."

It was a good story, and Huyberts told it well; his delivery was polished as a rock tumbled on the beach for many years. Probably, Maris thought, that particular story had been tumbled by generations of Barents colonials until it had a very fine polish indeed.

The something-in-a-white-sauce was removed and plates laden with shellfish replaced it. Maris watched in dismay as Dwendle Stoffelsen attacked his with two of the strange pieces of silverware whose use she had not yet figured out, elegantly extracting bits of pink meat without getting the least spot of grease on his fingers. She'd been able to fork up bits of the previous course by watching Stoffelsen and using the same implement he chose, but there was no way she could imitate this technique.

"The Diplomat does not care for our native *krebsi*? Do try some, they are delicious, almost exactly like Barentsian *kreb*," Stoffelsen urged her.

"So sorry . . . an unfortunate allergy," Maris murmured, and then realized she'd hardly been on Kalapriya long enough to discover any allergies to the local food. Better get back to the technical stuff. "So what's been going on since that first discovery? You guys must've had to do a lot of work to get the 'mats through Federation Approval and set up the business."

"Indeed, indeed," Stoffelsen agreed. While he told her all about the tests, the failures, the successes, the discovery that the bacteriomats were so flexible that they would mimic almost any missing or damaged brain or nervous system structure, Pledger van der Wessels unobtrusively signaled a servant who replaced Maris's plate of shellfish with something she could eat with a fork. It tasted like white insulation padding, but who cared?

"With the superb technical education available on Rezerval,

the Diplomat probably understands better than we do the mechanisms by which the 'mats repair and replace neural connections," Stoffelsen finished.

Cripes, the Diplomatic School turned out trained scientists on top of everything else? "I doubt that," Maris said sincerely. "I mean, uh, bein' on the spot like you are gives a—a depth of understanding where our overview must necessarily be superficial."

"Very well put," said Stoffelsen with a nod of approval.

It ought to be. She'd borrowed the line from one of the classic holos that most of Johnivans' crew didn't care to watch, being they were so slow and wordy. Nice to know these folks appreciated the classics. Maris finished her tasteless substitute dish and set her fork down with relief. Eating like a toppie was such a strain, she likely wouldn't have tasted anything anyway.

"The bacteriomats are a blessing for humanity," Pledger van der Wessels said solemnly. "It is a pity that we have not yet discovered a more efficient way to produce them than harvesting the sea caves. But every laboratory-grown strain has failed, and as the Diplomat doubtless knows, attempts to reproduce the environment on other worlds also have failed. There must be other organisms involved in the ecology that we have failed to detect."

He sounded so sad that Maris wanted to cheer him up. "Yes, Haar Teunis explained all that to me this afternoon. But after all," she said brightly, "if there was a lot of ways to grow them, you wouldn't get so much money for them, and if they could be grown off-planet, you wouldn't have the monopoly anymore, would you?"

There was a momentary silence; glancing around the table, Maris had the unnerving impression that two of her three dinner companions had been flash-frozen in place. Only Pledger van der Wessels continued to dissect his *krebsi* with apparent relish.

"I do hope," said Torston Huyberts at last, "the distinguished Diplomat is not suggesting that we would deliberately restrict the supply of these precious nanobacterial constructs for *personal profit?*"

Wouldn't you just, you old pig! If I was really a Diplo, I'd be suggestin' to Rezerval that here was something else needed lookin' into. "Such a notion never crossed my mind," Maris said. *Until you brought it up, that is.* For a moment she wished she really were Calandra Vissi, Diplomatic Envoy Extraordinary, with near-miraculous powers and advanced training in everything from nanoscience to unarmed combat . . . and a direct line to Rezerval. Because if Huyberts and Stoffelsen weren't involved up to the neck in procuring Johnivans' blackmarket 'mats or in something even worse, she'd . . . she'd eat a *krebsi!*

And maybe it was time to change the subject, and play the Diplo a little more convincingly with the knowledge she'd garnered from Gabrel Eskelinen on the way over here.

"The Barents Trading Society is, of course, above suspicion," Maris said loftily, stealing from another classic holo about toppie society life, "but one gathers the Society's control over the interior states is hardly complete."

"We have excellent relations with Ekanayana and Vaisee," Dwendle Stoffelsen said huffily. Maris recognized the names as those of the two large states which dominated the coastal plain.

"You have garrisons in both states," she corrected, "to enforce the mutual nonaggression agreement you forced down their throats fifty years ago." Good job Gabrel Eskelinen liked to talk so much.

"Neither state is unhappy with the agreement," Dwendle countered. "As a result of their proximity to our coastal enclaves, their economies are flourishing as never before. The profits from the bacteriomat trade mostly return to Kalapriya; we purchase furniture, food, all the necessities of life from Ekanayana, and most of our servants here come from Vaisee and are happy to have money to send back to their families. They also benefit from such limited medical help as we are permitted to give under the Prohibited Technologies Act. Their currency is stabilized, backed by the Barents thaler, and both regimes have enjoyed an unprecedented fifty years of peace and prosperity. We may have employed some unofficially coercive methods to achieve the original treaties, but that is long in the past, and Rezerval can find nothing to complain about in our current relations with the Indigenous Territories."

A bowl of fruit appeared on the table, a welcome change from the previous heavy courses. Real, fresh, whole fruit, not flash-dried slices! Maris remembered tasting a thin slice of apple once, a treat that Fingers had abstracted from a traveler's luggage and shared with the whole crew. Her mouth watered and she reached for the nearest piece of fruit, an oval lavender globe with a thin skin stretched over what looked like deliciously juicy purple pulp.

"It's nice you get along with yer—your neighbors," she drawled, "but I hear things ain't—aren't so peaceful up in the hills."

"The Indigenous Territories in the mountain regions," Torston agreed, "are smaller and more varied than the nations of the coastal plain and also less easily, ah, persuaded of the virtues of mutual cooperation."

Maris nodded intelligently. "You mean they're still at war with each other all the time." She bit into the lavender fruit and her mouth filled with melting sweetness. But how did toppies keep the juice off their hands?

"That has been unfortunately true," Torston conceded, "but it won't last long—oh!" He jerked as if somebody had kicked him under the table.

"You were saying, Haar Huyberts?" Maris inquired sweetly.

"I think my colleague meant to say that the quarrels of the more distant Indigenous Territories really have little effect on the Barents Trading Society. After all, the bacteriomats can be grown *only* in the sea caves along the coast—any child knows that!" Dwendle Stoffelsen boomed.

"In fact," Torston rejoined the conversation, "Valentin is the only city on Kalapriya with any claim to a distinguished visitor's interest. Even our other enclaves are little more than laboratories set up to take advantage of caves offering good 'mat breeding facilities. All off-planet trade must necessarily come through our port here. So you will be able to satisfy yourself in no time that Haar Montoyasana's allegations are pure fabrication."

"Oh, I don't know about that," Maris said, happy in finding a subject she actually knew something about. "You gents may *think* nothin' comes through Valentin you don't know about, but there's ways and ways of getting around any customs system. Bent inspectors, ship's crew taking an unofficial back door, masking projectors that'll make a sonic disruptor look like a lady's depilatory kit . . ."

Torston and Dwendle exchanged glances.

"NOT on Kalapriya," Pledger van der Wessels said

forcefully into the momentary silence. "You have seen for yourself the extreme care we take, even in our private homes here in Valentin, not to expose the natives to prohibited technology."

Maris glanced involuntarily at the short, slender, dark people who ceaselessly carried dishes, filled goblets, replaced napkins, and mopped up minor spills all through the hall.

Torston's face reddened and he launched on a confused explanation of why the servants here were a special case that didn't really count as violation of the Prohibited Technology Act, an explanation that might have rambled on indefinitely if it hadn't been broken off by a surprised gasp. Maris reckoned that this time, Stoffelsen had kicked him on the ankle bone. Hard.

"Rest easy, Torston. Diplomat Vissi is welcome to study the clauses in our contract allowing exemption for a certain number of servants, so long as those servants are not allowed to work on any offworld mechanical or electrical devices directly or observe their workings."

"I wouldn't dream of it," Maris said politely. "I'm sure all is managed exactly as it should be."

"And very shortly, I trust, we will be able to satisfy you that this is true of everything about the Barents Trading Society's dealings with Kalapriya," Dwendle said. "I'm sure you have no desire to prolong your visit on this primitive backwater, dealing with the ramblings of some delusional fool who's gone native himself. Not exactly a career posting, eh, Diplomat Vissi?"

At least they were in agreement on that much. Maris couldn't be out of here too soon to suit her. "Not meanin'— meaning any offense to Kalapriya," Maris said cheerfully around another mouthful of the lavender fruit, "but there *are* more pressing matters requiring my attention. As soon as we've settled our business, I need to leave . . . on the first ship not passing through Tasman."

Dwendle Stoffelsen coughed, choked, and finally favored her with a fruity laugh. "A fine jest, Diplomat Vissi. How would we all like to bypass Tasman and their extortionate passage tolls—although I suppose as a Diplomat on Rezerval business, you were not troubled with that particular semi-official piracy?"

"No joke," Maris said. "Okay by me if I never see that station again."

"Unfortunately," Torston said, "as the Diplomat well knows, there is no interstellar traffic from Kalapriya except by way of Tasman. That is the only Singularity point which serves our system."

"And a damned good thing those spaceway robbers have made of it, too!" put in Pledger van der Wessels. Maris noticed that he was eating his fruit with a fork and a small, crescent-shaped knife, in a bowl that caught the overflowing sticky juices. So that was how toppies handled the problem. Oh well, they could just decide that she was setting a new fashion. She had other things to worry about.

"No exit except through Tasman," she repeated mechanically. A fragment of juicy pulp was lodged in the back of her mouth; she chewed and swallowed carefully. Suddenly the fruit seemed to have no taste at all. "I—I knew that, of course." She actually had known it. Johnivans had made his fortune off smuggling to and from Kalapriya; Johnivans had killed the real Calandra Vissi to warn away what he thought was an intrusion into his monopoly of the Tasman smuggling business. But somehow, in all this crowded day, Maris had not thought of what this singularity in the fabric of spacetime meant to her.

There was no escape from Kalapriya—not for her. Going back through Tasman would be a death sentence if Johnivans had people watching for her; and he would be sure to hear about any shuttle manifest with Calandra Vissi's name on it.

And in the immediate future, then, no escape from the role of Calandra Vissi.

Chapter Six

Udara on Kalapriya

Lorum van Vechten, Resident in Udara for the Barents Trading Society, surveyed the Bashir's waiting room and unconsciously lifted his patrician nose slightly higher, as if avoiding a bad smell. No matter how many hours he spent in these antechambers, he would never get used to Udaran taste—all these vibrant, clashing red and orange silk pillows, glittering with embroidery in gold and silver thread, piled any which way on wooden benches carved into tortuous curves and fantastic shapes. He had a strong suspicion that some of the shapes represented human figures entwined in obscene embraces, but they were so distorted and decorated by so many unnecessary curlicues that one really couldn't tell. Not for sure. Not without getting down on hands and knees and getting a *really close* look.

Which, would, of course, be far too undignified an activity for the Udaran Resident—although he could almost swear the leg of that far bench was carved into the shape of an impossibly buxom and wasp-waisted girl doing something very improper to a grinning elephant-headed being—but in any case, it was too late now. The brocaded panels of the curtain before the door to the Bashir's audience room rippled and parted, and a small dark Rohini servant appeared and beckoned him silently to the inner chamber.

This was even worse than the waiting room: a shadowed place lit only by what light filtered in through elaborately carved window screens, the air thick with the musky fragrances the Bashir fancied, and completely lined with carpets and pillows, so that the Resident had no choice but to sit native-style with legs crossed and his knees creaking in protest. A low table of beaten brass before him held several empty cups and a tall pitcher.

The old man himself reclined comfortably on the long bed-bench that crossed the far wall, half smothered in pillows that his Rohini concubine was forever arranging and patting into place. He would not dispense with the girl's services even for the most private meeting; even his Minister for Loyalty to the State had to put up with Khati kneeling by the Bashir's head, pillowing it on her generous breasts, flaunting her half-naked charms behind some wholly inadequate tracery of gold net and embroidery. Lorum supposed it was safe enough; the girl was wholly uneducated, too ignorant to understand the import of political discussions, and she must, after all, owe her whole loyalty to the old man whose favor had raised her from a palace scrubber to the high status of most favored concubine.

Besides, she had been residing in the palace long enough to know exactly what the Ministry for Loyalty would do, in those dark cells deep within the mountain, to a girl foolish enough to repeat what she heard in the Bashir's audience chambers.

At least it was not necessary to greet the little whore; official protocol said that she was invisible. Lorum made his way through the customary greetings to the Bashir, as elaborate as the décor, as false as the gilded wood carved in the style of ancient metalwork, and was just drawing breath to inform the Bashir of the latest disturbing communications from Valentin when the old man raised a clawlike hand for silence.

"General Zahin wishes to speak with you. We will await his coming."

"But my news is most urgent!" Lorum protested.

"All the more reason for my dear friend and trusted

councillor to hear it with us. We will drink together while we wait."

Lorum tried to conceal his impatience behind the expected courtly mask of indifference while Khati tilted the pitcher to fill two cups with madira and added a few drops to a third cup. As was polite, she sipped from the nearly empty cup she had poured for herself; this was supposed to demonstrate that the madira had not been poisoned. Not that it proved anything; if the Bashir wanted to poison him, he could easily have rubbed the inside of Lorum's cup with any of half a dozen deadly substances sold in the bazaars. It was all ritual, and meaningless. Khati's bowed head and deferent movements were a mockery of formal court behavior, made so by the full breasts and slender brown waist almost totally exposed beneath that gold net . . . Lorum reminded himself not to stare; officially, the girl wasn't even there.

He stared instead at the clear liquid in his cup, wondering how little he could drink without being rude. The native-distilled madira was more powerful than Barents brandy, and Lorum suspected that the herbs they used to flavor it were mild hallucinogens. Even the fumes rising from the cup made him slightly dizzy. And how long must they wait for old Zahin? The Bashir's dearest friend, *fine*, but the ancient soldier was officially retired now that he was semiparalyzed, and in Lorum's opinion the disease that had attacked Zahin's legs had probably gone to his brain too; the old fart saw conspiracies and danger behind every curtain. And to wait on his convenience *now*, when they had a *real* problem, was intolerable!

Finally the Minister Emeritus's entourage arrived: first two tall, unsmiling Rudhrani guards who inspected the Bashir's chamber; then the Rohini bearers staggering under the weight of Zahin's special portable chair; then at long last, when that was set up, four more panting Rohini carried Zahin's sedan chair to the door of the audience chamber, lifted him from it, and settled him in the portable chair with its extension to support his useless legs in comfort.

Nothing could be said, of course, until all these servants withdrew. Lorum was amused to see that Pundarik Zahin appeared as anxious as he was himself to be rid of these unnecessary ears; the old man shooed them away while they were still patting at his cushions and arranging the brocaded wrap over his legs. He took the cup of madira Khati poured for him, drained it in one swallow and held it out for more.

As soon as the curtain fell behind them, Lorum drew breath to speak—but the Bashir was before him.

"Well?" he demanded, but he spoke in Kalapriyan, and Lorum was shocked to see the ruler looking to old Zahin, not to him, for news.

"The boy has been taken care of."

"Not—"

"Dead? No. That seemed excessive, considering his parentage."

"In a manner of speaking," the Bashir interpolated drily. "The late Minister Vajjadara was my good friend."

"But young Chulayen—"

"Was his beloved son, and entirely worthy of his father." Zahin said firmly. "I know the boy; his heart is loyal, and I can assure you he will give no further trouble."

"How, then?"

"His wife and children stand hostage for his future discretion—or so he believes."

"Very well. But if that does not suffice—"

"Further measures will be taken if necessary," Pundarik Zahin replied. "He can always go the same way as the outlander Montoyasana."

"Can you do that to your old friend's . . . son?" It seemed to Lorum that the emphasis on the last word was strange; but then the whole language was strange. He was struggling to follow the quick-voiced interchange and had no understanding of what they were talking about.

"Perhaps the matter should be turned over to the Minister for Loyalty," the Bashir went on.

"The family is already in his hands. Let me stand surety for the son's behavior. I have more to lose than any of us— if you have kept your promise?"

"There has not been time to raise the matter." The Bashir sounded, so far as Lorum could judge from the swift-flowing cadences of the liquid Kalapriyan tongue, shifty. But then, the Bashir was naturally a shifty bastard, or he'd not occupy his throne for long.

Now Zahin was looking expectantly toward Lorum, and the Bashir shifted back into Galactic, which he spoke better than most natives—well, of course, most of them never learned the speech of the outlanders at all, why should they? But the Bashir had picked Lorum's brains remorselessly until he was nearly fluent, at least in the simplified trade version of the language. It would not do to forget that the man, insane megalomaniac though he might be, was an extremely *intelligent* insane megalomaniac.

"My apologies, Resident. A small matter of internal security."

"If this 'small matter' involves our mutual interests, I should be informed," Lorum hinted. "Did I hear the name of Montoyasana?" No need to admit having understood most of what they said; he could reasonably have picked out the one name so well known to him.

"This has nothing to do with him," Zahin said quickly. "You know yourself that he is in no position to give further trouble."

Lorum wondered whether he dared point out that he actually knew no such thing. Zahin had assured him that Montoyasana had been among the first group sent to the Thamboon caves. But he had not visited the caves himself. It was always possible that Montoyasana had escaped, or that he had persuaded the Udarans it was too dangerous for them to perform the surgery on an outlander . . .

The Bashir sighed heavily and Lorum decided it was safer not to speak. "A young man, what do you call such trouble-makers, 'hot of head'? In our language we say that they cast fire into the water. This one has been meddling where he should not. Someone has been careless. A formal decree appropriating some caves in the former state of Thamboon to our use crossed the desk of an officious boy who knows nothing and thinks it his duty to question everything. The stated reason for taking over the caves was for saltpeter, which we should indeed require in great quantity were it not for our private arrangement." His smile of complicity made Lorum feel as if he were wading through vats of oil. "The boy saw fit to protest loudly and far that the caves, which he has visited on pilgrimage, are not appropriate for mining operations and that our decree will destroy a natural treasure. Worse, he has hinted at knowing the true use of the caves."

"I do not believe that," Pundarik Zahin said quickly in Kalapriyan. "He said only that it would only be worth industrializing the caves if they contained something small and valuable. He said it almost in jest, not like one hinting at a secret. He knows nothing."

"If he knows nothing, then he will be discreet in the hope that his wife and children may yet be returned to him," the Bashir pronounced. "If he continues to speak out, then he proves that he knows too much—"

"Or that he values honor over his personal well-being," Zahin interrupted. "In his family such a choice is not unknown."

The Bashir snorted. "He can hardly have inherited that madness from old Vajjadara."

"It might have been taught him."

"In either case," the Bashir said with a chopping gesture of one hand, "if he speaks further, he must be removed. Sentimentality cannot be allowed to endanger our project. There will never be a cure for you, Pundarik, if this boy brings all down about our ears."

Lorum started, then tried to look as if he were only studying the erotic embroideries on the wall hangings. The Bashir and his ministers did not know how much Kalapriyan he understood; on general principles he aimed to keep it that way. Only, this was the first time that anyone on the Udaran side had hinted at wanting a share in the 'mats themselves in addition to their usual payment. He could see all kinds of complications looming ahead—in addition to the one he had yet to inform the Bashir of.

As soon as the two Udarans fell silent, Lorum spoke. "Gracious lord, there is news from Valentin—"

"In due time, in due time," the Bashir said. "First let us discuss the matter of payment."

"The delivery of last time was not satisfactory?" Lorum inquired sweetly. They all knew it had been more than satisfactory; otherwise Thamboon would hardly have been subdued so easily.

"Adequate to our purposes," the Bashir said with an airy wave of his hand, "barely adequate. But we have no complaints on that score. However, it has been brought to our attention that there is some irony in our sending all the produce of our caves to outlanders while those in our own land suffer from ailments that could be readily cured." He looked pointedly at Pundarik Zahin's withered legs.

Lorum's heart sank. This demand had been bound to rise at some time; it was his curst bad luck that one of the Udarans in most need of a 'mat transplant was the Bashir's oldest friend. But why did it have to happen *now*, when they already had problems enough? "The proper application of the bacteriomats is not simple," he said slowly. "A neuro-surgeon should oversee the opening of the skull and insertion of the material. To bring such a skilled doctor from off-planet in secrecy will be difficult." And that was a major under-statement.

"We have surgeons," the Bashir said, "with quite suffi-cient practice in head operations."

Pundarik Zahin looked queasy, and Lorum seized his chance. "Ah, but would you entrust your dear friend here to those who practice only upon the 'disappeared'?"

"It will not be necessary," the Bashir said. "You yourself, Resident, have surgical training, have you not? Not just any training; you worked with Nunzia Hirvonen. One of the pioneers of bacteriomat treatment, I understand."

Lorum mentally called down skin-rot, boils, and the black heaves upon whatever officious Society bureaucrat had decided that it would be a bright idea to send each Resident's full curriculum vitae to the ruler of the Indigenous Terri-tory where he served "to show our good faith and coop-eration." And for the first time in his life he regretted the cleverness with which he'd managed to excise from the curriculum vitae any mention of the fact that Hirvonen had thrown him out of "her" surgical program—damned bitch, always picking on him! She'd even convinced his family that he would embarrass them all if he was allowed to continue practicing. Just because of a few natural, almost trivial errors! The child would probably have died anyway. It was all Nunzia Hirvonen's fault that he had been forced to give up the well-paid and comfortable life of a Rezerval medic for exile to a remote Barentsian colony planet. Should he confess now? No, the Bashir would just think he was making excuses.

On the other hand, excuses sounded like a really good idea, under the circumstances.

"That was . . . a long time ago," he said weakly. When it came to the point, he really could not bear to go into the humiliating details. After all, he hadn't exactly flunked out of the program. He'd just been *thrown* out. "I would hardly trust my skills to operate on so valued a member of your inner council as the Minister Emeritus."

The Bashir smiled. This time the image evoked was not oily; Lorum felt as if he were looking at a field of spear points. "We trust you absolutely, Resident. Not only our continued cooperation, but your life, rest upon a successful outcome."

Did the madman really intend to jeopardize the entire, highly profitable operations of the Consortium to do a favor for this one old man? Lorum looked at the smiling dark face before him, at the fixed stare of the dilated eyes, and believed it. The man who had just casually agreed to sending a woman and children to certain death to prevent awkward questions about Consortium affairs was willing to risk ending those affairs entirely for the sake of his best friend. Who was, incidentally, the man who'd signed the order condemning those innocents.

Of course, if Lorum performed the insertion, there'd be no doctor from off-planet, much less risk to the Consortium . . . but a totally unacceptable risk to Lorum himself. How . . . the heliograph news! Momentarily driven from his brain by this insane idea of the Bashir's, now it came back to him as salvation itself.

"I shall be honored to serve the Bashir," Lorum said, "as soon as this problem from Valentin is settled. Unfortunately, I shall have to travel to the coast to make sure that the woman does not imperil our entire operation—"

"What woman?" the Bashir demanded, and Lorum smiled inwardly. At last he had the man's attention.

"The Diplomat from Rezerval," he said slowly, "who has been sent to enquire into Orlando Montoyasana's allegations of prohibited weapons technology use among certain of the Indigenous Tribal Territories." He paused to lend weight to his next words. "I have just been informed by heliograph that she intends traveling up-country in pursuit of her inquiries." Another judicious pause. "To Udara."

"Pah!" The Bashir spat on a gold-embroidered carpet and waved for Khati to prepare him another cup of madira. "One woman, that is nothing."

"A Diplomat," Lorum tried to explain, "is more than just a woman. They have special capabilities—"

The Bashir grinned. "Any woman seems special, till you have had her. Then they are all the same." He caressed the concubine who knelt by his side, though she could hardly have understood what he said in Galactic. "We will send our agents to stop this woman. But you are our Resident. You will remain here and perform the insertion upon Pundarik Zahin." He raised his voice. "*Jamundari!*"

Lorum heard a metallic clash behind him, at the door to the entrance chamber, and turned with an unhappy feeling. The two tall Rudhrani guards were there, holding their long spears crossed to block the doorway. "You will, in fact, remain as our guest in the palace until the work is concluded," the Bashir said cheerfully, and repeated his instructions in Kalapriyan for the benefit of the guards.

CHAPTER SEVEN

Valentin on Kalapriya

The ball after the banquet was intended to make the ladies of Barents and the younger people happy while keeping the Diplomat harmlessly entertained and giving the leaders of the Barents Trading Society a much-needed rest. Dwendle Stoffelsen had personally seen to it that the first five days of the Diplomat's visit were crammed from dawn to dusk with formal entertainments, speeches, and tours of everything from a bacteriomat breeding cave to the processing hall where the 'mats were prepared for shipment off-planet. It would kill him to keep up the pace he'd scheduled for the woman; before meeting her, he'd entertained some hope that it would also kill her, or at least exhaust her to the point where she'd be happy to leave Kalapriya just to escape another round of speeches and tours.

His first sight of her at the banquet had destroyed that hope. She might have looked exhausted and frail on arrival at Valentin's spaceport, but with a couple of hours to rest she had bounced back, bright and lively and looking hardly older than one of his own daughters. She had to be at least thirty; Diplomatic School training took years, not to mention learning to manage the biomechanical implants, and

111

Diplos were not sent out alone to their first assignments. Dwendle had just forgotten how damned *young* thirty could be. And how resilient. He seriously doubted they could exhaust the Diplo without killing themselves in the process.

Now, of course, after the barbed hints she'd dropped over dinner, they had worse problems to worry about. He summoned Torston and Kaspar into one of the curtained alcoves that lined the hall for a whispered consultation and outlined his fears. The woman had obviously studied ways of slipping materials past the customs inspectors; all right, that was reasonable enough given that her orders were to investigate Orlando Montoyasana's allegations of prohibited technology being smuggled onto Kalapriya. But that remark about the bacteriomat monopoly—!

"It *could* have been an innocent observation," Torston suggested.

"Nothing a Diplo says is innocent," Kaspar said. As the only one of the three who'd actually encountered a Diplo before, he took the lead in this conversation despite being the youngest of the three and the only one who wasn't from a Founding Family. "They're trained to make provocative comments that will upset guilty people and cause them to betray themselves. And from the looks of you two, that's exactly what happened. I do hope you didn't spill soup all over yourselves when she said that."

"Certainly not!" Torston bristled. "We were eating *krebsi* at the time!"

Dwendle stifled a sigh and wondered, not for the first time, why he had been saddled with an officious youngster and a doddering old fool as coconspirators. He knew why, of course. These two were not only venal enough to enter enthusiastically into the Consortium he had created, they were in his power by virtue of the background sheets he held on each of them. He'd thought himself very clever to ensure that no one was invited to join the Consortium but those who had some secret weakness he could exploit.

"We betrayed nothing," he said to Kaspar, "but it's clear the woman knows too much. She knows it's a two-way trade, she was teasing us with her knowledge of our involvement, and she is far too conversant with the situation in the mountain Territories. And she's announced her intention of going wherever her inquiries lead."

"If she goes into the hills, she might get involved in the tribal wars," Torston said hopefully. "Not our fault if she dies there."

"It's hard to kill Diplos," Kaspar said gloomily, "and what's worse, it leads to investigations. What if she survives, and sees some of the weapons the Udarans are using?"

"If she gets as far as Udara," Dwendle said, "she might see a great deal worse than that."

In dismal silence, they watched the dancers. Diplomat Vissi looked like a young girl without a care in the world; she was laughing now, getting the steps of the twining promenade hopelessly mixed up as Gabrel Eskelinen tried to lead her through them. The peach-colored panels of her borrowed Kalapriyan-style dress fluttered around her ankles, revealing tantalizing glimpses of lavender underpanels and slim legs. Even that overserious prude Eskelinen was laughing.

"It's deceptive," Kaspar said. "She's probably had youth treatments. Don't imagine that's a girl you're looking at. Think of it as a snake. A *highly trained* snake."

"But if killing her will only lead to more investigations, how can we stop her?" Torston sounded close to tears. "All our fortunes, everything we've worked for, ruined because of this one woman poking her nose in. I *told* you Orlando Montoyasana shouldn't be given an upcountry pass, I told you the man was dangerous. No, no, you said, Dwendle, you said he was a known conspiracy maniac and nobody ever paid attention to him, everywhere he goes he fusses about native cultures being destroyed, even if he stumbles on something they'll write it off as more of Montoyasana's particular paranoia. That's what you said. And now look what's happened!"

"Montoyasana won't be making any more complaints. And if the death of the Diplo also brings about the end of the investigation," Kaspar said, "there'll be no more questions asked. We can end the whole thing now, tonight."

"But how?" Dwendle asked involuntarily.

"Eskelinen. You've no particular love for him, have you?"

"Another nuisance," Dwendle shrugged, "always wanting to be off up-country, mixing too much with the natives, but he's military—he can be kept under control. All we have to do is persuade his colonel that he shouldn't be given another pass to leave the regiment. I'll think up some good reason why I really need him in Valentin."

"But if he could be neutralized along with the Diplo, you'd have no objection?"

"Gods, no!" It sounded too good to be true. It probably *was* too good to be true.

"Then it's very simple." Kaspar sounded unbearably smug, but Dwendle could put up with that in the hope of hearing that smug voice pronounce his salvation. "Torston, you will see that their departure from the ball is delayed until most of our people have been gone for some time, so that they will be alone on the road back to House Stoffelsen. Dwendle, you need to arrange some large transfers of funds into Eskelinen's accounts, and fiddle the accounting programs so that they are back-dated over the last several months; can you do that?"

It would be easy enough to arrange, using the same backdoor accesses to the accounts that Dwendle already used to disguise the Consortium's illicit profits. "Yes, but he'll know—"

"After tonight," Kaspar said coolly, "he'll know nothing. Tomorrow morning you will be shocked to discover that Gabrel Eskelinen killed the Diplomat using a pro-tech weapon, unfortunately just before the city security forces could stop him by more conventional means. They were, of course, forced to kill him in self-defense. His possession of the weapon and the sums transferred to his bank account will demonstrate that he was the smuggler she came to investigate. We will present the evidence to Rezerval, together with Gabrel's cache of prohibited weapons—I'm sorry, but we must sacrifice the latest shipment to lend verisimilitude— explain that we are shocked and dismayed but that we acted immediately to retrieve the weapons from their native possessors, and here they are, and here's the guilty party, unfortunately dead, and here's their precious Diplo, also unfortunately dead, but she died heroically in the line of duty. That wraps it all up nicely; no need for any further investigation." He smiled sweetly at his colleagues.

"He's a soldier, she's a Diplo, how are you going to take them out?" Dwendle demanded.

Kaspar's smile brightened. "With some of those pro-tech weapons Leutnant Eskelinen has been smuggling, obviously. I'll catch them both in a tanglenet, which *she* won't be expecting, and bubble those pretty brains with a dazer set for maximum neuronal disruption before she has time to pull any dirty Diplo tricks or bring out any secret weapons. *He* will have no defences against a tanglenet, so I'll have plenty of time to put a sword through him. Then it's only to disable the tangler, put the dazer in his hand, and congratulate the security men on their prompt action. They'll be willing enough to take the credit, and the evidence will be sufficient to prove that he's the smuggler."

"If it works . . ." Dwendle said doubtfully.

"Trust me. I'll see to it personally." Kaspar sketched a parody of a military salute. "I'm off now—and you'd best leave soon too, Stoffelsen. Those accounts need to be in place before morning."

His insouciant manner was maddening. "*Haar* Stoffelsen to you, young man!" Dwendle snapped, "and I'll see to the accounting in . . . in my own good time."

"As you like, *Haar* Stoffelsen," Kaspar said patiently, "but remember that leaving the ball early will ensure that you and your good lady—and your charming daughters—are home long before any disturbances on the road tonight."

"I suppose that leaves me to entertain the Diplomat," Torston sighed with a long-suffering tone and a longing look at the pretty ankles he could glimpse under the Diplomat's layered skirt panels.

"I think Gabrel Eskelinen will do that quite adequately," Dwendle said. "Just make sure they do not leave before the last valsa is played. Make it a point of etiquette—Valentin tradition, bad luck for the guest of honor to leave before everyone else has had a chance to make their farewells." Not a bad "tradition," even if he had thought it up on the spur of the moment—and the best of it was that if old Torston started boring on about it, everybody would accept his statement that it was an old Founding Families tradition without question. Sort of thing the old bore was always coming up with anyway.

Now if he could just think of an equally good excuse to get Ivonna and the girls out of here, without arousing the Diplomat's suspicions!

As the older contingent of Society members drifted away, there was plenty of space on the dance floor for the younger ones to demonstrate the shifting patterns and changes of the paar-dansken for their distinguished visitor. "Diplomat Vissi" was so involved in remembering the complicated sequence of right hand across, turn to your left-hand neighbor, skip back to the right and thread down the arches that she scarcely noticed when her host and hostess made their farewells. Only the loud complaints of Faundaree and Saara at being dragged home so early caught her attention.

"Is it time to go?" she asked Gabrel in an undertone, between step-changes. "Should we leave too?"

"By no means, young la—I mean, Diplomat Vissi! By no means!" boomed an authoritative voice just behind her. Maris turned, startled, to find one of the old guys from the banquet table standing much too close to her—only, with an adroit move, Gabrel was somehow between them, and the old guy backed off a few paces, still talking. Something about a long-standing Valentin tradition that absolutely *required* the guest of honor to remain until the end of the ball; Maris didn't follow all the details and didn't much care. Paar-dansken were fun; she wasn't supposed to know the steps so she didn't have to pretend to be an expert in something she was totally ignorant of; and nobody in the gay young crowd that surrounded her had the least desire to talk about bacteriomats, or tribal treaties, or prohibited technology, or anything else she was supposed to know all about.

And Gabrel Eskelinen, who didn't know any better, was treating her like a toppie *lady*; a strangely intoxicating experience. This whole party was like living one of those holos she loved to watch whenever Johnivans could get them; not quite real, but much much better than any reality Maris had ever known.

Fine by her if they kept dancing till dawn. Had to be easier to handle than whatever was next on the Barents Trading Society's gods-curst schedule.

In fact it was well after moonset, if not quite dawn, when the band put aside the rapping sticks that dictated the rhythm of the paar-dansken and picked up traditional viols and flugels for the last valsa. Young officers in gold-braided uniforms and ladies in sheer dresses spangled with glittering dots took the floor, one couple after another, spinning and swooping with a grace that took Maris's breath away.

"I can't do this," she protested when Gabrel took her hand.

It wasn't like the paar-dansken, a bunch of people skipping around each other and everybody laughing when you got the pattern wrong. This was something else, magic, flying to music, something you couldn't fake from having seen it on historical drama holos.

"You can't *not* do it," Gabrel informed her. "Valentin tradition. Guest of honor must be the last one dancing. And the last dance is always a valsa."

Maris looked up at him suspiciously as he drew her into his arms, one hand firm on her back, the other holding her own hand. "Why do I suspect you made that up just now?"

"Not all of it," Gabrel said. "The last dance *is* always a valsa. Anyway, it's easy. Anyone can valsa. Just listen to the beat—one-two-three, one-two-three, and here we go . . ."

"Okay," he said a moment later. "You have to hear the beat and match your steps to it. ONE-two-three, ONE-two-three . . ."

"Ouch," was the next thing he said, but Maris, biting her lip in concentration, hardly noticed.

"I think I'm getting it!" she cried in delight.

"No," Gabrel said through lips tight with pain, "that was my left ankle you got."

The room spun around them and Maris found herself going backward and forward and sideways under Gabrel's firm steering, and most of the time now her feet were landing on the floor instead of on Gabrel's toes, and . . .

"It *is* like flying," she sighed happily as the music came to a halt.

"I hope you don't crash-land your flitters quite that often." Gabrel lifted one foot tenderly. "I should have worn cavalry boots."

Maris grinned. "Serves you right for inventing traditions!"

He put one finger under her chin and gently tilted her head up. "Diplomat Vissi, do you know that you look more like a seventeen-year-old girl at her first dance than like a mature and experienced graduate of the Diplomatic School?"

Maris froze for a moment. Seventeen wasn't a bad estimate of her actual age, assuming she'd been nine or maybe ten when Johnivans recruited her into his gang. Was Gabrel guessing—no. He *couldn't* have guessed.

She pictured Calandra Vissi's papers in her mind and tried to think herself back into the person who'd earned those diplomas and commendations and had been to all those worlds the travel records showed. How would Diplomat Vissi respond?

"You flatter me, sir," she said with a polite smile. "I'm nearly thirty, far past being able to pass for a girl. But—" she laughed lightly "—this *is* my first dance. We don't dance on Rezerval—not like this, anyway. Perhaps that has misled you."

"Nearly thirty," Gabrel repeated, while Maris repeated the mental arithmetic that had given her Calandra Vissi's age. "Hard to credit. Is there some magic about Diplomatic School, some secret youth treatments that we provincials wouldn't know about?"

"Rumors of our special capabilities are greatly exaggerated," Maris replied demurely. If it needed youth treatments to explain the disparity between her face and Calandra Vissi's recorded age, there would be a rumor about such treatments as soon as she could plant one with Saara.

Rumors could be quite useful.

They just might save her skin.

Gods knew what else would, given that she had no way off this world and out of this role except straight back into Johnivans' hands.

Torston Huyberts kept Maris and Gabrel by his side, making farewells to all the toppies of Barents, until they were the last to leave—that was, if you didn't count the slender dark-skinned servants quietly fluttering around the hall and cleaning up the traces of the evening's entertainment, the red puddles of spilled punch and the twists of paper that had been somebody's dance card, the garlands of waxy-white flowers now beginning to turn brown at the edges, a torn and discarded strip of lace with a dirty boot print as mute evidence of what had happened to it. While they were waiting for the carriage to be brought round, Maris looked back into the empty hall, automatically cataloging these details and wondering why the room reminded her of the corridors on Thirty where Johnivans' gang had hunted down and killed the last survivors of Ugly Benko's band. And why she felt the same way she had during that fight—tired to death, scared, and yet somehow exhilarated by the fast action and the intoxicating scent of danger in the air. Well, this evening had been a battle of sorts, only fought with words and wits rather than with dazers and tanglers.

And it was over now. What she had won, beyond another day's survival in her imposture, Maris didn't know; but at least she hadn't *lost*. Time to relax now; there would be more battles to fight tomorrow. Torston Huyberts's carriage had taken him away; there was only Gabrel by her side now, and she no longer thought of him as an enemy. Not somebody to be trusted with a secret that meant her survival, no, but not someone who was out to trick her and trap her either.

She took a deep breath of the warm Kalapriyan night air, soft and damp with a hint of sea salt, and tried to convince her overstrained nerves and hammering pulse that there was nothing, now, in the air but the oversweet scent of fading flowers.

"Tired?" Gabrel asked.

"Not in the least," Maris said. "Do you think we Diplomats are such fragile flowers that we fade after an evening's entertainment?"

"No. But it has been a long day for your first one on Kalapriya."

Yeah, and you'll never guess just how long and hard—I hope! Maris's thoughts went back to Tasman, to the panicked girl standing in Calandra Vissi's quarters and realizing, too late—*almost* too late, she corrected herself—that she had run just where Johnivans wanted her.

To kill her.

Had that really been only two watches—half a day, she corrected herself; must think in dirtside terms now—half a day ago? Seemed more like half a lifetime.

Maybe it was. After all, she was a different person now.

But the feeling of that discovery, the panic and the sense that all around her were enemies, stayed with Maris even as Gabrel Eskelinen handed her up into the carriage and they started out on the dark road back to House Stoffelsen. Well, and that made sense. These people *were* enemies of a sort, she argued against the prickly feeling at the back of her neck. Maybe they didn't know it, but that was only because they didn't know who she really was. They might make pretty speeches to Calandra Vissi, but they would be no friends to a nameless thief and smuggler from Tasman.

And some of them didn't seem to like Calandra Vissi all that much, either.

The feeling of danger was all around her, close and heavy like the overly warm night air and the strong sweet perfume of night-blooming flowers, and Maris couldn't shut down, couldn't keep from scanning the darkness on either side of the road as if Johnivans might spring out from the shadows.

The road itself wasn't that bright, just a line of white dust between the shadowy groves and mud-walled buildings, lit by torches spaced too far apart to show anything but the bare outlines of the way the carriage must go. Maris had learned long ago, in the disputed corridors of Tasman's lowest levels, that light and darkness themselves could be weapons; cut the lights to a partition, and incoming fighters with dark-adjusted sight could make mincemeat of those within who were temporarily blinded by the loss of light. Now she averted her eyes from each pair of flickering torches, watching instead the shadows within the angles of joined buildings, looking for what didn't belong even while some part of her laughed at her senseless fears.

What didn't belong was a glitter in darkness, a nearly invisible net of thread-fine light, and its movement was what caught her eye first; the graceful arcs of death swooping out toward the carriage. "Gabrel!" she shouted while diving out of the carriage and away from the tanglenet. She hit the dirt with a bone-jarring thump and rolled into a shadowed corner, *not* the one hiding the net. *Dirt's softer to land on than plastisteel, and thank the gods those boxes-on-wheels-don't move at any speed, come on, up, you're not hurt . . .*

The roll ended at a pile of rubble that scraped her shins and banged against her ribs with jagged edges. Piled stones, mortar, leftovers from something that had been torn down and left for scavengers to pick, who cared? Maris came up to a crouch with a nice heavy sharp-cornered rock in each hand and saw that Gabrel was half entangled in the net.

But only half. Warned by her shout, he'd moved fast enough to keep one arm and shoulder free, and he had drawn his sword. *A lot of good that's going to do.* The sickly pink sizzle of a dazer beam set for nerve disruption went through the tanglenet, but aimed at where she'd been sitting, not at Gabrel. *Two seconds to recharge, if they're using the old models—if they've got the new ones, we're fucked.*

The dazer had to have been one of the older models, because Maris had time to sling her first rock at a shadow behind the pink flare. The dark shape yelped, went down on one knee and would have clapped a hand over its bruised shoulder if there had been time, but there wasn't because Maris was on him now with the second rock in her upraised hand, grabbing his shoulder with her free hand and hammering down at where the head had to be and hearing a sickening soft kind of crunch. The man slumped, a soft dead weight against her knees, and she stumbled backward. Her hands were sticky; she dropped the stone she still held and tried to wipe her palms on the fine floating panels of her skirts. *Idiot, if there's another one you've just handed yourself to him on a platter.*

But there wasn't another attacker; only the one shape dark and limp in the shadows, and Gabrel still struggling with the tanglenet. At least the beasts pulling the carriage hadn't taken fright and bolted, there was a mercy. Maris gritted her teeth and felt along the dead man's body, found a small hard square shape, pressed down on the center where a button clicked and the lines of light entrapping Gabrel faded away.

Now the turagai wanted to run; they must have been caught in the tanglenet as well. Gabrel had his hands full with sword and reins, and for a few sweating, swearing moments it looked to Maris like a toss-up who was going to control the carriage's movements, Gabrel or the thrashing, panicky beasts. Then he jerked their heads back, said a few words more quietly, and the turagai stood still, panting and rolling their great eyes but apparently under control again. For the moment.

He looped the reins over a post and jumped from the carriage, seemed to stagger for a moment, then limped toward her. "Very—commendably quick reactions, Diplomat Vissi. My superiors will find it a most amusing story."

"Funny sense of humor they've got, then."

"After all," Gabrel pointed out, "*I* am supposed to be protecting *you*, not the other way round. Although I see the rumors are this far true, Diplomats need little protection." He leaned casually against the wall.

*God of Minor Fuckups preserve us! Do I have to deal with
wounded male pride on top of everything else?*

"You prob'ly weren't expecting modern weapons," Maris
said.

"And you were? I could wish you would have mentioned
the possibility."

"Not exactly. I just had this feelin' something wasn't right.
When somebody wants to make damned sure you're the last
to leave a meeting, and you've got a long dark road to
go . . ." Maris shrugged. You didn't need a Diplo's implants
to figure that out, just common sense; but saying so would
hardly sooth Gabrel's bruised ego. "You moved right fast
there, getting your sword free, for somebody as wasn't
expecting an attack."

"And a lot of good it did," Gabrel said drily. "Can you
bring one of those torches over here?"

He pointed down the road to where the next pair of inadequate torches flickered against the night. Naturally the attack
had been staged midway between sets of torches, to give
this guy the deepest shadow; it was what Maris would have
done herself, part of why she'd been hyperalert just there.

"I would go myself," he said apologetically when she didn't
move right away, "but I am not totally sure that my right
leg will support me without the help of this excellent mud
wall."

"Pins-and-needles feeling? Feels heavy when you try to
move it?"

"Somewhat of an understatement, but—yes, more or less."

"Nerve disruption backwash from the dazer beam. Must've
just caught you in the outer glow. It should wear off in a
few hours."

"Delighted to hear it. Now, about the torch . . ."

"How come?"

"I like to know who's just tried to kill me. Don't you?"

"I don't like knowin' people who are goin' to try and kill
me." *I really must do something about my social life; seems
like that's the only kind of people I do know.* But she fetched
the torch. If she'd just killed one of Johnivans' people, she
wanted to know whose ghost to appease.

The torch was easy enough to detach—just a bowl on a
stick, basically, dropped into the top end of a hollow pole
short enough for even Maris to reach—but no fun at all

to carry. She learned almost immediately that you wanted to keep the *bunu* bowl balanced just so, or some of the hot oil that fueled the burning wick dropped down your hand and arm.

"Not a nice sight for a lady," Gabrel said apologetically when Maris came back, "but anybody using tangler nets and dazers is more likely to be your acquaintance than—" He took the torch from her, lowered it cautiously to shed light on their assailant's ruined head, and took a sharp inward breath "—mine," he finished in a curiously flat tone.

Relief flooded Maris. It was somebody she knew, yes, but not one of her old gang; she would owe this ghost no remembrances. "I know him, too," she said. "Kaspar some-body."

"Slevinen," Gabrel said. "Kaspar Slevinen. New-come from Barents, which *could* explain the weapons, but why smuggle them in? And damned close with some of the Good Old Families, which I thought strange before, seeing they mostly keep themselves to themselves, but Kaspar damned near lives in Torston Huyberts's pocket . . ."

"That was the geezer who wanted to make sure we stayed till last," Maris said. She dropped to her knees, careless of the blood and dust on her borrowed finery, and picked up the slim dazer lying by Kaspar Slevinen's limp hand. She thumbed the power button experimentally. A faint pink glow shone out, then faded. "Careless," she said with regret. "He'd let the charge run down. That's why it didn't do you more damage." *And we can't exactly ask him where he kept the charger, now.*

Gabrel nodded slowly. "Slevinen, Huyberts, and Stoffelsen. Always had their heads together in some corner. And tonight . . . Stoffelsen left early, so that you were sure to be coming back alone with me. Huyberts kept us there until all others had departed. Slevinen attacks us with pro-tech weaponry. And you're here to investigate Orlando Montoya-sana's claim that somebody is corrupting the Indigenous Territories with prohibited technology. I do believe that someone doesn't want you to make that investigation."

"If there's anythin' to it, of course they don't want me pokin' my nose in," Maris said. "Don't take a nanotech designer to figure that much out."

"But why now? Stoffelsen was in charge of your schedule,

and as your escort I've seen it; the man was planning to waste as much of your time as possible with receptions and banquets and speeches and tours. What happened tonight to make him change his mind?"

"He decided death was better than sittin' through any more speeches," Maris suggested. "Specially if it was my death 'stead o' his'n."

Gabrel looked down his nose at her. "This is hardly a time for levity."

"Well, it ain't the best time and place for discussin' who wants to kill us, either," Maris pointed out. "First we need to get him out of sight, then let's get *us* out of sight. Your leg workin' now?"

Gabrel took an experimental step away from the wall and nodded. "Feels half dead still, but it'll hold me up."

"Fine, then you take his head—eh, shoulders?" Maris corrected herself as she remembered the bloody ruin that was the back of Kaspar Slevinen's head. She took the torch from Gabrel, jammed the supporting stick into a crevice of the low mud wall he'd been leaning against, and picked up Slevinen's heels. Between them they got his body over the wall and let it fall heavily into the ditch on the other side.

"Get his dazer and tangler," Gabrel suggested. "We might need them."

"Dazer's no good, it's out of power." But the tangler might still prove useful.

"For evidence." Gabrel took the two small devices from Maris and tucked them into his sash.

"Now what?"

"Well, I don't think it would be healthy for you to go back to House Stoffelsen," Gabrel said. "You leave anything there you can't do without?"

"My credentials." She hadn't packed very well for a stint as Diplomat; there was nothing else in her traveling bag but Calandra's fashionable clothes, unsuitable for this climate and illegal for this level of technology. Why hadn't she taken weapons? Because she hadn't seen any. *A Diplomat is a walking weapon.* That was rumor speaking, and a rumor she'd have a hard time living up to. Too bad Slevinen's dazer was drained and she didn't know where to recharge it. Maybe she could get the tangler away from Gabrel.

"I'll vouch for you. Come on, we've a lot to do. We need to leave before dawn, before Huyberts and Stoffelsen find out their plan didn't work."

Maris dug her heels in, resisting the pull of Gabrel's hand. "Leave for where, exactly? Think we can get off-planet without them noticing?" Gods, she hoped that wasn't what he had in mind! Off-planet meant going back through Tasman. That wouldn't be exactly safe either, but she could hardly explain that while Gabrel thought she was the Diplo. But if that was their only way out, she'd have to tell him. Everything. Couldn't let him walk into Johnivans' hands without a clue what he was about to die for.

"Off-planet? No way. You've got a mission, remember? I propose that we pursue it." Gabrel's teeth flashed white in the darkness. "The climate of the Hills is much healthier than these coastal lowlands."

Chapter Eight

Rezerval

Niklaas was deep in level four hundred and twenty-two of Geek Dungeons when the nursing aide tapped on his shoulder, throwing his concentration off and blowing his ongoing attempt to write a decryption program that would enable the screen jump spell before the Dark Nerd blew him away with a disk wiper.

"My apologies, Haar Silvan," the aide said. "A visitor."

Niklaas closed the game with a tap of his right forefinger and smiled politely, as if he really didn't care that she'd just caused him to pay a three-thousand-point early escape penalty that would probably prevent him getting to the five-hundredth level before his seventeenth birthday. After all, it wasn't like he had a lot else to do in the three months to go before his birthday. Or after.

Or ever.

Then he saw who the visitor was and his smile became genuine. "Tomi! But what—how—?"

Tomi Oksanen was *walking* toward his bed. His gait was somewhat stiff and jerky, but he was definitely walking. No float-chair, no visible supporters.

It had been a strange friendship in the first place; no one

would have expected the teenage son of a high Federation officer to join forces with the somewhat older black sheep of the Oksanen family, which itself was something of a black sheep on Rezerval—lots of money, even more unsavory rumors about where the money came from, and a family of bland, smiling towheads whose cherubic faces gave no hint about which of the rumors might be true.

Tomi, though, hadn't been much of a smiler even before the infamous party where some of Rezerval's young society died from popping tainted joytoys, and he'd had a lot less to smile about after the party. The poison that an embittered Oksanen ex-employee had laced the joytoys with hadn't killed him, but it had paralyzed much of his nervous system and landed him in the same intensive care ward as Niklaas. Nights that each of them spent listening to the other one struggling for breath, days punctuated by the torture sessions called rehab therapy, and the shared despair of knowing that neither of them would ever approach the top of the waiting list for 'mat implants had forged a bond between these two most unlikely of friends, a bond that had survived Tomi's removal from the medical center for home care by the phalanx of trained nurses and therapists the Oksanen family could hire for him. They'd still had net-letters, and, once Tomi could get around in a float-chair, occasional visits. There'd been times when only Tomi's sardonic black humor had given Niklaas the will to face another day in the prison that his body had become. As for Tomi, he claimed there were times when only the sight of Niklaas's invincible naivete and belief in fables like universal justice amused him enough to distract him from his own troubles.

"Muscle stimulators?" Niklaas guessed. "Braces under your pants?"

Tomi grinned and pivoted, holding his arms out so that Niklaas could see that there was no place where his skin-tight jumpsuit showed the betraying bulge of a lock brace or a stim box. "You *know* they said those wouldn't work for anybody'd t-trashed his central nervous system the way I d-did, Niki!"

The stutter was new, and would have worried Niklaas if the greater miracle of Tomi's walking hadn't overwhelmed him. They did say it wasn't good if new symptoms showed up months later, a sign that the nerve damage was ongoing. But who cared, if the nerve *repair* was also happening?

"How'd you get a 'mat?" Niklaas whispered. He tapped his finger nervously on the bedspread until Tomi drew up a chair with a jerky scrape across the floor and plopped down beside him. "I didn't think there *was* enough money to bribe your way to the top of the list."

Tomi gave the seraphic smile that was an Oksanen family trademark, the innocent look that warned older acquaintances of Oksanens to check their creds and keep a hand on their balls. "No bribery, Niklaas. It's a new, experimental t-tr- . . . t- . . . surgery," he finished, having given up on "treatment."

"I haven't heard about anything like that." And he called up the med journal abstracts daily, looking for some hope between the unavailable 'mat transplants and the wishful-thinking world of the dreamers who claimed yak milk and soy extract would cause natural nerve regeneration.

"It's not exactly being written up in the literature."

"Oh. *Very* experimental, then."

"No, just very expensive. T-t- . . . Couple of words, Niki." Tomi lowered his voice and whispered, "Cassilis Clinic."

"Where?" It was hopeless, of course. Anything that an Oksanen considered expensive was far beyond the reach of a Federation official's salary. But just in case . . . *"Where? Here on Rezerval?"*

"Castelnuovo P-pr-"

"Castelnuovo Province," Niki said before his friend could find a synonym.

Tomi's head bobbed in that strange jerking motion, like a chicken pecking for food. Niki didn't remember *that* happening before, either. Well, stuttering and twitching might not be one's idea of the perfect life, but it beat the hell out of being stuck in a Med Center ward working your way up to the five-hundredth level of Geek Dungeons or tapping the net screens with your one working finger to browse the literature on nerve regeneration.

"And it doesn't use 'mats?"

"Nobody on the list is losing a p-pl- . . . chance at a 'mat b-because of this," Tomi promised.

"You *swear*?" Niklaas had been fighting his conscience ever since he regained consciousness and figured out that his chances of a legitimate 'mat implant were slim to none, what with new cases of Fournier Syndrome being diagnosed faster than 'mats could be bred on Kalapriya. Okay, he'd tried a dumb kid trick with his new roloprops, and that shouldn't wreck his life . . . but neither should it wreck the life of some guy who'd been born before the gene-screens caught signs of Fournier Syndrome, and who now faced paralysis in his twenties and death before he was thirty. Even if Mom's connections in the Federation *could* help her sneak him to the top of the list . . . and the chances of that also were slim to none . . . he wasn't getting his repair at the price of some other guy's death sentence.

But seeing somebody else who'd had no hope of making the list, somebody who'd been worse off than him and had done something even dumber, walking around like a halfway normal human being . . . to see Tomi with a future, able to go places, maybe even able to have *sex* some day . . . this was twisting his conscience into a pretzel. It was one thing to pretend to accept your fate when there were other people in the same fix. It was a lot harder to keep up the pretense now.

"*Your* family wouldn't care whose place you took," he pointed out. "*You* don't have to uphold the honor of the Federation's Secretary of Internal Information." Life had been a lot easier when Mom was just another supergeek, before the high quality of her technical work got her bumped up the ladder until she was eligible for a Federation appointment where she didn't hardly get to do any technical work at all.

The Federation appointment wasn't a lot of fun for Mom, either. She never said so—the Silvan motto was "Serve with Honor"—but Niki knew she missed the freedom of geeking around in the Federation nets and coming up with clever fixes for problems nobody else had even discovered.

Tomi bobbed his head jerkily. "Right, we wouldn't care . . . but *you* would, right? You and Annemari, you are like something out of a historical vid sometimes, all your notions about 'honor' and 'service.' So while I was there, kid, I had some of our p-people check it out. They say this clinic is d-definitely *not* sneaking 'mats from any of the Federation medical centers. And they wouldn't bother lying t-to me, would they, because they know I wouldn't mind one way or another."

After Tomi's departure Niklaas didn't bother to reactivate the game. He put off calling his mother, too, and told himself the reason was that he didn't want to discuss this mysterious clinic in Castelnuovo Province over a com channel to Federation offices; not secure enough. She visited him every day, it could wait.

The real reason was that he didn't want to know for sure just yet. He didn't want to find out that the Cassilis Clinic was a fake, or that Tomi had been lying when he hinted that they had another source for 'mats, or that they could never raise the credits on a Federation official's salary. Just for a little while, he wanted to believe that he had a future.

The nurse-aide who'd interrupted his game stopped by again after a little while.

"Are you feeling all right, Haar Silvan? You haven't started playing again, and you look a little flushed." She put the back of her hand against his forehead. Niklaas started imagining what it would feel like if she put it somewhere else on his body, assuming he *could* feel the touch, and immediately became a lot more flushed.

"I'm not sick," he assured her. "Just . . . thinking."

"Must be pleasant thoughts, for a change," she teased with a smile.

"I was thinking," Niklaas said slowly, "of what life would be like if the only barrier to an active sex life were persuading some girl to get active with me."

The nurse-aide's smile froze in place. "I shouldn't think that would pose much of a problem for you, Haar Silvan," she said softly, brushing a lock of bronze-gold hair from his forehead as she removed her hand. She turned away quickly and hoped he hadn't seen the look in her eyes. Poor boy, he knew as well as she did that he'd likely never face that particular problem. Spontaneous nerve regeneration was a better chance for him than getting to the top of the 'mat waiting list.

She'd read about a case of spontaneous nerve regeneration.

Once.

And it hadn't been very well documented.

✧　　✧　　✧

Annemari Silvan's office had been designed to maximize
the peaceful flow of spiritual and mental energies, with the
usual color and aura harmonizer cooperating with a spirit
specialist. The result was a room perfectly suited to
Annemari's cool silver-gilt beauty and sharply concentrated
mind. The colors were calm silvers and greys, conducive
to concentration and with the added advantage that the
fading gold of her hair, the only color accent, seemed bright
by contrast. The reflecting vid screens on desk and walls
were carefully angled so that the light, and any ill-meaning
spirits, bouncing off them would be trapped in the fountain of moving mirrors in one corner or the swaying crystal chimes hanging from the ceiling in another corner. Tall
silver bins with angled lids were intended to conceal any
messy stacks of papers from sight.

It was a beautiful room for one person to sit in, alone
and undisturbed, concentrating on high intellectual problems.

Annemari reckoned that she had spent all of fifteen minutes doing that since taking office five years ago.

And that had been on a Sunday morning, at 3:00 A.M.,
when she slipped up to her office to kick her shoes off and
rest her smile muscles after a particularly draining diplomatic reception; *and* it had only lasted fifteen minutes
because one of her programmers had been working through
the night, saw her office lights and thought he'd found the
perfect time for an informal chat with the boss about how
she wanted the new info screen design to work.

Now, in midweek, the subtle silvers and greys of the
decorator's scheme were drowned in a rising tide of flimsies
in Federation green, urgent notes in Federation orange, diplomatic disks sealed with Federation red, and computer print-
outs in recycled beige. Annemari felt rather recycled beige
herself, as she tried simultaneously to cope with the usual
demands of her job and to follow up three separate lines
of investigation into the black-market bacteriomats. Some
of her official workload could be delegated to her staff; so
far she hadn't dared let anybody except Calandra know about
the bacteriomat investigation.

That might have to change soon, if she couldn't recon-
cile the scanty but mutually incompatible bits of information she had dragged off the data nets.

Niklaas's conversation with Tomi Oksanen was the first

lead she'd had since Calandra Vissi dropped out of communication. Unfortunately, he'd thought it over by himself for several days before asking her if she knew anything about the Cassilis Clinic, and in those days it seemed that Tomi Oksanen had disappeared. The Oksanen family was not known for divulging information readily, but usually it was the financial data that they buried beneath layer upon layer of misleading documents and false trails to nonexistent banking corporations. Annemari was extremely good at working through financial deceptions. Her twenty years of programming experience stood her in good stead here. The Oksanens and other upper-class financial criminals *hired* computoads and technonerds to conceal their dealings; Annemari had *been* a technonerd, and she could still think like one. She knew how all the major Federation databases were designed; she'd designed some of them herself. She'd even written the code for some parts herself. And the trapdoors she'd written for debugging purposes were extremely useful when she wanted unrecorded access to databases that she had no official reason for looking at.

If Tomi Oksanen had been, say, a credit transaction as part of a money-laundering deal between the Oksanens and some more openly criminal family like the Boghaert clan, she'd have tracked him down in no time at all.

Theoretically, a human being should leave far more traces in the system than a single credit transaction and should be correspondingly easier to track down. But Annemari's attempts to meet with Tomi Oksanen and ask him about the Cassilis Clinic had been met with the famous Oksanen blank-wall silence. Tomi? Oh, yes, one of the younger ones, they said casually, as if his playboy exploits hadn't been enlivening the gossip vids—and costing the Oksanen family—for years. In the Med Center? Yes, they *had* heard he'd been ill. Didn't Auntie Minna say something about his going to the South Coast to recuperate? Or maybe it had been the Valima Mountains. These young people, you know, always flitting about. No, his parents weren't on-planet just now. Couldn't say exactly where they'd be, complicated itinerary, could have been changes. Come to think of it, didn't somebody mention that Tomi was going to stay with one of his lady friends, Kaarina or maybe it was Kristi or could have

been Chiara, dear me, forget my own name next, that I
will . . .

Annemari made the requisite polite noises and closed the
vid channels. She hadn't had much hope for that line of
inquiry; she was no good at these games of conversational
fencing, couldn't keep her mind on how to corner her
opponent because it took all her energy to stop her screaming
at them that they were bloody liars. Should have put somebody from her staff on the job, someone like young Jeppe;
he was good with people. Except she daren't trust anybody
else with these inquiries, and anyway Jeppe was busy
smoothing ruffled feathers over in the legislative offices,
where Legist Kovalainen claimed the Information Department
was deliberately blocking his request for a statistical analysis
of all Federation employees sorted on six different properties, four of which hadn't been defined as data fields when
most of the employees were hired and processed, and three
of which couldn't be listed in the database because they
constituted illegal invasion of personal privacy. It would be
really, really nice if Jeppe managed to get Kovalainen to
understand the difference between "won't give you the
information" and "don't have it in the first place and aren't
legally empowered to get it" without giving him an excuse
to complain that Annemari's department was incompetent.
More likely, though, the best he'd be able to do would be
to point Kovalainen at some other department and get him
to harass them for a while.

Meanwhile, there was the ongoing credentials check on
spaceport officials, the request from Health for a program
to map possible disease vectors related to the new plague
on Junya IV, and the job of reconciling the data retrieval
programs embodied in the Information Freedom project with
the data concealment programs in the Right to Personal
Privacy project. Annemari had delegated all those jobs as
best she could, but her best wasn't good enough; two of
the three senior staff members entrusted with the projects
had already requested meetings, and one of them wanted
the meeting to include a representative from the legislative
office as the Freedom and Privacy acts, respectively, *were*
self-contradictory statutes already passed by the Legists. "Ask
Legist Kovalainen to join you," Annemari suggested, "I
happen to know he's very interested in information retrieval

issues." There, that would keep Kovalainen busy, and now she could get Jeppe back to work on something useful . . . like . . . like compiling a statistical analysis of non-Federation medical clinics on Rezerval, number of patients treated, qualifications of staff, whatever other details she could think of to bury the questions she was really interested in. With special attention to Castelnuovo Province.

She promised Vibeke a meeting that afternoon to discuss the Health Department request, reassured herself that Anders Ruggiero seemed able to write and run a simple background and reference checking request without her active supervision, and asked Jeppe for a full report on non-Federation clinics in Castelnuovo Province.

"More BS from the Health Department?" Jeppe moaned.

"Could be a little more interesting than usual," Annemari said without committing herself on the source of the request. "We want full staff lists and resumes, tax data, lists of patients and what they were treated for . . . and don't worry about Privacy Act restrictions on this one."

"Kovalainen will explode," Jeppe predicted.

"Kovalainen doesn't need to be told about all our internal business. That's why I want you on this, Jeppe; I need someone discreet. There are political considerations . . ." Annemari let her voice trail off. "I don't need to tell *you* about the possible complications here."

Jeppe nodded wisely, as if he actually had some idea what she was talking about. Which was convenient, because Annemari had no idea how she could justify this project if he asked. She'd been banking on the typical technonerd reluctance to admit there was anything at all he didn't already know, and apparently it had worked.

Once Jeppe left, Annemari scrawled *Gone for the day* on the back of a memo, closed and locked her office door, and set her desk console to route all incoming calls other than Jeppe's to a message list. She spared a moment's envy for the characters in one of the old-fashioned romantic comedy vids she'd seen, who had assistants called "secretaries" specifically to guard the door against visitors. If she didn't have to practically hide out in her own office to get a little uninterrupted time, how much more work she could do!

Of course, her work nowadays was to deal with the

interruptions. Ninety percent of her job wasn't technical at all; it was smoothing feathers and adjusting competing demands and setting priorities. And when there was any real computer work to be done, she had to delegate it to one of her eager young assistants.

But this couldn't be delegated. Mentally flexing her fingers, Annemari settled down happily to do a little personal, private research on the Cassilis Clinic, so she'd have some background with which to interpret Jeppe's results. The readily available public information was bland and virtually information-free; with little effort she was able to pull up vids of a long, low white building set in a beautifully landscaped park, short speeches from unidentified but impressive-looking men and women in white coats, blurred views of what were probably the latest in monitors and other medical devices, and testimonials from satisfied patients. "I looked and felt ten years younger after a thorough workup at the Cassilis Clinic," was the general tenor of the testimonials.

It would be interesting to see what Jeppe could add to this picture. So far, all she had was lots of surface pleasantness, no real data, and a general sense that the Cassilis Clinic was a cross between elective beauty surgery and an overpriced health spa for the rich and bored.

Felt like an Oksanen family operation to her. Would a list of employees prove enlightening?

While she waited for Jeppe's results, Annemari checked the progress of the infospyder she'd activated to track Tomi Oksanen's credit usage, transit vouchers, and other traces he might have left in the net. Like the Cassilis Clinic public site, the results were interesting, but not informative. Up to four days ago—the day of his visit to Niklaas—the program had turned up about what you'd expect from an Oksanen playboy. Lots of credit chits from fashionable restaurants, a major funds-verified transaction from a Rezerval jeweler. Annemari recognized the name. Splashy stuff featuring really beautiful Thyrkan rainbow crystals in really tacky gold settings; Tomi must have a new girlfriend, and her taste was about what one would expect from a girl willing to go out with an Oksanen.

The interesting part about that transaction was that Tomi had a girl and felt it worth splashing credits in the form of showy jewelry on her. The Oksanen men had a reputation for being generous with the women they ran around with, but only for services received.

If Tomi was in condition to receive any services at all from his new girl, the Cassilis Clinic had worked the kind of miracle Annemari had thought only bacteriomats could perform.

Niklaas said Tomi had sworn that nobody on the list was losing a chance at a 'mat transplant because of Cassilis Clinic. But what was the word of an Oksanen worth?

The rest of the record was the usual—no public transit records, of course, but a handful of dangerous-flying notices, two summonses for failure to appear and answer charges of causing a flitter accident, the kind of fines that would have got the attention of anybody but an Oksanen, and a large credit transfer to somebody Annemari had never heard of, who turned out to be the injured party in the flitter accident. Who had also failed to appear at the second hearing, the day after the transfer, so the matter had been dropped. Solved in the usual Oksanen family fashion: throw enough money at it and it'll go away.

The really interesting—and frustrating—thing was that there were no traces of Tomi Oksanen anywhere in the net for the last four days. For some reason the Oksanens must have decided to keep his recent activities private. Annemari tapped in a code that would open Rezerval's largest secure financial systems database to her. This would show any of Tomi's transactions that had been blocked from view.

Nothing showed up.

Annemari trawled through Rezerval's off-planet transactions and discovered that some of her colleagues were keeping surprisingly large credit accounts on Toussaint, a non-Federation world that was a favorite for tax evaders. But that was none of her business, so she ignored the information and asked for any transactions specific to the Oksanen family.

That brought up a flood of data, probably enough to keep Federation lawyers happily employed for years picking holes in the Oksanen financial empire if only there were a legitimate way of sending the information to them. Annemari narrowed the search to the last four days and to transactions involving Tomi Oksanen personally.

There were none.

No credits, no flitter tickets, nothing.

Of course even an Oksanen had the power to drop off the net for a while; anybody sufficiently rich and discreet could achieve that by using only personal flitters and private landing zones, making no transactions, entering no controlled areas, staying on-planet. It would not be trivially easy on Rezerval, where half the planet was made up of Federation offices and other controlled zones where proof of identity and time of entry were automatically recorded. But it was possible, even if not exactly in the notoriously flashy Oksanen style.

The *really* interesting thing was that this wasn't the first blank in Tomi Oksanen's records. He had "disappeared," in the sense of leaving no traces in the system, for twenty days following his release against medical recommendations from the Med Center and into the care of Oksanen family physicians.

Twenty days in the Cassilis Clinic? With no charges recorded—from what looked like a luxury spa and plastic surgery clinic?

A chime from the deskvid announced that Jeppe was sending preliminary results directly to her. Annemari wished she had told him to sneaker-mail them; papers carried by hand left no record, e-transmissions were not as secure. Oh well, she'd asked for enough stuff to disguise her real interests; it took long enough to sort the mass of data and pick out the records relating to Cassilis Clinic.

Jeppe hadn't been able to get at a list of patients and treatments; an attached note indicated that he had some ways around the Clinic's security but wasn't sure he could get in without setting off alerts. Good judgment call, that. Annemari didn't particularly want anyone at the Cassilis Clinic to worry about being investigated—not yet, anyway. And she also didn't want to tell Jeppe or anybody else about the extra bits of code she'd inserted into most Federation database systems as a programmer.

Because the tax information was in public Federation databases, Jeppe had been able to do a thorough job on that without breaking any regulations at all. Annemari would not have been surprised to find that as far as the Federation knew nobody had drawn any income from the Cassilis

Clinic—but no, that would have been obvious. The Oksanens were liars, cheats, and notorious tax evaders, but they weren't *obvious*; that was what made it such a pleasure to pit her wits against theirs. Jeppe's spyder had neatly sorted taxpayers reporting income from the Cassilis Clinic by amount, so that the list began with several blandly meaningless corporation names and ended with the pittances paid to daily scrubbers, groundskeepers and other low-level employees.

It was the ones in the high-middle part of the list that interested Annemari. These would be the top-salaried employees, the surgeons and medtechs. Lots of surgeons. You'd expect that. No, *lots* of surgeons, far more than it would take to staff the plastic surgery part of a clinic like that. Annemari randomly highlighted about ten percent of the names and set the spyder's parameters to pull up resumes; any licensed clinic was obliged to file resumes for all technical and medical staff, so those also had been available to Jeppe. She read the results, frowning slightly, then requested full resumes on everybody reporting income between—hmm, what did a Federation Level Five medtech get, 600,000 credits a year? Okay, make it everybody between 500,000 and 5 million; that would pick up some top techs and some of the smaller dummy corporations, but should cover everybody she was interested in.

And that list was *very* interesting. Annemari skimmed through it once, deleted the obvious and expectable entries— well, okay, maybe not so obvious. She had had no idea a "cosmetic consultant" could get paid *that* much, but right now she didn't have time to waste on the makeup people and the personal trainers and the groomers and buffers. With those culled out, she studied the list of surgeons and other specialists employed at the Cassilis Clinic with deep interest. The obvious cosmetic specialties were well represented, but there was another group whose areas of expertise seemed at first glance to have nothing to do with the clinic's public goals.

Time to activate another kind of data search, the kind she wasn't so good at. Annemari tapped her deskvid and sent a note to Nunzia Hirvonen asking her to respond when she had time.

Nunzia was on vocal almost before Annemari took her fingertip off the screen. The top half of her face, the liquid dark eyes and arching brows, showed over the spyder's resume spreadsheet. "Anni! What's up? You going to take up eating lunch? There's this new place on the Concourse—"

"Wow," Annemari said, caught off guard. "I didn't think you would be free right now."

"I'm not," Nunzia said. "Scrubbing for surgery, talking on voice control, thirty more seconds, slice and dice some poor guy's brain."

"Improving it in the process, I trust."

"Honey, how could surgery *not* improve it? He's a *guy.*" Nunzia's laugh was like warm honey flowing down into a pool.

"Fifteen seconds, now. Is that long enough for you to tell me if there's any reason a general health spa and plastic surgery clinic should need neurosurgeons?"

"Only if they plan to botch up customers' facial nerves on a regular basis, and want to do the repairs in-house," Nunzia said crisply, "in which case they shouldn't be in business anyway. Wait a minute—you said neurosurgeons? Plural?"

Annemari nodded, then remembered Nunzia had said she was on vocals only. "Right. Three at least, probably five— I'm not sure what some of these subspecialties mean."

"That," Nunzia said with her usual assurance, "makes *no* sense."

"That depends," Annemari murmured to herself.

"Now you *have* to meet me for lunch," Nunzia announced, "and Tell All. I want the full story. Gaetano's on the Concourse, twelve sharp. If you get there first, order us some bruschetta with lemongrass sauce for starters. See you there."

Before lunchtime Annemari dealt quickly and competently with three more requests for various statistical analyses, an attempt by the head of Data Entry to steal her best two nerds, and a complaint from Legist Kovalainen that the "girl" who'd asked him to join the meeting on the Information and Privacy Acts couldn't explain anything. She also comforted Vibeke— "Don't worry, *nobody* can explain anything to Kovalainen; he hasn't the basic equipment for understanding it. I just wanted him off Jeppe's back for the day, and now I owe you one. Okay, I owe you *two.* After lunch?"

While she handled data and personnel crises, the back of her head was turning over Tomi Oksanen's mysterious recovery and equally mysterious disappearance, the glorified health spa in Castelnuovo Province that kept three—or maybe five—highly paid neurosurgeons on permanent staff, and one puzzling little bit of data the transit-permits-search spyder had retrieved for her. Something she hadn't even been looking for, but it was a *smart* spyder program and remembered she'd previously been interested in this matter. Put together, these three matters weren't puzzling in the slightest; in fact, Annemari sailed off to her lunch meeting with Nunzia feeling that she had probably figured out almost everything she needed to know.

The one thing she hadn't thought of was the risk of encountering Evert Cornelis on her way out of the building.

"Annemari! Nothing wrong, I hope?" Evert looked toward the Med Center.

"No, no, I'm just going to lunch," she reassured him, and then realized she might have made a slight mistake.

"I have to see this," Evert announced. "You never take time off for lunch. What's lured you away from the delights of a fruitpak at your desk while yelling at your staff?"

"I don't yell at my staff," Annemari said.

"No, sorry, wrong word. You freeze them with a glance, of course. But what inspired you to take a break? Let me guess, you're avoiding Legist Kovalainen."

Annemari's pace quickened. "Is he looking for me?"

"I'd recommend a *long* lunch," Evert said obliquely. "Where are we going?"

"I'm meeting Dr. Hirvonen," Annemari said. "It's a business lunch. We have Federation business to discuss."

"Excellent! I love traditional Italo-Thai food."

"How did you—"

"Know you were headed for Gaetano's?" Evert beamed. "It's the only place on the Concourse that Nunzia considers serves decent food. She just doesn't appreciate the subtler pleasures of Franco-Mexican at Bistro Tapatia. No matter, I'll take you there another day."

"That would be lovely, Evert," Annemari said politely, "I'll look forward to seeing you then. Now, if you'll excuse me, I don't want to be late for this meeting with Dr. Hirvonen." It was as close to a brush-off as ingrained civility would permit her to go.

"Oh, I'm coming with you," Evert insisted. "Told you I like Italo-Thai, and as it happens, I've some business to discuss with you, too. That little matter you asked me about the other day, about your 'friend' on Kalapriya?"

After looking at the information the transit spyder had turned up Annemari no longer felt anxious about Calandra, but it would have been *really* rude to tell him so if he'd already gone to the trouble to contact his Aunt Sanne. She resigned herself to listening while Evert told a long involved story with a predictable ending, slowed her pace so that he could get the breath to tell his story in his preferred fashion, and wondered, while he nattered on, whether there was *any* way short of murder to shake him off before she met Nunzia at Gaetano's.

" . . . so, like you told me, and perfectly right you were, m'dear, as always, Sanne was only too happy to send me a long gossipy vid about all her social doings in Valentin. And I mean *long*!" Evert shook his head in wonder. "Gods, how that woman can rattle on. No idea where she gets it from. Rest of m'family can stick to the point and give you a straight answer to a simple question, but like my father always said—or was it Uncle Baar—anyway, one of 'em said, 'Ask Sanne if it was raining when she came inside and you'll have to hear all about the damage the water spotting would've done to her pricey new organic coverall if it had been raining, which is when you'll learn it wasn't.' " He paused. "Now where was I?"

"Sanne's news from Valentin," Annemari prompted.

"Oh! Right. Well, of course you didn't want me to ask a simple question anyway, so it's not her fault, but I just wish *you* had listened to the vid instead of me, Annemari."

"So do I," Annemari murmured against the protests of her better self.

Fortunately, Evert didn't take the comment as she had meant it. He patted her shoulder. "There, there, noble of you, but Sanne's a family misfortune—I mean, member—and I wouldn't really want to inflict her conversation on anyone else. Anyway, first word out of her mouth was about some grand banquet and dance they'd planned on having for the visiting Diplomat, so of course I thought I'd get to hear then whether Calandra had shown up or not, but no. *First* the woman has to tell me all about her new dress for the ball, and I give you my word, Annemari, I didn't know anybody could *say* that much about one dress—specially on a restricted planet where they're only allowed to use organics and native manufacture. Then all the gossip and matchmaking *before* the ball, and after all that it turns out . . ."

"Calandra didn't show?"

"Why, no!" Evert was startled into plain speech. "That's what I've been trying to tell you, Annemari. Calandra was there and she's perfectly all right. Sanne's husband, Pledger, was seated at the head table with her for the banquet, and he seemed quite taken with her. So did the young man they assigned as her escort, according to Sanne. She said they were having altogether too much fun at the ball and Calandra ain't dignified enough by half for a Diplomatic envoy."

Annemari stopped in front of the green pavilion outside Gaetano's. "Evert, that's impossible."

"What, for a Diplo to lighten up? Unlikely, maybe, but surely possible. I even have hopes of seeing *you* let your hair down, Annemari. Been meaning to tell you, it's high time you stopped spending every Joy Luck Fortune night home with a glass of milk and an old holovid."

Annemari devoutly hoped Evert didn't know the title of the last holovid she'd rented, presently flashing across the inside of her head in neon-pink lettering with little hearts attached. Not that there was anything *wrong* with watching something called *With All My Heart*. It would just be . . . embarrassing. And after the unauthorized searches she'd recently pulled off, she couldn't help thinking how easy it would be for anyone who knew his way around Federation computer systems to bring up a list of the last ten holos she'd rented.

But that somebody wouldn't be Evert, who called Tech Support when the cleaners disconnected the power to his deskvid. He was guessing about her habits . . . more or less correctly.

Unfortunately, he interpreted the pause as permission to continue dissecting her personal life. Or lack of one.

"It was one thing when Kaarle—when you were widowed and left alone with Niklaas to raise. I know you didn't want to leave him in the creche anytime you weren't working. But Kaarle's been dead for years now, Annemari, and Niklaas—"

"Still needs me," Annemari cut him off. "No, Evert, that's *not* what I want to talk about. Are you *sure* your aunt Sanne said she saw Calandra?"

"Just told you so," said Evert. "Said she danced all night. Calandra, I mean, not Sanne."

"And exactly when was the ball?"

"On the fourteenth."

Annemari frowned. "I suppose that's *just* possible. I should have checked the time on those transit records."

"You found records showing she was someplace else at the time?"

"Or just after . . . Is Tasman on Federation time?"

Evert shrugged. "Dunno, but that's easy enough to check. But I'll trust a live person over a computer database any day, and so should you, Annemari—*you* know how easy it is to hack into those things. If somebody tried to fake a journey for Calandra to some other place, you need to be looking into who'd want to do that, not questioning my family's eyewitness information!"

"I would," said Annemari abstractedly, as she tried to figure out what this latest twist could mean, "except it wasn't Calandra Vissi's travel plans I found."

"Then what—how—"

"Come inside and sit down, you two!" Nunzia Hirvonen swept up beside them, hugged Annemari and pushed Evert toward the door. "I'm starving. Order first, then gossip."

Gaetano's might serve traditional Italo-Thai food, but the décor had been managed by a thoroughly modern aura consultant, from the collage of antique coins over the door to attract wealth to the trailing red cords that dangled from beams to dissipate negative energies. The entire north wall was covered by a screen of falling water dropping onto rounded stones, and the rounded lines of chairs and tables supported a smooth flow of energy from the fountain through the entire room.

Over the *bruschetta con limone* Annemari gave up on discretion and decided to tell everybody everything. It didn't take much decision; Nunzia's warm pressure was almost impossible to resist. Besides, she didn't want to wait until after lunch to explain to Evert why Calandra couldn't have been at the banquet on Kalapriya.

First she had to fill Nunzia in on the background—the

offer of a bacteriomat implant for Nikki from an anonymous source, her dispatching of Calandra Vissi to look into the possibility that somebody was stealing bacteriomats from the Barents Trading Society's stock, her subsequent loss of contact with Calandra and request that Evert check on her discreetly through his family contacts on Kalapriya. "But while I was waiting to hear from Evert," she explained, "just this morning, in fact, one of my spyder programs came up with transit records for Thecla Partheni, leaving Tasman the day after I lost contact with Calandra, returning to Rezerval that same day. Or . . . I need to check what time Tasman is on; it could have been the equivalent of really late at night on Kalapriya, which would explain your aunt seeing Calandra at the ball, Evert."

Both Nunzia and Evert looked blank.

"Look," Annemari said, "this is really seriously classified information, and I never said anything, okay? But Thecla Partheni is one of Calandra's spare identities. Obviously her cover was compromised and she had to switch identities. Also obviously, she found some clue that sent her back here to Rezerval. And I would have thought, from the timing, that it all happened on Tasman. She couldn't have been on Kalapriya more than a few hours at most."

"But she *was* there," Evert pointed out. "Damn it, Annemari, you've talked with the Tasman officer who escorted Calandra to the Kalapriya shuttle, and I've just had a vid from m'aunt Sanne going on and on about what Calandra wore to the ball in her honor. Did your spyder show Calandra returning to Tasman? No? Well then, most likely one of those Tasman thieves lifted Calandra's spare ID and used it to get off-station."

"The spare identities aren't stealable," Annemari explained. "Nunzia, you know how they're done for Diplos, can you explain to Evert why we *know* nobody stole the Thecla Partheni ID?"

"It doesn't exist," Nunzia said promptly. "Not physically, not outside Calandra's brain. One of her neurochip implants allows her to activate a signal that will cause Federation computers and any system drawing on their databases to recognize her retinal scans and DNA as belonging to—what did you say the alternate name was, Annemari?"

"Thecla," Annemari said. "Thecla Partheni. We had to pick

something that would be ethnically compatible with her general physical appearance. Calandra's small and dark; she might be able to convince a computer her real name was something like Katrijna van Alstyne, but no human being would believe she was from Barents. Oh, why am I going on about this, it doesn't matter; the point is that the retinal and DNA scans confirm that Calandra left Tasman for Rezerval as Thecla Partheni. And I *haven't* found any records showing Thecla— or Calandra—returning from Kalapriya to Tasman."

"That just means they're misfiled," Evert said, "because she was definitely in Valentin on Kalapriya the evening of the fourteenth. And if you don't believe me, I'll drag you to my rooms and force you to watch m'aunt Sanne going on and on about the damned ball."

"I just might take you up on that," Annemari said absently. "Does Sanne say anything about seeing Calandra *after* the ball?"

"No, but she wouldn't, would she?"

"She might say something about the surprising early departure of the Diplomat . . . Evert, could you check with her again and find out if she knows what Calandra has been doing since the day of her arrival?"

Evert groaned.

"Or maybe you could ask somebody else?"

Evert's brow furrowed. "I've got a young relative in the Guards . . . no, that's no use; Moylen's only a leutnant, he wouldn't be in on high diplomatic doings. It'll have to be Sanne. But is it really necessary? I thought you had settled that she went back to Tasman."

"Maybe. The timing's funny. And . . . Kalapriya is technology-restricted; they wouldn't be checking bio-data the way the space stations and shuttles do. It's just barely possible that Calandra found out something at the ball that made her return to Tasman at once, without reporting to me. But it's also possible that the shuttle taking this person from Tasman to Kalapriya didn't run the passengers through proper security and ID checks. An impersonator might be able to make herself up to look enough like Calandra to fool some Tasman officer who'd only seen her once before, if that. And if somebody is impersonating *my* Diplomat on Kalapriya," Annemari said firmly, "I'd really, really like to know about it."

"Then look for Calandra and ask her. And why do you suppose she hasn't checked in with you already?"

"Possibly," Annemari said, "for the same reason that she chose to use an alternate identity. Perhaps she doesn't want somebody to know that she's a Diplomat. In which case she'd hardly be walking in through the front door of a Federation office building, would she?"

"You know, Annemari," Evert murmured, "your eyes go more grey than blue when you're being sarcastic. It's not becoming. We both know there are plenty of ways your pet Diplomat could reach you without 'walking in through the front door.' If you really think Thecla Partheni is Calandra and that she returned to Rezerval four days ago, you ought to be worried sick. Why aren't you?"

"Because I have reason to think she's following up the clue that brought her back here," Annemari answered.

"How can you think that if you haven't heard from her?"

"She left the Rezerval main port by the Garibaldi gate," Annemari said, looking at Nunzia rather than Evert. "Most of the public transit from there runs south . . ."

"To Castelnuovo Province," Nunzia nodded. "Let me guess. That's the location of the clinic you were asking about?"

Then it was Evert's turn to listen while Annemari described Tomi Oksanen's mysterious recovery, the visit to Niklaas in which he'd mentioned the Cassilis Clinic, and his subsequent disappearance. "On the public nets it shows up as a combination health spa and plastic surgery clinic for the rich and beautiful who want to stay that way," she concluded, "but they're paying a *lot* of surgeons, and they're not all reconstruction men. At least three neurosurgeons that I know of. Maybe more—Nunzia, what's stereotactic injection?"

"A technique used, among other things, for implanting neuronal cells," Nunzia said. "If they've got a specialist in *that* on staff—"

"Two," said Annemari with a brisk, satisfied nod.

"Then they're doing *something* in the way of rebuilding neural networks," Nunzia said. "And either it's something very complicated, or they're doing a lot of it, because 'mat insertion is actually a fairly simple procedure."

"Really?" Evert asked. "Personally, I'd as soon have as many highly paid surgeons as possible helping out before anybody puts a hole in *my* skull for therapeutic purposes."

Nunzia smiled slightly. "You're safe from 'mat reconstruction, Haar Cornelis. Even now, we can't repair what was never there to begin with."

"I do believe I've just been insulted," Evert said. He grinned at Nunzia and she returned his smile more warmly than her words would have suggested. Annemari began to see a solution to one of her long-standing problems. Not exactly one of the most urgent ones, still . . . But the possibility of Evert and Nunzia getting together was pleasant enough, and surprising enough, to divert her for a moment from everything else.

"Anyway," Nunzia said when she finally broke eye contact with Evert and dove into her *pappardelle al cinghale*, "cutting holes in the skull is hardly cutting-edge surgery. They've been doing it since the Stone Age to treat everything from epilepsy to osteomyelitis." She gestured largely with her fork. "Difference is, *we* know what we're doing and why it works. *They* just drilled a hole and hoped it would let the demons out."

"Whereas modern surgeons," Evert said with exquisite politeness, "do just the opposite—drill a hole and poke a demon in. Or am I behind the times? Does modern neuroscience have an explanation for exactly how the bacteriomats of Kalapriya work their wonders?"

"One point to you," Nunzia said without malice. "No, we don't know exactly how they work, and yes, before you say it, surgeons of the forty-first century probably *will* look pityingly upon us poor ignoramuses of the Plastic Age. What they do know is that they're a major advance on primitive stem-cell therapy. Back in the twenty-first century surgeons had found that stem cells injected into an adult brain would somehow figure out what kinds of cells were missing or damaged and grow themselves into replacements. That took care of a lot of problems."

"So what do Kalapriyan bacteriomats have over stem cells?"

"One word. *Structure!*" Nunzia jabbed her fork at the plate and pushed her food around into an undifferentiated mess. "Nobody ever did succeed in persuading stem cells to grow long enough axons to repair severely damaged spinal cords. But biofilms, like the 'mats, aren't just one species but a collection of microbial species working together. So when you get a biofilm that likes to live in human brains and nerves, it doesn't need to grow single supercells; it can create a whole community of linked, cooperating cells to bridge the gap." She pushed individual bits of pasta into a line across her plate. "*And* the 'mats mimic whole structures in the brain, the way stem cells mimic individual cells—which allows them to do repairs far beyond what was accomplished with stem-cell therapy. Bottom line, your chances of surviving demyelinizing infections, brain tumors, or latent Fournier Syndrome—not only surviving, but walking away—are better than ever before."

"Only if you can get on the list," Annemari murmured, blinking rapidly.

"Gods. I'm a tactless idiot," Nunzia said, putting her fork down. "Anni, can you forgive—"

"Annemari, I'm so sorry—" Evert began.

Annemari managed a smile, and a moment later had command of her voice. "Help me check out the Cassilis Clinic, and you're both off the hook. Otherwise, I'll make you feel guilty and miserable forever. Deal?"

CHAPTER NINE

Udara on Kalapriya

Chulayen couldn't remember how he'd reached the fortresslike building at the top of the mountain that housed the Ministry for Loyalty. He must have been running, because his throat burned for breath and his chest was heaving and there was blackness swirling at the edges of his vision, but he could remember nothing of the streets he must have passed through to get here, nor of what he'd been shouting as he ran. The only things clear in his mind were the shattered, empty rooms he'd left behind and the locked gate before him, and the guard who refused to pass him through.

"Dung burner! Ghay fodder! I am Chulayen Vajjadara, son of Minister Vajjadara, and I have urgent business with the Minister for Loyalty!"

The turbanned man behind the gate, smart and secure in the bright red uniform of the Ministry for Loyalty, scratched his nose and studied something on the guardhouse wall, beyond Chulayen's line of vision. "Don't see no Minister Varadajja on *this* list."

"Vajjadara, you half-wit! And of course you won't see his name on the list. He's dead!"

151

"Well, then," the guard said with a sly grin, "he won't be issuing no orders to let *you* in, will he?"

"You must let me in. Please. I *must* see the Minister for Loyalty at once. It's—" Chulayen groped for words. "It's a matter of national security."

The guard's look of smug certainty faded just a little, giving Chulayen renewed hope. He felt in the inner pocket of his sash and brought out a thousand-tulai note. "To show my appreciation of your understanding?"

The man's hand moved quickly to snatch the note through the bars of the gate, then slowly toward the great keys hanging from his gold-braided sash. Chulayen babbled in his relief. "So kind, yes, you understand, I would not be so importunate, but there has been a terrible mistake, my Anusha and the children, no reason to take them, no reason at all—"

The guard's hand stopped just short of the keys. "The wife and kiddies, is it?" His tone was kindly, but the back of Chulayen's neck prickled with unreasonable fear.

"It's all a mistake. I must see the Minister at once," he repeated, not knowing what else to say.

"That's what they all say," the guard told him.

"All?"

"The families. If there are any left. It's always a mistake, no reason for the Ministry to take *their* people away." The guard folded his hands over the gold sash and Chulayen's heart sank. "Go home. The Ministry for Loyalty doesn't *make* mistakes. By rights I ought to call the Arm of the Bashir on you now, for shouting treason in the street, but in view of your gen'rosity I'll let you go this once. Get along now, quick! There's nothing you can do here."

"No!" Chulayen grabbed the wrought-iron grille and shook it. He could feel the mortar crumbling around the ends of the bars. "No, you don't understand, it's a mistake!"

"Ministry for Loyalty doesn't make mistakes," the guard repeated.

"Doesn't make mistakes!" a high mocking voice behind Chulayen repeated. "Doesn't make mistakes! Let's hear it for the Ministry!" A clod of dirt hit Chulayen on the shoulder, crumbled before it hit the ground. He half turned and saw that the street behind him was full of onlookers, mostly low-class street sweepers and water carriers and servants, the scum of the Rohini slums down-mountain. How did they come to be in this part of town? Had they followed him? He shook his head, disoriented, and a rain of clods and small stones went past him. Mostly past him. They were trying to stone the Ministry, but their aim wasn't so good; if he didn't get out of the way something worse than a handful of dirt would hit him soon, they were prying stones out of the rain gutters now.

"Let me in!" He shook the grille again. "I'm not part of that *mob*. I have business with the Minister!"

"Stand aside," the guard warned. He whistled and more men in red uniforms with gold sashes poured into the courtyard behind him. They were armed only with old-fashioned muskets, but muskets were enough at this range. The guard made a strange throwing motion with one hand; it seemed as though a net of light fell over the crowd. A moment later, the line of muskets came up, leveled; there was a crashing roar and Chulayen's head exploded into darkness.

"He should be told what happens to the 'disappeared,'" Sonchai argued. "As soon as he comes round. It's not right, making him do our work under false pretenses."

"Nobody's making him do anything," said Madee wearily. "We'll tell him what he needs to know, and ask for his help. That's all." She drew the end of her shalin over her head and huddled within the thin fabric. The cellar was a cold, clammy place for an old woman with old bones to sit; even all the injured people lying on the floor or leaning against the damp walls couldn't warm it up enough for her. She was shaking with fatigue after an hour of working to stop bleeding, set bones in makeshift splints, give whatever rough-and-ready first aid she could to those injured in the riot. The room smelled of blood and madira: every Rohini midwife knew to rinse her hands in the clear, rough hill-distilled liquor, and Madee had a superstitious belief that it was better than water for cleansing most wounds. After all, few Rohini mothers died of the childbed fever—far fewer than the Rudhrani women who could afford the best physicians with the strongest charms.

And most Rohini women learned what they could of

healing, because Rohini didn't go to one of the Bashir's "public" hospitals. Especially, Madee thought grimly, especially not Rohini who sported suspicious-looking injuries after a riot in front of the Ministry for Loyalty; might as well walk up to the slightly damaged front grille of the Ministry and ask to be shot then and there.

If you could be so lucky.

She'd even extracted a musket ball from the chest of a boy not much younger than Chulen . . . not that it had done him much good; he'd died coughing out blood. Well, better dead in a Puvaathi cellar than taken prisoner by the Arm of the Bashir; they all knew where those prisoners went. The legendary saint Puran Bhagat, he who was thrown into a deep well after the wicked Emperor Salbahan cut off his hands and feet, had had a better chance than the "disappeared" of Udara.

They knew, but Chulen didn't. And Madee didn't think it was necessary to tell him just yet. He would have enough to assimilate as it was. He'd be no use to them—or to himself—if he couldn't remain calm enough to play his part. Besides, there was nothing they could do for his woman and children—she couldn't *do* this if she thought of them by name—until the next prison convoy left Puvaathi for the brainfarms. Whether they could do anything then might well depend on whether Chulen was able to get back into the good graces of the Ministers and what he could learn from his official position.

"He'll try harder if he knows there's a chance of saving them," Sonchai argued as if he had read her thoughts.

"He may be too demoralized to try successfully if he knows what he's trying to save them from," Madee said evenly.

"Don't you even *care* one way or another? Can you really think about it as if you're moving pieces in a game of chaupur? They're your—"

"I know what they are," Madee cut him off. "And I say we do not tell him yet. I have the right." She stared at Sonchai until he dropped his eyes.

"You have the right," he conceded sulkily. "But you are playing with dice made from the bones of the dead, Madee." Every child knew the story of how Rusala played at chaupur with the all-powerful Bashir Sarkap, and won back first his horse, then his armor, and finally his life.

"As Rusala learned," Madee replied, "such is the only way to win against the dice of the Bashir. And if I am Rusala in the story, what are you? The wise horse Bhaunr, who warned Rusala? Or the rat Dhol Raja who upset the pieces whenever Sarkap was losing?"

A groan from the inner room came most opportunely. "Go and see if any of the other wounded need water," she ordered him. Chulen's eyelids were fluttering; it was time to tell him—as much as he must know, for now.

"So many injured to save one man from the Arm of the Bashir," Sonchai grumbled as he left. That was Sonchai, forever arguing about something—if you shut him up about a future decision, he'd go back and argue about a past one. Such a pretty boy he had been, with those full lips and long dark lashes, but he had grown into a perpetually angry and discontented young man. Beauties—of either sex—didn't age well, Madee had noticed. She herself had never been a beauty.

The first thing Chulayen knew for sure was that the back of his head hurt. A lot.

Slowly his consciousness of other aches and pains returned, none of them much to compare with the ongoing explosion behind his right ear. He was stiff, and cold, and lying on damp ground in a darkness sprinkled with flickering lights. But not dead. When he saw the muskets pointing at him—

Then it came back to him in an unbearable rush, his attempt to get into the Ministry for Loyalty, the grille, the guard, the shattered empty rooms down the hill and everybody gone. This must be one of those prison rooms beneath the Ministry. "Anusha? Anusha!" He pushed himself up on one elbow; the small flames swirled about him and became stars, falling stars, the earth turning under him and acid bile coming up in his throat as his stomach also spun and swooped.

"Lie still, Chulen, lie still." A damp rag wiped his mouth, a hand steadied his shoulder. "You will be sick if you try to sit up too fast."

"You don't understand," he whispered. "Anusha—the children?"

"They are not here." It was a woman's voice, sad and

caring. Not what he would have expected to find in a Ministry prison; was it a trap? "Drink this, it will make you feel better."

Obediently Chulayen sipped from the rough-edged cup held to his lips. Something cold, a little bitter, but it awakened a raging thirst he hadn't been aware of. He tried to gulp down the rest, but the cup was taken away and the hand supporting his shoulders lowered him back down.

"Not too much at once, or you will be sick again."

"Nothing—to be sick *with*," he managed, remembering more of the long afternoon and evening he'd spent going from office to office. Worrying about some distant crystal caves, while the Arm of the Bashir was taking away Neena and Neeta and the baby. "Fool," he said. "I was a fool."

"You should have taken one of my *yai pao* when they were hot," said the voice. One of the flickering lamps came closer, and the face of the old pancake vendor swam out of the darkness.

"Old mother! Did they take you too? Were you there? Tell them it was a mistake, you were not part of it—"

"The Ministry for Loyalty does not make mistakes," mocked a voice in the darkness. Chulayen started, then groaned as his head exploded in another shower of throbbing pains.

"Sonchai, don't tease the boy. He is confused," the old woman said sharply. She turned back to Chulayen. "It is all right, Chulen—at least—this much is all right; this is not a Ministry prison."

"But I thought . . . Where are we, then?"

"It does not matter," the woman soothed him. "We are where the Arm of the Bashir will not look for us. Now lie quiet, Chulen! We cannot risk too much noise."

"We have risked too much already for this one, Madee," said the voice that had mocked him before. Its owner came nearer the lamp, and Chulayen saw a young man with full lips and a sulky look on his face. The vending woman kept one hand on his shoulder, as if to urge him to lie still.

"It's true, Sonchai, but we would have done the same for you."

"*I* would never have been such a fool as to challenge the Ministry for Loyalty before their own gates!"

"I hope not, but then you have the advantage of Chulen: you know who and what you are."

This whole exchange mystified Chulayen so that he was happy enough to lie still, eyes closed against the flickering lights that still tended to whirl in dizzying patterns if he tried to concentrate. So he was not a prisoner of the Ministry for Loyalty. That was good, probably. But it meant he had no chance of finding Anusha and the children in this place. "I have to leave," he told the old woman.

"Not yet," she said sharply.

"I'm well enough." He had to be, for the children, for any chance of saving the children.

"You don't *know* enough. We have to explain—" She sighed, settled back on her heels and pushed the folds of the faded, threadbare shalin away from her face. "I don't even know where to begin. Chulen, what do you remember of your childhood?"

"Are you holding me prisoner because of my parents? It won't do you any good. They are dead. They can't pay you any ransom—and I doubt their friends would, either. Not now," he said bitterly, remembering the bland, vague responses he'd had all day, and the crushing blow that had ended it. "I am not exactly in favor with the Bashir's present ministers. Or didn't you understand why I was at the Ministry for Loyalty?"

"Oh, yes," she said. "We understood. That was why we were there too."

Chulayen tried to laugh. "What, a bunch of ragged Rohini came to save my Anusha?"

"To save you," she said, "because you are one of us."

Chulayen shook his head. A mistake; the pain woke and sank claws into the back of his skull. "I don't know what you mean."

"Oh, yes, you do," she said urgently. "You were not so young when your parents were taken, you *must* remember something."

"I don't know what you are talking about. My father died two years since; he was ill with the winter fever, nobody took him anywhere. And my mother has been dead for some years." He sat up in his agitation. Better; his head still hurt, but the dizziness was receding.

"Vajjadara, the Minister for Trade, died two winters ago,"

the old woman agreed. "But Chulen, do you remember nothing of your first years? Before you played in the Vajjadara gardens?"

Wisps of dreams and nightmares floated through his muzzy brain. "There was a woman, a Rohini woman, who sang to me at night," he said at last. A dim memory of indescribable warmth and comfort, a sense of safety he'd never known since, that he sometimes returned to in dreams. "A nurse?"

"Your *mother*, Chulen."

"But—she was Rohini!"

"So are you. Your mother and father were brave people, Chulen, the bravest. They spoke out against the Bashir's growing power when Udara was still a small state, when the people still had a voice in the council—*all* the people, not just the high-born Rudhrani—and they were taken by the Ministry for Loyalty when you were not four years old."

"But my father, my mother—" Chulayen struggled for words to describe the parents he had been taught to honor above all else. "They never spoke of this. Why should I believe *you*?"

"The Minister for Trade and his wife had prayed for years for a son," Madee told him. "You were too young to have a part in what they called your parents' treason, and in those days the Ministry for Loyalty had not learned what profitable use it could make of prisoners. After your true parents were taken away, Minister Vajjadara's wife asked for you."

"No! My *mother*—"

"Was Sunanda Talap, a brave Rohini woman who died in a Ministry prison, Chulen." There were tears in Madee's eyes.

"Why would Minister Vajjadara agree to raise a Rohini boy as his own son?"

"It is said that he loved his wife very much. And her heart yearned for a child."

That much, at least, Chulayen knew was true.

"Those among the Bashir's servants who knew of your origins agreed not to speak of them. He said that he would raise you as Rudhrani and that you would uphold the high principles of his people."

"If no one spoke of it," Chulayen cried, "how do *you* know so much?"

"Sunanda was my daughter," Madee said. She stopped, struggling with her tears.

"Then why did you not raise me?"

"Idiot!" Sonchai snarled. "Do you know so little of what goes on beneath those fine buildings of your Rudhrani friends? If anyone had known Madee was Sunanda's mother, she would have been taken and killed also. Usually the children of the 'disappeared' are left to starve on the street. She waited for you, she prayed, she feared you had been killed with your parents . . . and she asked. Vajjadara had Rohini servants, and they talk to other Rohini."

"I have known for years where you were, grandson," Madee took up the tale again with forced calm. "But what could I do? Do you think that a Rohini pancake vendor could go to Minister Vajjadara and say, 'That boy you are calling yours is my grandson, give him back'? We watched over you, we saw you were growing up safe and healthy, they were good to you."

"They—were—my *parents*."

"And did you never wonder why you did not grow tall like the Minister, why your skin is so much darker than his and his wife's? Did no one ever say anything that made you doubt your position, even for a moment?"

"No! I—" Chulayen fell silent, remembering when his marriage with Anusha had been arranged. He had not been overeager to marry the tall, plain Rudhrani girl with her outspoken manner, but his mother had been so pleased by the alliance. "A girl of good Rudhrani blood, that's the most important thing," she had said over and over, and once, "especially for you, Chulayen." But she would not explain why it was so much more important for him than for any of his schoolmates to marry into an unblemished Rudhrani lineage, and when pressed, she'd denied she had said any such thing, claimed he must have misunderstood her.

And there'd been other things, nothing blatant, nothing he couldn't ignore at the time. Odd looks and comments from his father's friends: "So this is Chulayen! Well, well, he *does* seem to be growing up to be a proper Vajjadara," as if this were mildly surprising. Teasing from his schoolmates about his skin that tanned so dark when he played games in the brief mountain summer, teasing that was cut off promptly by the teachers—he had thought they were protecting him because he was a Vajjadara; perhaps, he thought now, they had been protecting him against the knowledge that he *wasn't* a Vajjadara.

Wasn't even Rudhrani.

He put the pain of that thought away for now. It would be impolite to acknowledge before this poor Rohini woman—he still could not, would not think of her as his grandmother—how shamed he felt at the idea that *he* might be a Rohini. One of the class that all educated people agreed was only fit for service, not for leadership. No Rudhrani gentleman was ever discourteous. He might not be Rudhrani, but he could still be a gentleman.

Besides, he might need the help of these people if he was ever to rescue Anusha and the children.

"At first they took Sunanda and Pra, left you in the empty rooms. We meant to get you after nightfall, but they came back for you first." Madee rocked back and forth, drawing the end of the shalin over her face and chanting as if to herself. "*Thora thora, beta, tun disin, aur bahoti disi dhur; Purt jinan de tur chale, aur mawan chikna chur.*" It was part of the Song of Rusala, the mother's lament for her son's departure: "The mother whose son goes away becomes as dust."

They left you in the empty rooms. Chulayen's recurring nightmare came back to him with such force that for a moment he thought himself dreaming indeed: an empty house, doors and window shutters shattered by rifle butts, empty rooms greeting him with the memory of screams. It had not been foreknowledge, then, but memory. Now he saw that in the nightmare he was looking *up* at high windows, at bloody smears on the walls above his head. A child's view. And the thin high wailing voice that accompanied the dream was his own crying.

"How did they die?"

Madee wrapped the shalin tightly around herself, shrinking down into herself, becoming a cloth-covered bundle.

"Don't ask," Sonchai said harshly. "No one taken by the Arm of the Bashir dies well."

"My children!" Terror lanced through Chulayen. Caught up in Madee's story, he had for a moment been able to forget the fear that had paralyzed his brain ever since he came home to that broken house. "They're not dead? Why would they kill babies? Why *take* babies?" A wild thought struck him and he cackled with hysterical laughter. "Let me guess, another of the Bashir's High Ministers has a barren wife who is just dying to take on a half-Rohini baby boy and a pair of hellion twin girls." It was better than believing them dead already. If they had been "adopted" he might still be able to get them back.

And Anusha . . . He had never loved Anusha properly. He had treated her with the deference a Rudhrani gentleman owed to his wife, he had given the proper gifts on the births of the twins and far more extravagant gifts when she bore his son, Vashi, but he had always felt that she looked down on him and resented their marriage. Maybe she did—maybe even she had known the secret that had been kept, it seemed, from him alone. Maybe her parents had forced her to agree to this marriage with arguments that still hurt her: "What do you expect, you who are too tall, too bony, too loud? Have old mothers been knocking at our door with flattering offers? He may be Rohini, but no one knows about it, and the family is good. Your younger sisters are settled, it's time you were married while anybody will still have you." Oh yes, he could imagine how they would have dealt with Anusha to drive her, stiff and resentful, to the marriage canopy. Two strangers marrying to satisfy their families; no wonder they'd never become true companions, small wonder that she'd turned in her loneliness to the crazy creed of the Inner Light Way. All that would change, Chulayen vowed, if—no, *when*— he got her and the children back.

"Oh, the Arm of the Bashir doesn't kill prisoners anymore," Sonchai said. "That would be wasteful. They'll be kept until the next convoy goes out."

"Goes where?"

"We might be able to free them when the convoy goes," Madee said without answering his question. "It's hard to find out when they leave; usually at night, always without warning. We had someone in the Ministry who could let us know when extra travel rations for prisoners were ordered, that always meant a convoy leaving soon, but I think they found out about him."

"Then what can we do?"

"Not very much," Madee admitted. "We've saved a few,

helped them to slip away from the convoys by night, but not enough; most of the 'disappeared' go straight to the . . ."

"To the caves," Sonchai said harshly.

"Caves?" Maybe they were using prisoners to mine the saltpeter from places like the Jurgan Caves. Maybe that was why nobody had seemed to care how hard it was to carry the stuff back; the object was punishment, not profits. Chulayen was thinking furiously. "They must give them long sentences, else some would come back and there'd be more talk about the caves here in the city."

"No one comes back," Sonchai said.

"Ever? Surely there must be an occasional escape—"

Sonchai's laugh was harsh. "The Ministry for Loyalty does not leave its prisoners in condition to escape."

"But you get some free before they ever reach the caves."

"Some." Sonchai stared at him with a challenging look. "We could do more if we had more help on the inside. There's only so much that sweepers and bearers and personal servants can pick up. And in case it has escaped your attention, there are not a great many Rohini in the civil service."

"You could help us, Chulayen, if you would," Madee said quietly. "We meant all along to ask for your help, one day."

"You picked a good day for it," Chulayen said. "I'm hardly in a position to refuse now, am I?"

Madee plucked at the folds of her shalin with nervous fingers. "We did not expect this. We thought that some day I would come to you, would explain—but you seemed so perfectly Rudhrani, so content, so sure of your life, there was never a good time. We did not intend to put this pressure on you, Chulayen, I swear it! Would I put my own grandson's children at risk?"

"How do *I* know what you would do? Only tell me how I can help them now." Whether these Rohini had planned the disaster that had consumed his family, or were merely taking advantage of it, made no difference now; they were his only hope.

Chapter Ten

Dharampal on Kalapriya

Indukanta Jagat was in a foul temper by the time he was admitted to the audience chambers in Dharampal, but he knew better than to show his anger at being kept waiting too openly. Instead he bowed deeply and praised the Vakil's even-handedness and independence and expressed his certainty that the Barents Resident in Dharampal would have been admitted no sooner than the representative of Udara.

"I fear you have been misinformed," said Yadleen. "Unlike Udara, the independent state of Dharampal has accepted no resident representative of the Barents Trading Society. So the issue of equal treatment does not really arise—does it? You are here. The outlanders are not."

And anybody who took that as an expression that Yadleen favored Udara over the foreign trading company was . . . doing exactly what the Vakil wanted, no doubt.

The Vakil of Dharampal was a slender young man, not yet thirty, whose slight build and clean-shaven face deceived many into thinking him a mere boy who would do whatever his senior counsellors advised. Jagat was not such a fool; this "boy" had maintained Dharampal's perilous neutrality between the growing powers of the Barents Trading

163

Society and the Bashirate of Udara for the five long and difficult years since his accession to the throne, with half his council leaning toward Barents and the other half toward Udara. It had not been an easy balance to maintain; and though Jagat intended to make it considerably more difficult, if not impossible, for Dharampal to remain neutral, he had a grudging respect for the Vakil for having pulled it off this long.

"If they are not here yet, they will be soon," Jagat countered.

Yadleen's calm expression did not change. "Forgive me," he asked in dulcet tones, "but has the honored envoy from Udara been favored with news that has escaped the Vakil of Dharampal? I was not aware that I had accepted a Barents Trading Society Resident. Or does the Society now send its armies against a peaceful state that has given them no cause for offense?"

Indukanta Jagat folded his hands before him and bowed his head like a mourner at a state funeral. Privately he thought the pose deliciously apt: this meeting was indeed the first stage of the funeral of a state. Dharampal could no longer maintain its neutrality, not with Udara at its northern border. "The ways of the Trading Society are well known, Vakil. First they establish the excuse, then come the armies. Traveling toward Dharampal now are two agents of the Society. They will find some excuse to claim insult in your treatment of them; the armies will follow."

"Foreknowledge of the future is no doubt an excellent gift," said the Vakil tranquilly, "but one which the gods have not seen fit to grant me. Our relations with the Barents Trading Society are peaceful, and Gabrel Eskelinen has proven himself sympathetic to our position. He shall be received as an honored guest; what happens thereafter is in the lap of the gods. And I think our country might be rather difficult for the outlander armies."

Jagat endeavoured to keep his face from showing alarm. If the Vakil knew that Eskelinen was one of the approaching envoys, what else did he know of them—or of their mission? The Bashir's instructions as to what he was to tell the Vakil were quite clear. They did not cover the eventuality that Yadleen might know he was lying.

"Young Eskelinen in himself would be no problem," Jagat

finally replied, "but the woman he escorts will not be so easy to deal with. Does the Vakil know of the *Diplomatai*?" He used the outlander word but gave it a Kalapriyan plural, and was pleased to see a slight frown appear on Yadleen's smooth tan countenance.

"Is this another race of star-traveling beings?"

"Almost, Vakil," Jagat replied. "Almost another race, indeed. These *Diplomatai* begin life as human as you or I, but they are selected young and given special training and magical powers which render them as difficult to overpower as a djinn of the air. They speak all languages fluently, carry maps in their heads, can render an armed man helpless with their secret fighting magic, and conceal on their persons offworld weapons more terrible than any you have seen. Indeed, they had better have been called Nagai, serpent-people! They are customarily sent into places the outlanders have found difficult to conquer by normal means; their mission is to stir up trouble, weaken the state, and prepare the way for outlander armies." The description of the Diplos came from the Barents Resident in Udara; the explanation of the mission was Jagat's own invention. In any case, the Vakil could hardly prove he was lying. He might know of the travelers' movements, but who could speak for their intentions?

"Shocking!" Yadleen said. His voice was tranquil as ever, but Jagat could see one lean bronzed hand tensing and relaxing, very slightly. Good—the Vakil was at least troubled by his arguments. He could build on that. "And is this how the Barents Trading Society obtained the Bashir's permission to install a Resident in Udara? My friend, you have my condolences. I had no idea that the Bashir was so frightened of outlander armies that have yet to reach Dharampal, let alone Udara."

"Udara's situation is quite different," Jagat said. "We have . . . mutually beneficial relations with the Barents Trading Society."

"A friendly arrangement, in fact."

"Just so."

"Yet you doubt that their relations with Dharampal would be equally . . . friendly?"

"These *Diplomatai*," Jagat said, "are quite a different breed from the men of the Barents Society. Why do they send one to you, if not to foment distrust and discord?" Gods take the boy! He was arguing the matter as if it were no more than a puzzle in statecraft from some dead history . . . and Jagat was losing the argument! He had to find some way to touch Yadleen's emotions again, to make fear of the unknown overpower this cool logic. "My lord, the Bashir has always felt good will toward Dharampal," he began feeling his way toward another approach.

"As he felt good will toward Thamboon and Narumalar?"

If Yadleen expected Jagat to be discomposed by this reference to the two formerly independent states most recently absorbed into the Bashirate of Udara, he misunderstood his man. "Exactly so," Jagat replied. "The Bashir was gravely distressed by the internal instability of those states, which forced him to take over their rule lest his own lands be threatened. I am certain he would be no less distressed should his friend the Vakil of Dharampal allow troublemakers to travel freely through his territory."

"In short, you offer me a choice—offend the Barents Trading Society, or offend the Bashir." Yadleen's right hand clenched on the carved armrest of his throne.

Jagat bowed. After a moment's respectful silence he ventured an apposite proverb from the times of the Empire. " 'My neighbor is at my right hand, and the Emperor is far away as the summer skies.' "

"You mean," Yadleen said drily, "that the Bashir's armies are at my border—now that Thamboon is no longer independent—and the Trading Society . . ."

"As your Majesty said, this land might be rather difficult for their armies." Jagat bowed again.

"A certain number of refugees from Thamboon came to Dharampal," Yadleen said. "They had wild tales to tell of sorcery in the Bashir's armies, magical nets of light that entangled men and left them helpless to the swords of their enemies, silent demons that killed invisibly. But then, men will always exaggerate the powers of those who conquer them, will they not? I have read that in the time of the Empire, ignorant people ascribed the Emperor's knowledge of the land to secret spies in the form of birds, rather than to the excellent system of roads and couriers which the Empire created as it grew."

"It would be impossible," Jagat said sincerely, "to underestimate the resources available to my master."

Granted, the Consortium had not approved the conquest of Dharampal; having no limestone caves, it was not seen as a profitable area for the Consortium's business. But— "My neighbor is at my right hand, and the Emperor is as far away as the summer skies." Having supplied the Bashir's armies with their sorcerous weapons, the Consortium could hardly dictate from distant Valentin the use to which they were put.

Yadleen drummed his fingers on the armrest. "The visitors will be detained and questioned as to their purposes," he said at last, "but if we determine that they mean no harm, then we cannot in conscience harm them; they will be set free, even as Emperor Dhatacharya set free the rebel soldier Eshana when he swore fealty, and Eshana became Dhatacharya's most trusted man. History teaches us that we cannot build trust by treachery, nor loyalty by deceit."

The boy's conscience, Jagat thought, was what would destroy him. His tutor had given him too many ancient histories of the Empire to read, with their men in white gowns making noble speeches in white-walled palaces. He should rather have been sent out for a year or two of rough living with the tribesmen, to hear the blood-red songs of this century's feuds and tragedies and to bloody his own hands in a minor border skirmish or two.

"My master the Bashir will no doubt be overjoyed to hear your decision," Jagat said with a low bow. "If it pleases the Vakil, this humble one begs the privilege of remaining until the outlanders are brought in for questioning, that he may better understand their motives. It may well be that we in Udara are grown too suspicious of strangers; the Bashir would be only to happy to have your reassurance that these two mean no harm to our lands." And once Yadleen had the outlanders detained, Jagat would find it easy enough to make certain that they did not survive to trouble the Bashir.

Valentin on Kalapriya

After the assassination attempt that night, Gabrel thought their best course was to leave immediately. Clearly somebody

in Valentin—somebody in the Society, not just a native!—
didn't want a Diplomat investigating upcountry. Which made
it seem more likely that there was some truth in Orlando
Montoyasana's allegations, or at the very least, *something*
that should be investigated and stopped.

Strictly speaking, Gabrel should have consulted his superior
officers in the Society's private army before setting forth on
this expedition. But what if they were part of the group trying
to stop Calandra's inquiry? It seemed better to leave as
quickly as they could, and without mentioning the fact to
anybody official in Valentin.

Anuman, the Kalapriyan merchant who'd outfitted Gabrel
for previous upcountry treks, was a friend as well as a
trader; he was good-natured about being awakened in the
middle of the night and almost as amiable about accepting Gabrel's chit in payment for food, traveling clothes,
and other supplies. Of course, he increased the cost of
everything by at least fifty percent; that was understood
as the price of being in a hurry, and no doubt contrib-
uted to Anuman's amiability.

Gabrel's best friend in the regiment, Leutnant Moylen
Cornelis, was not quite so pleased about having his quarters invaded in the dark hours before dawn. But after a few
jibes about the unusual duties involved in being the assigned
escort of a Diplo, and a few remarks about the possible
rewards thereof—which, couched as they were in Barents
slang, Gabrel devoutly hoped Diplomat Vissi had not
understood—he emptied his purse for them willingly enough
and even volunteered the services of his groom for the first
part of the journey.

"Moylen, you're too good," Gabrel protested.

"Not in the least, dear fellow. Naturally you'll take my
spare mounts as far as you can ride, and I'll want Sanouk
to bring them back. And you'll need gold to pay for a couple
of ghaya to carry your things into the hills. I don't want
you being tempted to sell my racing string to some hill-
country Vakil of two villages and a farm in trade for his
pack animals."

Moylen Cornelis was Old Trader Family on both sides and
could well afford to keep a string of racing turagai and otherwise live in the style befitting an Old Family scion; his
monthly pay as Leutnant in the Society army wouldn't have

paid his mess bill for a week. So Gabrel, whose father's military pension had to cover not only family expenses but also the education of his three younger brothers, was able to accept his friend's generosity without too great a struggle with his own pride and conscience.

"Besides," Moylen had added as the clinching argument, "if Sanouk's with you, he can't gossip about this in the bazaar. Your departure will remain a mystery for at least four more days."

"How did you know I wanted it kept secret?" Gabrel demanded, suddenly feeling suspicious even of Moylen. Kaspar Slevinen—whose body would be discovered tomorrow—had been close to Haars Huyberts and Stoffelsen. Whatever was going on, at least those two of the Old Trader Families were involved in it. Was House Cornelis also part of the plot?

Moylen gave him a mocking smile. "Dear boy, officers planning to travel upcountry on legitimate missions don't take off in the middle of the night with a pretty girl in tow."

"Diplomat Vissi," Gabrel said stiffly, "and she's not exactly a girl."

Moylen cocked an eye at Calandra, who was tactfully standing a few feet away and pretending deafness while studying the maps tacked to Moylen's sitting-room wall. She hadn't had time to change into the anonymous traveling clothes provided by Anuman; the borrowed ball dress, with its gauzy panels of peach and lavender dampened by sweat, clung to and emphasized the lines of her slender figure. Her hair was a mass of black curls, also damp with sweat and making a frame of ringlets around a delicate oval face. "No? But hardly a doddering old lady yet, wouldn't you say? Also, official missions don't begin with somebody half strangling my groom and scratching at my bedchamber door. I don't know what you're up to, Gabrel, and something tells me I don't want to know, but—be careful, will you? The regiment would be damned dull without you."

In the event, it had hardly been worthwhile borrowing Moylen's turagai; Calandra had never ridden before. At the end of the first day Gabrel had had to lift her from the saddle, and she'd managed only a few steps before her legs failed her and he had to carry her the rest of the way to their rooms in the Vaisee village where he'd planned to stop for the first night.

"Why didn't you *tell* me you couldn't ride?" he scolded her.

"Why didn't you tell me it was so *bunu* hard? Anyway, I'm learning. I'll do better tomorrow."

"You will not," Gabrel contradicted her, and walked out to make other arrangements.

Selling one of the turagai to a Rohini caravan leader provided enough extra money to pay both their passages on a boat going up the broad reaches of the Vaisee-jara as far as it was navigable, and left a little over for Sanouk to remain in the village a few days before returning to his master with the remaining two beasts. Gabrel hoped Sanouk's reluctance to tell Moylen that one of his prized racing turagai had been sold after all would keep him in the village until his money ran out; he hoped Moylen would understand the necessity and forgive him when they returned; come to think of it, he hoped they *would* return. He'd traveled upcountry before, but always as an officer of the Barents Trading Society's army, with all the might and support of Barents behind him. Now he was traveling as one half of a young, anonymous offworld couple with an inexplicable curiosity to sample Kalapriyan life outside the coastal enclaves. The difference was evident in the attitude of the innkeeper, who'd wanted payment in advance at three times the going rate; Gabrel had to waste time haggling with the man, demonstrating his fluent Kalapriyan and his intimate knowledge of both lodging rates and Kalapriyan curses, to get the price down to a mere one and a half times what a native would pay. The other purchases he made in the local market before returning to Calandra required a similarly protracted spell of bargaining; chaffering was Kalapriya's unofficial planetary sport, and if a Kalapriyan Olympics were ever organized, the herbalist in the market could have chaffered for Vaisee.

"Here," he said on his return, tossing the herbalist's round leather box at Calandra, "put this on your—um— where it's sore." He unstopped the stiff leather bag that had been his other purchase and took a drink of the contents to cover his embarrassment. The local madira burned like fire going down his throat; he was out of practice. "That salve will numb you up and help the skin heal over, and you'll have time to heal in the next few days; we're leaving the turagai here and taking a boat up the Vaisee-jara."

"All the way to whatsit—Darample?"

"Dharampal," Gabrel corrected, wondering what incompetent slob had created the Kalapriyan maps in the Diplomat's download. "And not all the way, naturally, the river's unnavigable once we reach the foothills. But you can't take turagai into the mountains. We'll have to buy a couple of ghaya to carry our packs, and we'll walk."

"All right by me," declared Calandra cheerfully, but her grin faded when she tried to stand up. "Um—I think I might need some help . . ."

It turned out that Calandra needed help not only to get from the rug she'd collapsed on to her narrow bed, but also to get the herbalist's salve on all the places that were sore, some of them being quite hard to reach in her present stiffened condition. Gabrel told himself that he should have thought of that and hired a girl from the marketplace to aid Calandra, then told himself that he'd have been an idiot to do any such thing. It was hard enough for a couple of outlanders to travel inconspicuously outside the coastal enclaves without setting any extra mouths chattering, and there was no impropriety in helping out a fellow traveler in difficulties. Then he concentrated on thinking of his fellow traveler as Diplomat Vissi rather than as the laughing girl he'd danced with the previous night. It took some strenuous thinking about other things to keep his reactions under control while he smoothed the salve onto the backs of her thighs. Every once in a while he stopped and took a drink from the leather sack of madira, not so much because he needed it as for an excuse to take his hands off the Diplo before they wandered where they shouldn't. Diplos probably had extremely *effective* ways of warding off unwanted attentions . . . And doing sums in his head wasn't enough distraction. He would have to find something else to recite . . . but the only poem he could think of offhand was the ballad of Rusala's adventures with the seven daughters of King Death. *Not* a good choice; Rusala had had entirely too much fun with those girls despite their unfortunate parentage.

"You don't have to curse," Maris said, her voice slightly muffled by the pillow she was biting.

"I wasn't cursing." Gabrel drew a blanket over the slender, girlish form and stood up, wiping little droplets of sweat from his brow. "I was—um—reviewing Kalapriyan grammar. *Ishti*-class verbs. In the past subjunctive."

"Find you get a lot of use for the past subjunctive, do you?" The Diplo had stopped chewing on the pillow and was propped up on her elbows, regarding him with a bird's bright inquisitive glance from under her mop of black curls.

"Easy for you to sneer," Gabrel said, finding a heaven-sent evasion for just why he'd felt it necessary to chant *ishti*-class verb conjugations for the last ten minutes, "but us ordinary citizens don't get whole languages downloaded into special chips in our heads. We have to learn them the old-fashioned way, by repetition and sweat."

Maris flopped back onto her pillow, facedown. "Those language chips aren't as great as everybody assumes," she said through the red and black embroidered pillow cover. "We don't come out, like, talking the language fluently or anythin'."

"Oh. More like a running start on learning the language?"

Maris sputtered into the woolen pillow cover. "Oh, yes. You could definitely say I got a running start." She shook with suppressed laughter.

"Now what's so funny about that?" Gabrel demanded.

Probably not a good idea to explain. "Uh, nothing. The, the salve burns a little bit," Maris improvised.

"That should stop soon. At least, the stuff my Gran used on nettle stings always burned at first and then made the skin go numb, and this smells like the same mixture." Gabrel sniffed at the pot of greenish-yellow grease. That and the fumes of the madira smelled like home to him, a rich mixture of stinging and floral perfumes that Barents could never match. Reminded of the madira, he upended the bag and took another mouthful. It didn't burn so much now. "Made it up from Kalapriyan herbs she gathered up in the Hills, she did, and never would tell me what went into it."

"I thought you were from Barents?" Maris propped herself up on both elbows and rested her chin in her hands; she wasn't ready to risk sitting up yet, but it was impossible to conduct a conversation with one's face in a pillow.

"In a manner of speaking," Gabrel said. "I'm the third generation of career military in our family. My grandfather was in on the pacification of the plains states. He did his best to see people treated fairly when they came under Barents law, and some of them remembered that when he retired. The ex-Vakil of Latacharya offered him a house on the slopes of the foothills, looking up at the mountains. I used to stay with him and Gran a lot when I was a kid; by that time my dad was in the Service here." He smiled, remembering those enchanted days in the freedom of Latacharya, and toasted them with another swallow of madira.

"And your mother stayed on Barents, did she?"

"Oh, no. Not Mam!" Gabrel chuckled. "She followed Dad wherever he was assigned. But—they were both only children, you see, and her parents hadn't approved of her marrying into the military; they were minor Barents nobility and as high in the instep as only impoverished minor nobles can be. So I think she planned on building her own extended family. I had three younger brothers, all born here on Kalapriya. Only trouble was, every time Mam was expecting she got hellish sick, so they'd send us kids up to Latacharya for the duration. And after my second brother was born Gran suggested we just stay there where she could school us until Mam was through with her family-building." Gabrel smiled reminiscently. "It's not like being in the true Hills, Latacharya isn't, but it's got that smell of conifers and snow-melt, and when the traders came through for a fair we kids used to sneak away from Gran and hang around the caravanserai all day, learning Kalapriyan words—some of which got our mouths washed out with soap when we tried them out at dinner, because Gran and Grandfather knew the language well enough themselves! And when I was ten I got my own hawk with her perch in Grandfather's mews; I was going to train her myself and go hawking with the native boys . . ."

"What happened?" Maris could tell from the way Gabrel's voice slowed that something had interrupted the idyll.

"My Dad took a saber cut across the thigh, dealing with some bandits along the river who hadn't quite understood

that Vaisee was under Barents protection now. He didn't
lose the leg, but—he couldn't ride anymore. They offered
him early retirement and three-quarters pension, and he
decided it was time for us all to go back to Barents. He
thought the climate in the plains might have been part
of Mam's trouble . . . she lost two babies after Number
Three was born. And he may have been right," Gabrel said,
"because Number Four came along ten months after we
moved back to Barents, only then the doctors said she
mustn't try to have any more. So she's been saving her
expansionist ideas for the next generation. She wants me
to get married to a nice fertile girl with a big family. She
must be the only mother on Barents who *wants* a lot of
in-laws . . . Sorry, I don't know why I'm boring you with
all this nonsense."

"Keep talking," Maris urged. "It takes my mind off." Not
to mention that when he was telling her about his past,
he wasn't asking *her* any embarrassing questions. "So how
did you wind up back on Kalapriya?"

"*Told* you," Gabrel said. Or had he? For some reason
he was finding it hard to remember exactly what he had
and hadn't said. "Career military. Oldest son, naturally
follow in m'father's footsteps. Grandfather's too. Besides,
cheapest education on Barents is military academy. For us
army brats, that is. With four sons to raise on a pension,
m'father couldn't very well feature sending any of us
anywhere else. Besides, got me back to Kalapriya." He tilted
the leather bag and was disappointed to find that only a
few drops of madira trickled out. Oh well. No need to
sit up if he wasn't drinking. He lay back on the rug and
stared at the criscrossing wooden rafters above them. "More
chance of promotion here, never know, could be we'll have
to take over the hill states, nice little war. Peacetime on
Barents, nothing to do but get older waiting for your
superior officers to get older and retire. No kind of career
for a soldier." He tossed the empty bag up in the air, failed
to catch it, and winked at Maris. "They think that's why
I volunteered for Kalapriya, y'see? Young fire-eater, looking for action. Actually . . ." He yawned. "Actually I jus'
love the place. Would've come back anyway. But don't tell
m'colonel that."

"I promise not to tell your colonel that you like Kalapriya,"

Maris said, "and . . . don't you think you'd better take your boots off before you go to sleep?"

But her suggestion had come too late.

Apart from his headache the next morning and the mystery of why he'd downed an entire bag of madira when he didn't even like drinking, Gabrel found the days of the boat trip upriver uneventful enough. Calandra was clearly still stiff on the first morning, but she assured Gabrel that the salve had worked wonders and that she would be able to apply it herself from then on.

The boat wasn't really designed for passengers; it was more of a one-size-fits-all, carrying crates of salt fish and tropical fruits and spices upriver, presumably returning with boxes of nuts from the mountain orchards and bales of the coarse, bright fabrics the hill people wove from the long hair of their ghaya. It veered from one side of the Vaisee-jara to the other, stopping at every little village along the river on either bank. An old grandmother took the boat back after a visit downriver to see the newest grandchild, a slightly younger midwife traveled upriver to attend the accouchement of a minor hill-Vakil's third wife; a Rohini jewel trader squatted over his brass-bound box of gilt-filigree trifles and scowled suspiciously at the Rudhrani soldier, on leave from his post with the Vaisee Royal Guard, who demeaned himself to take the boat for a visit with his upcountry family because, as he cheerfully explained, his last turag had lost her race with a colleague's gelding and had become that colleague's property, and he now meant to apply in person to his father for a loan to finance another string of racers.

Gabrel slouched against a stack of crates, his gold hair covered by an anonymous loose felt hat, his fair skin turning brown in the hot sun over the river, his height at least somewhat disguised by his slouch and by a coarse blanket of hill-country weave thrown over his shoulders. He breathed in the spice-scented air and the babble of dialects and felt himself at home in a way he never felt in Valentin, much less on Barents itself. *This* was where he belonged, in the field, soaking up local lore and stories. He listened to the midwife and the grandmother trading competing stories of difficult births, and learned much that a Barents Trading Society officer would not normally understand about the importance of a red cord under the bed and the disastrous possibilities inherent in offending Vasanti of the Three Breasts by leaving cooking implements in view during an accouchement. When a curtained box was carried on board by four dark southern men who stationed themselves at its corners, glaring at all passengers impartially, he recognized that a bride of good family was being sent north and understood, with regret, the old ladies' unspoken decision to stop telling childbirth stories for a while.

Soon enough their place was taken by a Rohini stargazer who offered to make the pilot's birth-chart in trade for passage to the next village, and who explained with great fluency the effects of the stars Lokaishana and Kanchana in guiding the pilot to a water trade, and the necessity of the man's placating the water demons also ruled by Lokaishana. This led to a theological argument with a dour man who now revealed himself as a hill-priest returning home from pilgrimage to the holy mouth of the Vaisee-jara, and who asserted categorically that demons could not be placated by offerings but must be controlled by amulets containing sacred writings. He just happened to have a supply of such amulets stitched into the seams of his bedroll and might be willing to part with some for an appropriate price.

The discussion became lively enough for Gabrel to pick up several interesting new terms of abuse concerning the ancestors, personal habits, and sexual preferences of both holy men; he felt some regret when the bride's guards bought up the hill-priest's entire stock of amulets, engaged him on the spot to protect them against malign influences, and took their cortege off the boat when it tied up for the night just downstream from the Ford of the Dead Emperors. Oh well, this part of their journey was nearly over anyway; half a day more would bring them to the rapids where the Dharamjara joined the Vaisee-jara and created a river deep enough for boat travel, and from there on they would have to go on foot.

He had to admit that Calandra's presence had been a help on this part of the journey, rather than the unmitigated nuisance he had expected. She didn't complain about having to squat on the deck of a creaking packet boat steaming slowly against the current; she didn't say anything about the clouds of midges that descended with the evening sun, or the burning heat of midday; she didn't object to scooping her share of the midday lentils and spiced sauce from the communal bowl with two fingers of her right hand or to washing them down with slightly muddy spice tea. In fact, for the first two days she said remarkably little; like Gabrel, she sat and listened. Unlike him, she bounced up and down with excitement at the sights revealed by the river: the painted villages gay with their patterns of red and black and ochre mud drawn on the walls; a troop of horned *bhagghi* drinking at a ford and throwing up their heads and fleeing into the forest as the boat approached; the great grey ruined walls and crumbling carvings of a long-abandoned palace of the First Empire. Somehow he had expected a Diplomat to be scornfully blasé about the sights of Kalapriya. He liked Calandra even better for her unabashed enthusiasm.

And the combination of silence and visible enthusiasm helped immeasurably, as the chattering old women decided that this quiet girl who looked so thrilled at what they considered everyday sights must be another bride, this one from a village too small to name, being escorted upriver to some mountain state whose ruler was wealthy enough to hire an outlander soldier as her guard. Gabrel felt a little chagrin that they'd seen through his disguise so easily—but what matter, as long as they told themselves a story that accounted for his presence in a way that wouldn't come to the ears of the Society representatives? It was their good fortune that Calandra was slim and dark enough to pass for an exceptionally tall and pale-skinned Rudhrani, and beautiful enough to make it plausible that she'd been sold as a bride to some mountain Vakil or Wazir. And it was his good fortune that she must have picked up on the old ladies' gossip and decided to help it along; all through the first day she spoke only to him, and that in an undertone, which helped immeasurably in creating her character as a shy girl being sent away from her home to an unknown husband.

Private conversation was all but impossible on the crowded boat; even at night the passengers slept shoulder to shoulder, rolled into their traveling rugs and crowded so close on the deck that the nightmares of one became the property of all. But toward the end of that first day, during the splashing and colorful curses that accompanied the off-loading of some crates onto a half-rotted village quay Gabrel found a chance to speak quietly to Calandra and to compliment her on helping him out. "You're acting the shy village bride very well. Keep it up; they made me for an outlander, and the explanation they've given themselves for my presence will do very well as long as they think you're a Rudhrani, too proud and too shy to speak to any common passengers."

Also, their blatant speculation about her probable destination helped to fill him in on the current political situation in the hill country. He knew, of course, that Thamboon and Narumalar had been taken over by Udara; that was the source of Orlando Montoyasana's complaints. He claimed that the Udaran army was using weapons of prohibited technology that could only have been smuggled in from offworld. But when Gabrel was called back from Dharampal to dance attendance on the Diplomat, there'd been no hint that Udara was menacing that state as well. Now the old women chattered about an Udaran envoy to Dharampal, assessed the probability that the young Vakil of Dharampal would meekly give in to the Bashir's demands and that his state would become another vassal state of Greater Udara, and debated the possibility that the Vakil was making a marriage alliance with Calandra's village as an excuse to bring in a whole troop of outlander soldiers against the Udaran threat.

The land where the Dharam-jara joined the Vaisee-jara was too rocky and precipitous to support a village, but over the years a small outdoor bazaar had grown up to meet the needs of traders and travelers. Here one could purchase anything—intricately carved nut shells with magic words carved into them to protect the wearer from evil spirits, sweet syrup with dozy-juice for a fretful baby, poison for a brutal husband, a birth-chart from a native astrologer or an earful of gossip about the doings of the hill kings. Having no particular desire to add more than necessary to the gossip of the bazaar, Gabrel overpaid for a pair of ghaya and refused the offer of overpriced lodgings in the mud-walled serai behind the bazaar. The sooner he and Calandra were out of here, he thought, the less chance there was that anybody would recognize her for an outlander.

That happy belief was rudely shaken by the gratitude of the trader who sold him the ghaya. While Gabrel was adjusting the harness on the great, shaggy beasts and demanding ointment for the sores left on their backs by the previous owner, the trader approached him and said quietly, "For the ointment, one tul; for a word more precious than all ointments, you have already paid enough. Two outlander men on turagai were here two days past, demanding word of an outlander couple, a man and a woman, whom they believed to have ridden this way. At the time, naturally, no one knew anything of interest to them."

"The noble lady whom I escort to her wedding . . ." Gabrel began.

The trader spat sideways into the mud around the ghaya stalls. "The noble lady," he said, "speaks Kalapriyan like a child of four years, and had never seen ghaya before, nor eaten *yao pai*. You may have dyed her hair and tinted her skin to make her pass for Rudhrani, but she is too ignorant to be anything but another outlander. *I* have no love for the men of Barents, but you have paid me well and those others offered little enough; I have no reason to babble tales of what I surmise to them. But they will be back, and some other will have noticed as much as I did and will tell it them for a handful of tulai. Get her out of here, and have your trouble with the other outlanders somewhere else, not in my bazaar."

The trail that snaked along the rocky side of the Dharamjara was quite rough enough if one took it directly from the place where the two streams met. After the trader's warning, Gabrel thought it prudent to follow the narrow stream that was the origin of the Vaisee-jara east from the bazaar until they were well behind the first range of hills, and then to cut back across the barren, rocky country to intercept the trail they really wanted. That made for some interesting and strenuous walking, interrupted periodically by the necessity to persuade the ghaya that they *did* want to take the thorny uphill path and did *not* want to lie down and roll on the thorns, luxuriously scratching their thick hairy hides and squashing the packs they bore. And in many places there was no path at all. Gabrel consulted his compass frequently, watched the passage of the sun closely, and wished devoutly that he had not packed his maps so carefully at the very bottom of one of the long leather rolls now bound in the pack-harness of the larger ghay. But there'd been no need to consult a map while they were on the boat, and—he hadn't exactly planned to leave the bazaar so precipitately, or in a direction so different from that he really wanted. He envied Calandra her Diplomat's head, doubtless loaded with detailed maps of Kalapriya as well as vocabulary, grammar, and whatever other information Rezerval had thought she might need. But he didn't want to ask her for help, as if he were such an idiot as to get lost as soon as he was out of sight of the Vaisee-jara. Besides, he knew where they were. Approximately. More or less. With reasonable certainty . . . oh, *devils*, what was that crag of rock doing in front of them? He'd intended to cut across in a westerly direction, to meet the Dharam-jara well before they got anywhere near the Old Man's Head, but the steep eroded gullies had forced them north and north again. Now, to reach the smoother going of the trail along the river before nightfall, they were going to have to go right across that eerily eroded hill.

The Dharampalis believed that such hills were the homes of the serpent-people, the Nagai and Takshakai, avoided by all right-thinking hill people, and that was just the *good* part; what really worried Gabrel was the maze of water-drilled holes that splashed across the surface of the limestone rock, perfect for catching and breaking a pack-ghaya's leg, and the narrow fissures that ran across the rock and gave homes to poisonous snakes.

Gabrel studied his compass again, squinted at the sun, and tried to convince himself that they could afford the time to backtrack and pick up the Dharam-jara somewhere south of the Old Man's Head. Even if they didn't quite reach the river this night, wasn't camping among the rocks better than crossing this pockmarked disaster area? *No*— the ghaya needed water, were used to drinking their fill twice a day, and there was barely enough water in the gullies they'd passed, this time of year, to keep a snake alive. Besides, he wasn't entirely sure they *could* find a better way through the hills; there was a reason why this triangle of land between the Dharam-jara and the Vaisee-jara was so empty. Only a madman or an outlander would attempt to cross it.

He caught Calandra studying him, a slight frown between her dark brows, and snapped, "If you know a better way to get back to the Dharam-jara, feel free to mention it!"

"If you feel we should go this way, I'm sure you're right," she said cheerfully. "Much farther now?"

"You know as well as I do. About three hours more to get back to the river." If they were lucky, if neither men nor beasts broke a leg crossing the Old Man's Head, if his guess as to their position was right.

In the event, it was nearly four hours, and the sun was down before they had a fire to light their campsite, and Gabrel was not *quite* sure that they had reached the Dharam-jara at the point he had been aiming for, well north of the two villages upstream from the bazaar but south of the Dharampal border. And he did not find leisure to study his map until all the work of camping for the night was done: pack beasts fed and watered, tent up, firewood collected. As he had expected, Diplomat Vissi had been quite useless at all these tasks; as he had *not* expected, she had been cheerfully ready to pitch in where she could and to learn what he wanted to tell her. She was hopeless with the pack animals, of course, probably had spent all her life on high-tech worlds; he had to tell her several times that they weren't machines where you punched a button and got a response.

"Got that," the woman said the third time he made this explanation. "They're *dumber* than machines."

"That too," Gabrel acknowledged with a smile. Nobody had ever accused Kalapriya's native ghaya of high intelligence. But they were strong, tireless, and reasonably obedient when handled by somebody who understood their limitations. "But they'll take us up into the High Jagirs on paths none of your machines could negotiate."

"Flitter could, though," Calandra said.

Gabrel mimed astonishment. "What, you'd take a flitter over these mountains and give these simple hillmen the surprise of their lives? And you here to investigate allegations of inappropriate technology importation? I'm shocked, Diplomat Vissi, shocked!"

"Didn't say I wanted to," Calandra pointed out. "Just said a flitter *could* do it. And a sight easier and faster than these ghays."

"Right. The plural, in case you're interested, is ghaya." Gabrel studied the Diplomat's face in the uncertain firelight. "I would've thought your language implant would tell you that much."

Calandra looked down. "I *told* you, the chips ain't like magic."

"That's clear," Gabrel said meanly. "The chap who sold me these beasts said you speak Kalapriyan like a four-year-old."

Calandra blinked hard and Gabrel wondered at his own snappiness. The woman had really behaved quite well; why was he suddenly being bitchy at her? He felt desperately uneasy and couldn't quite put a finger on the reason.

"'Scuse me, I gotta . . ." Without saying exactly what it was she suddenly needed to do, Calandra crawled into her tent and dropped the flap. Leaving Gabrel on his own to prepare their meal. Well, what had he expected of a pampered offworlder? It must have been quite a shock for Diplomat Vissi to live under the primitive conditions of Kalapriya outside the coastal enclaves; she'd taken the boat journey well enough, but trekking on foot over the High Jagirs with only the supplies a pair of ghaya could carry might well be more than she'd bargained for.

In the privacy of her tent, Maris stuck a plug into her right ear and settled down to concentrated study of the audio plugs of *Kalapriyan for Dummies* that she'd boosted from Moylen Cornelis's rooms. That had been a lucky find, but it wouldn't do her much good if she didn't get more time to use the plugs. The slow, lazy days of the boat journey upriver had been a gift from the gods; both Gabrel and the other passengers had invented their own story for why she didn't say much, and with her curly hair worn loose to cover the plug in one ear she'd been able to listen her way through a good half of the language lessons. By the time they reached the bazaar she had acquired enough vocabulary to get the gist of most conversations. If the people were speaking slowly. If she already had a good idea what they were talking about.

Was that enough to pass for a Diplomat's downloaded language capabilities? It would make sense that the download would help more with understanding than with talking; nothing substituted for actual real-time talking with real people, but apparently she hadn't learned enough yet. Okay, she would pretend exhaustion, spend as much time as possible in the minuscule tent, get a good grasp of *ishti*-class verbs. Just as well not to spend the evening out by the fire, chatting with Gabrel, anyway; the more she said, the greater was the chance that he'd catch on to her imposture. It was exhausting, watching every word she said, always trying to guess how a highly educated Diplo would react to these surroundings.

It was exhausting, remembering not to trust Gabrel.

It had been easy at first, when he was so stiff and full of resentment toward her. But that had started to change at the ball—and after, the attack in the dark alley—they worked together well, Maris thought sleepily. Concealing the body, cleaning up the mess, getting out of town fast and inconspicuously . . . the man had a natural talent for her kind of work, a talent that probably didn't get much exercise in the confines of the Society's military branch. No wonder he preferred slightly covert upcountry assignments, no wonder he'd resented being pulled back from the field to dance attendance on an offworld VIP. Johnivans would have tried to recruit him as a natural talent . . . but Johnivans wouldn't have had much luck, would he? There was something about Gabrel Eskelinen that would never bend to the sort of underhanded dealing Maris had grown used to on Tasman. He could lie fast and fluently, he could disguise himself, he could dispose of a corpse, and Maris didn't think he would have much compunction about killing somebody who attacked him. But she couldn't imagine him stabbing somebody in the back, or arranging . . . arranging to have a girl killed just because her dead body was more useful to him than her living self.

She swallowed hard. *Ishti*-class verbs in the past conditional chattered unheard in her right ear while the memory of her last hours on Tasman swamped her. Who did she think she was to make guesses about Gabrel's character? She had trusted Johnivans absolutely, damn near worshipped him ever since he'd seen a talent in her that made it worthwhile for him to take her into his gang and save her from working the corridors as a child-whore . . . and all the time she'd been nothing to him, less than nothing, a card to be played when convenient. And now she was tempted to trust Gabrel as she'd trusted Johnivans, to confess her imposture to him, because something about him felt straight and true and she was hating her lies more every day. Idiot! So she didn't *feel* that Gabrel Eskelinen would dump her if he knew the truth, so what? She hadn't *felt* any warning about Johnivans either, had she? Face it, she had no judgment for people. The only thing she knew was that she knew nothing and could trust nobody.

"Calandra?"

"*Dhulaishta*, I would have betrayed—*dhulaishtami*, you would have betrayed—*dhulaishtaiyen*, he, she, it would have betrayed—*dhulaishtamai*, no, you leave it out in first- and second-persons plural—*dhulamai*, we would have betrayed," Maris muttered under her breath, wishing whoever wrote the language plugs had picked a different example of *ishti*-class verbs. She'd already conjugated betrayal in present, simple past, simple future, and present conditional, and with each tense the choice of verb seemed more personal.

"*Calandra!*"

"*Dhulamiye*, you plural would have, oh shit." Between Gabrel's ratty mood and the *ishti*-class conjugations, Maris had temporarily forgotten her assumed name. She jerked the plug out of her ear and stuffed it into a fold of the embroidered sash that held her coarse woven shirt and leggings together, backed out of the tent and tried not to think about the impossibility of exiting these tiny tents with any degree of grace. Sitting up, she scowled at Gabrel and pushed her hair back. "What is it?" No great emergency, obviously; he was leaning against the broad back of a resting ghay while peering at some folding papers in the firelight.

"I just wanted you to compare this map with the ones your people downloaded to you," he said, holding out a page covered with spidery brown lines.

"Thought you knew this country backwards and forwards," Maris said.

"Last time I visited Dharampal," Gabrel said patiently, "I was officially there on official business, and I could simply follow the Dharam-jara upstream. This time I thought we might save time by cutting across where the river loops, here—" he pointed to a curved double line "—and then we could drop down from here to water the ghaya. Looks like about a day's travel, and then go back off-trail again and straight for Dharamvai—the Vakil's city. But I didn't make this map, some clerk in Valentin drew it up from Orlando Montoyasana's notes last time the man visited the Enclave, and he just might have left out a few little things like hostile villages or impassable cliffs on the route I'm thinking of taking. So I wanted to check it against what you know of the territory."

Oh, shit indeed! Maris blinked and stared into space, looking as she thought somebody with database chips and maps and languages planted in their head might look, and then said, "Looks all right to me, but then why wouldn't it? Rezerval doesn't have any more detailed maps of this area than you do."

"I thought the satellite scans might show some details of the terrain."

"Well, they don't," Maris said. "They're really not very clear at all. Sorry I can't help you and all that." She took the stick Gabrel had been pointing with, thrust it into the bubbling mess in the cook-pot on the fire, and stirred vigorously—perhaps a little too vigorously; the stuff slopped over and a few drops sizzled on the hot stones.

"Better let me do that," Gabrel said, dropping the map to rescue their dinner.

"I'm not much help to you, am I?"

"Well," Gabrel said, stirring the pot almost as vigorously as she had done, "it's not supposed to work that way, is it? *I've* been assigned to help *you*. Anyway, I don't suppose a Diplo's normal training covers situations quite this primitive."

"You could say that," Maris allowed. For sure she couldn't contradict it, anyway!

"And I think you more than did your share on this trip the night we started," Gabrel added.

"I—? Oh, that." Maris suppressed an internal shudder as she remembered the soft mushy place her rock had left in

Kaspar Slevinen's skull. She averted her gaze from the anonymous glop boiling in the cooking pot.

"Saving my life," Gabrel said with a straight face, "is usually good for one ticket into upcountry Kalapriya, all expenses paid, pack beasts managed, meals prepared, and tents erected. And you didn't even use any of your special weapons! You Rezerval types take this tech prohibition seriously, don't you?"

"Oh. Ummm . . ." Of course, a *real* Diplo would have done something much more elegant than bashing Slevinen over the head with a rock. Maris looked for a way to change the subject. "Would that be a one-way ticket, or round trip?"

"You don't think I can bring us out safely?"

"I've no worries at all about that," she lied, "just wondering whether I would have to save your life again in Udara or else learn to lead ghaya and set up me own—*my* own tent."

"I'd enjoy watching you attempt the latter," Gabrel said, "but the ghaya might not like it! Let's agree that you've earned a free ticket back to Valentin. Although if there *is* any useful information in those satellite maps in your head, to supplement my trail notes, I'd appreciate your sharing it. For instance, how do they show the elevation of Dharam-vai? I'd estimated it at about six thousand meters, when I was there treating with the Vakil, but of course I was restricted to the kind of prehistoric measurement instruments allowed under the technology prohibitions. I'm sure your mapping programs are much more accurate. How high above sea level would you say the city lies?"

"Oh, six thousand sounds like a pretty good estimate," Maris mumbled. Time for another change of subject. "Is that stuff ready yet? I'm so hungry I could eat a ghay!"

"I wouldn't recommend it," Gabrel said, "the meat tastes really sour. Something about the native grasses they eat. Or does your training as a Diplomat include a course in swallowing anything you're offered with a smile? You never have told me much about your studies. What exactly *do* Diplomats learn in that school?"

"Umm. It's mostly classified," Maris offered wildly. "Y'know, don't want to give away our systems and all that."

"Including what you had for dinner?"

"Ahh, just the usual. *You* know." At least she hoped he

did. Maris herself didn't have the faintest idea what toppies would eat in a fancy school, but she was pretty sure it didn't resemble the hodgepodge of dryfood stolen from shipping crates and odd dishes liberated from a Tasman dining hall on which Johnivans fed his gang. "I'd rather hear about how you found out that ghay meat tastes sour. I bet there's a story behind that?"

"Reconnoitering trip that went bad." Gabrel accepted the change of subject gracefully, leaned back against his bedroll, and launched into a tale of travels into uncharted territory, a native "guide" who'd never been more than a day's journey from his home village, and an early blizzard that effectively closed what he'd thought was the only pass back through the High Jagirs from their campsite.

Later that night, after the campfire was banked to a rock-encircled bed of slumbering embers and they had crawled into their separate tents, Gabrel lay awake with arms folded behind his head and considered the riddle of Calandra.

Basically, he liked the woman. She'd been a good companion so far on this journey upcountry, accepting the difficulties of travel without any of the whining he'd have heard from most of his colleagues in Valentin—and that was the men; he shuddered to think what a gently bred Barents lady, even one accustomed to the "hardships" of life in Valentin, would have made of a trip by turag, native packet boat, and foot into the foothills of the Jagirs. And—remembering that last night in Valentin—she was a *damned* good companion to have at one's back in a fight. Quick reflexes; if it had been up to him, they'd both have been trussed helpless in the tanglenet before he knew what was happening. Not that Slevinen would have left him alive long enough to be embarrassed by his stupidity, but that was scant comfort. Well, she was an offworlder and a Diplomat; she was *used* to watching for high-tech weaponry. He hadn't expected any such thing. No, that was no excuse, not after reading Orlando Montoyasana's letters about the prohibited technology he'd stumbled on in Udara. The fact was, he hadn't taken Montoyasana seriously, hadn't taken the whole *mission* seriously until Slevinen's attack on them. Putting that together with the trader's tale of the two Barents Society men who'd tried to cut them off at the junction of the Dharam-jara and the Vaisee-jara, Gabrel no longer had any

doubt that there was something in the mountains that somebody didn't want them to find. And given Slevinen's use
of a tangler, it seemed very likely that Montoyasana had
been exactly right about what was going on in Udara.

What was keeping Gabrel awake tonight, though, was his
inability to figure out what was going on right here and
now with Calandra . . . if that was really her name! From
the first she had not been what he expected in a Diplomat;
but then, one of the things you expected was that Diplos
would keep you off balance. So he had deliberately not
worried about the fact that she seemed too young and
innocent, and talked too bluntly, to be a Rezerval-trained
Diplo. That could have been part of the training, a way to
keep you off guard.

And on that day of her arrival, he'd hardly had time to
think about it much. What with formal dinners, ball gowns,
and assassination attempts, not to mention scrambling to
get out of Valentin at least half a step ahead of whoever
had it in for them, the occasional oddities in Calandra's
behavior had been the least of his worries.

The days of travel, though, had given him time to
observe . . . and think.

Calandra definitely did not behave like anything Gabrel
had heard of Diplos. Put that down to his ignorance, if you
would; but how could you explain the way she changed the
subject whenever he asked anything about her background
and training? And since she wouldn't tell him anything, what
could he go on but the rumors that passed for common
knowledge?

Diplos were supposed to have chips in their heads that
could be loaded with the basics of any language they were
likely to need. Calandra herself admitted that, but her statement that the language downloads weren't all they might
be was a gross understatement. She spoke Kalapriyan, as
the trader had pointed out, like a four-year-old or worse.
And she seemed to spend all her spare time muttering verb
conjugations.

Diplos toured many different worlds and were exposed
to many varied civilizations before they graduated into active
assignment work; Calandra reacted to the sights of Kalapriya
like a kid who'd never seen anything outside the four walls
of a study cubicle.

Diplos carried weapons unlike anything you'd ever imagined secreted on their persons and in their clothes; Calandra had bashed Kaspar Slevinen's head in with a handy rock. Wasn't there such a thing as carrying respect for prohibited technology a bit too far?

Was she some impostor posing as a Diplo? Obviously there were some Barents Trading Society people involved in the transfer of prohibited weapons to Udara; could they have disposed of the real Calandra Vissi and substituted one of their offword accomplices? Would such a woman have been cold-blooded enough to murder Slevinen—a coconspirator of hers, according to this thesis—just to establish her credibility in Gabrel's eyes?

Some women might. All Gabrel's experience of Calandra, though, said that she wasn't capable of such an act.

Besides—he remembered with relief—she had to have passed the routine spaceport ID checks in transit to Kalapriya. She had Calandra Vissi's retinas, fingerprints, and DNA. Gabrel shook his head. No, whatever the woman was or wasn't, she had to be Calandra Vissi of Rezerval. Pure logic, Occam's Razor, dictated against multiplying improbabilities in the service of his private paranoia; to suppose this woman an impostor was piling impossibility upon improbability.

So what *was* she? Perhaps a Diplomat in training, posing as a full graduate to improve her standing on Valentin. Someone who hadn't had the final tours yet, hadn't been issued the mysterious weapons, maybe didn't even have all the implant chips necessary to download languages and maps.

Gabrel chuckled quietly to himself. Yes, *that* made sense. Orlando Montoyasana's reputation as the galaxy's most paranoid and quarrelsome anthropologist had preceded him to Kalapriya. Probably the man had been pestering Rezerval for years, complaining about every world he studied. They weren't going to waste a real Diplo on a mission purely for show, to placate a crazy anthropologist; they'd use it as a training mission for one of the students.

And, of course, they wouldn't feel it necessary to mention to Montoyasana—much less to the Barents Trading Society—that the kid they were sending out wasn't a *real* Diplo.

Unfortunately, it seemed that she'd stumbled into a real

conspiracy. So what was he going to do about it? Head back to Valentin and demand a real Diplo, and preferably a contingent of Rezerval Guards, to investigate Udaran weaponry? With what that trader had said of Barentsians hunting for him, Gabrel had serious doubts as to whether they'd even get back to Valentin, much less get access to the ansible to contact Rezerval.

Pushing ahead seemed the better of the two alternatives. Anyway, if Gabrel had taken Montoyasana's complaints seriously, he wouldn't have wasted his time going back to Valentin and whining for a Diplo's assistance, would he? No, he would have started investigating on his own, right there where he was in Dharampal—close enough to Udara, and with his good Dharampali friends to help him.

No reason he couldn't do the same thing now. The only difference was, Calandra's arrival had caused the conspirators inside the Barents Trading Society to tip their hand. After Slevinen's attack and the trader's warning, Gabrel knew he couldn't risk taking any evidence he discovered to his superiors in the Society—not until he knew exactly who was involved, and how.

Calandra would come in handy there too; with her contacts in the Diplomatic School, she could take his report directly to Rezerval and hand it over to authorities who would think nothing of arresting half a dozen top officials in the Society, who would have the resources to clean up the nasty mess of corruption and cultural contamination they seemed to be stumbling into.

All he had to do, Gabrel reckoned, was penetrate a hostile Indigenous Tribal Territory, collect evidence of their use of prohibited offworld technology, find some leads as to who was supplying the weapons, get himself and Calandra back to the coastal enclaves, and smuggle her off-planet to deliver the report. Without the backup that a fully trained and armed Diplo could have provided. He smiled grimly. Wasn't there a character in some ancient children's book who believed in doing six impossible things before breakfast? At least he didn't have to do all this before breakfast—and now he thought about it, the phrase had been "*believe* six impossible things before breakfast." Fine, he'd start by believing they could accomplish their tasks with no difficulty.

But as he drifted off to sleep, he wasn't worrying about

the dangers ahead of him; a life of alternately soldiering and spying had taught Gabrel Eskelinen not to stay awake over next week's problems when there was a reasonably good chance tomorrow might kill you before you had to face them.

The one thing that really bothered him was that he wished, irrationally, that Calandra would trust him with the truth about herself.

Chapter Eleven

Udara on Kalapriya

"Name?" the Rudhrani guard at the gate of Pundarik Zahin's house snapped. That was a new thing; there'd been nobody barring the gate when he went there—was it only yesterday? It seemed like years ago.

"Vajjadara. Chulayen Vajjadara, with the Ministry for Lands and Properties," Chulayen said, head bowed. "If I could see the honorable general for just one moment?"

The guard sighed deeply. "What, does *every* two-tulai clerk in the Bashir's service have to talk to General Zahin before he goes into surgery? My master's been officially retired for years now, but you'd think no Ministry in Udara could function without him for a few days, the way you people have been pouring in with chits and last-minute requests."

"Surgery? I didn't know—" Chulayen stopped, started over. "Please, this is not a matter of government business. It is— my parents were friends of General Zahin's—I—we had words yesterday—I need to apologize before—"

The guard's expression softened. "Oh, personal, is it? I did hear as he was troubled by some quarrel yesterday. Would that have been you, then?"

"Yes," Chulayen said. "I was wrong. I wanted to apologize to him and tell him that I've seen my errors."

"Well, maybe it'll help him go in to the surgeon with a quieter mind, at that," the guard said. "But if you start arguing with him, I'll be sorry I let you in—and I'll make *you* even sorrier!"

"I only wish to express my humble duty and my complete submission to his judgment," Chulayen vowed.

He was shocked by the change in Pundarik Zahin's private rooms. The old, shady, dusty, cluttered study had been cleared of nearly all its furnishings, and a pair of servant girls was briskly scrubbing the floor on one side of the room while the old general sat in his invalid chair on the other side, irritably going through the stack of papers proffered by a clerk standing beside him. "Enough business for now!" he cried when Chulayen entered, pushing the papers away. "Tell the Ministers I'll be ready and happy to attend to them all in a few days, after we see how the outlander's medicine works. Well, my boy," he said to Chulayen in a softer tone, "I understand you've seen the error of your ways?"

"My loyalty has always been to the Bashir and to Udara," Chulayen said. "I deeply regret the misunderstanding which made me seem to be setting up my own will against the wiser judgment of the Minister for Defense, and my only hope is that the Bashir himself will understand and forgive my errors."

"Well said," Pundarik Zahin approved. "Perhaps—"

A bucket of water tipped over, sending a puddle splashing over the blanket that covered his legs, and he growled at the clumsy servant. "Wheel me out to the garden, boy, we can't talk in here. That crazy outlander!"

He continued his grumbles when Chulayen had maneuvered the clumsy wheeled chair out onto the paved, vine-shaded terrace overlooking the mountainside. "What *is* this mania outlanders have for cleaning and boiling and purifying everything? You'd think they were all born to be good Rudhrani housewives. Hah!" He laughed explosively at his own joke. "A little honest dirt never did any harm, and in our climate it's positively dangerous to strip the skin of its natural oils in the face of winter. At least that's how *I* was taught. But this man will have me scrubbed as raw as that room in there before he consents to treat me."

"It's outlander magic," Chulayen said. "I suppose we must allow them to cast out devils in their own way. What does he promise to do for you, sir?"

"Why, he thinks the devils are not in these useless things after all—" Zahin thumped one of his own legs "—but in my head, and he means to open up my head to let them out! Hah!" He laughed again, even more loudly.

"Truly, sir?"

"No, it's more complicated than that. Best I can understand it, he says our heads are supposed to be full of tiny demons that send orders to our bodies, and that some of my demons died when I had an attack of the falling sickness. So he's going to open me up and put in some of his own demons who will direct the work of my legs." Zahin scowled. "Truth to tell, I don't much care to think of the details. It all seems very improbable. I've cleaved a man's skull with my own saber—aye, fifty years ago it was, in the battle for the Sarai Pass, but I remember as 'twas yesterday. Blood aplenty there was on the snow, and a spill of grey stuff where his head opened, but I saw no demons coming out. Still, the outlanders pay well enough for the demons he grows—" Zahin checked himself as though he just now remembered whom he was talking to. "I suppose you understand all about that business now, boy? Been explained to you, has it?"

"Not fully," Chulayen said carefully, "but I know that my duty and loyalty are to the Bashir, and I hope that you, sir, will convey my deepest apologies to him and to the Ministry for Loyalty and tell them—persuade them—" His throat closed up for a moment before he could go on. "There's no need to keep my family hostage, sir. Anusha, Vashi, the girls, they had no part in this. The fault was entirely mine, and I see now that I was entirely mistaken. Please, sir, cannot you persuade them to set my family free?"

Zahin looked off into the blue distances beyond the terrace, stroking his moustache with one hand. "I'm only an old soldier, Chulen, not a diplomat, and it's a chancy business to bargain with the Ministry for Loyalty. I came close enough to being called traitor myself yesterday, because I talked them into leaving you free and only taking the womenfolk."

"And my son."

"And your son," Zahin agreed. "But you're young yet, Chulen. You can get another wife and make more sons. I stood surety for your good behavior, did you know that? Told the Bashir he might exile me if you did not come to your senses and give this up."

"You had better have let me be taken away with Anusha," Chulayen said bitterly.

"My boy, I am sorry. I did not know you cared for her so much. It always seemed to me your mother was much stronger for the marriage than you were. You might even have been glad to be free, for all I knew."

Chulayen felt a pang of guilt. He'd never loved Anusha. He had carefully done all his duty as the Rudhrani gentleman he thought himself to be; nobody could say he'd been a bad husband to her. He had treated her with respect, not even complaining when the first children were girl-twins, never reproaching her with the long years that followed until at last she gave him a son. He hadn't beaten her for getting herself mixed up in that low-class cult of the Inner Light Way; he'd even taken her on pilgrimage to those cursed caves.

He'd gone out of his way to be courteous and respectful and to indulge her, because he could not love her.

Love was not supposed to be important in marriage; doing one's duty was what mattered.

"And the children? You thought I would be glad to be rid of them too, I suppose?"

Pundarik Zahin sank back against the cushions of his invalid chair, looking very old. "Chulen, I can do nothing today; within the hour the outlander will come with his tools. When I've recovered from his work, when the memory of your offense is not so strong with the Bashir, I . . . will do what I can."

"Perhaps, before that, others will do more!" Chulayen snapped, turning on his heel.

Later he regretted that parting thrust most bitterly. But for now, all he could think was that Zahin had betrayed him. All his parents' friends had betrayed him. His *parents* had lied to him. If there was any help for him and his family, it lay in the hands of a raggle-taggle bunch of Rohini whom he had been brought up to despise—quietly and courteously, of course—as beneath his notice.

All he wanted to do, now, was to go back to that old woman, Madee—he could not think of her as his grand-mother—and make her arrange to rescue his family when they were moved from the prison to wherever the "disap-peared" were taken. But he couldn't. He who had been Chulayen Vajjadara, who had thought himself a Rudhrani gentleman and the son of a Minister for the Bashir, was now lower than the lowliest Rohini. He did not even own a name. He had no power to coerce Madee to do his bid-ding. But perhaps, if he learned what these Rohini wanted to know—if he turned traitor in earnest, instead of blun-dering into disfavor by his own slow-witted mistakes—perhaps he could buy her cooperation. Evidently he was not going to be arrested on sight; very well, he would do as she wished, return quietly to his job and listen for any scraps of information that might be useful to the traitors.

The undercellar where he and the others injured in the riot had been taken was somewhere on the lower slopes of the town, among the shabby patched buildings and tumble-down houses of the poorest Rohini; not an area Chulayen knew well. As evening fell, he was still wander-ing the alleys, looking for the particular pattern of rusted grilles and splintery posts that he remembered as the entrance to the maze of rooms going down below street level. He was not overly eager to tell the woman Madee of his fail-ure, and so he drifted along almost aimlessly, expecting that eventually he'd recognize the place. But in the blue haze of twilight everything looked the same to him, one indis-tinguishable stream of broken roofs, walls with layers of plaster falling off in great patches, naked children, street beggars, dusty ditches, piles of rags heaped up in doorways and corners. But no—one of the piles moved; for a moment he thought, with instant revulsion, of rats; and then it stretched out filthy feet and sat up and he saw a face appearing out of the mud-colored folds.

"You have walked past three times already," the face said, "but you fine gentlemen are all blind as cave-fish. Follow me to the place before your ramblings attract more cursed Rudhrani!"

And these are my people, Chulayen thought as he followed the beggar. *This is my true heritage: rude peasants and earthen-floored slums.* He felt shame at the thought, told himself that the true shame belonged to those who had taken all power and wealth to themselves, then remembered that until a day ago he had been one of those. He had never felt as if he was oppressing anybody. It had seemed the natural order of things. Rohini were simple folk, happiest in service positions with somebody else telling them what to do and arranging their lives; Rudhrani gentlemen organized and ruled and saw that the world was a well-kept and orderly place; Rudhrani women stayed modestly at home, watching the servants and children and generally keeping their homes as orderly and proper as their men kept the outside world.

Now—he did not know what to think, or even what he should feel. But it still seemed shameful to him to be in such a place as the subsurface rooms to which the beggar led him; worse yet, as he became aware of the smell of cheap, sweet incense and the sound of singing interspersed with wails and high-pitched shouts. His mother—no, Minister Vajjadara's wife, he corrected himself harshly—had taught him to scorn such meetings. Rudhrani worshiped the gods decently and with propriety, in the privacy of their own homes; even the poorest Rudhrani house was not without its wall niche for images of the gods and its offering bowl to set at their feet. The semipublic, hysterical gatherings of the Inner Light Way were—well, Rohini stuff, and not worth paying serious attention to.

And yet Anusha had been drawn into the cult; they must have offered her something she couldn't find at her home altars.

There were pallets around the sides of the low, dark room, with bandaged people lying on them. Chulayen thought he recognized some faces—and some injuries—from the previous day: that boy with the smashed-in dent on one side of his head, who breathed but neither spoke nor moved, and the woman with a mass of bandages where her right foot should have been. He frowned. It could not be good for them to have to put up with this noise and smoke; couldn't the cultists have found another place to hold their ceremonies?

The rhythmic noises rose and fell, never stopping completely. In the failing, flickering light of ghay-butter lamps the faces of the wounded, and of the worshipers, came into view and vanished as the little lights danced this way and that, as if people were passing into and out of the plane of this life all around him and at random. He craned his neck and searched for the old pancake vendor, Madee, who claimed to be his grandmother; somehow expecting her to be leading this cult ritual. But there did not seem to be a leader. Except for those lying on pallets, the occupants of the room sat in messy, overlapping circles on the floor, hands clasped on their folded legs, all looking toward the center of the room.

And there was nothing at all in the center.

Slowly Chulayen's ear began to separate the sounds. There was a simple, repetitive song; different voices chanted the short verses, while everybody joined in the chorus.

"*Ugme, soi, utme,*" a man chanted. "What appears, disappears."

"*Janne so mar jae,*" the rest of the room responded. "What is born dies."

"*Chhunne soi gir pare.*" That was Madee's quavery old voice: "What is picked up falls again."

"*Phule so kamlae,*" the listeners finished. "That which blossoms, fades."

That went on and on, the simple monotonous melody like a child's cradle-song; Chulayen told himself that it was boring and not at all musically interesting, but somehow his body kept wanting to sway in time with the singing. Finally he lowered himself to the cold floor, where he sat with hands clasped on his bent knees. Would they never stop?

Impatience is an error, his tutor had said. *Do not allow it to take over your mind.* And his mother had said, "A gentleman may feel impatience, but he never shows it."

Chulayen tried to still his mind using the techniques his tutor had shown him, and found that for brief seconds the music was soothing and not maddening; for just as long as he could keep from thinking about the past and worrying about the future. Then, just as he had learned to endure it, the low chanting stopped. The room full of people sat in a silence so complete that Chulayen found himself listening to the sound of his own breathing and trying to quiet it.

The silence lasted long enough for his legs to prickle with

cramp from the unaccustomed position; then, again without any signal that he could perceive, people began to stand up and stretch as casually as though they were awakening from a brief nap. Chulayen stood too, and the people nearest him looked at him with alarm.

"He is one of us, children, never fear," Madee called out, and came hobbling through the crowd to stand before him. Chulayen drew breath to speak at last, but she held up one finger and tapped her own lips, so he remained silent.

Chatting in low voices, in twos and threes, the crowd slowly dispersed. Chulayen wondered why they were so long about it; finally he realized that they were pacing their departure so that there would not be an obvious flow of people coming out of the building all at one time.

"Why take such trouble to keep your meetings secret?" he asked Madee in a low voice, once there was only a handful of worshipers dawdling in the room. "It is not illegal to follow the Inner Light Way."

"Perhaps not," Madee said drily, "but it is not exactly approved of, either."

"Anusha," Chulayen began, and stopped. What would he have said? That he wouldn't have let Anusha take up with the cult if he'd known they were so secretive, wouldn't have let her run such risks? He'd put her into far worse danger by his own thoughtless actions.

"Anusha," Madee repeated. She let his wife's name hang in the air between them.

Chulayen swallowed painfully. "I—cannot help as you requested."

"No? You thought better, perhaps, of showing yourself to the gentle Bashir and his kindly Arm?"

"Hush, Sonchai," Madee reproved the pretty young man without looking around, "Sarcastic speeches rarely help any but the speaker."

Sonchai's face darkened and he looked down. Chulayen noticed that he was standing by a girl lovely enough to be his sister; put Sonchai's long dark lashes and sensuous lips on a girl's face, and you saw beauty instead of effiminacy. The girl, though obviously Rohini, was dressed better than anyone else Chulayen had seen in the group—better than anyone he knew, for that matter; the gold embroidery on her dark red shalin sparkled in the light, and it was belted over matching gathered trousers in a way that emphasized all her womanly curves. The loose end of the shalin was not drawn over her head, modestly, but left to trail down her back, so that he could see her large dark eyes and the line of glittering gold that emphasized the arch of her eyebrows, the perfect oval face and the full lips, all within a frame of curling black hair that glinted red in the fitful light. She did not drop her eyes at his gaze, either, as a modest woman would, but stared back at him with a challenging look that surprised him in so young a girl.

"What happened, then, Chulen?" Madee prompted him gently.

With an effort Chulayen took his eyes from the girl, as surprising a figure in that dim basement as if he had found a statue of Red Radhana all gilded and decked out for war, and told Madee of his visit to Pundarik Zahin. "Then, afterwards, I went to resume my work at the Ministry for Lands and Properties," he said, "but Lunthanadi said I had been put on leave. She had been told that I'd had a nervous breakdown from overwork and that I must on no account return to my office before the Festival of Torches."

"Excellent!" Madee said.

"But—the Festival of Torches is not held until after the first snows. That could be days yet, maybe even weeks— and I thought you wanted me to listen and learn—"

"I did," Madee said, "but Khati here has come to us with information that changes everything. We need you far more, now, as a guide to the Jurgan Caves."

"The Caves! But what—"

Madee gestured for Khati to join them. She came forward at once, without even a pretence of shyness; but Sonchai followed her as closely as any brother wishing to protect a modest young sister.

"I am sorry I could not tell you before, indeed I am," Khati began apologizing to Madee as she came up, "but the Bashir is . . . he wishes me by him at all times, and when he cannot have me by his side I am watched. He is jealous beyond reason. It was not until today I could get away, on the excuse of visiting my mother, and I must be back at her house before the guards who escorted me become suspicious."

"Yes, yes, you explained all that," Madee said absently,

but her gaze softened as she looked at the girl. "It is a hard task the gods have set you, Khati, and you are a good brave girl. You should not have had to take the risk of coming to me; from now on one of us will be by your mother at all times, to take any messages you bring or send."

"I was there," Sonchai interrupted, "but she *would* come with me."

"I needed the comfort of the meeting," Khati said simply. "The Light does not shine brightly in the Bashir's palace."

"The Light is within you as it is within us all, Khati." Madee smoothed the girl's wavy dark hair away from her forehead. "But Sonchai should take you back now, as soon as you have told this young man what you told me before the meeting."

"Envoys from the coast—from Valentin," Khati said, "suspecting that the Bashir has been buying outlander magic to help him conquer all around Udara. And one of them is from the stars, and she is a demon who speaks all languages and knows all things and who can call down fire from the sky, and will do so, if she learns about the brainfarms. So the Bashir has sent his servant Indukanta Jagat to Dharampal, to persuade the young Vakil to imprison the envoys as they pass through his territory—he will *ask* no more than that, but his real task is to kill them once the Vakil has taken their weapons. But in case they should escape the trap at Dharampal, the Bashir has ordered all the brainfarms in Udara cleansed. The only one remaining will be in the Jurgan Caves, where even if it is discovered he will be able to claim it was Thamboon's doing and unknown to him. Oh, and all the prisoners waiting assignment were sent away last night, to be farmed in Thamboon."

Chulayen blinked in astonishment. The report had been delivered so quickly and concisely, as if an experienced man had taken over the pretty little girl's body! And now that she was finished, she didn't babble on, but stood quietly waiting for Madee's response.

Those were matters he could think about. The rest—the content of Khati's report—was full of mysteries he did not want to unravel. A terrible fear possessed him; he felt a cold sweat all over his body. If he stayed here what would he learn?

Where else could he go, now?

"Thank you, Khati," Madee said. She laid her hand on the girl's head again. "You are a good brave girl and the Light will be with you. She had best return now, Sonchai. You will take care she is not seen until she is safe in your mother's house?"

"With my life," Sonchai promised, showing no trace of his usual petulance.

The two slipped away into the shadows at the back of the meeting room and seemed to vanish like smoke into clouds. Chulayen blinked again. There were more ways than he had realized through this maze of underground rooms.

"You see, Chulen," Madee said now to him, "we need someone who knows the world, who can travel to meet these outlander envoys and warn them before they are taken up by the Vakil's men. And then you must tell them that they will find all the evidence they need at the Jurgan Caves, and guide them there. You understand?"

"No—I understand *nothing*," Chulayen said. "Know the world? I have traveled no farther than Thamboon—what was Thamboon—and only once."

"You went there on pilgrimage to the Jurgan Caves," Madee said. "Can you find the way again, without asking for help?"

"I think so."

"Very well, then there is no problem with that part. As for intercepting the envoys before they reach Dharamvai, that is simple enough. You have only to go on pilgrimage again. Tell your neighbors, and anyone you meet on the way, that you have decided to make a visit to the holy shrines at the mouth of the Vaisee-jara, to purify yourself of the demons which possessed you yesterday."

"But that is at the coast," Chulayen pointed out.

Madee raised her eyes to the low ceiling. "Give me Light," she said in a decidedly unprayer-like voice. "To reach the coastal shrines from Udara, Chulen, you must first go through the Sukhana Pass, then follow the Dharam-jara down until it meets the Vaisee-jara. Now, how do you think the outlanders will be coming upcountry from Valentin?"

"Oh!"

"You are not known to be connected with our group, you

have just suffered a tragic loss, you have been told to go on leave, and you have the funds to make a private pilgrimage if you wish. It's perfect!"

"And—when I meet the outlanders—what then?"

Madee raised her eyes again, briefly, but said nothing. "Why, you will tell them that they must go to the Jurgan Caves, not into Udara. You will tell them that their lives are in danger here and that they will find all the evidence they want in the Caves."

"Evidence of what? And in any case," Chulayen finally found words for one of the problems buzzing in his head like angry bees, "I am sorry about the outlanders, but I must stay here until you help me to free Anusha and my children. Then, yes, I will go anywhere you ask."

Madee looked at him with pity. "Did you not understand what else Khati said? They have been taken already."

"I *know* they've been taken, the Ministry for Loyalty is holding them. That's why I need your help."

"No, the Arm of the Bashir does not have them anymore," Madee interrupted. "That is the other thing Khati came to tell us. All the prisoners the Arm held—*all*, Chulen—have been sent to the Jurgan Caves. The convoy left last night, while we were still tending the wounded from the riot."

"Then I'll follow them."

"And do exactly what? Chulen, be sensible. We have people in the mountains as well. If there is a chance to distract the guards on the convoy and free some of the prisoners, they will take it; and they will do better without your interference. They would not trust someone coming from a Ministry, you know."

"You could send Sonchai—or anyone they do know—with me, to *tell* them to trust me, that my own family is in the convoy," Chulayen argued with a growing sense of helplessness.

"You would be no help there," Madee said. "If they can be freed in that way, so much the better. But you should know that very few escape in the mountains. Your best chance is to find the outlanders and lead them to the Jurgan Caves. When they see what is being done there, they will call down their sky-fires to destroy the Bashir."

"What, because the pretty crystals are being ruined by saltpeter miners?" Chulayen laughed. "I do not think the outlanders consider those caves a holy spot as you Inner Light cultists do."

Madee looked so sad that his laughter died. "Chulen, Chulen. Do you still believe the Bashir meant to use those caves for mining saltpeter? You yourself proved that would make no sense."

"Then what *does* he use them for?"

"There are molds and slimes growing in the sea caves that the outlanders value for their magics," Madee said. "The outlander Vhana Vekhatan, may his light be extinguished for all time, has found a way to cultivate the same things in our mountain caves."

It took Chulayen a moment to recognize the Kalapriyanized name of Lorum van Vechten, the Barents Resident in Udara.

"They will hardly object to that—he is doing them a favor!"

"They will object to the way he farms the mold," Madee said grimly. "You have not been told about that yet; we feared it would upset you too much for you to serve us."

"Nothing will upset me too much to try and save my family!"

"I hope that is true," Madee said. And she explained the brainfarms to him.

CHAPTER TWELVE

Thamboon on Kalapriya

On good days—or rather, in good hours, for there was
neither day nor night in this glittering prison—he knew who
he was and how he had come to be here, but without any
of the fear and revulsion that had led him to strike out
against his jailers when they brought him here and he saw
what he was to become. Perhaps, he speculated in those
lucid times, the part of him that felt emotions had been
excised by the saw that cut through the top of his skull.
Or perhaps there were drugs in the food to keep them all
calm. There would certainly have been much more wastage if the prisoners flailed in their chains and flung themselves about in fear and agony. Even the ignoramuses who
kept watch over the caves could understand that much,
though they had no idea of how to keep a sterile environment that would delay infections and subsequent deaths.
If van Vechten had troubled himself to oversee the caves
he would probably have been much more efficient, but the
Resident never showed himself in the brainfarms and the
guards were so ignorant that most prisoners died after only
a few days of being farmed and harvested.

Which was, probably, a mercy—except that it meant the

Bashir's need for fresh, living bodies was never sated, and so there must be more wars and more of his own people taken by the Ministry for Loyalty and more suffering. When would it end? When he ran out of bodies to use? And when would *that* be? After he had enslaved all Kalapriya save for the coastal enclaves? Somewhere, sometime, this insane expansion must halt. The growing realm of Greater Udara would come up against the borders of those lands which were under the protection of the Barents Trading Society and their private army, and then it would be impossible to keep the Bashir's use of outlander weapons a secret, and somebody *must* stop him.

He had hoped to bring observers from Rezerval to witness the prohibited technology being more and more openly flaunted in the Bashir's army, observers with the power to enforce the Federation's rules about cultural contamination even against a world as rich and powerful as Barents. Now he despaired of that ever happening. Possibly the Bashir had intercepted the coded letters he sent out with a trader. More likely the letters had come into the hands of whoever was supplying the Bashir with weapons, and had been destroyed in Valentin. Or if they'd reached Rezerval, the bureaucrats there had dismissed his concerns as they had so many times before. No culturally protected community was wholly free from contamination where it came into contact with outlanders, and he had always reported even the most minor breaches of Federation rules, and usually the best response he got was a bland form letter thanking him for his concern. They probably would not see that this was *different*, this was *important*.

He hadn't realized, himself, just how bad this case was; because he couldn't figure out how the Bashir was paying whoever supplied him, what was the benefit for the Barentsians who had to be involved in smuggling the weapons upcountry.

Now he himself was part of the payment, and he knew that supplying prohibited technology to an Indigenous Tribal Territory was the smallest part of the whole monstrous scheme, and that the profits were incalculable. It might even be that Rezerval was involved, that everybody who knew deliberately turned a blind eye to the flouting of regulations and destruction of a culture. There was enough profit here—

and enough benefit, even to people who'd never even heard of Kalapriya—to make that entirely plausible.

He shifted restlessly until the chains that held him sitting upright, back to the wall, clanked and drew a suspicious glance from the bored guard. At least he could see the guard today. Some days the man's figure was haloed with red and orange flames; some days the entire cave disappeared behind waves of pulsating color. That, like the days of merciful confusion when he did not know who and where he was, was probably a sign that the inevitable infections were at last taking hold. He'd heard the guards speculating on why he'd lasted so much longer than most prisoners; they thought he might be protected by powerful outlander demons. It was as close as their primitive worldview could come to what he himself thought the more reasonable hypothesis: that the bacteria which caused infections in this world were not quite accustomed to his outlander blood, found him a less tasty snack than the native Kalapriyans.

He wondered, vaguely, if the same thing was true of the slime being carefully nurtured on parts of himself that he could not see. Probably not. There'd never been any trouble getting the 'mats to mimic any patient's brain function; whatever they did worked quite as well on outlanders as it did on Kalapriyans. And the technician, when he visited, seemed pleased enough with what he harvested. At least the stuff would go to somebody who really needed it. Probably at a hugely inflated black-market price, to someone who would never qualify for a 'mat transplant under Rezerval's stringent rationing system; that was a logical consequence of the whole scheme; but nobody took a transplant who didn't need it. It should be some comfort to reflect that there was a good outcome to this diabolical scheme.

The part of his mind that was capable of feeling comfort seemed as dead as that which should have felt fear. All that was left him, now, was this oddly dispassionate reasoning; and waiting for the infections in his open head to gain ground and give him release at last. He could tell that his brain was not functioning as well as earlier. Some days he forgot how to speak; other times were filled with the flickering red-and-yellow fire of visual hallucinations, or discordant music grating on his auditory nerves. But how could you measure the failure of your own brain? The progression itself interfered with your ability to measure it. Reminded him of some scientific paradox he'd learned in school, something about the act of measuring something influencing the thing you measured. Only this wasn't the same, he didn't think. That was the trouble, he *didn't* think anymore, not properly. Moments of clarity floating like islands in the fog. And now the auditory hallucinations were starting again, screams and wails of lost spirits and something eerily like the crying of a child.

Not hallucinations. He blinked, thankful that he retained that much control out of his eyes, and concentrated on the dimness at the far end of the cave as if by sheer will he could make the indistinct figures emerging from the tunnel shine out bright and clear. Brown faces, short slender forms clothed in colorless rags, limping and clinging to one another. But indisputably *real*; his hallucinations never showed such details as the livid scar on that young man's face, the dirty hair tumbling in elf-locks around the old woman's face, the long black braids of the little girls who clung to her knees. As they moved forward, stumbling, into the dim intersecting spheres of light cast by the oil lamps on the walls, the woman stood straighter and he saw that she was not old at all; just exhausted and in despair. She was taller than the other prisoners, and the sharp slant of her cheekbones marked a lineage of pure Rudhrani blood. Must be a political, then; most of those brought here were Rohini "criminals" or prisoners of war from the recent conquest of Thamboon.

"A hard journey, Udaka?" the cavern guard remarked to the man in MinLoy uniform who held the end of the chain binding the prisoners one to another.

"Hard enough." The MinLoy man spat into the shadows at his feet. "Got ambushed by a bunch of raggedy-ass Rohini bandits, first night out. They grabbed two before we cut them down. Had to kill the prisoners too. Damned waste. I'd hoped to bring the bandits here alive to add to your little 'farm,' but those Rohini fools never know when to stop fighting." He jerked his head at the tall woman who stood at the head of the line, her face a mask of death. "Her baby got killed in the fight."

The cavern guard shrugged. "Not much loss there. Kids

never live long. Whose are these brats, then?" He indicated the shrinking girl-children.

"Oh, they're hers too. Picked the lot of them up at their home. Seems the father'd been making trouble, but he's got powerful protectors; so instead of taking him, we took the family and let him know he wouldn't see them again unless he behaved himself." Udaka grinned. "Not that he'll *want* to see them, once we cut them and start farming their heads . . . but there's no need to go into those little details."

"You brought rations for them, I hope?"

"Some. It's the devil of a chore, hauling food up here, and for what? They all die in a few days anyway."

"Not all." The guard turned so that he could see his whole face. "That one there—" he jerked his chin "—he's lasted two weeks since we started using him for a breeder. And that was *after* a spell in your palatial underground residence! Anyway, we're supposed to keep feeding them as long as they can swallow. Less wastage that way."

Udaka shrugged. "Well, it won't take much to feed this lot. We had some bad weather after the bandit attack—early storms—and the way some of them are coughing, frankly, I'm surprised they made it up the trails this far. I'll lay a dozen tulai that half of them don't survive the cutting."

"Make it two dozen," said the cavern guard, "enough to pay for a good night's drinking when I go off duty, and you're on. We've had a *lot* of practice setting them up by now. All you have to do is make sure they can't move when you're going through the skull—that's the part that hurts, see—and then once the head's open, you can cut a little bit in the right place and they *don't* move much. That outlander showed us the way of it."

So that was why everybody was so still! The traitor had showed them how to injure the motor cortex in just the right place to inhibit all voluntary movement below the neck. The chains were only to hold them upright, not to stop people thrashing around. Orlando Montoyasana blinked furiously, trying to hold that moment of understanding in his mind, feeling with sick despair that he had learned this much before, and forgotten it, and learned and forgotten again. Probably he had. Everything went away in the foggy periods. Why did he even try? He was a dead man; there was no escape from this place, and the infections that claimed the other prisoners would eventually kill him too.

Because my understanding is all I have left. He clutched it as a starving man would clutch a crust of bread, knowing it wasn't enough, but still feeling it as infinitely precious. As the MinLoy guard completed the paperwork and other formalities of handing over his prisoners, Orlando Montoyasana had a glimmer of something else he might be able to save, at least for a few days.

"Mind you give me a fair count of living bodies after the cut!" Udaka called as he left. "We'll settle up when I bring the next lot in. Devils take you, I'll double it again if you keep them all alive till then! I'll even say, all but the children—even you won't be able to make them last!" He laughed heartily, clearly not thinking he risked much by the promise.

"Bhalini!" Montoyasana whispered as soon as the sounds of the departing convoy had died away. The cavern guard couldn't hear him over the wails of the new prisoners. He tried again, with all the strength left in his wasted throat. "Bhalini!"

"Hush up, you lot, or I'll give you something to whine about!" Bhalini commanded, striking out at random with the short white cane he carried as a sign of authority. The new prisoners cried, cringed away from the blows, and fell silent. Only the tall Rudhrani woman did not shrink, even when the cane landed on her. She seemed totally indifferent to all that went on around her, even to the two little girls trying to hide behind her.

"Ma, it's *talking*!" one of the girls whispered, pointing in Montoyasana's direction. "It's *alive.*"

A low moaning began as first one, then another of the bodies chained to the wall began to register the stares of the new captives. Montoyasana cursed the incoherent babble of his fellow prisoners and tried to speak clearly enough to be heard through the noise. "Bhalini, I can help you win that wager. I have—" *outlander science*, he was about to say, but changed in time to something that the guard would be more likely to believe. "I have strong magics. See how long I've lived here! Would you have all these new bodies last as long, and get your drinking money twice over from Udaka?" Perhaps he could cast van Vechten's instructions about sterilizing instruments and keeping the caves clean in terms of rites to cast out demons with fire and boiling water.

Bhalini struck out with his cane at the prisoners along the wall until they quieted, then squatted in front of Montoyasana. "Aye, share thy magic, then, outlander demon!"

"At a price—nothing good comes without a price."

"What can *you* use, dead man? A little more dozy-juice to help you sleep away the hours?"

"Nothing for me. But keep the little ones back from the cutting."

"It's as much as my life is worth, if the Arm of the Bashir should hear of it."

"You said yourself, children hardly last long enough to be worth the work of preparing them. And these are girls— weaker, to begin with, and they look sickly." Actually they looked no worse than one would expect of terrified children who had just been dragged away from everything they knew. And weren't girl-children constitutionally stronger than boys? But it didn't matter; Bhalini looked half convinced already. "It's not as if they were even part of your wager," Montoyasana pointed out. "Keep the rest alive longer, and . . . and . . ." His mind wandered, and a momentary numbness assailed his tongue. What had he been talking about? A child cried, and the mother stooped and gathered it into her arms, and he remembered. "Keep the rest alive longer, win your wager and get the Bashir's praise for serving him well. Or cut them all now and kill half of them for lack of the—the strong magics I know. It's all one to me."

"Aye, that it likely is, to a dead man talking," the guard agreed, without malice. "But two is overmuch risk. They'd be playing and quarreling and get themselves noticed. Tell me your charms, and I'll keep one child with me—for a time."

"As long as you can?" There might yet be a miracle. Rezerval might find them and intercede. In all probability he was buying the one girl only a few days of life in terrified misery. But if she were old enough to understand, she would take any chance of life, however slender.

"As long as I can," Bhalini agreed. "Gods know she'll eat little enough, a scrawny little thing like that."

"Which?"

"How should I care? Let the mother decide." And before Montoyasana could gather his wandering wits enough to protest this casual cruelty, Bhalini stood up and called, "You! Rudhrani traitor woman, one of your girls goes with you now, and the other stays with me. Which do you keep?"

The girl already in the woman's arms redoubled her wailing and clung with the force of hysteria to her mother's shoulders. "There, there, Neeta," the woman said. "I'll not leave you."

"*I'll* stay with the ugly man," said the other girl distinctly, squaring her thin shoulders. "I'm not afraid." Her voice quavered on the last word.

Bhalini grinned down at Montoyasana. "See there? They choose for themselves. All right, all of you!" He raised his voice. "Traitor scum, down this passage. I'll see to you in a minute. You, girl, stay with me." He grasped the child's wrist to keep her with him. Montoyasana closed his eyes against the heartbreak of the mother's face.

"Now, outlander," Bhalini muttered, "tell me your charms!"

Chapter Thirteen

Rezerval

Annemari didn't bother to look up and down the hall before trying the door of the Cassilis Clinic's business center. Whether anybody was there to see her going in was really beside the point; it went without saying that the organizers of this satin-smooth operation would have spycams installed in any place they wanted to watch. Her only hope was to act like somebody with nothing to hide and hope that they assumed her to be an arrogant rich lady who thought she was entitled to go anywhere she wanted. Such behavior shouldn't draw too much attention; from what she'd seen of the clinic's clientele, most if not all of them were rich assholes.

The door was unlocked; that was the good news. The bad news was that it was unlocked because somebody was working late. A slim girl with a really excellent strand job of alternating silver and black hair, tapping a deskvid and muttering imprecations under her breath, looked around at the sound of the door opening.

"We're not really open right now, Honored Fru," she said, with a stiff artificial smile that clashed with her frowning brows.

"Oh, don't let me disturb you," Annemari said brightly. "I just wanted to use one of your screens for a moment. Would you *believe* it, I was in such a frazzle about getting my darling boy here that I absolutely forgot to pick up any supplies from my personal colorist. If I don't have him send some toner out immediately I'll be an absolute *fright* before the week's out; this color has to be refreshed almost daily." She passed a hand through her silver-blond locks and thanked the gods that had given her a young-looking face and prematurely greying hair. The silvery tint was so becoming against her smooth, creamy skin that Nunzia Hirvonen was always accusing her of having had it done on purpose to make herself look younger by contrast.

"There's a screen in your room for personal transmissions, Honored Fru," the girl said.

"I know, but the silly thing isn't working. I can't even get a local connection for room service!" It had taken Annemari half an hour of delicate fiddling to remove the back of the deskvid in her room, break two vital connections, and insert a dead moth as a possible explanation for the minor damage. Getting the cover back on had been the hardest part of the job.

"Oh. You want me to see if I can get a tech out to fix it tonight?" the girl offered reluctantly, glancing at her own screen.

"Oh, no, there's absolutely no hurry." Annemari had counted on the tech support staff working regular hours and had timed her own visit for well after hours. "If you'd just be a dear and let me slip in and use a screen for one teeny moment to reach Aristide?"

The name of Rezerval's top stylist and colorist worked its magic on the girl. As her eyes widened, Annemari silently blessed Nunzia Hirvonen for keeping up with all the fashion nonsense that bored Annemari herself to tears.

"You go to *Aristide*? I should have guessed, nobody else could get that color—it's really wonderful, such a pale gold without looking grey at all."

Annemari had always thought it *was* grey. Names really were magic.

"Clients aren't really supposed to use these screens . . ." the girl added reluctantly.

"Oh, fiddlesticks, I won't do any harm. I'll just slip in

and out so quietly you'll never know I'd been there!" More to the point, the inquiry Annemari really planned to make wouldn't raise any red flags if it came from a screen in the business center. She was perfectly capable of hacking through the clinic's firewalls to get the information from her room screen, but she wasn't quite sure she could do so without tripping hidden alarms.

"I sure wish *I* could afford a consult with Aristide," the girl hinted. "But even if I could, I hear he won't even take appointments from somebody who isn't already on his personal list."

Annemari smiled sweetly. "Oh, you can always get around that sort of thing. If the right person recommends you, I'm sure he'll make time for you. What's your name, and when's your next day off?"

"Jenna . . . Jenna Berg, and I'm off every fifth-day . . . Can you really do that?"

"It won't be any trouble at all," Annemari said, quite truthfully. If anybody went to the trouble to setting something up with Aristide, it would have to be Nunzia; he'd never even met Annemari. "And as for the costs, why don't we just add it in to my clinic bill?" And Evert would pay *that*. Her friends were certainly coming through for her in style— even if they didn't know just how much style, yet.

She took a chair facing the now helpful girl, so that Jenna would be unable to see exactly what she was doing, and tapped the deskvid to activate it. As she'd hoped, these screens automatically gave every user full system privileges. Lousy security; if Cassilis Clinic was still in business next year, she'd have to suggest to one of her friends in the private sector that they demonstrate the loopholes and bid for a complete overhaul of the system. But for now, the clinic owners' carelessness made her life incomparably easier. It took only seconds to bring up and memorize the information she wanted; then she sent a message to Aristide after all, so that the log would have something to show if anybody checked it. The colorist wouldn't have any idea why he was getting urgent requests for toner from someone who wasn't even one of his clients; she added a suggestion that he check with Nunzia Hirvonen, and hoped Nunzia would pick up from there.

"All done!" she announced brightly, rising to go.

"And . . . my appointment?"

"He'll have to see when he can work you in. Otherwise it might be *months*," Annemari lied. "I'll let you know when something is arranged."

"I could probably switch shifts with one of my friends, if he's got something free on another day."

"Good, that'll make it easier. See you soon!" The longer she stayed chatting with Jenna Berg, the better the chance that somebody a little more intelligent would show up and want to know what she was doing here; Cassilis Clinic security couldn't be *that* bad. Annemari slipped away with a few more promises to let Jenna know as soon as Aristide could fit her in. If the information she'd just gotten off the system screen was correct, she had just a short time to make it to her next destination—and first she had to look in on Niklaas.

"Doing all right?" she asked, probably unnecessarily. Niklaas was sipping something icy and lemon-colored through a transparent straw that went through several acrobatic loops between the flask and his lips, and watching one of those disgusting war vids that filled the room with booms and bangs and screams.

"Fine," Niklaas waved a languid hand to acknowledge his mother's presence.

She sniffed the air suspiciously. "What's in that flask? You know you're not supposed to—"

"Little muscle relaxant, s'all. Nice nurse brought it. They're taking me down for scanning prett' soon," Niklaas slurred. "Said they want me nice and calm first."

"So soon!" Maybe she should stay with him and catch up on her other plan later.

"Y'can't come," Niklaas said when she mentioned that possibility. "Told me . . . restricted area . . . near surgery, y'see."

"You mean they won't even let your *mother* in?" Annemari put one hand to her throat, fingering the ornate necklace she wore, and then placed her palm on Niklaas's shoulder. She sighed as if in resignation. "Well then, darling, maybe I'll try out the spa facilities while you're busy, and meet you for dinner after the tests." She went behind the head of Niklaas's bed, dropped her silky grey tunic and pants on the floor, and wrapped herself in one of the fluffy pink robes provided by the clinic. No time to hang anything up; she had only minutes now to reach her destination.

Annemari had to pass her right hand through a palm scanner to open the door to the Rejuvenating Chemical Soak Therapy Room. Inside she found a small, steamy tiled room with a circular tub of greenish gunk bubbling away in the center. Annemari hung up her robe and groped through the steam to dip a cautious foot in the tub. The stuff wasn't all that hot; there must be subsurface air jets making the bubbles. It stung her skin, but not too badly.

She let out a small sigh of relief as the steam cleared enough to show her that there was only one other person in the tub, a small woman with a cloud of dark curls surrounding an olive-skinned oval face. The schedule she'd sneaked a look at in the office had been accurate, then. Annemari nodded to her companion, found a comfortably curved bench under the surface of the bubbling gunk, and sank slowly into what the Cassilis Clinic described as their rejuvenating chemical soak. After the first sting it wasn't bad at all; more stimulating than actually painful.

"This is really quite pleasant," she said to the other woman. "Perhaps I'll sign up for a course of regular treatments while I'm here." She tried to trace a message on the surface of the mud, but the aerating bubbles erased the lines as fast as her finger could move.

"Oh, yes, it's wonderful for the skin, and you feel so fresh and relaxed afterward!" the other woman babbled. "Aren't you here for the treatments, then?"

"No, I brought my son for some . . . rehabilitation therapy. I hear they do miracles with hopeless cases here."

"I've heard that too," said the other woman. "But as long as you're here, you really ought to take advantage of the facilities yourself. I'm doing art therapy after this. Good for the nerves, you know. Modern life is so stressful, it's wonderfully relaxing to do simple work with your hands."

"Sounds good," Annemari said casually. "Will anyone object if I join you?"

"No, just give the palm scanner your hand and it'll record that you've joined the group and put the charge on your bill. Those scanners are wonderful, they let the clinic staff keep track of all the clients all the time and if you don't remember what's next on your treatment schedule, or can't find the room, they send a staff member to guide you. So restful!"

Annemari nodded to show she had taken in the information, and lay back to enjoy the aerating bubbles and the stimulating chemical skin bath for the few minutes before her companion indicated that it was time to move on to the Art Therapy Room. After showering they found fresh pink terry pajamas laid out for them—two pairs, and in the right sizes; the palm scanner had done its work.

"You'll really like art therapy," Annemari's new friend said cheerfully as they paced down the corridor. "It's very freeing, you just express yourself with great splashes of color and draw whatever you want, and it's amazing what messages come to you. I'm Thecla Partheni, by the way."

"Annemari Silvan." They had reached the art room; Annemari and "Thecla" joined the line of pink-clad ladies passing their hands through the palm scanner and kept up a bright meaningless chatter until they were stationed side by side with drawing screens and a pile of art supplies.

"These screens are supposed to be wonderful for working out ideas," "Thecla" said. "You just trace out your design and indicate the medium effects you want to apply—pastels or oils or whatever—and you get a nice clean printout with no blots or mistakes. But to me it's just not the same as getting your hands in the actual medium, you know? Call me old-fashioned, but I really like the primitive act of making colored marks on paper, like this. She scribbled *Anything on the screens can be read by the central monitor*, held her paper pad so that Annemari could read it, and quickly covered up the writing with a scrawl of energetic dark blue spirals.

"I think you're right," Annemari said, "the real therapeutic effect is in working with your hands." *Calandra, why haven't you reported in? And what brought you here?* It was easy to cover up her light pastel writing with a crude spring rainbow.

"That's right, you're really getting the hang of it!" *No chance to report. We forgot to give Thecla's identity administrator privileges. Am I glad you're here! Can you get me central database privileges? I want to download this place's construction permit blueprints and anything else on record. There's a lot of space unaccounted for—places we're not allowed to go.* All that required a vigorous execution of a cityscape in glowing colors, followed by a muttered imprecation, ripping the paper off the pad, and dropping the crumpled page into a recycler that hummed into action, instantly reducing the paper to an indistinguishable mass of bright pigments and cellulose shreds.

I might be able to get some information directly. But this is going to take forever. Isn't there any place around here we can talk safely? Annemari stared at her own paper, sighed, then tore up the sheet and dropped it into the recycler. "I just can't make this picture come out right!" she said aloud for the benefit of the art therapist, who was looking their way with a frown of concern.

For the rest of the "art therapy" hour Annemari and Calandra chatted out loud about nothing in particular and covered paper with brightly colored shapes, none of which they recycled, just in case the "therapist" should want to inspect their work. Afterward Calandra invited Annemari to join her in a healthful stroll in the clinic gardens. "I have a free recreation hour now, if you're not scheduled for anything?"

"I don't have a schedule," Annemari said as they paced along a soft path of close-cropped grass between flowering hedges. "I'm just here with Ni—with my son. He's the one who really needs the clinic treatments. They more or less told me to run away and play while he was having the preliminary tests done. I'm not even allowed back in the area where the testing happens."

"Poor little boy," Calandra cooed. They came to a branch in the path and she turned to the left, away from the attractive fountain playing at the end of the right-hand path. "Will he be scared without you?"

"Goodness, no, he's nearly seventeen. More likely to be embarrassed by my presence!"

"What lovely flowers!" Calandra exclaimed, pointing at a nondescript shrub with small puce blossoms. "Let's break a teensy rule and get a closer look at them." She hopped over the low shrubs bordering the path and led Annemari across the grass. "Right *here,*" she said in a lower voice just as they reached the shrub, "there's a spot none of their monitors cover."

"How did you—oh." Annemari nodded as Calandra tapped

the side of her head. "I may not have all the downloaded files I'd like, but my scanners are still working. We can talk here, but not for long; there's a limit to how long even a couple of total idiots would spend admiring this filthy bush. Now fill me in. Are you really going to get Niklaas a 'mat implant here? They charge an arm and a couple of legs, you know."

"Evert Cornelis transferred enough into my account to cover the charges," Annemari said. "But I still don't know where they're getting the bacteriomats. Are they stolen from the Barents Trading Society's stock?"

Calandra shook her head. "I'm *almost* sure not. What led me here was a 'mat transport canister addressed to the Clinic. It wasn't a BTS canister—for what that's worth. But it was coming off Kalapriya. I've been trying to find out more, but they've got most of my time so scheduled I hardly have a chance to snoop. I checked in as Thecla Partheni with a case of nervous prostration brought on by too many high-stress social activities. Fortunately they don't do a really thorough workup on the public-side clients. I must have appeared convincingly stressed out; they took one look at me and assigned a nutritionist, an exercise counselor, art therapy, and daily chemical soaks. I may not find out much, but I'll sure be healthy when we get out of here."

"Why Thecla? Oh, well, I suppose you wouldn't want to use your own ID here, they might check and find out you're a Diplo assigned to my office," Annemari worked out. "But you traveled here under the Partheni ID."

"The Calandra Vissi ID is compromised," Calandra said. "Somebody tried to kill me on Tasman."

"Tasman? Not Kalapriya?"

"I never even reached Kalapriya."

"But—"

"I'm telling you, the Tasman smugglers were following me from the moment I got there. Whatever's going on, that end of the investigation has been well and truly leaked. And what's more, somebody among the smugglers is a good enough hacker to recode the partition locks on the lower levels of Tasman—either that, or my data download for Tasman was badly out of date. I had to deduce one of the partition lock codes from scratch to get away from those creeps."

"I didn't think you could do that."

"You probably couldn't," Calandra said, "but I did Cryptography and Ciphers for my optional at the School. Of course, it helps that my augmented retinal implants let me scan the keys for recent fingerprints; that cut down on the number of combinations I had to try. Still, it was a near thing. Those are very determined people. And very unpleasant." She massaged one hand with the other as though rubbing away a painful memory.

"And they caught you?"

"Yes, but they didn't keep me. And they think I spaced myself to get away, so they didn't follow me back here, either."

Annemari felt her head whirling. "Why would they think you'd do that?"

"They were going to torture me," Calandra said calmly. "They gave me a little taste on account, and thought I was scared witless."

"I put you in that much danger?"

"Annemari. It's part of the job. You didn't think 'mat smugglers were going to be nice people, did you? Forget about it; I have. Now, can you sign on from your room screen and authorize Thecla Partheni to access Rezerval databases? Because if you'll do that, I can probably get enough data to map out exactly where the concealed areas of the clinic are and where we need to be snooping."

"Probably," Annemari said. Her head was whirling. "Wait a minute, there's something else we need to clear up first. *Somebody* showed up on Kalapriya as you, right on schedule. She toured a 'mat cave and attended an official dinner and ball and disappeared that night. I'd been assuming that was you, that you found out something on Kalapriya that sent you back here."

Calandra shook her head. "Nope. Told you, I never even got that far."

"Then who was impersonating you?"

"I don't know," Calandra said, rather grimly, "but from what you say, she isn't doing it anymore. Being Calandra Vissi doesn't seem to be a healthy occupation these days. Now what about the authorization? I feel half blind without my data accesses."

"That's easy. I'll send Jeppe a list of stuff to do while

I'm out of the office, a *long* list, and somewhere in the middle I'll put in a general statement about giving all Diplo IDs full security privileges. That way your name won't show if they're intercepting my email, and the actual access permission will happen completely off-screen as far as the clinic's concerned. *And* we can probably find out a little more about the reserved areas right now, a little more directly."

"How?"

Annemari grinned. "I slipped a spyder under Niklaas's skin before they took him off for testing. You think I'd let them wheel my boy off to parts unknown with no way for me to track him?"

In a locked, soundproof room deep in the surgical section of the Cassilis Clinic, Tomi Oksanen moaned and twitched. An aide checked the tubes that kept nutrients flowing through his unconscious body while his primary neurosurgeon conferred with the head of the clinic.

"It can't be the bacteriomats. I've done three hundred installations now and hardly any have failed."

"To be precise," said his superior in a chill, knife-edged voice, "in the first year of operation, a five-percent failure rate was reported, mostly from implants that failed to mesh with the recipient's nervous system as desired. All dissatisfied clients were of course given a full refund, which was a nontrivial cut in our profit margin. The reported rate of such failures in this year has been less than two percent."

"You see? It's getting better, not worse."

"But there have been over thirty cases *this year* of total system failure, like this one. And that's just the ones that have been reported back to us; there may be others that the clients concealed for fear of scandal or investigation." The clinic head gestured at Tomi Oksanen's naked, thrashing body. "The clients—or rather, their heirs—are not going to be satisfied with a refund and an apology. God of Chaos, man, the Oksanens alone could close this place down! What are you *doing* with these patients?"

"I have followed accepted surgical protocols for bacteriomat implantation," the surgeon replied stiffly.

"And how many such cases are reported in the literature?"

"Well . . ."

"Never mind hedging," the clinic head snapped. "I can tell you. *None!* But far too many of our patients are becoming—like *that*. First twitching, then full-blown paranoiac insanity, then convulsions, then coma, then death."

"Young Oksanen's not dead."

"Yet." The head of the clinic looked coldly at his chief neurosurgeon. "If you want to keep your job here—if you want there to *be* a clinic to give you this job—if you want to stay out of a Federation prison, then I *strongly* suggest you find a way to reverse whatever error you made in his surgery before he does die."

Annemari and Calandra pressed their ears to the back partition of a storage pantry off the clinic kitchen. They could hear nothing but occasional anonymous bumps and thuds.

"Are you *sure* this wall backs up against the surgical sector?" Annemari whispered.

"Are *you* sure the clinic's construction permit blueprints are accurate?" Calandra retorted. "Because that's what I downloaded and that's all I have to go on."

They were both sweaty and somewhat irritable, having moved a number of heavy cases of very boring health food supplements to get access to the partition. Calandra was especially irritated because Annemari had kept remarking that if the health food supplement cases were painted pink and placed in the gym, moving them would be part of the aerobic exercise program that Calandra's alter identity, "Thecla," was paying big credits to enjoy.

"I don't enjoy it," Calandra finally told Annemari. "I look on it as one of the sacrifices I make for my Federation. And I hope the Earthlady sees to it that the clinic fees aren't another of the sacrifices I make; I've poured enough libations to her. I want full reimbursement for every credit these blood-sucking bastards have extracted from Thecla's account."

"That account was set up with Federation funds in the first place, as part of adding realism to your alternate identity," Annemari pointed out.

"Oh. Right. I guess that means I don't get any of it back, then." Calandra sat on a box labeled AMINO ACID FORTIFICATION EXTRACT and brooded. " 'Thecla' should have taken off for an exotic play world when she had the chance, instead of risking her life and literally working her butt off for the Federation."

"Nonsense," Annemari said, "you'd have been bored in a week at one of those resorts. And your butt has never looked better."

"You think?"

"I—ssh. Someone's finally saying something."

In a single sinuous movement Calandra was off the box and had her ear pressed to the partition.

"I can't make anything out," Annemari whispered in disappointment.

"Shurrup. *I* can." Calandra tugged her earlobe once, then again, to initiate the highest possible level of hearing enhancement. If anybody shouted now she'd go temporarily deaf . . . but she could hear the faint creaks of the partition supports, the rustle of a cockroach somewhere beneath the floor, and the quiet conversation going on in a back office of the clinic's restricted-access sector.

"Has there been any change in the way the 'mats are cultured?"

A snort of disgust echoed in Calandra's enhanced hearing like a minor hurricane. "How would I know? I don't even have any direct contact with van Vechten. You know how it works. His contacts in Valentin send the cases to Tasman. That Hongko gangster on Tasman, Johnivans, adds his own extortionate fees and forwards the cases here. One of our dummy corporations buys arms for a perfectly legitimate shipment to the Feuding Worlds—which just happen to lie the far side of a Tasman jump. We let Johnivans know when the shipment's coming through, and he diverts it to Kalapriya. How would *I* know how van Vechten's culturing the 'mats? He's the only man who's figured out how to grow them outside the coastal caves, and that's as much as we know about his process."

"All right, but you need to—what's that?"

"That" was the chime-timer on Calandra's wrist, announcing with increasing urgency that she was late for her aerobic acrobatics session. She snatched her hand away from the wall and tried to bury the timer between her thighs, but it was too late; the chatterers were nervous now, and left the office with no more discussion. She was disappointed to have to tell Annemari how little she'd learned.

"More than you think," Annemari said as they restacked the cases of nutritional supplements. The chime-timer rang at intervals, each time a little louder. "Can't you shut that thing off?"

"The rich idiots who come here for the spa environment aren't supposed to be able to figure out how," Calandra informed her. "I don't particularly want to blow my *second* cover, thank you."

"Then you'd better take one of these." Annemari reached into an open box and tossed her a stick of something that looked like seeds rolled up in dehydrated apricot skins.

"Why?"

"Don't ask, just start munching!"

A moment later two undercooks showed up to investigate the chiming sound. "Ah-ah, ladies," one of them said, wagging a finger, "trying to sneak in a between-meals snack?"

Annemari pouted prettily. "Don't tell on us, will you?"

"We won't do it again," Calandra promised. She took another bite of the sticky concoction. "What *is* this, anyway?"

"Bhlepti seeds and whole grains in apricot leather. Very nutritious." The cook grinned. "You ladies *must* be hungry if you're willing to snack on those. I'm surprised you didn't go for the chocolate."

"We couldn't find it," Annemari said glumly. "Come on, Ca—Thecla, you're late for aerobics. We'd better cut across the gardens." She batted her eyelashes at the cook. "You won't tell on us for that either, will you?"

She managed to look suitably hangdog until they were running past the ugly little shrubs with the puce blossoms, then stopped and grabbed Calandra's arm.

"This is a dead spot, right?"

Calandra nodded.

"Okay—what did you pick up?"

When she heard Calandra's summary of the overheard conversation she hugged her. "I love you, I love you, I love you," she announced. "You are a pearl among Diplos. Do you *realize* what you just gave me?"

"Confirmation that somebody is selling high-tech weaponry to Kalapriya in return for black-market bacteriomats. Which we can't use because it's just an overheard conversation."

"Didn't you record it?"

Calandra pushed the soft spot behind her right ear and a series of creaks, rustles, and inaudible voices came floating eerily out of her tousled black curls. "I can pick up more with the enhanced hearing than the recorder gets," she apologized. "That was due to be checked next time I went in for repairs."

"Oh, well, it doesn't matter," Annemari dismissed the problem of the faulty recording blithely. "The important thing is that now we have the information to put the whole plot together *and* track down the source of the 'mats."

"We do?"

"Calandra, *think*. Orlando Montoyasana registered a complaint that somebody was introducing prohibited technology into one of the highland Indigenous Tribal Territories of Kalapriya. Remember?"

"Yes, but he's always complaining about—"

"There'd be no need to smuggle high-tech weaponry into Valentin; they've got the Barents Trading Society's private army keeping the coastal Kalapriyan states under control, and the Society doesn't care what the mountain states do as long as it doesn't cause them any trouble. Obviously the weapons are going to an Indigenous Tribal Territory, and that's what alerted Montoyasana."

"And just how is some state hundreds of kilometers inland from the coastal caves going to produce bacteriomats for trade?"

"I don't know," Annemari said triumphantly, "but I do know who this van Vechten they were talking about has to be. His name came up in Montoyasana's messages. Access your Kalapriyan political database download!"

Calandra blinked twice, stared in an unfocused way out over the gardens, and then nodded. "He's the Barents Resident for the state of Udara, which has recently . . . expanded . . . taking over the formerly independent ITTs of Thamboon and Narumalar. Oh!"

"And what do you want to bet the Udarans had the help of some offworld weaponry for those surprisingly easy takeovers?"

"Okay," Calandra argued, "but we still don't know how van Vechten is getting the 'mats. He could be stealing them from the BTS supplies on the coast."

"If the coastal growing facilities were the source, Udara would have no leverage for special treatment and prohibited technology. Besides, those jerks you eavesdropped on *said* he'd figured out how to grow them outside the coastal caves. What we have to do next is very simple."

"It is?"

"We need to go to Udara and *ask* Haar van Vechten how he's doing it. Politely, of course," Annemari added, "but with a nice solid backup of Federation peacekeeping forces to underline the request."

"You mean *I* need to go. You can't leave Niklaas here, especially when he's scheduled for surgery. And it'll take me forever to trek into the mountains."

"*And* your identity is already compromised." Annemari frowned. "You might not even get there. I wonder . . . Are there flitters on Kalapriya?"

"I doubt it, and even if there were, it would be against Federation regs on protected worlds to take them inland."

"Then we'll have to take one with us," Annemari said.

Calandra blinked. "Can you authorize that?"

"No, not anymore than I can order the peacekeeping forces to accompany us, but I can hack into Enforcement's database and forge the orders . . . Well, really, Calandra, what are you staring for? Have you forgotten I was a technonerd for twenty years before they kicked me upstairs into Admin? What did you *think* I was doing all that time, data entry and accounting programs?"

"I just . . . don't . . . get it," Calandra said faintly. "You're a Silvan. The Silvans are so ethical; if you try to get them to break a rule, they bend it back the other way. You wouldn't even use your position to jump Niklaas up the list for a 'mat transplant."

"You really don't get it, do you? That would be unethical; this is merely illegal. And it's necessary."

"It is?"

"Do we know who's smoothing the path for the Cassilis Clinic on Rezerval?"

"Oksanens?"

"Got to be somebody official in on it as well. Until we know who, we daren't alert anybody. And the same thing goes for Valentin; we mustn't depend on the Barents Trading Society for resources, we have to take our own."

"Career suicide," Calandra muttered.

"Not if it works."

"And if it doesn't work?"

"In that case," Annemari pointed out, "the Federation's displeasure will probably be the least of our worries. Now come on. We need to do something about Niklaas and then get going. You'd better cut aerobics."

CHAPTER FOURTEEN

Dharampal on Kalapriya

When the soldiers from Dharampal surrounded them, Gabrel immediately demanded to be taken straight to their Vakil. He went on demanding this, with increasing loudness and firmness, while the soldiers tied their hands and feet and went through their packs.

"There's no need to play with *those*," the captain of the troop reproved a young soldier who was looking with interest at some fibrous plugs that had fallen to the ground when he shook out Maris's packed clothes.

Gabrel stopped his loud complaints for a moment to listen. He recognized what the young recruit had found, if the captain didn't.

"Looks like outlander magic to me," the soldier said defensively.

"Red Radhana take you, fool," said the captain. "They're obviously some of the things women use at, you know, their private times."

"Huh?"

The captain's face turned dark reddish brown and he pressed his lips together while one of the older soldiers shouted an offer to take young Varisha aside and explain about women to him. "*Later*, Odaka," the captain said. "Later you can take him to a brothel and *demonstrate*, if you like, but right now we're to bring these two in unharmed." He looked reflectively at the red marks on Gabrel's chin, where bruises would soon rise. "Reasonably unharmed. Now put all their outlander stuff back in the packs, and since you and Varisha are so interested in it, Odaka, the two of you can carry them. We'll turn the ghaya loose; they'll find good enough grazing along the river."

"Worth good money, those ghaya," Odaka grumbled, but he followed the captain's orders.

"Ghaya can't manage the paths we're taking," the captain said, "although why I bother to explain anything to you blockheads I do not know."

Hands bound in front of them, led on short ropes by two soldiers, Maris and Gabrel had a hellishly uncomfortable stumbling journey over mountain paths steeper and narrower than anything Maris, at least, had encountered before. The captain made no allowance for light or dark, and in the interval between sunset and moonrise they both collected a number of fresh bruises and scrapes from falling over rocks and thorn bushes that the locals avoided as if by instinct.

"I want to see the Vakil," Gabrel repeated at intervals, whenever the steep scrambling climb left him breath to make the demand.

"That's up to the Vakil, not to you or me," the captain said, reasonably politely, the first five or six times.

"He will be most annoyed to find that his good friend Gabrel Eskelinen has been mistreated this way."

The captain snorted. "That why he told me to bring his good *friend* Eskelinen at a rope's end? And the witch who travels with you, she a buddy of the Vakil's too?"

"Did he issue his orders personally?" Gabrel demanded. "Or did you have them from someone else—Minister Kansiya, perhaps? Does Yadleen even *know* what's going on?"

"The Vakil, may his beard increase, knows and sees all that is within the bounds of Dharampal," the captain said, but after that he allowed the marching pace to slacken a little and even loosened Gabrel's bonds so that he could catch himself when he stumbled. "Sorry about the witch," he said, looking at Maris, "but I daren't take any chances with *her*."

Gabrel started to complain again, but the captain interrupted him. "And if *either* of you say anything else, I'm to have you gagged. We've been warned that these outlander witches can corrupt honest men's thoughts, and maybe work worse magic, with their spells. I can't take the risk she might be working through your speech . . . you understand?"

"You'd better hope my friend Harsajjan Bharat, the Vakil's adviser, understands," Gabrel warned him.

The captain sighed. "And just who do you think signed the orders to bring you to the palace under guard? And told me to waste no time about it?" He patted the embroidered pouch tucked into his tunic sash, where stiff papers crackled under his hands.

After that Gabrel stopped arguing and saved his breath for getting up the mountain paths, and helping Maris when he could. At least the soldiers didn't seem to object to their walking together, though they were quick to interrupt any whispered conversation.

They reached the crest of the hills overlooking Dharamvai just after dawn, when the crude buildings of wood and mud were given a fleeting glory by the slanting red-gold light of the sun, the carvings that decorated every doorway and balcony thrown into high relief, and the piles of ordure in the gutters mercifully concealed by morning shadows. Gabrel could have wept at the irony of it. He'd dreamed of showing this mountain kingdom he had come to love to this girl whom—whom he had come to like a great deal—in just such a light, hoping that she would see the beauty and the decayed grandeur of this relic of empire as he did.

His dreams had not involved their being dragged down the mountain trail at a rope's end, jerked this way and that and staggering with weariness, hands bound before them like prisoners on their way to execution.

Not that it would come to that, of course. As soon as he had a chance to speak with Harsajjan, or even the Vakil, this foolish mistake would be cleared up. Gabrel resolved that he would beg the Vakil not to deal too harshly with the captain, who had dealt fairly with them within his understanding of the orders. He seemed to be a decent man overall; the mistake was doubtless not his fault.

And it was less troubling to think about begging the Vakil's mercy for the captain than to wonder whether he might be in need of it for himself and Maris.

Once within the walls of Dharamvai, after following tortuous narrow passages between leaning houses to a muddy and desolate walled yard, Gabrel was so tired that he actually sat down and fell asleep against the wall. He woke with a shock from a pleasant dream whose details vanished into the air even as his consciousness returned. It was close to noon, the sun falling as directly into this narrow yard as it ever could, and his pillow was the lap of the Honored Diplomat Vissi. He jerked upright, a stammered apology on his lips.

"It doesn't matter," the Diplo said. "I wouldn't have waked you now, only I *think* something is about to happen."

Something was indeed happening. The heavy gate of the courtyard swung open, pushed by a dark man in a blue and silver uniform who glanced at the prisoners and said, "On your feet, and quick about it!"

"I demand to see the Vakil," Gabrel said.

"You come with me, then."

The stranger's demands were interrupted by a file of soldiers in the red and gold of Dharampal, headed by the captain who had taken Gabrel and his companion prisoner the night before.

"Honorable Envoy Jagat," the captain said with a low bow that somehow was not at all respectful, "*I* am commanded to escort the prisoners to the Vakil's midday audience."

"My master wishes them brought to him."

"Should the Vakil, may his beard increase, so direct me, I shall be honored to bring the outlanders to the borders of Udara for your men to take over. Naturally the Bashir of Udara would not so insult the Vakil as to send soldiers into a country with which he still has peaceful relations. But for now, as I told you, my orders are to bring them before the Vakil himself."

Gabrel observed Calandra blinking rapidly and looking from side to side as though she were doing her best to follow the conversation. "They're arguing about who takes us out of here," he explained in a cautious undertone. "If we get any choice, we want to go with the guys in red."

"Why?" Calandra whispered back. "They're the ones who tied us up in the first place!"

"They're locals. I used to have a friend at the court here; if I can speak with him, everything will be all right. The other fellow is from Udara. We *don't* want to be prisoners of the Bashir of Udara, trust me." Gabrel wasn't sure exactly what happened to all the political opponents of the Bashir who had "disappeared" over the years, but then he didn't much care about the details—whether they had been beheaded, or strangled, or simply dropped over a mountain cliff hardly made much difference. The one thing they didn't do was come back from the Bashir's prisons to discuss their experiences.

After some more reasonably polite fencing, the man in blue and silver, whose name appeared to be Indukanta Jagat, gave in to the irrefutable argument of the twenty soldiers behind the captain and agreed that the Vakil might have audience with his own prisoners. He insisted on accompanying them, which did not reassure Gabrel, but he comforted himself with the thought that the alternative would have been much worse.

The palace of the Vakil was unfamiliar to Gabrel; on his previous visits to Dharampal, he had stayed in private houses—in the sprawling compound of Harsajjan himself, last time—and the Vakil had met him incognito, in the unconvincing disguise of a young merchant, which everybody politely pretended not to see through. It had been that dangerous, already, for the ruler of a state close to Udara to show favor to a representative of the Barents Trading Society.

On the way to the palace, he occupied his mind by thinking out the politics of the matter. Udara itself had had a Barents Society Resident for some years, one Lorum van Vechten, of whom Gabrel knew little except that the man had been completely unhelpful as to local information about the Independent Tribal Territories of the High Jagirs. He came of an Old Trader family, had studied offworld, and done some kind of scientific or medical work before returning to Kalapriya, and the way people in Valentin avoided talking about him had left Gabrel with the impression that van Vechten was a minor family black sheep who'd been shipped off to a conveniently distant position of little importance, where he would have few chances to embarrass the family.

But though the Bashir of Udara had accepted a Barents Resident, he resolutely opposed any of the neighboring Independent Tribal Territories accepting such a resident or having any direct diplomatic relations with the Trading Society. The events of recent years made the reasons easy enough to understand. One by one, the states neighboring Udara had come under the Bashir's control and lost their independence. A Resident in a conquered state might have complained to the Trading Society, might even have got official support against yet another Udaran conquest. So long as Udara was the only state in the High Jagirs with a resident representative of Barents, the Bashir could presumably count on Udaran interests being represented in Valentin to the exclusion of those of the conquered territories. Phalap, the Seven Villages, Rudhatta, Thamboon, Narumalar were just names to the Barentsians of Valentin, fragments of an empire that had dissolved into feuds and chaos long before their arrival. Udara itself was scarcely more than that in the general Valentin consciousness.

All of which was too complicated to explain to Calandra in the few muttered words they had an opportunity to exchange on the way, and of no particular use to them anyway, as far as Gabrel could see. The only lever he might be able to use was the fact that at least some of the advisers to Yadleen, Vakil of Dharampal, were evidently not in favor of lying down while Udara trampled over them. Certainly Harsajjan wasn't—

But Harsajjan himself, according to this young captain of infantry, had signed the orders for their detention. Gabrel felt himself lost in puzzles and ancient intrigues beyond his capability to decipher.

That was, however, no excuse for not at least trying.

Yadleen's "palace" turned out to be merely an open, airy building perched, naturally, at the very top of the mountain. It had an air of rustic simplicity and freshness that matched Gabrel's impressions of the young Vakil as a direct and honorable man, trying to do the right thing by his subjects while treading a political maze laid down in the days of the ancient empire. Wide, low-ceilinged rooms roofed with cedar and walled with white plaster opened onto dazzling blue-and-gold vistas of sky and mountains; the snowy breezes of the highest Jagirs blew straight through the rooms when the screens were rolled up, as they were today. The air was chill for travelers coming direct from the lowlands, whose ghaya-skin cloaks were still rolled up in the packs that had been confiscated, but Gabrel preferred it to the usual stale air and sweet smoky smells of rooms closed up against the winter cold. Even Yadleen's chair of state was just that, no throne, but a plain straight armchair of dark wood whose only decoration was the patina of decades. The Vakil inspected his prisoners' faces with a searching stare as they entered, and Gabrel straightened as well as he could in the ropes that bound his arms.

"Leutnant Eskelinen." Yadleen made hard work of pronouncing the foreign rank and name, but they were recognizable. He went on more easily in Kalapriyan. "You may explain yourself."

"Explain?" Gabrel decided there was nothing to lose by taking a high hand—verbally, anyway. "The explanations are due to me! Is this how the Vakil of Dharampal greets his friends? Or is the Vakil about to apologize for a gross error? The Honorable Trading Society of Barents can forgive a mistake. A deliberate insult to its representatives is another thing."

The soldiers lined up against either wall stirred, but the Vakil motioned them to remain where they were.

"Most of my 'friends,' " Yadleen said mildly enough, "come to Dharampal openly, not sneaking across its borders. You have been accused of attempting to smuggle an outlander witch into our territories for the purpose of creating internal disruption." His glance toward Indukanta Jagat left Gabrel in no doubt as to who had made the accusation.

"A *witch*?" Gabrel tried to look indignant and surprised. "My lord Vakil knows that we of Barents do not believe in witchcraft."

Yadleen waved a negligent hand. "Please do not waste my time in arguing theology. Witches undeniably exist, as do ifreets and spirits of the air; you may say you do not believe in the High Jagirs, but that will not save you from freezing in the snow if you try to cross the wrong pass in winter. The question here is whether you brought this woman into our lands knowingly, or whether you are innocent of her plans."

"She is not a witch, but an ordinary woman of my people."

"She does not look like your people." Yadleen's casual glance contrasted Maris's short, slender figure, olive skin, and tumbled black curls with Gabrel, a standard-issue tall fair Barentsian. "Although I must admit she does not look like a powerful witch, either."

"May the Vakil's wisdom and beard increase," Indukanta Jagat put in. "These Diplomatai are clever enough to conceal their otherworldly powers until such time as it benefits them to use them."

His indiscreet use of the foreign word gave Gabrel the clue he needed. "Has the Vakil been told that this woman is a *Diplomat*?" He laughed loudly. "What a tale! If she were a Diplo, we'd have flown out of our prison as easily as a bird leaves a tree. What has the Vakil heard of Diplos?"

"Our honored friend Indukanta Jagat," Yadleen said, with a glance toward Jagat that was anything but friendly, "tells us that the Diplomatai—what were your words, Jagat? They 'speak all languages fluently, carry maps in their heads, can render an armed man helpless with their secret fighting magic, and conceal on their persons offworld weapons more terrible than any you have seen'—was that not it?"

Indukanta Jagat bowed.

"Well then!" Gabrel nodded toward Maris. "Why did this so-powerful Diplo allow your soldiers to capture us?"

"Perhaps she was taken by surprise," Yadleen suggested.

"And does the Vakil know why she has not yet spoken to him?"

Yadleen's eyebrows shot up. "A woman speak to the Vakil, when there is a man to speak for her?"

"Ah. But by the account of your 'friend' Indukanta Jagat—" Gabrel allowed a little sarcasm in his voice "—this is no ordinary woman but a Diplo. Don't you think she would speak for herself if she could? But she has so little mastery of your tongue that she does not even understand what we are saying now. She has been studying the language on our way here but has not yet reached the point where she can carry on an ordinary conversation, much less speak for herself before the Vakil."

"It is difficult to prove that someone does *not* speak a language," Yadleen observed.

"Well, I can certainly prove that she has been studying it!" Gabrel shot back. "Ask your captain, here, to bring forth our packs, and I shall show you the evidence."

There was a necessary delay while the packs, left behind in the courtyard where they had been held prisoner, were sent for. While they waited, the Vakil ordered chairs brought for Gabrel and Maris, had his servants bring them cups of fruit sorbet chilled in the mountain snows, and even allowed their bonds to be loosened so that they could hold the cups for themselves.

"We're making progress," Gabrel muttered to Maris.

"How? What have you been saying? I can't understand more than a word here and there."

"Good, that's maybe going to help get us out of here. Keep right on not understanding. I'll explain later." Indukanta Jagat was protesting to the Vakil that the prisoners should not be allowed to confer in their outlander tongue, and Gabrel didn't want to upset the delicate progress of negotiations by letting their conversation become an issue.

When the packs were brought, Gabrel requested the captain to open the one belonging to the woman and bring out "those articles which one of your men thought were used for women's purposes."

One of the soldiers upended Maris's pack and spilled the contents out onto the polished wooden floor. With an expression of distaste on his aristocratic features, the captain picked through the litter and eventually retrieved one of the small fibrous plugs. "This?"

"Yes. If you look at it closely, you will see it is far too small to be used for the purpose you mentioned."

The captain shrugged. "Village women use sundhu bark. It expands when, ah, with moisture. Besides, outlander women may be, um, *smaller.*" Reddish-brown splotches of color rose on his face.

"She is made after the manner of all women," Gabrel asserted, "but it is not necessary to humiliate her by putting this to the test. Just insert the plug in your ear, Captain."

"*What?*" The captain's face was quite red now, clashing vilely with his scarlet uniform.

"It's not a joke, Captain," Gabrel said. "These are not what you thought, but tools for learning languages. You will hear an elementary lesson in Kalapriyan grammar if you insert the plug into your ear."

The captain brought the plug close to the side of his head with a dubious expression.

"It doesn't activate until it's fitted into the ear," Gabrel said.

"Activate?"

"Ah—speak."

With a look of determination, as if he thought it equally probable that his head would explode as soon as he inserted the thing, the captain compressed the plug in two fingers and pushed it into his own ear.

"Ai! Devil voices!" he exclaimed, reaching to pull it out.

"No, *listen!*"

A moment later the captain looked more amused than apprehensive.

"What do the voices say, Captain?" Yadleen demanded.

"Um—Dhulaishta, dhulaishtami, dhulaishtaiyen," the captain recited. "Varaishta, varaishtami, varaishtaiyen. Kudjiishta—"

"Enough," Yadleen said, smiling for the first time, "you will make me think I am back with my tutor!" He looked at Gabrel. "It really is a lesson in the grammar of our language."

"I told you," Gabrel said, smiling back, and too relieved to remember the polite mode of addressing the Vakil in third person only.

"But it is also a strong magic, to capture these voices and imprison them in such a tiny thing."

"No magic," Gabrel said, "only the skills of my people. The Vakil *knows* we come from the stars; there are many things we can do which we are forbidden to reveal to the people of Kalapriya. The point is, this woman doesn't speak your language, and she is having to work just as hard at learning it as I did, or any other outlander. These stories of her special powers are tales to frighten children."

"And the weapons?"

"The Vakil may ask if any were found in our packs."

The captain was shaking his head before the Vakil even framed the question.

"The Vakil may remember that the Diplomatai are said to carry weapons concealed in their bodies," Indukanta Jagat put in.

"An assertion rather difficult to test without killing the subject," Yadleen commented.

"And one the Vakil already knows to be ridiculous," Gabrel said quickly, "since if we were in possession of such wonderful weapons, surely we should not have allowed ourselves to be captured and brought here like this!"

"At least have them searched more thoroughly," Jagat said.

Gabrel tried again to straighten his shoulders against the ropes that bound his arms. "Search me if you like," he said, "but an insult to this woman under my protection is an insult to the Barents Trading Society!"

Jagat shrugged. "If the Vakil is *afraid* of the Society, of course there is no more to be said."

His words raised a flush of anger on Yadleen's dark-ivory cheeks and Gabrel tensed. What if Calandra were in fact carrying secret weapons? He dared not ask her now.

"The Vakil of Dharampal fears neither the Barents Trading Society nor the upstart empire of Udara," Yadleen said after a moment's visible struggle to control his anger. "We will convene our council to consider this matter further. In the meantime, Captain Thanom, you shall escort the prisoners to a place where they can be kept in safety and all reasonable comfort."

"The cells of Dharampal's Stone House are comfort enough for such as these!" Jagat interrupted.

Yadleen turned an icy glance on the Udaran envoy. "Indukanta Jagat, if you think that Dharampal maintains prisons like those of Udara, your spies have much misinformed you. *We* have no need to confine so many of our subjects. Let me inform you of two things." He paused for so long that Jagat's face paled with the fear that he had gone too far.

"First," Yadleen said, "we have found a better use for the Stone House than the ancient Emperors who built it. Being of stone and quite solidly built, it makes an excellent granary; it can be kept almost free of rats. And second," he added as Jagat began to relax, "the last man to interrupt a Vakil of Dharampal upon his chair of state had his mouth closed by filling it with salt. That was, of course, in the time of my father of blessed memory," he went on, "but for some reason it has not been necessary to apply the penalty for many years."

"An envoy of Udara is not subject to the laws of Dharampal!" Jagat protested.

"No? But what, then, of these envoys of the Barents Trading Society?" Yadleen asked with brows slightly raised. "At one time, Indukanta Jagat, you were pleased to praise our even-handedness. Surely you would not have us treat these Barentsian envoys with any less courtesy than we have shown to your honored self." He glanced at Captain Thanom. "Escort them to the private house of my trusted councillor Harsajjan Bharat. They will not, of course, be permitted to leave the house while the council deliberates, but I would have them used with all possible courtesy short of giving them their freedom. Oh, and cut off those ropes. If we start tying up envoys from other states now, we just might get carried away and tie them *all* up."

By the time Maris got a chance to talk to Gabrel in reasonable privacy she was close to dying of curiosity. It clearly hadn't been safe to confer while he was—she supposed— talking for their lives in front of the ivory-skinned boy who carried himself like a great king in a historical holodrama. And even after they were untied, he had discouraged her from talking while the soldiers in red and gold escorted them to their new prison. If it *was* a prison? She didn't know what to make of the endless sprawling compound, with its big and little courtyards and balconies and three steps down and two steps up leading through a maze of rooms that seemed to have been designed one at a time by people with vastly differing sensibilities. And almost as soon as they got there they were separated. Gabrel seemed to understand why they were being led off in different directions and not to be worried about it, so she copied his manner of lofty unconcern.

She was surrounded by women who fluttered around her talking too quickly for her to catch more than an occasional word, all waving their hands from swathes of tissue-light shalin dyed in brilliant jewel colors until Maris felt as though she were being abducted by a flock of talkative butterflies. They touched her hair and skin lightly, as if to reassure themselves that she was human like them. The middle-aged woman who seemed to be in charge clucked with disapproval when her fingers caught in the snarls of Maris's tangled curls, and kept saying, *"Ghur, ghur!"*

At least that was one word Maris knew from her surreptitious ventures with the audio plugs. "Dirty, dirty, is it? Well, I'm sorry to inform you of this, but the washin' facilities in this wonderful country leave something to be . . ."

She stooped to pass under a low door curtained with layers of hanging tapestries, and came into a dark place glowing with banked fires and moist with aromatic steam.

" . . . desired," Maris finished with a longing look at the great cedar-lined sunken tub of steaming water that occupied the center of the room.

The women smiled at her and started taking off her clothes.

"I can do that for meself," Maris protested, but to no avail. She gave up, abandoned herself to events. After all, they all wanted the same thing: to get her clean.

Thoroughly, blissfully clean and totally relaxed, she corrected after an hour of their ministrations. There'd been hot steam and warm water and cold water, gentle scrubs with wads of bark that were just scratchy enough and that released a scented, soapy foam, oils and powders and massages and soft warm towels to wrap up in, more washing and combing and oiling for her hair, and finally, clean clothes in what seemed to be the style of the country—that was to say, soft loose trousers, an indecently tight upper garment, and a long pleated shalin with enough fabric in it to clothe a dozen people.

The butterfly ladies had a fine time trying to show her how to pleat the shalin into her sash so that it would stay up, and Maris had a bit of trouble getting the thing adjusted so that she could walk in it. They seemed to feel that a "proper" length was trailing an inch or so of fabric on the floor; the first step Maris took like that, she tripped on her own hem and almost fell. She tugged the fabric up above her sash to ankle height.

The middle-aged woman, whom Maris had privately christened "Boss Lady" promptly tugged it down again.

"I can't *walk* like that," Maris said. She searched her brain for some scraps of Kalapriyan. "*Sajja, meer sajja.*" That meant "much long." She pulled the pleats of the shalin up into her sash again.

"*Hai, hai, meer sajja,*" Boss Lady agreed, pulling the shalin down again.

"Much" wasn't getting her meaning across. How in the name of the God of Minor Fuckups did you say *"too* long"? Demons take it, she'd have to rely on sign language. Maris pulled the shalin up again, not quite as high as before, and said, *"Sajja?"* When Boss Lady reached for her, she skipped back, shaking her head. "Uh-uh. This here is plenty bunu *sajja* enough, get me?"

They compromised on a length hovering just below her ankles, which had the dubious virtue of leaving everybody dissatisfied; Maris felt constrained to take tiny, mincing steps, and Boss Lady clearly felt the occasional glimpses of bare toes verged on indecency.

"This," she announced as soon as she was back in a room with Gabrel, "is the *bunu* weirdest country! They don't want me to wear me good hiking boots, but they throw a fit if me toes show under this thing. And all the while their midriffs are bare as an egg and what's up top might as well be the same, for all the cover this thing gives." She tugged at the neckline of the thin, tight-fitting bodice that was supposed to preserve decency while the upper folds of the shalin floated around like butterfly wings.

"I've seen worse fashions," Gabrel said. His blue eyes were curiously light in his tanned face, as though some inner fire had been lit. "I won't complain if they concentrate on concealing the feet instead of . . . other areas."

Maris felt uncomfortably warm up top, even though her feet were still freezing from walking barefoot over floors of polished wood and stone. She curled up on one of the oversized cushions that furnished the room and wrapped the free end of her shalin around her shoulders. "So. Are we still in jail, or what? And what *happened* back there? I couldn't understand more'n one word in ten," she confessed.

Gabrel grinned at her; flash of white teeth against that tanned face, light sparking from blue eyes and gold in his hair . . . the man would cause a riot down in the levels on Tasman. Unfairly distracting, it was. "I know you couldn't follow the talk. That's partly what saved us. It seems the Udaran envoy has been filling the Vakil with terror-stories about the unearthly powers of Diplos and trying to convince him you're here to overthrow his throne. He relaxed considerably once I explained that you were no Diplo."

Maris felt her stomach sinking as if she'd just been dropped into free fall without warning. "You did *what*?"

"Oh, give it up," Gabrel said with a trace of impatience. "We haven't the luxury of playing games here. I know what you are and I can't afford to preserve your pride at the risk of my mission—and our lives."

Worse than free fall, Maris thought. She'd never wanted to throw up in zero-g, as some less fortunate Tasmans did. Right now, though . . .

"How—did you find out?" she managed through a mouth gone suddenly dry. *And are you going to send me back to Tasman?* No, he couldn't do that—not from here. She relaxed just a fraction.

"I've had my suspicions for some time," Gabrel said. "You just didn't seem old enough—or sure enough—or knowledgeable enough for a Diplo. And you were too open-minded. Diplos usually think they know everything *about* everything and wouldn't be caught dead listening to a local's information; as soon as you asked my opinion on the Kalapriyan situation I began to wonder."

And I thought I was being so clever, finding out enough from him to let me pass with the others. Maris shook her head at her own stupidity.

"Oh well. I never really thought I could get away with it," she said, as much for her benefit as his.

"You didn't have maps, your Kalapriyan was terrible, you just didn't have the prep a Diplo would require," Gabrel went on. "But what really clinched it was when I searched your pack—"

Maris let out a hiss of outrage before remembering that she wasn't in a position to *be* outraged.

"—and found the audio plugs of *Kalapriyan for Dummies*." Gabrel grinned unrepentantly. "You gave it a good try, Calandra, but that made the situation obvious."

"It did?" *Then why are you still calling me Calandra?*

"You might as well admit it, I've figured everything out. You haven't graduated yet, have you? You're still in training school. You haven't even had the surgery for the download implants. But Rezerval figured, it's only another complaint by that raving paranoiac Montoyasana, why waste a fully trained Diplo; we'll send out a trainee and let her get some practice and make it look like we're taking

Montoyasana seriously. Put you in a hell of a spot, didn't it?"

Maris slowly let out her breath. "You—could say that." What Johnivans had taught her was still true, even if Johnivans himself was a lying treacherous SOB. *If you get caught out, say as little as possible. Let people make up their own stories about who you are and what you're doing off your proper level.* Would she be in more trouble, or less, if she told him how far off his guesses were? Probably more. Gabrel wouldn't be pleased to find out he hadn't been that clever after all, and he probably would be furious to learn he'd been wasting Barents-style courtesy and chivalry on some ragamuffin from a Tasman smuggler's gang.

He might be even more furious, later on, if he found out she was *still* lying.

It was too dangerous. Once he found out the truth he'd probably despise her.

Eventually he'd despise her anyway. Was it so bad to let him believe his own story for a little longer? To have him treating her like a person who deserved courtesy and respect? She'd probably never get that again. She wanted just a little more of it.

They were in a dangerous situation, in foreign territory, and *he* deserved to know the exact truth of it.

What difference did it make? He wouldn't be expecting her to do any magical Diplo-type stunts now, either way.

Gabrel sat down beside her; his weight squashed the cushion down so that she slid against him, feeling the warmth and strength of his body. "What are you looking so worried about?"

"What happens next," Maris said truthfully.

She meant, what *she* did next, but Gabrel took it as a question for him and that let her off the hook for a while, anyway.

"Well, we're not exactly in jail," Gabrel said. "But we're not exactly free to go either. I guess it's a kind of house arrest—but the house belongs to my friend Harsajjan Bharat. We'll be comfortable enough, and at the moment Yadleen—that's the Vakil—seems to be considerably more pissed off at the Udaran envoy than he is at us."

He stretched his long legs out and leaned back into the cushion, hands behind his head. To avoid rolling onto his chest, Maris edged back until she was perched insecurely on the very edge of the mattress-sized cushion.

"On the other hand," he went on, "the Udaran envoy seems to think we ought to be executed out of hand."

"How can you be so calm about it?"

"Oh, Yadleen isn't going to have us killed; he can't afford to be seen as giving in to Udaran demands. Half his council would resign in protest."

"That makes me feel *so* safe. Can't we get out of here? We're not, like, under guard or anything, right?"

"The other half of the council is pro-Udara. *They'd* resign in protest."

"That," Maris said tartly, "strikes me as Yadleen's problem, not ours."

Gabrel sighed. "Calandra, by the time you graduate from Diplo School, you'll hopefully understand a little more about not upsetting the balance of power in a region. It will be much easier to carry out our mission if we leave Dharampal with the Vakil's blessing. It will also make the Udarans think twice about assassinating us on the road. Unless," he added, his face falling, "they are ready to attack Dharampal. I hadn't thought about that . . . Yadleen letting us go, or even seeming to collude in our escape, would make an excellent *casus belli*."

"Cassus belleye," Maris repeated. "And what might that be when it's at home, a Kalapriyan dessert? Thanks very much, but I don't want to be served up on the Bashir of Udara's dinner table. *I* vote we leave here, quietly, now."

"Don't you understand *anything* about diplomacy? That would be the worst possible—"

Gabrel broke off as the gold-brocaded hangings over the door stirred. A middle-aged Kalapriyan man in tunic and trousers as stiffly brocaded as the hangings parted the curtains. He looked tired.

"Eskelinen! I had hoped to have more time to spend with you. I am sorry to be inhospitable, but you must leave here, quietly, at once," Harsajjan Bharat announced.

Maris just managed not to say "I told you so," when Gabrel translated for her. She listened attentively while Gabrel and his Dharampal friend talked, and found that now she wasn't tied up and scared out of her wits it was a lot easier to catch bits of the conversation. Especially since she knew pretty much what it had to be about. Harsajjan Bharat thought the Udaran envoy was going to arrange to have them assassinated tonight, and he didn't want that to happen. She would have felt more grateful if it hadn't seemed to her that his main concern was the way such an event would affect the honor of his house. Oh well, maybe that wasn't true; it could be due to her not understanding court Kalapriyan real well. In any case, it appeared that they were going to get their traveling clothes and their packs back and that some of Harsajjan's people were going to smuggle them out to . . . there her limited Kalapriyan vocabulary gave out, because what came next wasn't what she was expecting. She'd thought he would say that his guides would set them on the way to Udara. Instead there was excited talk about some other place that she'd never heard of.

When Harsajjan finally left, she pounced on Gabrel for explanations and details. "All right, I got that part," she cut him off when he started to translate the whole conversation word for word. "He wants us out of here so we don't get killed in his house. What I didn't get is where we're *going* from here. Not into Udara, I got that much, but why? Too dangerous?" Not going to Udara seemed like an excellent idea to her . . . but she sure didn't have any better ideas. Returning to Valentin would probably not work out real well; obviously she wasn't keeping up the Diplo act well enough to fool anybody for long. If Dharampal hadn't suffered from the minor defect of being, apparently, full of Udaran assassins, she thought she could have been happy to stay right here as an involuntary guest of Harsajjan Bharat. Hot baths and clean clothes and regular meals and not even having to steal anything to justify her existence—sounded pretty good.

The likelihood of getting stabbed, beheaded, poisoned, or dismembered in the night was a definite drawback to that arrangement, though.

"Where we're going may not be any safer than Udara," Gabrel said now, "and it'll definitely be a harder journey."

Maris sighed. "More scrambling up forty-five-degree slope trails designed for goats, like we did to get here?"

"Oh, much worse than that. If this world were ever opened to tourism, rock jockeys from all over the galaxy would be coming here to climb the High Jagirs." He sounded obnoxiously cheerful at the prospect.

"Let me guess," Maris said, "rock climbing is one of your hobbies."

"How did you know?"

"Diplo intuition!" she snapped. "And in case you were wondering, mountaineering is *not* among my favorite sports."

Gabrel shook his head. "Rezerval must have known what the interior of Kalapriya is like. Why didn't they send somebody who could—oh, well, I suppose they only expected you to poke around Valentin for a while and then report back that Montoyasana was raising a fuss about nothing as usual." His sudden smile warmed Maris down to her freezing toes. "You have done much more than Rezerval could possibly have expected of you. I hadn't thought even a fully trained and experienced Diplo would be willing to trek into the Jagirs, much less a kid who hasn't even finished the course work or had the surgeries yet." He looked thoughtful. "That's another thing that made me wonder about you. You're not thirty, Calandra. Nowhere near. How old are you really?"

"Does it matter?" Maris fenced. Give Gabrel time and he'd probably tell her how old *he* thought she was, then all she'd have to do is agree.

"Let's see, Diplo School doesn't take candidates under eighteen, and they wouldn't have let a first- or second-year student go out alone; you must be almost through with the classes and on a waiting list for surgery. So, twenty-three, twenty-four, something like that?"

"Something like that," Maris agreed. Sounded a lot better than the truth, although she did wonder—briefly—how Gabrel would react to that. *I'm almost seventeen . . . I think.* Definitely not the right thing to say at this point. She kept her mouth shut and let him go on explaining their immediate plans.

Apparently Harsajjan Bharat meant to smuggle them out of his compound as soon as it was dark, guiding them out of Dharamvai to meet a messenger from the Udaran resistance.

"There's a resistance movement?"

"Even the Bashir of Udara hasn't managed to kill *everybody* who disagrees with his methods."

This messenger knew a Diplo was being sent to investigate the allegations of illegal weapons trading, and according to him, the place to look was not in Udara proper but in a remote complex of caves in the former state of Thamboon. There, he had told Harsajjan, the outlanders would find evidence and explanation of all that was going on.

"Or a quick death," Maris suggested. "How do we know we can trust this guy?"

"We don't," Gabrel admitted. "But Harsajjan seems to think he's genuine . . . and anyway, you have a better idea?"

Maris shook her head.

"Well then. Fortunately, they haven't washed our traveling clothes yet, so we can put them right back on."

Mixed blessing, Maris thought. All that bathing and massaging and here she was going to smell like a goat again after ten minutes in that filthy outfit. On the other hand, it would be nice to be able to walk again.

"And, Calandra . . ."

It took Maris a moment to remember that Gabrel still didn't know her true name. "Yes?"

"There's no need to let this Chulayen Vajjadara, the Udaran resistance contact, know you're not yet a fully trained Diplo. It might shake his confidence in us."

"Understood," Maris murmured.

She did wish, irrationally, that Gabrel would call her by her own name just once. But obviously this was no time to explain just how unlike a fully trained Diplo she really was, and he was too sharp for her to think she could confess to the one lie without getting into the whole tangle.

Besides, she reminded herself, he wouldn't like or respect Maris Nobody from the slums of Tasman. It was "Calandra Vissi" he was being nice to.

Chapter Fifteen

Udara on Kalapriya

Lorum van Vechten prodded his patient's bandage-swathed head gingerly. Everything *seemed* all right. Just to be on the safe side, though, he supposed he had better change the dressings. At least, he told himself as he unwrapped the strips of organic fabric, at least this wasn't one of those truly disgusting wounds that people in primitive areas tended to get. No great gaping slashes just begging for infection to set in; just the neat line of stitches holding the skin together over the hole he'd opened in the skull. And that wasn't a very *big* hole; just enough to let him insert a syringe full of fresh 'mats in solution.

The physical results of the surgery were healing well enough. He contemplated sniffing the wound for a hint of gangrene, then decided that was really *too* gross, and besides, the skin tone was good and it looked clean enough. He settled for swabbing the shaved head with madira, which was foul stuff to drink but sufficiently alcoholic to be a reasonable disinfectant, and wrapping a somewhat lighter turban of fresh bandages over the old man's head. Gods, he didn't even have plasti-stik—in a decent hospital, this whole unwieldy contraption could have been replaced by a squirt of Disinfecto and a square of plasti-stik gauze right over the site of the incision! Primitives!

"Well, boy?" Pundarik Zahin demanded in his usual testy tones. "How much longer do I have to look like a damned turbanned Rohini fetish t-talker?" His right hand twitched; the man must be even more impatient than usual.

"Only a few more days, sir," Lorum promised.

"You've been saying that for almost a week now."

"In my medical judgment," Lorum said stiffly, "the site of the incision should remain covered until healing is complete. The risk of infection—"

Pundarik Zahin snorted. "I've had *incisions* aplenty in my fighting days, boy. Back when the Bashir was making Udara, making a *state* out of a collection of miserable hill t-towns— you think everybody understood his vision, went along peacefully? Hah! One damned rebel laid my leg open from hip to knee, and if I'd taken to my bed to pour strong wine over the slash and wrap myself in bandages, why, Shatha t-town wouldn't be part of Udara now—there might not *be* a Greater Udara! None of my wounds ever festered. You know why? Because I've got clean flesh, boy! Clean flesh and a dove every t-torch festival to Red Radhana, the warriors' lady; that'll do more than all your outlander magics." His right knee jumped suddenly under the blanket that covered both withered legs. "Look at that! Mention Red Radhana and she sends a sign of healing!"

"Doubtless, sir," Lorum van Vechten said woodenly. Dealing with General Zahin reminded him of what he'd *really* hated about studying under Dr. Hirvonen. The fear of screwing up during a surgery was bad enough, but even worse was her insistence that he follow up personally on the recuperation of each and every patient. The damned woman didn't seem to understand that the whole point of specializing in neurosurgery was that you didn't have to deal with patients at all, just with the immobile head in front of you on the operating table. Once the head regained consciousness and began talking again, you were supposed to be able to leave it to the nurses and go on to another interesting problem.

Patients were definitely the downside of a medical career, just as natives were the problem with being the Barents Resident in Udara. If only someone would devise a 'mat modification that would make people's brains work *properly*, so that they recognized and respected his genius and *let him alone . . .*

Higher up the mountain, in the palace that overlooked all of Puvaathi, the Bashir's brain was working far from properly by Lorum van Vechten's standards. In fact, it was about to boil over with rage and frustration.

"What do you mean, the envoys escaped?" he bellowed at the man standing stiffly before him. The red and golden hangings of his audience chamber vibrated as he pounded his fist on the low table in front of him. The concubine Khati, who always attended him, dressed like a festival-day idol in gold-embroidered red silk, shrank back against the folds of the hangings as if she hoped to disappear among them.

Indukanta Jagat bowed stiffly. "Doubtless my lord the Bashir will wish to punish the Vakil of Dharampal for his insolence in letting the prisoners go."

"I thought you said they escaped."

Jagat lifted his shoulders slightly. "That they are gone is certain. Whether it was with or without the connivance of young Yadleen is not so certain; I can only say that he refused to have the Minister responsible for their house arrest publicly impaled when I suggested the suitability of some such measure, claiming the escape was no more Harsajjan Bharat's fault than it was his own. Whether he had the insolence to contermand my lord's expressed wishes, or was simply incompetent to keep two outlanders under control, hardly matters; in either case he is clearly not fit to rule a country on our borders. In my opinion, we should take over the state before internal unrest turns it into an anarchic threat—"

"Your opinion? *Your opinion?* Hah! And in your opinion, Indukanta Jagat, which are *you*—corrupt or merely incompetent? You should have assassinated those envoys on their first night under house arrest."

"I had arrangements to do exactly that," Jagat protested, "but when my men reached the Bharat compound, the envoys were no longer there."

"So which was it? Were you too incompetent to post a guard . . . or were you in a conspiracy with the Vakil to thwart my wishes? It seems to me that Harsajjan Bharat is not the only one in this affair who has earned a sharp stake to rest upon."

"My lord!" Jagat paled. "My lord the Bashir will recall that it was I who brought the first news of these outlander envoys, I who warned him of their supernatural powers and evil intentions."

"Perhaps you did so only to put yourself in the perfect position for seeing that they went about their way unmolested. What, after all, has been the result of your meddling? They were brought to Dharampal—very well; they had to pass that way in any case. Now, instead of traveling openly on from Dharampal, where we could have had them killed on the road, they have been forewarned of their danger. Now they are traveling by secret ways, so secretly and cautiously that even you and your men could not find them at any of the passes into Udara—*or so you say.*" The Bashir invested those last four words with a menace that sent Jagat to his knees, babbling pleas for mercy.

"Remove this scum," the Bashir said to the two guards who stood immobile, arms folded, on either side of the door.

Before they could lay hands on him, Jagat had flung himself forward to grasp the concubine's knees. "In the name of love and pity, let my lord forgive my incompetence! Let my lands and houses be given over to the state for the glory of Greater Udara, only let me remain to serve the Bashir—"

"As you served me in Dharampal?" The Bashir laughed loudly, his voice cracking at the end. "The estates of a traitor are forfeit to the Bashir in any case. Take him!"

The guards grasped Jagat under the arms and lifted him. A portion of Khati's brocaded shalin tore away in his desperately grasping hands. She reached forward, tears in her eyes. "My lord, have mercy!"

"You dare to speak in my audience chamber?" The Bashir whirled and turned his wrath on her. "By Red Radhana, I should have you stripped and impaled together with this traitor!" He laughed again, a high-pitched, nervous laugh, as she shrank back among the hangings. "No, not yet. A pity to ruin such a lovely body. I shall just give you a little reminder to show more respect."

Khati curled on the floor, arms wrapped around her head,

as the Bashir kicked her. She gasped once or twice when his foot found old bruises, but managed to keep from crying; tears excited the Bashir in dangerous ways.

It could have been worse, she repeated to herself over and over, trying to make of the words a mantra that would take her mind off the repeated blows. *It could have been worse.* On the Bashir's whim she could have been dragged away with Indukanta Jagat to be impaled, or held down by the guards while he flogged the flesh from her bones. Someday, when he ceased to desire her, that would happen. If he guessed at her part in warning and diverting the outlanders, it would certainly happen. For now . . . he would probably want to use her as soon as he had tired of kicking and hitting. *Worse happens every day to some poor Rohini who attracts the wrong sort of attention.*

"My lord Bashir!" It was one of the guards who had dragged poor Jagat out; what was he doing back here so soon? "My lord must come . . . must see . . ."

"Must?" the Bashir repeated sharply.

"The Bashir would wish to see what is in the skies," the guard corrected himself. "There is a flying dragon hovering over the palace!"

"Have you been at the madira?"

"No, truly, my lord!" The guard prostrated himself. Khati relaxed slightly as the Bashir's attention was removed from her, and concentrated on taking slow, deep healing breaths. She was one dull ache all over, but there were none of the sharp flares of pain that usually came with a broken bone. It really hadn't been so bad . . . this time. The Light was with her.

"I think it is a flying dragon, but of a kind that I have not seen before—I mean, not that I've ever actually *seen* one, but you know, my lord, the pictures in the temple— anyway, it is smaller than I thought it would be, and much more shiny. I suppose it would be hard to paint the light flashing off it, that's part of the problem . . ."

The Bashir stepped over the prostrate, babbling guard and strode down the hall. The guard's terrified ramblings died away. After a moment both he and Khati raised their heads. It was Vedya, she saw. Part Rohini, though that was a carefully kept secret, but she thought he had sometimes tried unobtrusively to help her. "If you made that up to distract him from beating me," she whispered, "you'd better start running *now*."

Vedya shook his head. "I'm not that smart—or that brave," he confessed. "Really, it is a flying dragon. Come and see." He offered a hand to help Khati up, and she compressed her lips to keep from whimpering at the pain of movement.

"He is a madman and I am ashamed to be in his service," Vedya said under his breath as he saw what it cost Khati to get to her feet.

"It's not that bad," Khati assured him. "Truly." She was about to say *I've had worse*, but this was not the time to start trying to recruit Vedya to their cause. Besides, she wanted to see the dragon in the sky!

"It's landed," Vedya said, unnecessarily, as they reached the crowd at the front of the palace. Khati swallowed her disappointment and stood on tiptoe, trying to see over all those tall Rudhrani. Maybe the dragon had been sent by the gods to destroy the Bashir in its flaming breath.

"Will it hurt you if I set you on that?" Vedya asked, seeing her struggles to see through the crowd and indicating a pillar that rose from a low, squared-off base.

"No," Khati lied, and managed not to gasp when Vedya's hands closed round her bruised waist and lifted her up to the base of the pillar. It was worth it; from here she could see everything in the square.

"It doesn't look like I thought it would," she said with some disappointment. The dragon glittered brightly in the sun, that much was true. But otherwise it looked . . . well, rather small, for a dragon, and boring. Its hide was smooth, not scaly, and instead of coruscating with brilliant flashes of color it seemed to be a dull grey all over except for some patterns in blue along its flanks. And where were its wings?

The dragon's side opened and two demons with glittering skin stepped out. No, they were only outlanders in some strange costume, Khati realized with even more disappointment. One was tall and unnaturally fair-haired, like the Barents Resident; the other was just an ordinary person, rather pale, but of normal height and with curly dark hair like Khati's own.

"It's not a dragon," she said sadly. "It's just a flying box."

"Don't be silly," Vedya said. "Have you ever seen a box fly through the air?"

"No, but I've never seen a dragon do that either," Khati pointed out. "Hush! I want to hear what they're saying."

The small outlander was doing all the talking, and maybe she wasn't an outlander at all, because she spoke as well as any Udaran—quite unlike the strongly accented, simple words that Lorum van Vechten used. She didn't get a chance to say much, though, barely started introducing herself before the Bashir interrupted with a command to his guards. Khati saw the telltale glitter of the Bashir's magic nets and sighed with grief. She *had* hoped to see more of the outlanders before they were destroyed. But nobody ever survived the magic weapons that Lorum van Vechten had given the Bashir. They would be caught immobile in nets of light, and hacked to bits by ordinary unmagical swords, and if she had any sense she would get out of here before it started, but the crowd of palace servitors was too close around her and she couldn't see Vedya, he had been pushed away by the curious crowd, all *right* then, at least close her eyes so she didn't have to see . . . or would it be worse, hearing and not seeing? Khati had not quite decided when the small outlander's hand flicked outward, for all the world as if she were sowing seed on a fresh-plowed field. But instead of seed, what fell from her hand was a kind of dark emptiness that consumed the flickering lights of the Bashir's nets.

"Demons," sighed a clerk standing by her pillar.

"*Outlanders*," Khati corrected scornfully. It made perfect sense; why hadn't she seen it coming? The Bashir's magic weapons came from the outlanders, didn't they? *Of course* they hadn't sold him their strongest magics; they kept those for themselves. She should have foreseen it.

So should the Bashir. He'd been used for too long to winning too easily, Khati thought as she saw him foaming with impotent rage. He ordered his guards to strike, but invisible walls around the outlander women caught and held their swords.

"The penalty for attacking a Diplomat of Rezerval is stasis," the small woman remarked, in a pleasant tone that somehow carried quite clearly through the square and up the palace steps, more clearly than if she had shouted. "We are willing to assume that the Bashir was surprised by our visit and gave his orders before he had identified us as peaceful emissaries." She paused, one dark eyebrow arched, and waited—quite clearly waited—for the Bashir to back down.

Which he did, stumbling and stuttering.

Khati thought she had never enjoyed anything so much in all her sixteen years.

But when the outlander envoys demanded a private meeting with the Bashir and the Barents Resident, and suggested that the onlookers go on about their business, she regretfully melted in with the crowd and slipped away to one of her secret hiding places in the palace. This would definitely not be a good time to catch the Bashir's eye; if he had been looking for somebody to beat after Indukanta Jagat's unwelcome news, he would be looking for somebody to *kill* after being publicly humiliated by the envoys he had failed to assassinate in time. And this time he might not remember how much he enjoyed Khati's body in time to prevent his ordering her impaled on a stake beside Jagat.

If she had any sense, she would disappear from the palace now and take refuge with her own people. Meer Madee would not expect her to stay here and spy on the Bashir any longer, not now; she had always warned Khati to run when it started feeling too dangerous.

But she *did* want to know what would happen at this meeting.

And why Indukanta Jagat's information had been wrong. He had clearly said the Diplo was being escorted by a man, a soldier of the Barents army.

And most of all, she wanted to know whether Chulayen had intercepted the Diplo and her escort, and if so, why had they come on into Udara instead of going with him to Thamboon?

Chapter Sixteen

Udara on Kalapriya

"That," Annemari said with a long sigh, "was not *quite* the most frustrating meeting I've sat through in the last twenty years. But it came close."

After the long and extremely formal diplomatic discussion, they had been ushered to what must be the most luxurious guest quarters in the Bashir's palace. No indoor plumbing, Annemari noted, but lots of tapestries and cushions to soften the raw cedar walls and packed-earth floor, and basins of beaten metal for washing in. The ubiquitous red and gold that the Bashir favored made her eyes hurt after a while, especially the clashing of soft vegetable reds with imported chemical dyes from Valentin. And the gold embroidery made the cushions rather scratchy. Still, it did seem they were being treated with appropriate respect. For what that was worth.

"They're being very polite," Calandra agreed, "and very good at not telling us anything. Do you believe the Bashir's story about where his prohibited weapons came from?"

"A Barentsian fugitive, under sentence of death in Valentin, fleeing inland and buying his safety in Udara with a pack full of tanglers and nerve dazers? And now conveniently dead?" Annemari's laugh cracked a little. "All very convenient, isn't it? I especially liked the part about the Bashir being shocked—*shocked*! to hear that the weaponry is seriously illegal, being far beyond the technology level approved for Kalapriya."

"Umm." Calandra rolled over on the pile of embroidered cushions that served as both chair and bed, and nibbled the end of one curly frond of hair. "I notice you didn't point out that Lorum van Vechten had to have known the weaponry was pro-tech."

"Why bother? I'm sure their story will be that he had no idea the Bashir was using tanglers; he's the Resident, not an arms master. He'll claim he thought Udara was extending its territory by legitimate means, diplomacy and traditional warfare, and none of his business to interfere. And if we question that, he'll point out that nobody in Valentin questioned the speed of the Udaran conquests either."

"I rather suspect Valentin doesn't know much about what goes on among the hill tribes," Calandra said. "Remember, communications outside the coastal enclaves are limited to native technology. They've got some sort of primitive system of signaling by electric wires in the coastal plain—"

"That's not pro-tech?"

"Hand-cranked generators," Calandra explained, "and it was actually a Kalapriyan who invented the concept. They get wire for the electrographs through the Barents Trading Society, but that was approved because it isn't different in kind from the wire they can hand-draw through a plate, just smoother and a whole lot cheaper."

"It must be nice to have everything there is to know about Kalapriya, including the language, downloaded onto a memory chip inside your head," Annemari said with a trace of envy.

Calandra put one hand to her temple, where the ache came after a download. She didn't know if that was where the chip was located or whether some confusion of nerves made it hurt there instead of in the socket at the back of her neck; she just knew that absorbing a mass of information in seconds usually cost her a few days of headache. If she was lucky. Really heavy downloads meant migraines with flashing lights instead of ordinary headaches; she was lucky that there hadn't been all that much information this time.

Or not, depending on how you looked at it.

"Not everything there is to know," she corrected Annemari, "just everything Rezerval knows. And I have a feeling there's a *lot* about this world that isn't in Federation databases." She sighed. "It may have been a mistake to let them find out I speak Kalapriyan; we might learn a lot more by eavesdropping than in formal meetings."

"Seeing that our alternative would have been depending on Lorum van Vechten as a translator," Annemari said drily, "I think it's an exceedingly good thing you do speak Kalapriyan." A flicker of movement on the tapestried wall caught her attention; was it just light from the water in a nearby basin reflecting off the golden threads? She was so tired that all her surroundings seemed a mystery of moving lights and shadows.

"Yes, but I might have learned a lot by listening to how he translated you."

"And he almost certainly would *not* have made it clear to the Bashir how important a Diplo is, and how many people—not just in Valentin, but on Rezerval!—know exactly where we were going, and how much trouble it would make for the Bashir if he had us quietly assassinated," Annemari pointed out. The tapestry was definitely trembling; and there was no wind blowing through the crude windows in the outer wall. "So you would've had to step in and use your Kalapriyan anyway, to make sure he understood that it would be a really, really bad idea to make us disappear. I'm sorry, Calandra, but eavesdropping really never was an option."

She threw herself flat across the layers of carpet and grabbed a handful of stiff brocaded wall hanging, and something else inside the hangings, something firm and yet yielding like flesh, something that squeaked in distress as she yanked with all her force and brought down a whole wall of tapestries over a small human figure.

" . . . for us, anyway," Annemari finished, slightly out of breath. Years of sitting behind a desk and tapping her fingers on a vid screen were no training for wrestling with unseen adversaries. She sat on a portion of the eavesdropper to keep it from getting away while Calandra excavated the rest from the heap of tapestries.

"It's a little girl!" Annemari exclaimed in surprise when

the tapestries were finally separated from the red and gold
organic fabrics of the child's clothes.

"What are you doing here?" Calandra demanded in harsh
Kalapriyan. *"Khush? Mal sooree, bai-chha!"*

The girl shook her head frantically, long dark plaits
whipping back and forth. *"La soree! La! Ebh-bashir
dhulaishtaiyen . . ."*

Calandra listened for a moment to the flood of Kalapriyan, inserted a sharp question and got back more
questions in response. Annemari chewed her left thumb-
nail and muttered, "I will not interrupt, I will *not* interrupt, what the *hell* is going on here, I *will not* interrupt,"
under her breath until the colloquy was finished.

"Well?" she demanded when both Calandra and their
eavesdropper at last seemed to be through talking.

Calandra sighed and pressed one hand to her forehead.
Making such heavy use of the language implants always
made her temples throb. The medtechs on Rezerval claimed
a slight adjustment could fix that little problem . . . but then,
they'd also described the initial surgery as "minor."

"The girl's Rohini—oh, we never went into that, did we?
The Kalapriyans think they belong to two distinct races,
although DNA analyses don't support that belief. Castes,
maybe; races, no. The Rohini tend to be smaller, though,
and darker-skinned than the Rudhrani, and the farther away
from the coast, the more the natives make of the distinction. The Trading Society doesn't recognize any distinction
in law, and that seems to be having a good influence on
the coastal states, but up here in the hills the Rohini are
practically slaves. In Udara, anyway. Rudhrani run the
government, command the army, have all the good jobs.
There was an independent Rohini state—Thamboon—but the
Bashir conquered it recently."

"Please tell me," Annemari said in a voice that could have
chipped ice, "that you and this child have not been discuss-
ing comparative sociology and the history of Kalapriya for
the last ten minutes!"

"Hold on. It's relevant. The thing is, evidently the Bashir
and his buddies have been rather overdoing the Rudhrani-
superiority thing. That, plus a nasty habit of secretly
assassinating political opponents, plus the way he's been
taking over neighboring states recently—it's a recipe for

revolution, Annemari. And this young woman is one of our revolutionaries."

"In the Bashir's palace? Wearing his colors?"

Calandra sighed. "Annemari, you may not have the Rezerval data on Kalapriya packed into your head, but you *did* study history, no? Or were you too busy with your computing and engineering classes to pick up even the basics of historic political structures and their consequences? One thing tyrants do—male tyrants, mostly, although there were some odd stories about one of the Russian empresses of Old Earth—they become sexual predators. This girl—her name's Khati—was kidnapped from one of the Rohini slums down the mountain by a Rudhrani palace guard who thought she might be a nice present for the Bashir. Now she's his favorite mistress and the palace guard has become the principal assistant to the Minister for Loyalty, which is the Bashir's secret political police."

"And she wants us to help her escape?"

Calandra rolled her eyes. "Annemari, she could 'escape' anytime just by walking back down the mountain. The Bashir's personal guards would just go out and pick up some more pretty girls for him to play with. She's stayed because her position gives her lots of chances to spy on the Bashir and his council, and she passes on the information she gets to her brother, who just happens to be in the underground resistance movement. For which, I might mention, she will be tortured to death if any of the Rudhrani in the palace catch her. Annemari, she didn't come seeking *our* help; she came to offer *hers*. There were a few little misunderstandings to clear up first, but I think we've got it worked out now. For starters, she was expecting us . . . sort of."

"What do you mean, sort of? And how *could* she be expecting us? I didn't even file a flight plan out of Valentin." As a department head from Rezerval, Annemari had used her authority to commandeer a flitter without explanation or discussion of her travel plans. She and Calandra had decided that with no way to tell which members of the Barents Trading Society were involved in the bacteriomat black market, they would do best to get out of the city before anybody figured out what they were doing there . . . and leaving behind as little information as possible about what they intended to do next.

"Apparently it has been the gossip of the bazaars for some weeks that a Diplo was coming into the hills, escorted by an officer of the Society's private army," Calandra explained. "Now *I* can't explain how they knew we were coming here before we knew, unless the native fortune-tellers have some technology that *they* have been keeping from *us*, but—"

"The other Calandra," Annemari said slowly.

"The who?"

"Remember, I told you in the clinic? When you dropped out of contact, Calandra, I went looking for you."

"Yes, yes, I know. And you found 'Thecla Partheni' traveling from Tasman back to Rezerval, to the Cassilis Clinic."

"That was what the travel records showed," Annemari agreed. "But I had also asked Evert Cornelis to make some private enquiries; he has an aunt, or something, whose husband is fairly high up in the Barents Trading Society. And *she* told Evert that Calandra Vissi had arrived in Valentin and made quite a social splash—something about a banquet and a ball in her honor. And the ball was *after* you, as Thecla Partheni, had taken passage from Tasman to Rezerval. At the time I couldn't understand it—and once I found you, and you confirmed that you hadn't set foot on Kalapriya, I thought it must be some silly misunderstanding. Because nobody else could be traveling as you. Could they?"

Calandra shrugged. "They couldn't use my papers or travel chits, because they wouldn't pass the routine retinal and DNA scans . . . but Valentin and the other Society enclaves along the coast try to keep the technology interface with the natives as small as possible, to reduce the chances of accidental cultural contamination. We never left the spaceport area, so you wouldn't have seen what the rest of Valentin is like. But supposedly there are only a few well-guarded Society facilities outside the port that have any nonnative technology at all. The Trading Society families make rather a fetish of living under primitive conditions— you know, no climate control, wearing nothing but organics, using the local beasts to pull wheeled transporters, all that sort of thing. They claim it's to reduce the chances of cultural contamination, but by now I gather it's developed into a sort of inverted snobbery—they feel superior to most Galactics because they *can* put up with the hardships of life on Kalapriya. So if somebody got outside the spaceport area and then claimed to be me, yes, she might well get away with it; they certainly wouldn't run a retinal scanner over her, anyway . . ." Her voice trailed off and she frowned with concentration.

Annemari touched the neckline of her intellitunic. The fabric softened and draped lower as if she'd been tugging at it from discomfort. "You're telling me that we person-ally have just introduced more cultural contamination than the entire Barents Trading Society has committed on Kalapriya in the last four generations?"

"We knew that would happen when we took a flitter to get here as fast as possible," Calandra pointed out. "Any-way, you're not responsible for the tanglers and the other pro-tech weaponry the Bashir has been buying. So I wouldn't feel *too* guilty. Seems to me this world has been well and truly technologically contaminated already. I don't think smart fabrics, or even flitters, are going to mess up the culture more than a hill-country megalomaniac armed with military surplus galactic weaponry. What interests me is . . ."

"Yes?"

"You didn't tell anyone on Rezerval where I was going, did you?"

"No. I wanted to get some *information* before I made it official." Annemari made a helpless gesture. "Instead, all I'm getting is more and more confusion."

"Then the only people who knew my name and desti-nation," Calandra said, as if thinking aloud, "were the Tasman underworld gang who captured me. So they're the only people who could even have *thought* to impersonate me on Kalapriya. And the one thing we know for sure about them is that they're smuggling 'mats off Kalapriya. So they're probably smuggling pro-tech weaponry the other way."

"Somebody in the Barents Trading Society has to be involved too," Annemari reminded her. "Probably several people."

"Yes, but nobody in the Society could impersonate me; it's a small clannish group and everybody knows everybody else. Don't you see, Annemari, this fake Diplo has to be one of the Tasman gang! And the officer who's escorting her is either part of the smuggling group, or in danger of his life. Because she has to be coming here to cover or destroy evidence; why else would they risk such an impersonation?"

The girl Khati touched Calandra's hand and whispered something.

"Hai, hai," Calandra said, nodding absently. Then she stopped and paid attention to Khati's increasingly urgent whispers, only saying "Hai" or "Vedya" at intervals.

"Khati thinks we should get out of here," she told Annemari. "Her friend in the Resistance was sent to guide the other 'Calandra' to some place called the Jurgan Caves, in what used to be Thamboon, where she would find evidence of the Bashir's bacteriomat smuggling. Khati says the Bashir shut down everything in Udara when the gossip about the envoys was heard and if we stay here we won't find anything."

"I wouldn't call tanglers exactly 'nothing.' "

"No, but we do want to tie it in with the 'mat smuggling, don't we? And if the others get there first they may destroy the evidence. Why else would one of the Tasman gang team up with a Barents Trading Society officer to trek upcountry? And I think Khati had better come with us. The Bashir is bound to find out she came to our quarters, and once we leave her life won't be worth a Kalapriyan tul." Calandra spoke to Khati again in Kalapriyan. The girl shook her head at first, then as Calandra said something else she bowed low, almost prostrating herself.

"She wanted us to pick up somebody else from her group who's made pilgrimage to these caves, to act as a guide," Calandra explained to Annemari. "I told her it's all right, that I have the location of the caves in my head. Of course I can't explain implants and download chips. So—well, it seems that the caves are holy to some religious sect that's mixed up with the resistance—she seems to think *I'm* holy by extension." Calandra shook her head. "I've been called a lot of things in my career, but being a minor goddess of the Inner Light Way is definitely a first."

"Let's hope," Annemari said, "her faith in you is sufficient to keep her from going hysterical on her first trip in a flitter, O blessed lady of the Inner Light Way."

Chapter Seventeen

Somewhere between Dharampal and Thamboon on Kalapriya

The morning sunlight flashed off the High Jagirs, turning their snow-covered peaks into a fantasia of gold and crystal. Below, the shadows covered a world of rocky cliffs and deep green forest; above, there was nothing but an endless blue so pale and thin that it made Maris even colder to look up at it. As Gabrel sighed with satisfaction at the vista opening before them, she reflected that it would probably be *hours* before any of that sunshine reached the hillside where they were making their way up something that might be laughingly referred to as a path. The disadvantages of dirtside living never ceased to amaze her; imagine having to wait for hours just to get the lights turned on!

"There's Bald Wizard," Gabrel pointed out a slightly rounded peak to the right side of the range, "and Old Snow Lady beside him." Maris supposed that the double cones of the second mountain's outline made the reason for the name obvious enough. If you thought like a man.

"And *there*," he said with a reverence that Maris found intensely irritating, "there is Ayodhana herself." He indicated a distant peak that dwarfed the others into mere foothills.

"If we have to walk all the way to the top of that mountain, we'll maybe get there some time next century," Maris grumbled. "Might as well go back to Valentin now." Valentin had been looking better and better to her during the long hours of night climbing. She had a blister on her right heel, and she felt as filthy as she had before that lovely bath in Harsajjan Bharat's house, and there were permanent wires of pain running from her feet up through her hips—and for what? All that walking to get them into the middle of nowhere? Valentin might be primitive, but it had houses and food stalls and places to sleep that didn't have sharp rocks sticking into your hip bone.

"*Nobody* climbs Ayodhana," Gabrel said, sounding shocked. "She is the sacred mountain."

"Yeah, and these caves yer friend wants us to go to—they're sacred too, right?" Maris pointed out. "And that doesn't seem to've stopped the Bashir from turning them into some kind of weapons locker, or whatever."

Gabrel looked sick. "I'm afraid it's not exactly—"

Chulayen interrupted him and said something in a low, agitated voice, pointing back the way they had come. "Hai, hai," Gabrel agreed before turning back to Maris. "We need to keep moving. There are tribesmen in Dharampal who know these trails much better than Chulayen does. If they realize we haven't gone straight back to Valentin, they'll have trackers out checking the trails. But if we can cross into Thamboon before they catch up with us, the Vakil won't send anybody over the border. Probably."

"And what if it's not the Vakil tracking us, but that ugly bastard from Udara?"

"That," Gabrel said, "is an *extremely* good reason to keep moving."

Fortunately, the next segment of the trail was not as grueling as the rocky slopes they'd covered in darkness. It wound about the shoulder of the mountain, well below the treeline, and almost level as such things were counted in the ranges of the Lower Jagirs—which meant they had to scramble up and down over rocks and around tree roots, but at least it wasn't the constant, monotonous climbing that had made the night walk such a misery. The narrow path passed through alternating bands of shadow and light. There were forested areas where the great trees enclosed them like walls and filled the air with a resinous scent that gave Maris new energy, and there were sudden openings into grassy meadows where the shelves of stone lay too near the surface for trees to flourish. In one of the glades Chulayen held up his hand as a signal to pause. While Gabrel and Maris froze, listening for the sounds of somebody following him, he climbed a few feet up one of the gnarled trunks and came down with his hand full of what looked like dark, sticky chunks of quartz. He said a few words to Gabrel and popped one of the rocklike things into his mouth.

"Sundhu resin," Gabrel explained to Maris. "He says chewing it will give us more energy for the trek and we won't need to load our bellies with food."

Maris had been rather looking forward to a stop for something to eat, and she had not been thinking in terms of chewing on something that smelled—she took another suspicious sniff to confirm her suspicions—like paint thinner. Still, Gabrel was munching away now with every evidence of enjoyment, so she cautiously took the smallest sliver of gunk she could find in Chulayen's open hand and stuck the end into her mouth.

Yep. Paint thinner.

She bit down on the stuff and almost gagged as the resinous texture and sharp taste flooded her mouth.

It would doubtless be considered *extremely* rude to spit it out again. Once they were walking, maybe, if she could manage to be last in line . . . but right now Gabrel and Chulayen were both watching her.

She chewed, swallowed the bitter saliva that filled her mouth, chewed again. It didn't taste quite so bitter now. A few more bites, and the chunk of stuff she'd taken had disintegrated into fibers, and she felt as if she'd just popped a couple of stimmers. And the taste . . . Her eyes widened, and the men laughed.

" 'S *good*!" she said in surprise.

"It's also addictive," Gabrel told her as they shouldered their packs and started forward again, "but Chulayen says the only people who get a chance to be addicted are the mountain tribes—it has to be taken fresh from the tree, and whatever active compounds make it such a good stimulant break down within hours. Someday I'd like to get a biochemist up here to analyze the freshly harvested sap."

"Mmm," Maris nodded while sucking the last delicious, tangy resinous flavor from the fibers in her mouth. Chulayen, ahead of them, spat his mouthful of fibers onto the trail, and she followed his example. "Synthesize this stuff, you could make a fortune selling it as, I dunno, chewing gum or something. Maybe make a drink out of it."

"That," said Gabrel, sounding shocked, "would be immoral. Didn't I tell you it was addictive?"

Maris had thought that was the point. Nothing like having a monopoly of something that people not only liked but *had* to have more of. If Johnivans could get his hands on an analysis of this stuff, he'd . . . kill the biochemist, and then . . .

What had seemed simple, clear, and profitable when she thought with her Tasman mind *did* seem immoral when she thought like Calandra Vissi, who was dead but who seemed to be taking over her head anyway. Maris remembered the kids who'd gone the dreamdust way on Tasman. Not just the ones in Johnivans' gang, but the young prostitutes who used the stuff to make their short lives bearable until the 'dust killed them. Would she have died that way if Johnivans hadn't taken her in?

So what was immoral? Providing dreamdust? Or leaving people in lives so miserable that dying of slow starvation on a constant dreamdust high seemed preferable to reality? Damn, trying to be a real person instead of a scumsucker was *complicated*. Too bad she wasn't really Calandra Vissi. The Diplo probably knew the right thing to do without having to think about it.

Anyway, she couldn't climb and think at the same time, she was too tired. She rubbed the sweat off her forehead—funny how you could sweat so much when it was so *bunu* cold—and tapped Chulayen's shoulder, holding out her hand for another chunk of sundhu resin.

Breakfast turned out to be a stale, flat onion pancake, handed out by Chulayen while they were still walking the level—and the sundhu resin, or her hunger, made even that taste delicious. Maris started scanning for likely trees every time they entered a band of forest, pointing them out to Chulayen until Gabrel reminded her that there was no point in stockpiling the resin; what they couldn't chew as they walked would lose its stimulant qualities in storage.

When no one was watching, she broke off half the next piece Chulayen gave her and tucked it into a corner of her pack. She could test it tomorrow; no need to take everything some total stranger told her at face value, just because Gabrel believed him. After all—Gabrel believed *her*, didn't he? He might fall for any lie—he hadn't trained with professionals, like she had.

That is, she could test it if she was still alive tomorrow. When they finally stopped for a rest and another yummy stone-cold onion pancake, Gabrel had time to translate what Chulayen had been telling him. And it didn't sound good to Maris.

"I thought this guy said the Bashir was storing his pro-tech weapons in these caves we're going to."

"That's what I thought at first," Gabrel admitted, "but you can see that wouldn't make any sense. You don't use some location too remote for anybody but mountain goats as a weapons locker; can you imagine carrying heavy machinery up this trail?"

"Tanglefield generators and nerve dazers aren't all that heavy."

"In large quantities they are."

"So what *does* he use it for?"

Gabrel's lips tightened for a moment; he looked sick. "According to Chulayen, he uses it for . . . making what he trades for the weapons. He used to do it in Udara, but because of the rumors that somebody was going to investigate, he moved everything to the Jurgan Caves in Thamboon."

"So what *do* you manufacture in 'some location too remote for anybody but mountain goats,' then?" Maris threw his own words back at him, and the answer came to her before Gabrel could speak. Those bio-shielded cylinders that Johnivans got from Kalapriya, that went out to Rezerval as "medical supplies" . . .

"Bacteriomats," she answered her own question. "He's found a way to culture 'mats outside the coastal caves, and instead of selling them to the Barents Trading Society, he's trading them to . . . somebody . . . for pro-tech weaponry."

Gabrel nodded. "So he can conquer more territory, so he can take more prisoners, so he can culture more bacteriomats, so he can get more arms . . . It's an endless spiral."

Maris thought it over. "I don't quite get the bit about the prisoners."

"I'm not quite sure either," Gabrel said, "but Chulayen insists that they're being used to help culture the 'mats, and that it kills them, so the Bashir needs more and more people. He used to condemn his political prisoners to the 'mat culture caves, but that's not enough anymore; he's taking people from the conquered areas. I don't quite get what's so toxic about the 'mat culture process; our people in Barents do it without dying or even getting sick, and my Kalapriyan isn't good enough to understand what Chulayen is saying. I keep asking how the prisoners culture the 'mats, and he says the prisoners *are* the 'mats. Something is getting badly mangled in translation."

Chulayen broke in here with a flood of Kalapriyan in which Maris managed to make out the words "wife, son, daughters—everybody, all my family!" and some names.

"His family was taken by the Ministry for Loyalty," Gabrel translated. "Fairly recently. They were sent to the Jurgan Caves before he could do anything. He wants us to get there as fast as possible in case there's a chance of saving them."

Maris blinked back tears, angry at herself for the weakness. So Chulayen had lost his family, so what was that to her? She'd never *had* a family. But the little clerk's grief made something ache inside her. She focused on practicalities.

"And exactly how are we going to do that?"

"We may not be able to," Gabrel admitted. "We'll have to see what the situation is like when we get there. I'm not going to risk your life in some desperate attempt to save the prisoners in the caves. You're too valuable for that; you're the key to our whole success."

"Who, me? How? I don't feel all that valuable," Maris said. "I mean, I don't *want* to die, or anything, but . . ."

"Don't you see, Calandra? You're our link with Rezerval! Even if you're not fully trained yet, you're a Diplo intern. You've got contacts with people who can stop this whole filthy business, and they'll believe *you*. I can't risk going to Valentin with the story, because *some* of the senior Trading Society people have to be in it, and I don't know which ones. But *you* can take it directly to Rezerval."

Maris took a deep breath and let it out slowly. The thin mountain air seemed a bit short on oxygen; that must be what was making her feel so dizzy. "Gabrel. Tell me that's not your only plan—having me get help from Rezerval?"

"Can you think of a better?"

"Almost anything," Maris said, "would work better than *that.*" *Stop!* screamed a voice within her. *We never tell outsiders the truth.*

So who's more of an outsider than me? Maris argued back at her own protective voice. *Johnivans was gonna kill me, remember?*

That just goes to show. You can't trust anybody.

But if that was true—if she couldn't trust Gabrel, who had been so patient, so helpful, who had supported her a hundred ways without ever once complaining—well, what was the point of living in a world where you really *couldn't* trust anybody at all?

"Calandra? Are you all right?"

Maris realized that she had closed her eyes, wrapped up in her internal dialogue for what must have seemed like forever to Gabrel and Chulayen.

"I'm going to do it," she said, half aloud. "And if he hates me, so *what?*"

"Calandra." Gabrel took both her hands in his. "What's the matter? Of course I don't hate you. I couldn't hate you. Damn it, Calandra, you *know* how I feel about you."

"You won't anymore," Maris said bleakly, "when I explain." But there wasn't any other choice, now. Somehow, traveling with Gabrel Eskelinen and trying to think with Calandra Vissi's head had fatally messed up her own head. She had become infected with outsider notions about doing the right thing instead of looking after yourself first, last, and always.

"Explain what?"

No way to put it off any longer. No excuse to put it off any longer. "Gabrel, you didn't quite get it right—about who I am—"

"You're not an intern?"

"No."

"But—I could have *sworn* you weren't a fully trained Diplo with all the implants."

"I'm not that either," Maris said. "And me name ain't even

Calandra! I'm Maris! Maris Nobody from Tasman, got that?
I'm a damn fake and you been too *bunu* dumb to catch
on, all this time! Calandra's *dead*, you idiot! I—I needed
to get off Tasman real quick, they was gonna kill me, and
I had her ID and I used it and I was gonna run off soon's
I got away safe only there wasn't never no chance!" Angry
tears choked her and she realized she'd been shouting like
a Tasman scumsucker. She took a deep breath and let the
memory of Calandra Vissi fill her with borrowed calm.

"I didn't kill Calandra," she said, more quietly. "Nobody
meant to kill her. It was an accident. But afterwards—" She
could not bear to tell him how Johnivans had meant to throw
her life away. That she was a person so worthless, her best
friend in all the world had no more use for her living self
than for her corpse. "Well, I was in trouble. Real bad trouble.
And I look a little bit like Calandra, and Ny—a friend," she
substituted, "hacked into the databases and fixed it so my
DNA and retina scans would go on her ID, so I could use
it to get away. That's all I wanted—to get away."

"To *Kalapriya*?"

"Anywhere off Tasman, and that's where Calandra was
s'posed to be going, so I thought that would be easiest. I
didn't realize until I got here," Maris confessed, "that the
only way out was back through Tasman again. So I was
stuck."

Gabrel sat down at the base of a tree and leaned forward,
resting his arms on his bent knees.

"I . . . didn't mean to get you stuck with me," Maris ventured after a while, and then, after another silence, "I'm
sorry."

Gabrel raised his head and Maris looked away, afraid of
seeing scorn in his eyes.

"You've never even been on Rezerval."

"Right."

"You're here because your friends killed the real Diplo."

His voice was flat and dead. He hated her. He had to;
look at the mess she'd gotten him into, and how she'd been
lying to him since the day they met. She might as well spell
out the whole sorry story. When you had nothing left but
pride . . . well, what good was pride?

"I'm here," Maris corrected, "because when the Diplo
spaced herself, my 'friends' needed a substitute. If a Diplo'd

just disappeared on Tasman, there'd've been a search that could've messed up Johnivans' whole organization. So his idea was to hack into Rezerval's databases and substitute my physical data for Calandra's, then let them find my dead body in her quarters and report she'd died of natural causes. Only when I put the story together, I decided I'd rather impersonate a live Diplo than a dead one. I got out of Tasman one step ahead of Johnivans . . . I don't *have* any friends," she finished, swallowing hard. "I'm nobody. I can't do you no *bunu* good." At least she could quit trying to talk toppie now.

She could feel Gabrel studying her face. Maris hoped she didn't look as miserable as she felt.

"You're wrong about that, you know," he said.

Maris lifted her empty hands. "And just what do you think I *can* do? I'm for sure not your contact with any Rezerval toppies!"

"You have friends now," Gabrel said. "You saved my life in Valentin, and you've been a damned good marching companion all this way. No accredited Diplo could have done better. Don't run yourself down, Cal . . . umm . . ."

"Maris." She folded her arms, as if she could hold on to herself, hold on to her misery. Words cost nothing. If she let herself believe them, it would just hurt worse when Gabrel showed the truth. Whatever he might say, he *couldn't* feel the same about a Tasman scumsucker as he would've about a Rezerval Diplo. "You always do jump to conclusions too fast," she told him. "When you've had time to think about it, you'll hate me for getting you into this. So why don't we just fast-forward to that part now and skip the nice talk?" And skip the part where she started to feel good again and then it was taken away. The remembered pain of discovering Johnivans' betrayal shot through her again, almost taking her breath away; it felt like a hand squeezing her heart. She couldn't go through that again with Gabrel.

Gabrel sighed. "Maybe we should just forget about personal relationships and decide how we're going to finish the job."

It did hurt.

"Fine by me," Maris said tightly.

"Okay, then."

"Okay."

After a long, tense silence Gabrel finally spoke again . . . in Kalapriyan this time. Chulayen answered, no, asked a question. Gabrel said something that sounded way too short to be a summary of her confession to him. In fact, if she knew Kalapriyan any better, she'd have thought he said, "Go away."

He had; Chulayen turned his back to them and walked down the path they'd come up until he was lost to sight among the trees.

"Wait a minute!" Maris cried. Never mind her personal misery, there was more than that at stake. "You can't just send him away like that. We got to try and rescue his *family*, don't we?"

Gabrel stood up. Maris dropped her eyes so she wouldn't have to see his face. All she could see was the toes of his boots coming closer until they stopped, inches from her own toes. "This isn't going to work, Maris."

"We could try, couldn't we? Oh, gods take it. Call Chulayen back. Him and me'll *bunu* try and get in there. We don't need you!" *I don't need you. Leastways, not any more than I need air and water.*

"I didn't mean that," Gabrel said. "Of course we're going to try. But we can't go in with our minds on other things, and I don't know about you, but *I* can't forget about our personal relationship and leave things like this. We've got to clear the air."

Maris looked up, avoided meeting his eyes, glanced from side to side at the conifer-studded hills. "Looks plenty clear to me," she said.

"Stop. Playing. Word. Games." Gabrel said through clenched teeth. "Oh, *gods* . . ." His hands closed on her shoulders and his mouth came down over hers, at first hard, then soft and warm and . . . Maris lost track of her thoughts and everything else. She'd imagined this a million times, only not like this, not with him knowing who she really was—

That brought her back to reality and she wrenched her head away. It hurt to stop. Hurt worse than anything yet.

As soon as his own mouth was free, Gabrel was talking, saying nonsense, not letting her get a word in edgewise. "Maris, I love you, don't you understand? I don't care who you were before, you're *mine* now."

"You don't love me," Maris told him. "I was being Calandra Vissi. It's her you love, and she's *dead*."

"Calandra Vissi didn't save my life in Valentin, and ride until her thighs were scraped raw without a word of complaint, and lead pack ghaya up into the hills with me, and make camp in the mountains with me," Gabrel said. "*You* did. It doesn't matter what you were calling yourself at the time. The girl who made this trip with me is the one I love."

He bent his head to kiss her again, but Maris twisted away. "Wait," she pleaded. "I got to think."

Love her? That couldn't be true. There wasn't anything about her to love. If there had been, Johnivans wouldn't have tossed her life aside so casually.

Unless . . .

Johnivans was a different sort of person than Gabrel, wasn't he?

Actually, Johnivans wasn't up to Gabrel's class at all. Now that she thought about it.

Maybe the problem wasn't that she wasn't worth anything, but that Johnivans didn't know how to care about people.

And Gabrel did.

He knew a lot more than that, too. While he was ostensibly giving her time to think, his left arm was holding her very close and his right hand was roaming in a most distracting fashion. It would be so easy to quit thinking altogether and give in to what felt so very, very good and safe. But she wasn't quite ready yet.

"You always fall in love with girls who drag pack-ghaya up a mountain trail?" she demanded. "Because if so, I'm gonna have too *bunu* much competition in these hills."

Gabrel tried to look serious, as if he were thinking it over, but the corners of his mouth kept twitching up. "Actually," he said, "I think I fell in love with you when you bullied me into talking to you, that first evening in Valentin."

"Huh! You mean when I *listened* to you all the way to the meeting hall."

"No," he said, "I think it was when you half crippled me by stepping on my feet during the valsa."

"I never!"

"Oh, yes, you did, my love. You are entrancing, maddening, beautiful, brave, and a terrible dancer. But I'll teach you to valsa properly."

"I am *not* a terrible dancer!"

"You should have seen the bruises."

"You're making it up, you walked fine afterwards didn't you?"

"A soldier is trained to bear pain," Gabrel said solemnly, "and if you don't stop talking, I'll have to shut you up again."

"Yap," Maris said. "Yap yappity yap. Yap yap ya . . ."

The second kiss was definitely better than the first. She was seriously tempted to keep arguing and kissing, just to see how much better it could get, but they did have a job to do.

She and Gabrel evidently realized that at the same time. His grip on her loosened and he stepped back.

So did she.

It felt like having part of her self torn away.

"I suppose," she said, "we'd better call Chulayen and get on with it, then."

"I suppose so," Gabrel agreed.

When they resumed the council of war, Maris was seated on the ground beside Gabrel, in the curve of his arm. And Chulayen looked at them and looked . . . not happy, perhaps, but less miserable than he'd been since they met. He said something to Gabrel that Maris couldn't follow, but she was pretty sure the word "love"—*khariya*—came in there.

"Okay," Gabrel said, trying to sound businesslike. "We need to figure out where we are and go on from there, right?"

"Going on" was painfully slow, since he had to say everything twice, once in Galactic for Maris and once in Kalapriyan for Chulayen—they couldn't risk anybody missing anything, not now—but there wasn't that much to say, really. You could only say "hopeless situation," and "forlorn hope," so many ways.

"The way I see it," Gabrel summarized, "we've got people trying to kill us in Valentin. And we've got people trying to kill us in Dharampal. And we've probably got people trying to kill us in Udara. And that's the *good* news."

And people trying to kill me on Tasman, Maris added mentally, not that it would make any difference—so why bother saying it aloud?

"I don't think it would work to head back from here to

Valentin and try to tell them all that we've decided to drop the investigation. They might not give us a chance to discuss it. They might not even believe us. Besides—" Gabrel gave a wry smile "—I'd really, really hate to have come all this way for no result."

"And besides," Maris said, "we got to get Chulayen's wife and kids out, don't we?"

"If we can," Gabrel agreed.

"After which we'll also have people trying to kill us in Thamboon."

"Ah. But with any luck we'll also have evidence that ties the whole scheme together. *Then* we try to make it back to Valentin—no, to Rezerval—and take what we've got to . . . whatever authorities we can find."

"You reckon our chances of getting back alive are any better this way?"

"No," Gabrel admitted, "but they're no *worse*, and at least this way, if we do get back, maybe we can do something worthwhile. Mathematically, it makes perfect sense; our choice is between probably getting killed with no outcome, and probably getting killed with a possible good outcome."

"I can't begin to tell you," Maris said, "how much better it makes me feel to know we've got a mathematician on the job. Makes all the difference. Okay, which way do we go from here?"

After a brief consultation with Chulayen, Gabrel reported that the pilgrim route to the cave was a relatively gentle downhill walk from the glade where they rested.

"Too good to be true!" Maris exulted.

"Well, yes. They're bound to have guards posted. However, Chulayen is almost sure there's another way into the cave complex. When he was there on pilgrimage with his wife he noticed there was a constant slight breeze blowing against his face. Also, the Inner Light Way priests appeared very suddenly from the back of the main cave. He's pretty sure there is a series of chambers back beyond the crystal caves with some opening to the outside, and he thinks he can figure out how to work around the main entrance to that one. So we're going to go *that* way—" Gabrel pointed at a discouraging rocky slope "—and then around *there*, and then with any luck there'll be a rope bridge . . ."

"Don't tell me any more," Maris implored. "I think I'm happier not knowing."

There was a rope bridge. Maris wasn't sure that counted as good luck, though. The thing consisted of two ropes, count them, two: one to stand on and one to hold on to while you shuffled over a lot of very hard- and spiky-looking rocks a very long way below. And in full gravity! Another minus for dirtside life: not only couldn't you turn on the lights, you couldn't turn off the gravity.

You had, in fact, very little control at all. But when had she, personally, had any control over her circumstances? Surely not on Tasman, where Johnivans had used her as a spy, runner, and thief until it was more convenient to discard her. Certainly not since she'd run from Tasman. She wasn't even sure she'd had any control over falling in love with Gabrel. It felt more like giving in to a force of nature, like gravity.

Not that she really wanted to think about gravity just then . . . "What the hell," Maris said, and followed Chulayen over the double rope. Actually she crossed a little faster than he did, and a lot faster than Gabrel, whose weight made the device sag and creak alarmingly.

"In a holo," she said when Gabrel finally crossed the chasm, "the native guide would scamper across without even using the top rope, 'stead of gripping it with all ten fingers the way *he* did."

Gabrel grinned and translated the comment to Chulayen, who was looking rather more olive green than his usual light brown color. Chulayen replied with a spate of words ending in a shaky laugh. "He says he's a soft clerk in a Udaran government office, not a mountain tribesman," Gabrel translated, "and the pilgrim path to the caves is quite bad enough for him. After the pilgrimage he vowed never to go near one of these rope bridges again. Furthermore, he is beginning to hope we will all be killed attempting to enter the caves, so that he won't have to come back this way."

Maris looked with new respect at the little brown-skinned man. Just a clerk in some government office, but he'd joined the Udaran resistance movement, traveled across country to meet unknown foreigners, and led them back through the mountains because his family *might* still be alive in these mysterious caves of Thamboon. And even if he had gripped the handrope so tightly his knuckles turned white and taken half of forever to shuffle along the footrope, still he'd been the one to show them the way across the bridge. "Well, tell him if that's what the old softies of his country are like, I hope I never run across a tough young one!"

After the bridge they went more slowly; there was nothing so well defined as a path to guide them, only narrow trails through the bent grass. Chulayen studied the outlines of the surrounding hills intently. Gabrel flipped the curved Kalapriyan-style dagger he carried upside down and revealed a primitive compass concealed in the hilt. He and Chulayen stopped and conferred so often Maris began to wonder, then to suspect, then to feel certain—

"We're lost."

"Not *lost*," Gabrel said defensively, "we just aren't sure exactly—"

"Do you know where we are?"

"Well . . ."

"Does *he* know where this supposed back entrance to the caves is?"

"I . . . look out!"

Gabrel's shoulder caught her in the midriff and knocked the breath out of her, sending them both tumbling down among the stiff thorny bushes. A moment later Chulayen dove on top of them. Something caught the hem of Maris's long tunic and dragged it upward—*damn thorns*—and she had just time to think that Chulayen's weight on top of Gabrel's would drive the thorn bushes right into her bare back—and now she heard the buzzing that had alerted Gabrel; *some kind of machine?*—but she couldn't see over his body pinning her down, wriggled sideways and got room to breathe again, no, more than that, falling into darkness— She landed, hard, on something entirely composed of hard knobbly lumps and sharp edges.

"A flitter," Gabrel said under his breath. "Gods, they're getting blatant about it, not even trying to hide their smuggled technology anymore! *Stay* down, Maris, if they see us— Maris?"

The breath that had been knocked out of her body came back in, lovely beautiful oxygen, and the bruises—well, one good thing about the dark, she couldn't *see* the extent of the damage, but it didn't feel like anything was broken. She wasn't even bleeding. Much. Just the one scraped elbow that had found a rock face on the way down. "I think," Maris called up, "I've found it. The back way. Into them caves."

After some discussions about how deep the hole was ("Not bad," Maris reported, "I didn't break nothing."), whether Chulayen and Gabrel could climb down rather than falling in ("Try climbing. Falling's not fun."), and whether there were passages leading into the interior of the mountain ("Why d'you *think* I said I'd found it? 'Course there's passages!") Gabrel first lowered Chulayen down the precipitous sides of the hole, then swung himself over, hung by his hands for a moment, and let himself drop. A vigorous Barentsian curse helped Maris identify his shadowy form.

"Reckon you found the same ledge I did," she said, not without satisfaction. "Scrape yer elbow?"

Gabrel didn't deign to reply. He asked Chulayen something and got back an answer most of which Maris understood; her Kalapriyan seemed to be improving rapidly with all the practice she got listening to Gabrel and Chulayen. The little clerk didn't think this was the back way that had been used by the priests, and Gabrel agreed that there were probably easier entrances to the cave complex somewhere else; however, the faint continual draft of air past their faces made this one seem as promising as any other.

"Help if we could see anything," Maris complained, and even as she finished speaking a faint glow lit up Gabrel's face. It looked as though his cheek and forehead had intercepted the ledge on which Maris had scraped her elbow; no wonder he was testy. But showing off his light source seemed to be cheering him up.

"Built in with the compass," he explained. "Only turns on when I twist this little knob on the side of the hilt—see?" And he demonstrated by clicking the light on and off several times.

"The Bashir supplies his troops with magic lights also," Chulayen said—that was short and simple enough that Maris could understand it, especially when the clerk also produced a glowing disk from the folds of his sash.

"I thought you were just an office clerk," Gabrel said with suspicion.

"My . . . friends . . . occasionally divert some military supplies," Chulayen explained.

Maris threw up her hands. "This *bunu* world! Everybody except me is already carrying pro-tech, and who got arrested in Dharampal on suspicion of having outlander weapons? Me!"

After some time crawling along the one useful passage leading from that deep hole, Maris wished Gabrel and Chulayen had been carrying a little more prohibited technology. Something to map the cave complex would have been nice. She wasn't entirely happy with following the faint breath of air moving through the tunnel as evidence that somewhere up ahead were the larger caverns of which Chulayen had spoken. Still, it wasn't like there'd been a lot of choices. The other apparent passages had been only deep crevices with no openings; if this one petered out they'd have to backtrack, climb out of the hole she'd accidentally discovered, and look for another entrance.

Back through that narrow bit where they had to crawl single file on their bellies through slimy puddles . . . She really, *really* hoped they were going the right way. Then she realized that once they got to the crystal caves, they would have to find something they could steal that would be enough to get the attention of the authorities on Rezerval, lift whatever-it-was without being killed by the cave guards, then go back through that slimy tunnel, trek over the mountains, not get killed by Udaran assassins, find a boat back down the river to Valentin, not get killed by *Barentsian* assassins, get themselves to Rezerval from a planet whose only access station was Tasman, not get killed by Johnivans . . . She moaned softly to herself. They'd never make it. She might just as well lie down and die right here in the tunnel, except . . .

"What is wrong?" Chulayen asked. He spoke slowly and clearly so that she could understand him.

"Nothin'" Maris said. Her Kalapriyan definitely wasn't up to explaining all the ways they could die on the way back. "I . . . don't like tunnels." Okay, so she'd slipped through narrower spaces in the maintenance shafts on Tasman, but even there you could turn on the lights . . . and she knew her way around Tasman.

"There is nothing to fear," Chulayen promised her. "These mountains are very old. Nothing will fall to close our way."

Gods, she hadn't even thought to worry about that possibility!

"And the crystal caves are . . . were . . . very beautiful," Chulayen went on. "You and Gabrel will be the first outlanders to see them. Walls lined with crystals, you understand? Light everywhere. In darkness, one lights a candle first, and light dances everywhere."

That was something good to think about while she crawled on hands and knees through the stinking mud. After a while the passage opened up a little. They couldn't stand up, but at least she didn't have to keep her head down where her nose was practically in the mud. So the smell should have been better . . . but instead, as they progressed, it got worse.

Much worse.

If the roof hadn't raised up so that Maris could stand, she thought she would have thrown up. Chulayen stood up too, with a smothered groan of relief and a hand at the small of his back. Gabrel was too tall; he had to walk in a half-crouch that looked even more uncomfortable than crawling. Still, the change of position must be some relief.

And that cloying, sickly sweet smell kept getting worse.

"Watch out for crevasses," Gabrel warned in a low voice. He angled his dagger hilt so that a faint light showed the broken ground before them. Maris realized that the black areas weren't just deep shadows but actual openings in the cave floor, falling down who knows how far? She certainly didn't want to find out. Fortunately they were mostly narrow. She stepped across the openings carefully, holding Chulayen's hand for safety, then helped to balance him while he crossed each one.

"Bigger ones coming up," Gabrel murmured, "and we must be close now. Somebody else has been using this part of the cave." His light illumined a roughly planed plank that bridged a wide crevasse ahead.

"Smells like something crawled in here to *die*," Maris muttered.

"Maybe somebody fell through." Gabrel dropped to his knees, then to his stomach. One hand over his mouth and nose, he lowered his other hand with the light down into the gaping crevasse, then gasped suddenly and jerked backward, gagging.

"What is it?" Maris whispered.

"Don't look!"

Chulayen squeezed past her and whispered something in

Kalapriyan to Gabrel, then took the light and lowered it at arm's length into the crevasse, peering intently. When he straightened up he looked even greener than before, but maybe that was just the effect of the dim light among the shadows of the cave.

Or the effect of the smell.

"I can look or you can tell me," Maris said, carefully taking the shallowest breaths she could, "but I ain't going out on that plank until I know what's underneath me."

"Bodies," Gabrel said reluctantly.

Maris supposed she had already known that, because she didn't feel shocked or surprised. Just cold. *"His* people?" She jerked her head at Chulayen.

"He didn't recognize anyone . . . There's no way of telling for sure," Gabrel said. 'They've been . . . their heads are . . . I don't understand it. Why drag prisoners all the way up here just to execute them?" He turned to Chulayen and repeated the question, got back a long answer whispered so fast that Maris couldn't follow a word of it.

"He doesn't really know either, I don't think," Gabrel told Maris. "He keeps saying that Meer Madee told him they use the prisoners to make the bacteriomats and then they die."

"I guess we got to go on, then," Maris concluded. "Us seeing a heap of mangled bodies isn't going to count for evidence, is it? Even if you had a rope and could get down there and bring one back . . ."

"It might prove something," Gabrel said, "or it might not, depending on what's been done to the bodies. Unfortunately, we do not have a rope." He didn't sound that unhappy about it.

For once Maris found it easy to obey Gabrel's injunction not to look down as she crossed the plank across the crevasse. She *really* wished there were some way to turn off the gravity for that few seconds, though.

On the far side of the crevasse things improved. A lot. The cave was high enough for even Gabrel to stand up in, and wide enough that they could walk side by side. If you could call what they were doing *walking*. Gabrel evidently figured they were getting close to where the action was, so he insisted on what he called "slow advance mode," which was apparently a military term for sneaking up on some place really slowly and carefully.

Accent on *slowly*.

First Gabrel twisted the hilt of his dagger so that only the faintest light came from it, barely enough to show the uneven floor of the cave; and even that was shielded by his hand so that nobody in front of them would be likely to see it. He would take three steps forward, then pause and listen. He'd motion to Chulayen, who did the same thing, a lot more quietly than Gabrel. Last came Maris. Another pause to listen. Then they repeated the whole thing.

After a minor eternity of three-steps-and-listen, Maris realized that the cave was slowly getting brighter. She could see sparkly bits on the sides of the passage, and long back-cast shadows where those bits stuck out. She tapped Gabrel on the shoulder and pointed to the shadows. He nodded acknowledgment, twisted the light off and tucked his dagger back into the sash of his tunic.

Moving even more slowly than before, they came from the shadows of the crevasses to a world of glittering lights. The walls around them flowered with crystalline shapes, some like sharp-edged flowers, some like stars, others like broken bits of space debris, with no recognizable form to them, but a sense of some underlying purpose in their structure. The reflections from the crystal facets danced and swam around them, making Maris so dizzy that it was hard to reason out the cause: the light source must come from torches somewhere ahead. Torches, people . . . they slowed even more. A murmur that had at first seemed no more than the sighing of the cave now sounded like water, then like voices babbling indistinguishable syllables. Gabrel put his finger to his lips, listened intently, then turned to Chulayen with brows lifted. Chulayen shook his head; Maris deduced that he, too, was unable to make any sense out of what they were hearing. But at least it proved there *were* living people in the caves before them.

An outcropping of crystal-encrusted stone partially blocked the way forward. They crowded behind it and peered at what they could see of the lighted cave. The moving sparks of reflections from the crystal walls were so confusing that it was hard to make out details even close to the torches affixed to the walls at intervals, but it looked to Maris as if there was just one person walking around, and any number sitting against the cave walls—shadow upon shadow, moaning and mumbling singsong nonsense that chilled her even while she told herself that she couldn't *expect* to understand *Kalapriyan* mumbling. No matter what the language, the tones were those of madness.

"One guard," she breathed to Gabrel, and he nodded. They moved back a few (agonizingly careful) steps and held a whispered conference. What would be the best way to get rid of the guard so they could free the prisoners? Her appearance, or Gabrel's, would be sure to alarm him. Could Chulayen pass as another guard for long enough to lure the man back here where they could capture him? He looked dismayed at the suggestion but said something that Maris thought would have sounded snobbish, if he could have got enough intonation into his whispers.

"What'd he say? What's he going to *do*?" she demanded under her breath as Chulayen inched toward the cave opening again.

"He says he isn't dressed right to be a guard but if he tries really hard he thinks he can imitate a lower-class Rohini accent long enough to get the man back here."

Maris nodded. Like she thought—snobbish. She remembered Gabrel's brief explanations about the class differences between Rudhrani and Rohini. Hmm. If this Chulayen was Rudhrani, and a Udaran government employee at that, what was he doing with the resistance movement? Was he leading them into a trap?

Chulayen called out in Kalapriyan. The guard's pacing stopped, and Gabrel didn't seem to be worried by whatever Chulayen had said, so probably it was all right. But the guard didn't come toward them. Chulayen said something else and the guard took a step closer. Would he—

"*Baba! Babaji!*" A child's cry of delight echoed from the walls of the cavern, and a small figure ran past the guard, all the way to the outcropping of crystals that concealed their party. Chulayen leapt forward, dropped to one knee and embraced the child, heedless of the torchlight falling upon his exposed face. Tears glittered on his face as he rocked the child back and forth in his arms. His story had been true, then; Maris had been worrying about the wrong thing, as usual.

What she should have been worrying about was the number of guards. The first man, the one they'd tried to lure

back here, gave a shout—for help?—and suddenly there were
three, no, five men all coming at them, the others must have
been sleeping, and now they were really sunk—

"Back here!" Gabrel pushed her unceremoniously back into
the deepest crevice between the crystal pillar and the cave
wall, then strode forward into the torchlight and said something in Kalapriyan. The guards seized him and Chulayen,
tore the child from Chulayen's arms, and dragged all three
of them out of Maris's sight.

They didn't search further. She huddled in the crevice and
alternated between wondering what to do next and cursing Gabrel. She'd recognized the Kalapriyan word for "two"
in what he said, so presumably it was something like "It's
just the two of us." Nice that they took his word for it!
But what was the good of leaving her free on her own?
Anybody would think he'd forgotten that she wasn't a real
Diplo with wonderful weapons and secret powers—just a
Tasman scumsucker with no skills but lying and evasion.
Demons take the man—if only they'd both hidden—well,
okay, there probably wasn't room in here for both of them;
it was a tight fit for her alone. So fine. *He* should have
hidden and let her be captured, then rescuing them would've
been his problem. Talk about getting noble and chivalrous
at the wrong moment! Johnivans would have dived for cover
without a second thought, probably first pushing her out
into the light to distract the guards, and . . . *Would you really
prefer that?* Okay. No, she wouldn't. Gabrel was worth a
hundred of Johnivans. He was brave, Chulayen was honest, and she, Maris, was a nasty suspicious little liar who
thought the worst of everyone until proven wrong and who
didn't *deserve* to be the only one of them left free.

Maris sighed—quietly—and prepared to see what she could
do with her own skills. Being a Diplo and probably able
to call up reinforcements from Rezerval would've been nice,
but being just herself, she'd have to rely on lying and
evasion. Eavesdropping would've been a good supplement,
but she couldn't follow the guards' mumbling, slang-filled
conversation. Who was she kidding? She could barely follow a very slow, clear conversation in very basic Kalapriyan.
If she already knew what it was about. Besides, she could
barely hear the guards now . . .

A cold hand tugged at her arm. Maris started, cracked

her head on something hard and sharp jutting out of the crystal pillar, and—it was only the child.

Who'd given them away to the guards, she reminded herself.

But probably not on purpose.

Now the child—a little girl, she thought, with those long black braids—was whispering something urgently. Maris bent down to hear. A lot of good that did—it was still bloody Kalapriyan. She fumbled for words and managed something like "No understand, talk slow please."

What she wouldn't have given for a Diplo's language implant.

Finally the little girl calmed down enough to put it in words of one syllable for the dumb outlander. "Guards gone now. We get my *babaji*. You come help!"

Maris realized that the voices of the guards were quite inaudible now; all she could hear was the continual low-toned babbling and moaning of, she supposed, the prisoners. Inaudible didn't necessarily mean *gone*. She risked a cautious peek around the crystal pillar and saw nobody standing, not even any long shadows of standing men.

Yeah, right. So maybe the guards were sitting down like everybody else.

The kid tugged more urgently. Maris dug in her heels and pulled right back, enough to get the girl's attention, then squatted down to bring their heads together. "Go slow," she whispered. "Careful. No talk loud." She *hated* trying to talk this language; it made her feel like an idiot. She added in Galactic, more for her own satisfaction than because she really thought she'd be able to communicate, "Look, kid, you are with an *expert* at sneaking around now. You just stay back and let me handle things, you hear?" Not that she had any idea *how* she was going to "handle" the situation, but at least she could scope it out better if this kid would just calm down and stay put.

Something in her tone seemed to work—maybe it was just the universal Voice of Adult Authority—and the little girl stayed quietly in the shelter of the crystal pillar while Maris slunk to the next bit of shadowy cover, thinking nobody-here-you-don't-even-want-to-look thoughts to discourage anybody who just might *be* looking.

The torchlight was some distance away, and anyway it

did a terrible job of lighting this back part of the cave; patches of crystals sparkled in occasional pools of light, surrounded by dark shadows. Even if somebody saw a bit of movement, they'd probably take it for a crystal flashing in the wavering light. And the irregular walls of the cave provided plenty of solid cover. Maris couldn't have had a better environment for sneaking up on somebody if she'd custom-ordered it. Compared to following a mark along the brilliantly lit corridors of one of Tasman's toppie levels, this was a piece of cake.

Of course, last time she'd tried to do *that*, she hadn't been such a great success. But who'd have known the mark would turn out to be a Diplo? A bunch of stupid Kalapriyan guards had to be easy in comparison.

How do you know they're stupid?

Maris slipped from the shadows cast by a boulder sparkling with iridescent white snowflakes, across the narrow cavern and into the shelter of a stalactite cluster that seemed to be dripping half-melted crystals. *This isn't exactly the kind of job that goes to the sharpest guys around,* she answered the carping voice in her head.

And speaking of "around," where *were* all those guards who'd piled onto Gabrel and Chulayen? Maris peered between two flows of crystal and squinted into the uneven light of the cavern where it opened out ahead of her, carefully taking stock of every bit of information her senses could bring her.

Torches were fixed into the walls at head height every two or three meters. She avoided looking directly at the flames. Even the sparkling walls revealed by the torchlight were bright enough to mess up her vision. She directed her gaze down toward the cavern floor, where huddled dark shapes lined the walls.

People. Chained to the walls? Not moving much, anyway. Here and there she saw a head or an arm moving in a kind of aimless flopping motion, that was all. Some of them were moaning or babbling; nearly all the shapes looked *wrong* in some way that she couldn't make out from here.

None of them looked like Gabrel or Chulayen.

And they smelled—gods, how the place stank! You'd think they were sitting in pools of their own excrement.

As she moved into the open space, so slowly it was more like flowing than walking, Maris saw that was exactly what they were doing. The prisoners were chained by the neck to bolts driven deep into the cavern walls. Some flopped so limply against their chains that they had to be unconscious or dead. Just before her, two chained bodies sat in the frozen stiffness of death. Beyond them, a head wavered, fell forward into torchlight and revealed a gaping wound in the skull that exposed the brain matter.

Maris swallowed hard and ordered her stomach to control itself. She couldn't do anything about this, not now; she had to find Gabrel and Chulayen first. No point in even thinking about what tortures were being inflicted here *what they might be doing right now to Gabrel don't think about that don't think.* She managed a few more cautious steps and came to a halt right beside one of the torches. The flickering downward light showed the bodies beneath all too clearly and she could not resist a horrified look *there's something growing out of his head don't look don't look . . .*

"Ca— Maris!"

Gabrel's voice. "Go back, Ca— Maris," he called. "Something's distracted the guards. This is your chance to get away. Go back the way we came."

"Demons fly away with the way we came!" Maris followed the voice, kept her eyes averted from the parade of horrors against the cavern walls, finally came to where Gabrel and Chulayen were chained but, not, thank God, tortured yet . . . she felt his head to make sure.

"This is an order," Gabrel said in an urgent undertone. "You can't save us. Someone must tell Rezerval what's going on here."

The chains were some kind of antique metal, actual links, nothing programmable; she felt for a keypad or some device she could fiddle and cursed primitive worlds. "Mebbe you forgot," she told Gabrel while feeling down the length of the chain to the wall bolt and back again, "I ain't in yer army. Anyway, I don't take orders from somebody as can't even remember me right name." Ha! There was some kind of a catch here, holding the chain tight around Gabrel's neck.

"You'll do what I tell you—arrgh! Whose side are you on anyway?" Gabrel complained. "You trying to strangle me?" She had jerked his head sideways and cut off the slack in the chain while trying to get a view of the catch.

"The idea," Maris said between her teeth, "is not without its attractions. Gimme your dagger."

"Guards took it."

"Well, don't you have anything useful in those sash pockets?" Maris dug into the recesses of her own clothing and came up with a bone comb. That might work, if she broke off the inside teeth and used one of the strong outside teeth as a probe. She twisted the chain just a little more, using it to break off part of the comb and turn it into a tool, and Gabrel made gagging noises.

"Just hold *on*, I got to see what I'm doing," Maris muttered. Push the long bone tooth into this opening, feel gently, gently . . . Gabrel jerked and she lost her grip on the catch. "Hold *still!*"

"Not much point in picking the lock if I'm strangled first."

Maris was beginning to think she couldn't pick the lock anyway; the triangle of the bone tooth was too broad to slip deep enough into the catch. She could probably file it down on the metal of the bolt, but that would take time . . .

Steps at the mouth of the cave startled her. She crouched between Gabrel and Chulayen, trying to blend in with the huddled prisoners.

Light blinded her for a moment—not torchlight, but a proper light that you switched on and off; like Gabrel's dagger, only about a hundred times brighter. Maris blinked and squinted at the figure behind the light. It wasn't a guard returning. Maybe worse—a tall, fair-haired woman who walked confidently, as if she thought she owned the caverns, and openly carried a flash that was way beyond anything legal to have in Kalapriya.

One of the arms dealers, come to inspect the bacteriomats they took in trade for their offworld weapons? Had to be—who else would be let past the guards like that? For that matter, who else would be foolhardy enough to just walk in like this, alone?

Of course, she thought everybody in the cavern was chained to the wall.

Maris let her get two steps farther in; the light shone on a man just beyond Chulayen, and she heard the woman make a gagging noise as though unprepared for the sight. *Now.*

It was a beautiful move, if she did say so herself, one

that Ice Eyes had taught her back on Tasman: propelling herself straight out from the wall without worrying about the coming fall, arms out to grab the arms trader around the knees and bring the woman down in, hopefully, a surprised and breathless heap.

Of course, the way Ice Eyes taught the move, you were supposed to wind up on *top* of your adversary, not squashed between them and the floor. The extremely rocky and uneven floor, in this case. Fortunately the arms trader was not only surprised but also considerably older than Maris, and *slow*; Maris managed to reverse their positions and got a knee resting on the older woman's throat before the trader had recovered from the shock of being knocked flying.

"Call off the guards," she said, "or I'll choke you now."

The arms trader made a series of whooping, breathless noises. Someone else appeared behind her and cried out, "Annemari!" Another woman, from the voice. What *was* this weapons consortium, anyway, the first female-run business on Barents?

"If you're at all fond of Annemari," Maris said, "you just stay right where you are. All I gotta do is lean forward a little—"

A point of light flickered, burst into a spreading network of lights and settled over both Maris and her captive. Immobilized, Maris looked up at the new arrival as she came forward. It was like looking at her own face—with a bit more mileage on it—olive skin, black eyes, artful mop of black curls.

"You?" they both said at once.

"I thought you were a Diplo," Maris said.

"*You've* been pretending to be me, haven't you? Of all the nerve!"

"Oh, gods. If there's a *Diplo* in on this, Gabrel, there ain't nobody we can go to for help."

"You've got that right, anyway. Your guards are nice and secure in another tanglenet."

"*My* guards? You got them bastards in a tanglenet? I thought you were with them!"

"Aren't *you* working with them?"

A wheezing noise under Maris's knee reminded her of her hostage. The tanglenet allowed neither of them much freedom of movement, but she was able to draw her knee

up a little and give the arms dealer a chance to breathe—
and to speak.

"Delightful as it is to wander unchecked through this
garden of bright images," the arms dealer said, "perhaps
a little explanation would help here. Calandra, can you get
this thing loose from me?"

"Not without letting *her* free," said Calandra, jerking her
head at Maris.

"I suspect that won't be a problem," said the arms dealer.
"Allow me to introduce myself."

For an old lady who'd just been knocked off her feet,
half strangled, and caught in a tanglenet by her own side,
Maris had to admit that she did have an impressive degree
of aplomb.

"I," said the arms dealer, "am Annemari Silvan, of
Rezerval. The lady wielding the tanglefield generator is
Diplomat Vissi. We are here to investigate the source of the
black-market bacteriomats recently appearing in Federation
worlds, and—if this *is* the source—to put an end to the
trade."

A chain clinked, off to the side. "Leutnant Gabrel Eskelinen, Barents Trading Society," Gabrel said. "My companions and I are investigating allegations of illegal technology
imported onto Kalapriya." He looked pointedly at the tangler
in Calandra Vissi's hand.

"There's a lot more illegal stuff than this floating around,"
the Diplo said, but at least she switched off the generator.
Maris straightened with a sigh of relief, then offered her
hand to the woman she'd knocked down, who was being
a bit slower about getting up. Once up, though, she stood
erect, brushed the dirt off her beautifully cut beige silk suit,
and started talking as though she'd been in control of the
situation all along. Maris had to wonder what *would* get
this woman rattled.

"If what you say is accurate," she said, "it would seem
that we are all on the same side."

"If you got them guards in a tanglenet, you bet we're on
the same side," Maris said.

"Without wishing to give offense, have you any way to
substantiate your statements?"

Maris was still trying to parse that when Gabrel spoke
up.

"My companion let you up."

"Only after mine trapped her in a tanglefield net. Agreeing to break a stalemate is not the same as active cooperation. After a war, it is not unusual to find that the entire civilian population of the defeated country claims to have been secretly against their own leaders."

"If this is a war," Gabrel pointed out, "it's not exactly over."

"Oh, yes, it is," said Annemari. "Too much has been brought to Federation attention for anybody to hush it up now." She thought briefly of the colleagues whose surprisingly large secret credit accounts on Toussaint she'd discovered, back at the beginning of this investigation, and wondered how many of them would have some serious explaining to do when all was uncovered. And how many of them would have stopped her coming here if they'd known her plans. No, she'd been right to act alone and with no more authority than her title and a confident approach could give her . . . but this disheveled young man in chains might be right, too. The war was only over if she could carry off her bluff a little longer.

"Chulen!" a girl's voice called, joyous.

"Khati!"

A Kalapriyan girl appeared behind Calandra and Annemari, ran to Chulayen and knelt beside him, shooting off questions like a machine gun. Chulayen answered at the same speed.

"What are they saying?" Annemari demanded of Calandra.

"It's all right," Calandra answered obliquely. "They really are part of the underground resistance movement." She asked a sharp question in Kalapriyan and got a distracted agreement from Chulayen and Khati. "And these two are with them." She pulled a slender laserknife out of the decorative barrette holding back her curls and used it to slice through Chulayen's and Gabrel's chains. As soon as Chulayen was free, he grabbed for Annemari's flash.

"Let him have it," Gabrel said wearily. "He's . . . looking for his family." He swallowed. "You're right. This is the source of the bacteriomats. Chulayen tried to explain it to me on the way here, but my Kalapriyan isn't *that* good, and he didn't really have the background to understand and explain it. But it seems that somebody has figured out a culture medium that works for bacteriomats. *Living human brains.*"

The flash, in Chulayen's hands, illuminated one scene out of nightmare after another: sunken faces, eyes glazed over with madness, wailing mouths. And, over and over again, opened skulls with greenish-grey mats of slime oozing over the exposed lobes.

"We have to get medical help for these people." Annemari turned to Calandra. "Can you transmit direct?"

"Not from in here, no. I'll have to go back to the surface."

"Transmit? Medical help?" Gabrel seemed to be having as hard a time as Maris in keeping up. It didn't help that they were talking over the moans of prisoners crying to be freed.

Annemari looked faintly amused. "You didn't think I'd go after a planetwide conspiracy without any backup at all, did you? But the medical problems, those I was *not* anticipating." Her lips tightened as she looked where Chulayen knelt, holding what seemed to be a living corpse in his arms, a bag of bones held together by tight-stretched skin.

"Anushka, Anushka," he mourned, then something in Kalapriyan. Maris recognized one of the words; that was enough.

"Gimme the laserknife," she demanded, all but snatching it out of Calandra's hand. "We gotta cut that one loose. That's his *wife*. That's why he came here."

"We shall free them all," Annemari said mildly, but Maris wasn't waiting to hear. The laserknife sliced through metal chains as if it were cutting soycakes; Chulayen stood with the bag of bones in his arms and said something else, urgently.

"Tell him we're *getting* doctors, Gabrel!" She looked at Annemari. "Aren't we?"

"Can your medical staff in Valentin help? Which of them can you trust?" Annemari demanded of Gabrel.

He shook his head. "*Some* of Valentin is in it. I don't know which ones—though I could make some guesses. But there had to have been a doctor helping them do this butchery."

"I think I know which one," said Annemari tightly. "Did you know that the Barents Resident in Udara was kicked out of surgical training for incompetence and unethical behavior? I didn't know that until I happened to mention his name to the right person. He had been studying under Nunzia Hirvonen, the leading neurosurgeon on Rezerval. I would be willing to bet this is his work. Ask any of these people—any who can talk," she corrected herself.

"Lorum." The thread of a voice was almost lost amid the moans of other prisoners, but Annemari heard the name that had been in her mind, took the flash from Chulayen and illuminated a section of cave wall where an emaciated man, taller and paler than the other prisoners, knelt in a puddle of filth.

"Montoyasana!"

"Lorum van Vechten . . . was the surgeon," Orlando Montoyasana said weakly. His eyes rolled. "It's coming back."

"*What* is coming back?" Annemari knelt beside Montoyasana and reached out a hand for the laserknife.

"Rainbow colors, they sound so sharp . . . Intrinsic disharmonies . . . I'm *not* mad." Montoyasana said. "Hallucinations. Infection in the cortex . . . oh, it sounds so bright," he moaned, and his eyes rolled up into the top of his head.

"Would you believe there are *no* flitters on this entire *world*?" Calandra burst back among them, her tight dark curls crackling with frustrated energy. "We'll have to ferry them back to Valentin one load at a time. It'll take forever, but they're making up a medical ward for them right now."

"Return trip," Maris said. "Don't waste it. You can bring back stuff we need here. People too."

"What—oh, right! Calandra, tell them we're bringing in the first group there, and they should have inflatable personnel carriers ready for you to bring back, and have them send a medic with whatever antibiotics they've got and, oh, whatever emergency medical supplies they can think of. We can start treating people here while the flitter shuttles cases to Valentin. Calandra, send half our people back with that first load, and tell them I'm putting Leutnant Eskelinen in command; he knows the local situation. Leutnant, you can draw a sidearm from one of my people, and if anybody in Valentin makes a move you don't like, you have my authority to neutralize them. Calandra, you go too. I want you to get on the ansible to Rezerval and tell them to send more flitters and a full division from Enforcement; the two squads I brought with me won't begin to do the job. We're going to place Valentin under military law until this mess is sorted out . . . Oh, *hell*. I need to keep somebody who speaks Kalapriyan here to interpret for us."

"I c'n try," Maris said shyly. "If they don't talk too fast."

"I'm not," Annemari said, "too worried about understanding what *they* have to say. I just want to be sure *they* understand *me*. Can you do that much? Good. Start with telling these people they are all—*all*—going to be freed and cared for, and that those who put them there will never have power over them again."

It took Maris a while to put that together in words from her extremely limited vocabulary, but perhaps, she thought, it wasn't such a bad idea to keep it simple. A lot of these people looked as if they were past handling complicated concepts. They worked down the line together, Annemari cutting the chains, Maris promising the freed prisoners they would be cared for, Calandra doing a rough triage on each wasted body. "For the first load we have to pick people who can sit in the flitter seats," she explained when Maris wondered why she was choosing the healthiest prisoners to go first. "After that we'll have carriers to immobilize them in comfortable positions, and we can start sending out the worst cases while the medics work on the others."

Maris nodded. "Okay, makes sense. But could you explain it to *them*?"

Calandra gave her a strange look. "Why don't you give it a try? You did well enough just now."

She painfully constructed another couple of Kalapriyan sentences, explaining to the prisoners why most of them would have to wait for a while. The verbs were all jumbled up, wrong tense and mood, but the people who still looked sane seemed to understand her okay. And Calandra nodded as she went along.

"Not bad," Calandra said when she finished. "You know, I thought on Tasman that you were just some gang kid trying to pick my credits, but maybe . . . are you a student or something? Language specialist?"

Maris felt her cheeks turning dark red. "You were right on Tasman. I ain't no student. Just . . . well, Diplos are s'posed to have implants so they can speak the language where they're going, right? And I was s'posed to *be* a Diplo . . . so I studied real hard, every chance I got."

"You did well."

"Not well enough," Maris said ruefully. "*He* caught on to me right away." She jerked her head toward the mouth of the cave, toward Gabrel.

"Did he indeed? Hmm . . . I wonder why he brought you so far upcountry, then?"

"Well, maybe he didn't catch on right at first," Maris allowed. "He thought mebbe I was some kinda baby Diplo, like somebody who'd been to the School all right but hadn't graduated yet."

"*And* you cheated the retinal and DNA scans that were supposed to check for my ID," Calandra said wonderingly. "Sometime you must tell me how you pulled that off."

Maris didn't really want to dub on her old pals on Tasman, so she murmured something noncommittal and pretended to be having a hard time making the Kalapriyan prisoners understand her. Fortunately they had nearly enough people to fill the flitter with its first load; a few minutes later the flitter was gone, and Calandra and Gabrel with it. Maris told herself that the sick empty feeling inside her was relief. Now she wouldn't have to evade Calandra's questions about how the Tasman gang had hacked the Federation database. Now she wouldn't have to apologize to Gabrel for lying to him all along.

"Only thing is," she muttered to herself, "what *do* I do now?"

"You can help get these people more comfortable," Annemari said at once, "and as soon as the flitter is back with medics, you can be a great deal of help by translating what they wish to ask the prisoners."

And after that, what? Well, it wasn't Annemari's problem. Wasn't anybody's problem but hers, really. And she'd been taking care of herself long enough, she had no business feeling daunted by the prospect now. She wasn't going to be too popular here on Kalapriya, she didn't suppose. And she could hardly go back to her old life on Tasman. But with the redoubtable Annemari's help, she could probably get through Tasman alive and go on to—well, anywhere else. Some place where nobody wanted to kill her; that would have to do for a start.

Chapter Eighteen

Rezerval

There were, of course, innumerable details to take care of. There were so many details that Annemari was seriously tempted to retreat into geek mode and write a program to handle it all.

"No computer program could *possibly* handle all the ethical and legal issues involved," Evert Cornelis told her when she voiced this threat. They were back in the Rezerval park, seated on Annemari's new favorite bench. Unlike the one in front of Hans Joriink's statue, it did not have such a good view of the central pond. But it had an excellent view of the new memorial statue of Orlando Montoyasana.

"Oh, I'm not so sure," Annemari said. "We humans haven't been doing so well with the issues, you know. A good neural network with intelligent heuristics . . . all right, all right, I'm just kidding!"

"Breed a better bacteriomat to solve problems," Evert suggested, and then, when Annemari looked interested, *"No!* Lorum van Vechten's brainchild has caused enough havoc already."

Remembering what van Vechten had done with his black-market 'mats, and how he'd cultured them, sobered them both. The full number of victims of the faulty 'mats would probably never be known; most families rich enough to buy illegal neurosurgery were also rich and powerful enough to conceal the disasters that followed. Annemari would never know for sure just how many cases like Tomi Oksanen's were discreetly locked away in closed wards for "nervous problems." But the ones who'd surfaced so far were enough fuel for a lifetime of nightmares. The 'mats were indeed adaptable far beyond the imaginations of anybody who'd worked with them. Given living human brains as a culture medium, they absorbed and replicated not only the basic structure of the brain but the experiences and feelings processed by that particular brain while the 'mats were growing on it. Fear, terror, sensory hallucinations, despair, fever, and insanity were carefully cultured in Udara's limestone caverns, carefully harvested and transported and eventually transplanted, with exquisitely careful neurosurgery, inside the skulls of those desperate enough to pay any price for the promise of a repaired nervous system. And once the 'mat was fully adapted to its new habitat, it set about enthusiastically reproducing its store of raw emotions and insane hallucinations for its new home.

"Pundarik Zahin threw himself over a cliff, when he realized the 'mat transplant was making him insane," Annemari said. "He must have been a brave man." With no knowledge of the medical science underlying his "cure," he had decided that Lorum van Vechten had implanted actual demons in his head. He had clung to life through agonizing days of insanity and uncontrollable muscular twitches, using his ever-briefer periods of clarity to write down what was happening to him and why. Only when the document was copied and safely deposited with two of his most trusted friends did he allow himself the release of death.

That document, together with the eyewitness testimony of those who'd been in the "cave of minds," provided enough information to justify the full Federation involvement that Annemari had asked Calandra to demand. The subsequent inquiry had brought on a wave of suicides, disappearances, and arrests of those not quick enough to take one of the other two ways out. The governing structure of the Barents Trading Society was decimated; four of the High Families that "owned" Rezerval had fallen; careers had been made and broken; and the claim of Barents to the world of Kalapriya had been unconditionally revoked.

"More exhausting than terrible, really," Annemari said now, thinking back over the cataclysmic changes her attempt to get a transplant for Niklaas had brought on.

"But when you found out about Zahin, you must have been terribly worried about Niklaas. After all, you'd left him at the clinic to get one of those same bacteriomat transplants—and I loaned you the money for it! I would never have forgiven myself if they'd done that to him, Annemari."

"Oh, I wasn't the least bit worried," Annemari told him. "You see, I didn't want them operating on Niklaas while I was away."

"Yes, but how could you be sure they wouldn't do just that?"

"I blocked the funds transfer. You see," Annemari explained, "you're quite right, I couldn't trust the Cassilis Clinic to abide by my wish for them to delay surgery. But I felt *quite* sure I could trust them not to do an operation that hadn't been paid for. After all, they weren't exactly in a position to recover the cost from my Federation health insurance package."

"No tickee, no washee?"

"Something like that." Actually Annemari had been almost suicidally worried about Niklaas once she found out about the effects of the black-market 'mats; what if her funds block hadn't worked for some reason? But if she confessed that to Evert, he'd just go all protective on her again, and that was the last thing she wanted. "So you see," she told him with a smile almost brilliant enough to disguise her secret sadness, "everything worked out all right. Niklaas didn't get a black-market 'mat, and I can give you back your money."

"Leaving you exactly where you were before all this started," Evert pointed out. "Don't you think you deserve better than that, Annemari? For personally bringing down a three-world criminal smuggling, torture, and prohibited-technology ring?"

Annemari shrugged. "I also broke a few rules along the

way, and nobody's said anything about that either. I sort of figured the Federation had decided it all worked out all right—I don't get any rewards but I'm also not going to get busted down to datatech for bringing flitters and other pro-tech to Kalapriya."

"They could not logically punish you for that," Evert pronounced, "given that Lorum van Vechten and his colleagues in the Barents Trading Society were engaging in mass smuggling of far more destructive pro-tech devices."

"*Dear* Evert. And when has any government, anywhere, been *logical?*"

"This one certainly isn't," Evert said, "but with a little discussion in the right quarters, the right people can *occasionally* see reason. It has been decided that you are to receive the Hero of the Federation award."

"Oh?"

"It's a little silver star on a cobalt-blue background," Evert told her, "with the Federation logo in holographic rainbow silver over it."

"That sounds very nice," Annemari said, "I'm sure I have some evening outfits it'll go with . . ."

"Annemari, don't you *ever* ask the obvious question?"

"Always, when I can think of it," Annemari said. "I'm afraid this time the question escapes me."

"Aren't you interested in what goes with the award?"

"A ceremony, presumably."

"Better than that."

"A pension?"

"Better than *that*." Evert was openly grinning now. "Do you realize there have been only nine Hero of the Federation awards given in all of history? You're the tenth. And the other nine, like you, have been the kind of insanely disinterested people who can't really be rewarded by meeting the rich and famous, or being granted a pension, or being given a sinecure diplomatic position, or any of the other plums a government likes to hand out as minor favors. So instead, the Federation, in its infinite wisdom, decided that a Hero of the Federation gets one free pass."

"One what?"

"If, for instance," Evert explained, "you should ever want to murder someone, you could trade in your silver-and-blue dress accessory for an acquittal—in fact, you wouldn't even have to go to trial. Or if you wanted to get a dearly beloved relative off a quarantine world, or . . ."

Annemari felt something warm and beautiful glowing within her, bubbling with promise. "Tell me, Evert: do you think a Hero of the Federation could get somebody moved to the top of the 'mat transplant list with her one free pass?"

"I should think that would be well within the bounds of the rewards envisaged by the Federation," Evert said solemnly. "In fact, they will probably feel you are asking for too little. After all, the fifth Hero of the Federation, Hans Joriink, asked for sole possession of one of the moons of Daedalus . . . and got it."

"I don't want the moon and the stars," Annemari said. "Only a chance for Niklaas."

"Who, *me*?" Chulayen Vajjadara repeated.

"You cannot seem to say anything else these days," Madee commented. "Yes, Chulen, we want you to take temporary care of the Ministry for Lands and Properties. There will be some significant changes in the way the Ministry is organized, and somehow I doubt that the previous Minister and his subordinates have the necessary . . . er . . . flexibility of mind."

If those changes were anything like those that had swept over Udara in the weeks since his return from the Jurgan Caves, Chulayen doubted that *anybody* was flexible enough to deal with them. The confiscation of the Bashir's prohibited weapons had left his army powerless to resist revolts in Thamboon and Narumalar. While he was reeling from those blows, the Rohini resistance had risen and quickly toppled his regime. The Bashir and several of his ministers had fled, not quite believing in the Rohini promises of amnesty for anyone who surrendered. And the old lady he'd first known as a beggarly pancake vendor was currently in charge of organizing an interim government to keep essential state services running until elections could be organized for the new People's Democracy of Udara.

Chulayen had a strong feeling that the elections wouldn't make much difference to Madee's plans. If she had half as strong an effect on the general Rohini populace as she had on him, she would simply tell them who they wanted to vote for and the Ministers she had chosen would be confirmed in office by an overwhelming majority. The Rudhrani were too few to make a difference in a state with suffrage for all adults—and they grew fewer every day, as prominent families quietly disappeared from Udara to live in careful retirement on some distant estate.

Which meant that if he accepted this "temporary" appointment he would be in charge of the Ministry for Lands and Properties while the entire Udaran land ownership system was dismantled and rearranged to give every Rohini—and those Rudhrani who chose to stay—a working plot of cultivable land somewhere on the terraced hillsides of the mountain realm. Chulayen couldn't see Madee settling for anything less. And the magnitude of the task staggered him. The paperwork alone—

"Grandmother, you want somebody older and more experienced for a position like that," he protested.

Madee nodded. "This is true. Unfortunately, we do not *have* anybody older and more experienced. For some reason, very few Rohini have any experience at all with government work. I'm afraid it'll have to be you, Chulen."

"If you can call our fine Rudhrani gentleman a true Rohini," put in Sonchai, who was, as usual, lounging in a corner to provide a sarcastic counterpoint to Madee's comments.

Sonchai's little sister slapped his face and ran to take Chulayen's hand before her brother could retaliate. "And who are *you* to say who is a good Rohini, brother?" she demanded. "He has lost more to the Ministry for Loyalty than you can even imagine. Why do not you take a wife, and get children, and see all but one murdered for your part in the resistance, and *then* perhaps you can talk about Rohini and Rudhrani!"

Sonchai's face reddened where Khati had slapped him. "You mean to hold it up to me that I could not protect *you* from the Bashir's lusts—"

"I never asked for your protection," Khati interrupted him. "I served the Resistance, and I am proud of it, even if *you* think our family shamed forever."

"You will please remember that it is now *my* problem to

find a decent marriage for you, and if you think that will be easy now—"

"Children!" Madee clapped her hands once and they fell silent, glaring at her like sulky children indeed. "Enough of this foolish squabbling. You are both putting words into one another's mouths. Khati, go to the outer rooms; somebody needs to amuse Chulen's little daughter while we are settling this matter of the Ministry. Sonchai, if you were doing your job as my recording clerk, you would not have time to make so many sarcastic comments. Now get to work, both of you!"

Khati left, muttering things better not said clearly about her brother, and Madee turned to him. "Sonchai, record Chulayen Vajjadara as Minister *pro tem* of Lands and Properties, and—"

"Wait a minute," Chulayen began. "I have not—I cannot— Grandmother, at least give me some time to settle my personal life! You know what long hours this position means; I must find somebody to watch over Neena if I am to take it up. She has . . . nightmares," he finished lamely.

Madee cocked an ear toward the sounds of a clapping-and-singing game in the outer room. "Oh, I think Khati will do well enough to take charge of Neena. After all, she is out of a job now."

"Somebody must be with Neena at night, and if I am to be Minister *pro tem*—"

"So Khati will live in your house." Madee lifted an eyebrow. "Surely the Minister for Lands and Properties has a household big enough to accommodate one small girl-servant?"

"Her place is in my mother's house, with me," Sonchai protested.

"Absolutely not," Madee told him. "Do you forget that *I* live next door to your mother? Do you think I wish to be disturbed by your childish quarreling all day and night?"

She quashed Chulayen's remaining protests without mercy and sent him away to begin the monumental task of sorting through the previous Minister's records, which had been left in some disarray.

"Khati living in his household, caring for his daughter," Sonchai brooded. "I don't like it. You will have those two married before they know what happened to them."

"Weren't you just complaining about the difficulty of finding a husband for her? Stop looking at the dark side of everything, Sonchai. Khati needs some time with a gentle man
who can help her forget the Bashir, and Chulen needs a
girl to protect to help him forget Anusha. Trust Mother
Madee, she knows best."

"That sounds," Sonchai commented, "remarkably like a
campaign slogan."

Madee smiled.

Elsewhere, similar rearrangements were taking place with
similar complications and protests.

"Isn't this slightly illegal?" Calandra Vissi asked.

Evert Cornelis shook his head. "Kalapriya is now a direct
protectorate of Rezerval. It is definitely the Federation's job
to provide liaisons with each of the independent tribal territories. And do you have any idea how *hard* it is to find
people who know anything about Kalapriya, have some
concept of Federation law, are willing to work under primitive
conditions, and have no ties whatsoever to Barents?"

"What makes you think you've found one now? I'm a
Diplo, not a bloody administrator. I don't know anything
about running a state!"

"I don't have to ask you," Evert said simply. "You took
the Diplomatic Oath to serve where assigned."

"As a *Diplo*, not as a Resident or Liaison or whatever you
call it!"

"The oath doesn't say anything about choosing your role.
Annemari has ceded your services to my office on account
of the emergency, and I'm assigning you to Udara." Evert
smiled. "Don't fret, Calandra, you won't be the only Diplo
stuck on Kalapriya. Anybody with a language download chip
who isn't presently engaged on work of Federation security is in danger."

"I don't see why you can't use Barents Trading Society
people. They weren't *all* involved in the 'mats-for-arms plot,
you know."

"Officially," Evert said, "no member of the Barents Trading
Society may act in any role whatsoever on Kalapriya, public
or private, until the special commission has officially investigated and exonerated them. Unofficially, we're reassigning
the ones we're sure of to administrative posts wherever we

can slot them in, appointments to be confirmed and back pay made up only when the inquiry has finished. So if you think *you* have it bad . . ."

"No pay until a Federation Special Commission completes its inquiry," Calandra said. "That could be *years.*"

"They should have cleaned their own house when they had the chance," Evert said. "A few years on Kalapriya without pay or offworld luxuries beats a Federation prison."

"I'm not so sure of that," said Calandra, "and anyway, what makes you think they're going to have to do without offworld luxuries? It seems to me that the Federation needs to rethink its entire position on cultural contamination. What did we learn from Kalapriya, anyway? That some Barentsians are greedy and corrupt and not to be trusted with power? Give me a break. Some of *every* group will be greedy and corrupt and not to be trusted with power. Most, probably. I think the real lesson is that you can't *have* contact with primitive cultures and not have an effect on them. You can't quarantine technology like a communicable disease. The primitive cultures of the Dispersal are going to have culture shock and a giant technical leap forward. The only question is whether the Federation exerts some control over the flow of technology, or puts down a blanket ban and leaves it to the criminals and smugglers."

Evert's smile grew broader. "And I thought you didn't know anything about governing? As soon as you're settled in Udara I want a position paper from you on that very subject."

"I haven't agreed yet," Calandra warned him. "Would you rather have a cooperative Diplo-Resident or one who does the absolute minimum required?"

"That," Evert said, "rather depends on the price of the cooperation, doesn't it?"

Calandra told him exactly what it would cost.

Gabrel and Maris were still on Kalapriya, in Valentin. As one of the few Barents Trading Society members who was known to be absolutely clear of any involvement with the 'mats-for-arms trading ring, Gabrel was temporarily filling three different executive positions and consulting daily with Federation committees on the reorganization of Kalapriya as a direct protectorate. And he hadn't made a move toward Maris since they got back, which was extremely frustrating.

It seemed as though getting back to Valentin had reactivated all his proper Barents officer-and-a-gentleman training.

Granted, they didn't have a lot of privacy, but she could have stayed with him in his quarters, couldn't she? Instead, Maris was living at House Stoffelsen, now a sort of elegant boarding house for Federation employees; the Stoffelsens had departed Valentin rather hastily and without filing travel plans after Tasman. A number of their fellow Society members had followed suit; Valentin was notably empty of traditional colonial types, and notably full of Rezerval bureaucrats whose climate-controlled suits kept disappearing, requiring them to indent for replacements on a continual basis.

"The Kalapriyans are taking to outworlder technology like a Rudhrani bureaucrat to graft," Gabrel observed of this trend one evening when they were taking a decorous walk down the long shaded avenue that led from House Stoffelsen to the streets of Valentin. "What do you suppose they'll do when the power packs run down?"

"They're solar-powered," Maris told him. "They won't *run* down. And if they did, I expect the Kalapriyans would find a way to steal new power packs too. They don't seem to be sufferin' from whaddyacallit, cul-something?"

"Culture shock?"

"Righto. Except it *is* something shocking the way they get hold of them climate suits. Good thing the climate control unit for the office buildings ain't portable."

Gabrel coughed, seemed about to say something, then stopped.

"What is it?"

"I—oh, nothing."

Maris regarded him with exasperation. "It's *been* 'oh, nothing' for *days* now. If you've come to your senses and repented getting involved with a Tasman scumsucker, why don't you come right out and say so?"

"If I didn't want to be here with you, I wouldn't have to," Gabrel pointed out. "I could be too busy with work. Actually I *am* too busy with work; you can't imagine how many lies I have to tell before I can sneak off to spend an hour with you."

"Good practice for you," Maris said heartlessly. "Anyway, why do you work so hard to get a free hour or two if we're going to spend it walking up and down in the park like this?"

Gabrel went dark red. "I'm trying to treat you with respect. Maybe you aren't used to that, but—"

"Huh. I *thought* it wouldn't take you long to remember what I was."

"I—" Gabrel took a deep breath and stopped. "Maris, are you *trying* to pick a quarrel with me?"

"No! Well, maybe. Sort of." She *was* trying to break through the formal Barents courtesy that had separated them since they got back to Valentin. Quarreling wouldn't have been her preferred way to do it, but she had to do something to find out how he really felt—and to break her news to him. Come to think of it, Gabrel wasn't the only one who'd been unnaturally reserved. She'd been keeping a lot back too. But she couldn't keep it back any longer, not now that Calandra had confirmed it for her; the news was about to bubble out of her. "I . . . I'm not sure what you want."

Gabrel regarded her with exasperation. "I want to marry you. I want everybody in Valentin to *see* that I respect you and am treating you like my promised wife. I've just been waiting until I knew what position I could offer you."

"Do you think I *care* about that?"

"Well, I do!" Gabrel stopped shouting and controlled himself with a visible effort. "And I just got confirmation of it today. If you happen to be interested. I can support a wife now."

"You don't *need* to support me. I'm getting a position too, so there!" Oh, the God of Major Fuckups was sure on the job tonight. This wasn't the way it was supposed to go. She had meant to tell him her news, cry on his shoulder a bit about having to be separated for a while, get him to promise to wait for her. Having a fight wasn't on the agenda at all.

Gabrel went on as if he hadn't heard her, which was probably a good thing . . . or was it? Maybe the Valentin Gabrel *couldn't* hear the words "job" and "girl" in the same sentence. That would be a more serious problem than the years of separation that lay ahead of them. "I've just had formal confirmation that when the Federation completes its take-over here, I'm to be posted as assistant to the new Resident in Udara. The post carries a liberal allowance for lodging and dependents, so we can be married as soon as my orders are cut."

"Well . . . there's one problem," Maris said. "It looks like I'm going to have to go away for a while."

"Not back to Tasman?"

"Of course not, I couldn't go back to that life even if I wanted to. They were gonna kill me, remember?"

"Yes, well. Your—um, 'friends' aren't operating out of there anymore, you know. You'd be perfectly safe."

The upheavals of the 'mats-for-arms scandal had caused a much more thorough shaking up of Tasman than the search for a disappeared Diplo would have done. The disused tunnels that Johnivans' gang had made their home were mapped now, and filled with foam sealant. Johnivans and Keito had spaced themselves rather than be arrested; most of the rest of the gang were serving lengthy sentences on distant prison worlds. Maris had been unable to find out what had happened to Nyx; she hoped the computer hacker had hacked herself a new identity and vanished into the databases of the Federation.

"Well, where are you going, and for how long? I need to tell my family and set a date. They'll want to come here for the wedding. Or maybe we should be married on Barents," Gabrel mused. "My mother would like that, and it would be cheaper for us to go there than for the whole clan to come out to Kalapriya . . ."

"We've got time to work that out," Maris said uncomfortably.

"Not all that much. I expect my posting will be finalized within a few weeks, and I'll be expected to go right on upcountry when that happens. Good thing, really, my mother won't have a chance to make a Big Society Deal out of our wedding. There won't be time."

"Um . . . I expect she'll have plenty of time," Maris said in a small voice.

"Why? How long are you going to be gone for, anyway? And you never did tell me where you're going."

"I'm going," Maris informed him, "to Rezerval. I got a scholarship to Diplo School."

"You what? Why didn't you tell me?"

"I *been* tryin' to tell you, but you kept interrupting! The Calandra Vissi Diplomatic Scholarship," Maris said dreamily. "Imagine, me, a Tasman scumsucker, learnin' all that stuff about other worlds and unarmed combat and political science and astrogation and diplomacy and languages and . . ."

"But you said you were going to stay here and marry me."

"I want to go to school first."

"I thought you loved me!"

"I *do* love you! But I don't hardly know who 'I' am, Gabrel, don't you see? First I was what Johnivans wanted me to be, then I was trying to be Calandra, and now . . ." Maris couldn't find words for it. "I never had no real education, you know? And I never seen anywhere but Tasman and Kalapriya. And not even the upper *levels* of Tasman. Now I got a chance to learn something and be somebody. To be a real person. With an ID that ain't a forgery, and skills that count for something. And . . ." She was out of words to convince Gabrel. If he hated her for going away to school, it would break her heart. But she would go anyway.

"And you're only seventeen," Gabrel said gently. "I keep forgetting."

"Nice Barents girls get married at seventeen," Maris argued against herself.

"And you," Gabrel said, "are definitely not a 'nice Barents girl.' That's one of the things I love about you." He took her by the shoulders, holding her very gently, as if he were afraid she might disappear if he held on too tightly. "You need to fly, and I'm trying to clip your wings. Go to Diplo School, Maris. I can wait."

"You *want* me to go?"

"Gods, no! I want to drag you back to my quarters and ravish you until you change your mind."

"Okay by me." Maris glanced at her shiny new chrono-calculator, a parting gift from Calandra. "Like you said, I'm not a nice Barents girl. And after going off upcountry with you, I don't think I got much reputation left to ruin. We got three days before me shuttle leaves. How much ravishing you think you can get in by that time?"

"Enough to change your mind about going away to school?" Gabrel said.

Maris grinned. "I don't think so. But if you want to try, I think it's only fair to give you a chance!"